HIGH TOWERS

HIGH TOWERS

Thomas B. Costain

Special Index

Garden City, N. Y.

DOUBLEDAY & COMPANY, INC.

1949

With the exception of actual historical personages identified as such, the characters are entirely the product of the author's imagination and have no relation to any person in real life.

TO

Philippa

INTRODUCTION

GUY FRÉGAULT, whose biography of Pierre le Moyne d'Iberville is the most reliable and the only definitive book about that fantastic fighting man and leader, says that nothing exists on which even a physical description of him can be based. There is an equal lack of personal detail with reference to the other nine Le Moyne brothers who as a group have been called the Canadian Maccabees. They are shadowy figures, these French-Canadian heroes. They achieved remarkable things under extraordinary circumstances, the most notable being the conquest of Hudson's Bay and the discovery and settlement of Louisiana. The hint of a great conception can be sensed in the things they did, nothing less than the mastery of a continent. Apart from this we know when they were born, when they married and when they died. They were raised in Montreal and on their father's seigneurie across the river at Longueuil. Charles, the eldest, succeeded his father and built at Longueuil a great château with four high towers, at the same time amassing what in those days was a considerable fortune. Jean-Baptiste, the eighth brother, was governor of Louisiana for thirty years and the founder of New Orleans. Joseph became governor of Rochefort and Antoine of French Guiana. All of the other brothers, including the great colonial paladin Pierre, died in the service of France.

Beyond this brief record of their achievements and the vital statistics in the archives at Montreal, what is known of the ten stout brothers? What manner of men were they? Were they typical of the French-Canadian people of this early period, brave, resolute, devout, lighthearted? The only clue to them as human beings is an occasional revealing reference in the scanty annals of the day, such as an early indiscretion of D'Iberville's and the fact that the Iroquois called Paul le Moyne Little-Bird-Always-in-Motion. To deal with them as characters in a novel, therefore, is a task approaching that of the scientist who tries to reconstruct a monster of prehistoric times with nothing more to go on than a broken rib and a fragment of jawbone. The result is certain to raise doubts in the minds of historians who are skeptical necessarily of anything stemming from the imagination. In my opinion, nevertheless, the only way to tell the saga of the Le Moynes, and to attempt the rescue of these remarkable brothers from the oblivion into which they have sunk, is to set down their story in the guise of historical fiction. There are too many gaps in the record for successful factual treatment. Any apologies that I have to offer are not for attempting the task on this basis but for my shortcomings in carrying it out.

When real characters are involved in a story it is often necessary to surround them with creatures of the imagination in order to create a personalized background. Only the members of the family and a few figures of official standing are real in *High Towers*. Félicité and her mother, Philippe, Joseph de Mariat and Auguste of that ilk, the settlers and servants at Longueuil, the minor citizens of Montreal, the people of New Orleans where the story reaches its climax—none of these ever existed. It follows that the events in which they figure have no basis in fact, except that the lives of the Le Moyne brothers, and those about them, must have followed some such course.

I desire to extend my warmest thanks to the many who assisted me in gathering the necessary material. Help was extended in many quarters, in Montreal, Longueuil, Quebec, Paris, New York, New Orleans, Annapolis. I realize that, without the aid thus generously supplied, it would have been impossible to give anything in the nature of a rounded picture of the lives and times of this truly fabulous family.

THOMAS B. COSTAIN

HIGH TOWERS

Book One

CHAPTER I

NO WORDS can convey an adequate impression of the small settlement known as Ville Marie de Montréal as it was in the final years of the seventeenth century. It was a town of contrasts. Lying near the mouth of the Richelieu River, which spewed out the hostile Indian war parties, Montreal (as everyone was beginning to call it then) lived its days in suspense and fear. With such a precarious hold on mere existence, it was deeply moved to religion and at the same time gay in all its moods. The fur trade had made this town under the mountain its center and countinghouse, and so Montreal had grown lusty and rich and colorful beyond compare. Grave-faced priests in black or brown habit walked its streets, and long files of devout girls wearing curiously shaped gray cloaks and with wicker baskets in their hands in which they carried to school their books and their daily allowance of wine; but in perhaps greater number were the swaggering *coureurs de bois* and Indians in meager moosehide and beads (when not actually naked); and soldiers in buff jackets and with bandoleers of bleached leather and black hats with metallic galloon. There were plenty of minor characters to lend liveliness to the narrow streets along the river—quacks with wondrous remedies found in the woods, travelers with tall tales of adventure, and proud officials with four-cornered hats and much lace at neck and wrist.

It could easily be conceived that the spirit of Adam Dollard, brooding over the Place d'Armes, would ask, "What manner of town are ye making of this Montreal which my companions and I gave up our lives to save?"

Perhaps similar thoughts filled the mind of Dollier de Casson one very warm day in mid-July in the year 1697 as he paced about the fine gardens of the Seminary and talked to a companion who pattered with short steps after him. Before becoming the head of the Sulpician Order in Montreal, and thereby lord of the whole island and the lands adjoining, this bent old man had been a soldier, and one of his particular cares had been to improve the defenses. The main object of his stroll this morning was to cast an appraising eye over the completed condition of two stone towers which had been three years in the building. He sighed as he turned back through an avenue of young plum trees.

"We are free of Indian attacks now," he said to his companion, "but I promise you that a brace of English cannon would reduce these walls in an hour's time—and so make an end to all this money changing and this selling of brandy to the poor wild fellows of the woods!"

The Sulpicians were all gentlemen but so unassuming that they dressed in the plain garb of the parish priest with its white rabat and navy-blue cuffs and they were addressed simply as "monsieur." The pudgy little member, who had long before given up the effort to match steps with the tall Superior, did not seem much disturbed. "But first, monsieur," he puffed, "they would have to make a landing and mount their cannon. It's nothing to lose sleep over."

The Superior, who had been the strongest man in France in his campaigning days, smiled down over his gaunt shoulder. "It would take a very great calamity to make you lose sleep, Monsieur Ambrose."

"There will soon be peace." The priest made this pronouncement with a cheerful nod of the head. "Every letter we have from France speaks of the ending of the war with the English."

The smile left the deep-sunken eyes of the old man. "There will never be an ending to the wars with the English," he declared. He gave vent to a second sigh. "Not until one of us has prevailed."

The small priest began to laugh. "*Monsieur le Supérieur,* there is this matter of prevailing to be considered in all things. Consider first the groaning of the sick in the *Infirmerie* and the snores from the *Salle des Lits* next door. Which will prevail there? It's a seesaw which keeps many of us awake at nights."

"It was a mistake in planning to have them side by side. That I grant you."

"Last night," went on the priest, making the most of this opportunity to pour a grievance into the ears of the head of the order, "there was so much groaning and wheezing and blowing of breath and calling for this and that and praying in feeble supplication that not one of us who were well could catch a wink of sleep. And so we fell to discussing among ourselves such questions as, Who is the bravest man in New France?"

"It surely took little talk to settle *that.*"

"You are right, *Monsieur le Supérieur.* We were in quick accord there. Our great D'Iberville, of course."

"Of course, monsieur. No one can compare with that fine captain of ours."

"And then we fell to asking, Who is the holiest man? There is no need to ask me this time. The answer, monsieur, was *you.*"

The old man indulged in a dry smile. "Could they have arrived at any other conclusion when I happen to be the head of their own order?"

"And then we set ourselves to a problem which led to much disputing and backbiting and spitting out of contempt. Who, we asked ourselves, is the worst man in Montreal?"

The Superior paused. "I confess to some curiosity in this matter. What decision was reached?"

The priest wagged his head vigorously. "I prevailed this time, monsieur. It was my candidate who was awarded the palm for wickedness and meanness and lechery. Who, monsieur, but that sly snooper into the affairs of other men, that *tabellion* who fawns on the rich and robs the poor, that practitioner of evil, Jules Alcide Benoit!"

The old man sighed more deeply than before. "I concede it is hard not to think ill of Jules Benoit and yet we should strive to be charitable. This craving for money is a fault in so many. How much meanness and avarice can be shown in the smallest matters of property! This morning, Monsieur Ambrose, I went over the final papers on the Lachine settlement claims. The disputed lands are being portioned out at last. And none of the claimants will yield as much as an inch of land to the boy."

"What boy, monsieur?"

"I forget sometimes that you are a new arrival and not familiar with all that has happened. After the massacre at Lachine a baby was found, a boy. He was never identified, Monsieur Ambrose. Clearly he's entitled to the lands of one of the families which perished that terrible night. But which? I've made the suggestion that all the claimants give a small slice of what they are to receive and so make up a fair portion for this poor lad. But no, all four contend that he's no relation of theirs and that they shouldn't be expected to suffer loss for him."

The priest nodded. "I can see much justice in what they say."

"Justice, perhaps. But," with a worried shake of the head, "it is very hard on this poor young fellow whose parents labored to clear their land with the intent that he would someday reap the benefit."

They had reached the end of the walk and were turning in under an archway of gray stone when another member of the order came out to meet them, his soutane rustling in his haste. "Monsieur," he said, "the Seigneur of Longueuil is here to see you."

The head of the institution paused to catch his breath. The walk up through the gardens had been a hard one and his heart was showing the effects. "Bring Monsieur le Moyne here," he said, seating himself on a stone bench. His eyes turned toward the east. "If we were just a little higher here, we might see the towers of that great château he has built."

Charles le Moyne proved to be a man in the middle forties, a little inclined to stoutness and rather more elegantly dressed than was usual among the landowners of New France. He had been wearing a fine hat of the kind known as a *tapabord,* with a turned-up brim and scarlet silk lining, and he carried it now in his hands as he bowed respectfully to the head of the order. His gray coat was well tailored and his sleek silk stockings were of a matching color. Despite the unusual heat of the day, he was wearing gloves trimmed with ribbon. He was a handsome man and seemed amiable as well as shrewd.

"*Monsieur le Supérieur,*" he said, "I've come to beg some information. About a—a certain lady."

The head of the institution motioned him to take a seat on the bench. "It will be, I think, about the lady who lives in the house—well, not actually on the wall like Rahab, as is being said, but quite close to it."

Charles le Moyne nodded in assent. "Yes, it's about Madame Halay. I hear conflicting stories about her."

"This much I may tell you at once. She doesn't make her living as the harlot did on the walls of Jericho."

The Seigneur of Longueuil asked quickly, "Are you sure of that, monsieur?"

"Quite sure. The morals of this community are our responsibility and when a strange woman—a young woman, moreover, and a most attractive one who dresses with much richness and style—when she comes to Montreal alone, save for an infant daughter, we see to it that her movements are watched. Madame Halay has been under our eyes from the day of her arrival. I may tell you as fact that she has earned nothing that hasn't come from her diligent needle."

"She would be easier to deal with if she were the other kind." Charles le Moyne frowned thoughtfully. "All I know about her is this. She was coming out with her husband and the ship got into difficulties off Little Miquelon. Her husband was drowned."

"She was brought on to Quebec." Dollier de Casson took up the explanation. "At Quebec they didn't know what to do with her and after a time they conceived a most convenient way to handle the matter. They would send her on to Montreal, where there were many men in need of wives. And so—she became our problem."

"There *are* many men hereabouts in need of wives. Why does Madame Halay persist in refusing to consider candidates?"

The multitude of wrinkles about the fine dark eyes of Dollier de Casson drew together in a smile. "There are two reasons. First, the young woman professes herself undesirous of marrying any of the young men who have offered. Her first experience, it seems, didn't leave her enamored of the institution of matrimony. They were sent to New France by her husband's family, who considered her an unsuitable wife for him."

Charles le Moyne looked up with surprise. "That is very interesting. I hadn't heard that part of her story."

"She was in charge of his younger brothers and sisters. A second marriage, you understand. She wasn't well enough educated to be a governess, so I assume she was a nursemaid. The family was furious when he married her, particularly when the child arrived to complicate the matter of property succession. I sometimes wonder, monsieur, if the world would not be better off without property!"

"You said there were two reasons for her remaining unmarried. May I ask what the other is?"

"The other reason is that fine young brother of yours. He has always been a favorite with me, that Jean-Baptiste, and I am not surprised the young woman displays a preference for his company."

"De Bienville is barely eighteen." The seigneur used the title which their father had selected for the younger brother. There had been ten sons and so it had been necessary to draw on the names of villages in Normandy where old Charles le Moyne had been born. "He's of a romantic turn of mind. What can you expect at that age? He saw her at church and liked her looks so much he followed her home. It's certain she encouraged him because I hear he has been to see her many times since——"

"Four times in all. We have been keeping an eye on things. Your brother has been attentive but also most respectful toward the fair stranger in our midst."

"He wants to marry her." The seigneur spoke brusquely. "He has stated his intention to me most emphatically. Naturally, it can't be allowed."

"No," said the old man. "It wouldn't be a suitable match for one of the Le Moynes. I'm sorry I must agree with you, because it's going to be a blow for poor Jean-Baptiste."

"He's a favorite of mine also, monsieur. He's young but I think he has much promise. I foresee the day when the Sieur de Bienville will play a big part in the empire we propose to create for His Majesty the King on this new continent. When he marries it must be a match in keeping with his prospects. He mustn't be allowed to throw himself away."

Dollier de Casson asked quietly, "Is there anything you desire me to do?"

"Can she be sent back to France?"

"You must know that the King thinks only of sending people out here and that he frowns on any suggestion of allowing them to return. I question if the necessary permit could be obtained in this case."

"Then," said Charles le Moyne, "there's only one course open to me. I must see this young woman and make some arrangement with her."

A look of distress had settled on the old priest's face. "It is too bad, Charles, but I suppose it must be done. But please, in speaking with her be as considerate as you can. I'm convinced she's of gentle intent and that she's doing her best in a difficult situation."

He had spoken with so much solicitude that Charles le Moyne asked, "Have you seen her yourself?"

"I have seen her twice. Once at church and once in the room she has taken."

"And what is your opinion of her?"

Dollier de Casson smiled warmly. "I liked her, Charles. She has a tongue in her head and she didn't hesitate to tell me what she thought. And she's so pretty, so very pretty. Have you seen her?"

"No. But I hope to within the next hour. I—I will heed what you've said and spare her feelings as much as possible. May I encroach on your time again later to let you know the result?"

A hint of authority showed itself in the voice of the old priest. "I must stipulate that you acquaint me with everything which is said between you. This unfortunate young woman has become a charge, a responsibility. I feel most well disposed to her."

Le Moyne rose to leave but the priest made a gesture to restrain him. "I hear there have been further successes in Newfoundland," he said eagerly. "That great man, your brother, is winning everywhere! What a leader he is! God has given him to us for a purpose. . . . Have you heard directly from him?"

The Seigneur of Longueuil gave a quick nod of his head. His eyes had begun to shine. "I had a letter a week ago. He, D'Iberville, expected to have the whole island in his hands soon. He hadn't encountered a single setback."

Dollier de Casson's face had lost all trace of the fatigue and disillusion of age. "Perhaps," he exclaimed, "this is a sign that we shall be the ones to prevail!"

He saw his visitor to the gate and waved him on his way with an admonitory "Remember your promise, Charles, and be gentle with her." Turning back, he walked slowly up the hard clay path between the two wings of the gray stone building. In his prime he had been known to set the wheels of a mired cannon to turning without any help; but now he walked with stiff knees and seemed dependent on a knobby cane. He was so bent that he did not notice there was another visitor awaiting him in the entrance. This one was a very tall and stout man with a great round face like an uncured cheese and a pair of sharp eyes set rather closely together in its dead white expanse.

"Good morning—ah—monsieur," said the other man in a voice which carried a suggestion of water sloshed in a jug. "I'm informed that you've had a caller. Monsieur Charles le Moyne."

The old man painfully straightened his back until his eyes were on a level with the visitor's. He did not like this official from the court of Versailles who had been in Montreal now for the better part of two weeks and had preferred to stay at the Seminary rather than at any of the inns of the town. Some of this feeling could be read in his manner.

"Good morning, Monsieur de Mariat," he said. The many speculations in which all Montreal had indulged about the mission of the stranger came flocking back into his mind. He frowned uneasily. "Yes, Charles le Moyne has been here. He has just left."

"That is too bad." The official rubbed a finger along the flattened ridge of his nose. "I must see the wealthy and influential Seigneur of Longueuil today. I have—ah—saved him for the last." He began to laugh and the convolutions of his lower face shook like jelly. "For the dessert, you might say."

The movements of any visitor, particularly one as conspicuous as this massive member of the King's secretarial staff, could not be kept secret in a place as restricted as Montreal. Everyone knew that Joseph de Mariat had been closeted for long talks with many of the merchants of the town, all of whom were connected with the fur trade. He had made the rounds of the fur stores and had poked his nose into countinghouses and had talked to the captains of river craft, not neglecting the humblest members of the crews. He had not wasted a single moment of his stay.

It was evident that Dollier de Casson knew all this and found it hard to be polite to his inquisitive guest. His eyes ran over the portly form of De Mariat, noting that the latter, who was always arrayed rather resplendently, had outdone himself this morning, particularly in the matter of buttons. It took many years for a new fashion to penetrate as far as this distant colony but Canadians had known that in France men were discontinuing the use of the time-honored *aiguillettes* for holding their clothes together and were using a novel device. De Mariat was carrying the idea to such an extreme that he seemed to be literally festooned with buttons. They were not modest buttons, displaying themselves with a fit diffidence as though saying, "Bear with us now while we seem wrong and absurd and in time you'll discover there's good sense to us after all." These particular buttons were gaudy things of Florentine point and in a variety of glaring colors.

The old man began to count them but gave up in despair when he reached thirty. His eye then turned to the De Mariat coat, which was a handsome garment of Levantine cloth, most elaborately damasked.

"Can it be," he asked himself, observing the stiffness of the tails, "that he uses whalebone like a woman in her stays? Good St. Homobonus, what are we coming to!"

"I fear you will have difficulty in seeing the seigneur today," said Dollier de Casson after what had been a long pause. "He leaves for Longueuil at noon and in the meantime he is very much engaged."

"Excellent!" said the visitor. "I shall go with him. It may be that the air across the river will have less of this pestilent heat. I presume"—the sharp black eyes displayed a sudden trace of uneasiness—"there's no danger of—of Indians being out on the warpath?"

"No, Monsieur de Mariat." The old man's face did not change but deep inside himself he was indulging in a smile. "There will be no danger from the Indians. In any event, the château at Longueuil is like the strong places the Maccabees built, a fort of stout walls and high towers. You will be safer there even than here, behind the shaky palisades of Montreal."

II

Charles le Moyne had asked directions of a friendly Sulpician at the gate and had received a prompt reply which suggested to him that the affairs of the young widow were matters of general knowledge. "You must go to the shop of the gallipot"—it was not surprising to hear a colloquial term on the lips of the priest, for the Sulpicians were close to the life of the town—"the one above the Rue Notre Dame. She has rented a room over the shop."

Walking down the sloping street, the Seigneur of Longueuil carried his hat in his hand and occasionally used it as a fan. The heat was becoming more intense and he thought regretfully of the distance he must walk to reach the chemist's shop. There was not the faintest hint of a breeze, although below he could see the wide stretch of the river. The people he passed saluted him with the greatest respect.

A bell jangled when he opened the door of the shop and the proprietor, Damase Lafleur, came out from a back room. When Le Moyne stated his errand the chemist pointed to another door at the rear and said, "You will find her in, monsieur," a superfluous piece of information as a light footstep could be heard on the floor above.

The head of the great family of Le Moyne, the wealthiest and most justly respected and talked-about family in all New France, climbed a dark staircase. His tap on the door above elicited a clear *"Entrez!"* which made him sure he had selected the right one, for the natives of Montreal were more inclined to say, *"Ouvrez."* He turned the knob and found himself face to face with a young woman in a camisole of the high orange shade known as nacarat. She had a veil of the same color wrapped about her head and she had a broom in one hand.

"Good morning, monsieur," she said with a rising inflection which turned the greeting into a question.

Charles le Moyne had been startled by her attractiveness. She had dark brown eyes which looked unusually large under the impromptu head covering, her nose was delicately and piquantly modeled, her mouth vivid both in color and shape. She was Parisienne in every line: the careless chic with which the camisole was wrapped about her (on closer inspection the garment seemed worn and in need of the needle with which she made her living), the fineness of the lace which showed briefly under the rolled-up sleeves, the trim and diminutive tip of a slipper seen at intervals under the frayed hem of the skirt.

"I apologize for intruding on you at such an early hour," said the seigneur, bowing. "Perhaps the fact that I must leave Montreal at noon will seem to you an excuse."

"You are forgiven, Monsieur le Moyne," said the girl. He was so startled by her recognition of him that she laughed and added: "I've been expecting you. You will come in?"

He walked into the room, continuing to study her as he did so. She was tall and quite slender and she carried herself with an unmistakable air. "She's no cocotte," he said to himself. "One might easily be deceived into thinking her a lady."

"You will take the chair, please," she said. "There's only one, as you see. This," seating herself on the side of the bed, "will do for me. And now, monsieur, you have come, I think, to speak of your brother."

"Yes." Le Moyne nodded his head approvingly. He liked the directness of her attitude. "Jean-Baptiste has been coming to see you. It seems that he has become—I suppose 'enamored' is the word."

The girl said with dignity, "He has done me the great honor of falling in love with me and has asked my hand in marriage."

"Indeed? You will pardon me for betraying my surprise. You see, Jean-Baptiste is a boy. He's barely eighteen. Hardly the age, you will agree, to be thinking of matrimony."

The girl's eyebrows went up. "A little early perhaps. But the Sieur de Bienville seems very mature for his age. And, m'sieur, he has property of his own."

"Under the terms of his father's will," said the seigneur quickly, "he has no control over his inheritance yet. *That* is in my hands. Madame, do you care to tell me your age?"

"I am twenty," she answered. Then she smiled. Her face became so lovely that her visitor wondered uneasily if he could maintain a proper degree of firmness in dealing with her. "You thought older, perhaps? I'm not surprised. I have been married and I am a mother. But I am being truthful, monsieur. I am twenty. Your brother is only eighteen. Is it an obstacle?"

Charles le Moyne saw no reason why he could not use the direct methods he found most useful in matters of trade. "Are you in love with my brother?" he asked.

"No." The girl shook her head and then smiled again. "You see how truthful I am being? But, m'sieur, I am fond of Jean-Baptiste. I am *very* fond of him. I thought once I was in love but—but after a *very* short time I realized I had fallen out of love most completely. I don't think, m'sieur, I shall ever find myself in love again."

"You are being frank indeed. But under these circumstances what answer have you given my brother?"

"I've given him no answer. If I am to stay in this wild country I must marry again. Could I find a more congenial husband than my sweet and gentle Jean-Baptiste? That is what I have said to him. I have been most frank in all our talks. . . . But, m'sieur, I don't want to stay here. This country, it frightens me! I hear stories of the Indians and of terrible dangers. I hear of the great cold and it makes me shudder, even on a warm day like this. I have one desire and only one. To return to France. To Paris. To go back on the very first boat!"

A sense of satisfaction had taken possession of her visitor. "I can arrange this," he said to himself. "How deftly she puts her case! She threatens us but in a most agreeable way."

As he was thus turning matters over in his mind his eyes had been fixed on a woolen robe thrown carelessly on the floor at the foot of the bed. Noticing the direction of his gaze, she gave her head a barely perceptible toss. "It's not a covering of flax stalks, m'sieur," she said. "And there are no men hidden under it."

The seigneur was puzzled. He was a devout man, as were all the people of New France, but it was apparent that his devotion had not led him to much reading of the Vulgate.

The girl proceeded to explain. "You must have heard what I'm being called. The woman who lives on the wall." She motioned toward the one window in the room and he became aware for the first time that it looked out directly on the palisade. "There was a woman once who lived on a wall and she hid the spies of Joshua under stalks of flax. Don't you understand what I'm trying to tell you? Or is it that you don't want to believe?"

"I don't need to be convinced," he declared. This was true. He had become sure since seeing her, and talking with her, that her morals were above question. "You seem to have been educated somewhat above the—the station in life in which you started."

She shook her head. "No, m'sieur. I had no education at all. But I *wanted* to get above my station in life and so I watched and listened and asked questions." She stopped and looked up at him with appeal in her eyes. "Have you any idea what it's like to be a servant? No, m'sieur, you couldn't know about it. It is—a most unpleasant life, I assure you."

"Have you any money left?"

"No, m'sieur. When my husband's family decided to send us here they gave him quite a lot of money. At least it looked a fortune to me. But Jacques was a quick spender. When we got on board the ship there was little of it left." She hesitated. "He was a great drinker. I seem to remember him most when he was drunk. At the end I was—I think I was beginning to hate him."

He studied her in silence for several moments, realizing that he had already begun to like her. Finally he said, "It would be unfortunate if a second marriage involved you in more family complications."

The girl gave him a steady look. "Yes, m'sieur."

"Perhaps it could be arranged to get you back to Paris."

Before going any further the head of the Le Moyne family walked to the window to allow himself a chance to give the situation final consideration. He noticed as he crossed the room that the furniture was homemade and consisted of only the most necessary pieces. Although the bed and the table and the single chair were square and solid, they exhibited nevertheless a few characteristic touches which raised them above the level of the commonplace: a nicety of proportion, a care shown in the finishing of the wood, a suggestion of grace even in some of the simple detail. There was artistry in the work of the Norman peasants who had settled the new land.

There was a cradle at the foot of the bed and he became aware of a pair of solemn eyes peering at him from behind it. They vanished immediately.

His mind was made up when he returned from the window. "I see my way to meet your wishes," he declared, resuming his seat in the chair. "It will be a matter of some difficulty and expense but the permit can be secured. I shall pay to you a sum adequate for the journey and to keep you two years after your arrival in Paris. In return I must have your promise not to see the Sieur de Bienville again."

"This makes me feel a very mercenary person. Still!" She paused and then gestured resignedly with her hands. "I'm willing to have it this way. But naturally, m'sieur, we will have to find ourselves in agreement as to what is meant by 'adequate.'"

He nodded briefly. "Naturally."

A pause followed. It was clear she had something else to say and that she hesitated to do so. Finally she turned her head and called: "Félicité-Anne! Come to Mother, my child."

The child emerged slowly and reluctantly from her place of concealment. She was barely able to balance herself by holding to the side of the cradle. She stopped and raised a pair of eyes which looked unnaturally large in her thin face. Frightened by his scrutiny, she dropped them immediately.

"It's my desire that a home be found here for my little Félicité."

The seigneur was so surprised that he swung around in his chair and stared at the child's mother. "It's hard to understand such a desire. A few moments ago you spoke of life here with fear and distaste. Why are you ready to leave the child to a way of living you shrink from yourself?"

"It's different with children." There was a trace of defiance in her tone and manner. "If she's raised here she will never feel about it as I do. I hear children playing in the streets and laughing. They look so strong and healthy. It will be the same with my Félicité." She leaned forward in her eagerness to justify herself. "M'sieur, there are the best of reasons for leaving her. If I take her back I am chained forever to my past. What will there be to do but go back to being a servant? She in her turn, my poor little girl, will become a servant. M'sieur! I beseech you to consider, to believe, it will be much better for her if she's put in a home here." She straightened up and looked at him with an air which had become completely defiant. "And there's my own life to consider. I refuse to put myself again under the thumb of another woman, to live on scraps of food, to sleep in dark closets! I have a plan, m'sieur, to start my life all over again. And I have a story ready to account for myself. An imposture, yes, but a very clever story. I've thought it all out and know I can carry it through. But it's not a story I could tell, and expect people to believe, if I had a child with me. I've explained to *Monsieur le Supérieur* about the child and he thinks it best to leave her."

He found enough reason in what she said to overcome his first feeling. "Perhaps it would be better for the child if a fresh start could be provided for her."

"I've been told," said the mother quickly, "that many families have settled on your land at Longueuil."

"There are nearly three hundred in the seigneury now," said Charles le Moyne proudly. "And twenty-seven houses. It's quite possible that a home could be found with one of the families. I'm willing to try."

The child ventured another glance at the stranger, at the same time taking a timorous step forward. He smiled and held out his arms to her. "Come," he said. "You see, Madame Halay, she likes me already."

"My poor little Félicité!" said the girl. "She isn't a pretty baby, as you can see, m'sieur. But it's nothing to be concerned about. I was an ugly little creature until I was about eight years old. Then I changed." She favored him with a sudden smile. "Would you say I turned out badly, m'sieur?"

"No," answered the seigneur with a suggestion of haste in his voice. "You turned out so well that we must get you back to France as fast as we can."

III

During the last few minutes of his visit with the woman who lived near the wall, Charles le Moyne had been conscious of a hubbub rising from the street below. As he emerged into the open air he perceived that the noise came from the intersection with the Rue Notre Dame. A curious specimen of a man was pacing up and down in front of the general trading store which stood there and indulging in a steady stream of abuse while a constantly increasing group of spectators watched the proceedings from a safe distance.

The chief actor in the scene was, obviously, a member of that colorful band of traders known as the *coureurs de bois*. They were familiar figures on the streets of Montreal but it was unusual to encounter one this late in the summer. The King's Fair had been held weeks before. It had been a great success. There had been nearly five hundred canoes in the flotilla which had left Green Bay and swept down the Ottawa River, all of them packed with skins, beaver for the most part but also plenty of otter and mink and the hides of the moose. With the canoes had come hundreds of Indians and, of course, all the French woodsmen. The latter had led the flotilla, making the waters and the woods resound with their songs of King Castor (Beaver) I. Merchants had come to Montreal from all parts of the colony and had set up their booths along the palisades; and for ten days there had been trading and bargaining (and much drinking of brandy and fighting and wenching) until all the furs had changed hands.

Long before this the canoes had started back up the Ottawa and the woodsmen had gone with them. This one laggard was an unusually tall fellow with an unkempt shock of red hair above a hook-nosed, sickle-mouthed face. The oddity of his appearance was added to by the incongruity of his attire. Naked from the waist up, he nevertheless wore a felt hat with a bedraggled plume hanging from it, and his leggings, though worn and patched, had been made of fine imported cloth. A smoked eel was tied around his neck, possibly as an emergency supply of food.

This curious individual was in a great rage. He was prancing about and doing ludicrous dance steps which generally ended in abrupt leaps into the air with a cracking of heels before landing. Each time he did this he would let out a screech of laughter. "Come up, come up, town rats!" he would cry. "Come a little closer, you flyblown scum of the streets, and let me kick your rabbit heads right off your shoulders!"

His anger, however, was directed at the proprietors of the trading store, who had not yet met his terms. He kept shouting that they wanted to rob him and that he would stay where he was, allowing no one to enter the store or even pass it until justice had been done him. The owners did not seem much disturbed. One of them sat in the window of the establishment and kept a supercilious eye on him as he indulged in his tirades—and a hand on the muzzle of a gun resting across the sill.

"Liars! Thieves!" the angry woodsman was shouting. "You skunks, masquerading in human guise! You crawling batfowlers! Cheats! Assassins. Didn't I break all records by bringing fifty bales of fur in one canoe, I, André Beaufils? And you, you greasy grice, trying to prig me down on the fair price we agreed to first!"

A very young man turned into the street at the same time as the Seigneur of Longueuil arrived on the scene. He was walking with lowered head and did not become aware of what was going on until he had made his way through the ranks of the delighted spectators and had invaded the forbidden territory in front of the store. He stopped only when an infuriated hail assailed his ears. He looked up then and frowned at the prancing figure of the woodsman.

"Keep away from me!" roared the latter. "I, André Beaufils, have been cheated. No one passes until these Judases, snuffling over their pieces of silver, pay me what's my due. And that means everyone from old Onontio himself to stinking town rabble like these frightened little penwipers! And it includes you, Jean-Baptiste le Moyne, Sieur de Bienville, and make no mistake about that!"

The young man, who was of slender build and had a rather studious air about him, looked startled at this outburst but at the same time somewhat amused.

"So! You are André Beaufils," he said. "I've heard a great deal about André Beaufils—and none of it pleasant. Now what's this you're saying? That you won't allow anyone to pass? But that's absurd. You see, André Beaufils, I've a visit to make farther up this street and so it's necessary for me to pass—and that without any delay."

The woodsman drew back his right leg. "Take one step more, my fancy gentleman!" he bellowed. "And I, André Beaufils, who cares nothing for man, God, or devil, will drill a hole through your skull with this toe of mine!"

Charles le Moyne found it hard to resist the impulse to interfere before his brother could meet with any injury but he held back, realizing that the situation had reached a stage where Jean-Baptiste must see it through himself. He darted an anxious look at the boy and was relieved to find him quite cool.

The Sieur de Bienville paused a moment and thoughtfully rubbed a hand along his nose. Then he said: "There are only twenty-five licenses issued to fur traders. What's the number of yours, André Beaufils?"

The woodsman checked himself on the point of another outburst. His mouth dropped open.

"It's a matter of very great difficulty and unpleasantness when anyone is caught trading without a license. I've heard the governor intends to revive the old laws and have those who break them branded and then sent to the galleys in France. Of course he may not go as far as that. I noticed that all three who were caught and fined during the fair were noisy fellows and always making trouble. The quiet ones without licenses weren't disturbed." He stared at the woodsman intently. "It might be quite awkward for you if it was found you hadn't a license."

He began to walk past the now silent trader, moving his feet slowly and casually. Beaufils stared at him as though unwilling to let this defiance go unpunished. The muscles of his right leg quivered and the spectators held their breaths, expecting him to launch one of his terrific, leaping kicks. But he made no move.

"By St. Joe!" he muttered. "Can I hurt this boy—a son of good old

Charles le Moyne and a brother of my friend Pierre? No, no, that I can't do!"

The youth said over his shoulder as he calmly passed the trader, "It would be wise if you were on your way by nightfall."

Charles le Moyne stepped forward and dropped a hand on his brother's shoulder. "That was well done," he whispered. "I was proud of the way you handled this fellow, Jean-Baptiste."

The younger brother seemed disturbed as well as surprised at meeting the head of the family. He glanced up the street in the direction of the chemist's shop and frowned uneasily. "I think perhaps, Charles," he said, "you've been seeing Marie."

"If you mean the young widow—yes, I've just left her."

"I—I expected you would go to her."

The seigneur turned toward him and was amazed to find that the boy's face had gone white. "Jean-Baptiste! You shouldn't take this so seriously!"

"I shouldn't take it seriously! Charles, it's the only thing that counts at all."

"But, my boy, this young woman would never make you the right kind of wife. Surely you see that yourself."

"I won't listen to anything against her!" said Jean-Baptiste fiercely. He was breathing hard. "I've already told you that I love her. I've told you I intend to make her my wife!"

"All I meant to say, Jean-Baptiste, was that she isn't happy in this country and that an unhappy woman never makes a good wife. She wants to return to France. Perhaps you already know that."

The boy looked down at the ground. "She said she wanted to," he stated in a low tone. "I didn't believe her. I thought she was—saying it as a test of my devotion." He lifted his eyes and regarded the head of the family with a belligerent air. "You've been making the most of it, Charles! You've been encouraging her to go back! You won't be content until you've destroyed my chance for happiness!"

The older brother flushed unhappily. "I've always tried to be fair with you. Surely you've realized how fond I am of you and that what I do is in your interests. I'm not trying to destroy your chance for happiness, Jean-Baptiste, I'm trying to preserve it." He paused for a moment and studied the unhappy face of the boy beside him. "I give you my solemn word that she mentioned her wishes without any suggestion or prompting from me."

"Charles!" said Jean-Baptiste, swallowing hard. "Charles! I must know. I must know at once! Are you going to help her to go?"

The Seigneur of Longueuil nodded his head reluctantly. "I'm going to arrange for her return. I repeat, my boy, it's at her own most earnest request. I know it will prove the best thing for all concerned." The pallor of his brother's face led him to add in a compassionate tone: "I know you are going to feel badly about it, my little Jean-Baptiste, but before long you'll be glad. You'll come to see that it wouldn't have been wise to marry her."

The boy cried in a despairing voice: "Now that you've done this to me, you must let me sail with Pierre! All that's left to me now is the chance to die for my country!"

The sound of an angry shout from the corner caused the seigneur to look in that direction. The woodsman was starting another tirade and was waving his arms in the air. "I must attend to this noisy fool!" said Charles le Moyne impatiently. Then he noticed that his brother had turned his back and was walking away from him.

"Jean-Baptiste!" he called anxiously.

The boy paid no attention. He broke into a run which carried him past the angry woodsman and out of sight around the corner of the Rue Notre Dame.

IV

Hippolyte Girard, the builder and carpenter of Longueuil, sat at the head of his table and supped up his soup with an angry air. Because of the heat he had stripped off his clothes on returning from work and had put on a dirty cotton nightgown in which he looked like a rather unhealthy and quite unhappy monkey. In contrast with the cheapness of his shift, a new cap of braided velvet with a gay tassel perched jauntily on his long and knobby head, and his feet had been thrust into the finest of embroidered moccasins.

"We are ruined!" he announced, glancing about the supper table with his dark and beady eyes. "Why do we sit here filling ourselves with costly food when blows of adversity rain upon us? Soon we'll have nothing left, no money, no house, no business. And all"—he turned and glared at a boy of about ten years who sat on his left—"and all because of this greedy fellow here, who lives on my bounty and who'll never be able to pay me back a sou of all the money I lavish on him!"

His son-in-law, Prosper Viau, paid no attention but went on spooning in his soup with the noisy haste of a huge appetite. His daughter looked at the boy and flushed uncomfortably.

"Father!" she protested. "What has Philippe done now?"

"Philippe! There you go again, Cécile. Calling that boy Philippe!" The old man's eyes were snapping angrily. "You know I call him Thomas. You know Thomas is the patron saint of architects and you know I want to make an architect of that boy." He went back to his soup. "You and your Philippe! You're like all women, Cécile. You haven't a patch of sense in you."

"I call him Philippe because that was the name he was given. Was he christened Thomas, Father? You and your Thomas!" Cécile reached out and took hold of his arm. "Wait! The soup is hot anyway. Now you will tell us what is wrong."

The old builder's nostrils flared with the struggle of emotions inside him. "It's the land!" he cried in a piteous voice and putting down his spoon. "The papers were signed and filed today. Jules Carré brought me the news from across the river. And that boy—that boy who has lived with me for nine years, who has been stuffed with the richest food——" There was nothing rich about the platter of soup and the knob of bread which constituted the boy's supper. Life, in fact, had been rather plain and hard for him at every stage of the nine years. "—that boy, to whom I have even given my name——"

"Well, Father, out with it! Don't keep us in suspense in this way. What does Philippe get?"

"He gets nothing!" cried the old man. He picked up his spoon again and began to beat on the table with it. "Nothing! I tell you I've been robbed by those cheating, thieving officials of the court in Montreal. I'm of a mind to enter a suit against them. I'll go to M'sieur Charles to-night——"

Cécile looked up at that. "Is M'sieur Charles at the château?"

Prosper spoke for the first time since the meal began. "Yes. He came this afternoon. There was a man with him. A big man. As big as me."

"Did you see them?" asked his wife anxiously. She knew how bitterly her father objected to his men leaving their work. The mill, on which they were now engaged, was some distance from the château.

"I saw them." Prosper's mouth was full of bread and he spoke indistinctly as a result. "I'd gone to the château to ask about the supplies we need. I saw M'sieur Charles. I saw the big man. He was dressed"—Prosper's dull mind struggled vainly for words to describe the grandeur of the visitor—"he was dressed *fine*."

"It was that man from Versailles," put in the old builder. "He's up to no good, that one! They say he's going to put a stop to the fur trade. What will happen to M'sieur Charles then, *hein?*" An idea occurred to him suddenly. "This M'sieur de Mariat returns to Quebec in two days. I'll write a letter to His Majesty and demand that justice be done me about this land. I'll make it strong. And I'll give it to this M'sieur de Mariat and tell him he must place it himself in the hands of the King." He got up from the table. "I'm going to write the letter now."

He turned and shuffled across the room to a door which opened into the other half of the ground floor of the little house. With a hand on the knob, he turned and said to the boy: "You've had your supper. Go and get your book and start on your studies. I'm going to make an architect of you." He paused and then barked at the boy, "Why do we paint rooms blue inside?"

Philippe, who had given up eating long before, answered in a low voice, "Because it keeps the flies out, m'sieur."

"That is right." The old man, obviously, was disappointed that the proper answer had been forthcoming. "Well, then, tell me this, what do you use in building under the coping of walls?"

"Cogging bricks, m'sieur."

"How did you know I was going to ask you those questions?" demanded the old man. He gave the boy the benefit of a final glare and then disappeared into the room, slamming the door after him.

Cécile looked at the empty plate in front of the boy and asked in a kindly voice, "Would you like more soup, Philippe?"

The boy shook his head. "No, thank you, Cécile. I've had enough."

Cécile, who was a plump and comfortable-looking young woman without any trace of physical resemblance to her father, looked across the table at the steadily munching Prosper. "Well, he'll be busy now for the rest of the evening and we'll see nothing more of him. Writing a letter to the King! Did you ever hear of such nonsense! Prosper, would you like a slice of cake?"

Before her husband could respond with the expected affirmative a knock sounded on the door. A man put his head in without waiting for permission and demanded, "Where's Old Kirkinhead?"

"If you mean my father——" began Cécile, tossing her head angrily.

"I mean your father. Does anyone call him anything else but Old Kirkinhead? Where is he?"

"He's gone to bed. You can't see him tonight, Jacques Simon."

The visitor looked carefully about the room to make sure she had told him the truth. Then he gave his head a surly shake. "So! I can't see him tonight! Well, my girl, you tell him I'll be here in the morning. You tell him that I'm missing that silver harness clasp of mine and that I wonder —that I'm wondering if *he* knows anything about it!"

CHAPTER II

THE HEAT was more intense the next day. No sounds could be heard in the wooded country where the great rivers met, no evidences of human activity were to be seen in the narrow farms. If the Iroquois, who had wiped out the settlement of Lachine in a thunderstorm, had chosen this time to strike again, they would have found the inhabitants of the seigneuries sleeping defenselessly in the shade of their fruit trees or plying drowsy needles in the repair of harness.

The only person at Longueuil who did not seem to be minding the heat was the Sieur de Bienville. The eighth of the Le Moyne brothers had arrived at the château the evening before and had gone immediately to the tower room used by the seigneur for the transaction of business. The talk between them had been a long one and Jean-Baptiste had emerged from it with an unhappy face and a dejected air. A bed had been provided for him in one of the other towers in the hope that it would prove cool. This, as it happened, had been unnecessary. He had been so full of his troubles that he had been unaware of the heat. Sleep being impossible, he had spent the hours of darkness pacing up and down or writing in his small and precise hand in a book which he always carried with him. A dozen times he had reached a decision. "I'll throw everything to the winds!" he said to himself each time. "I'll follow her to France where I'll have a chance, perhaps, to make her change her mind about me." Each time, however, he had realized that to leave now was impossible. He was a Le Moyne and must do his share in the Great Plan (as the younger brothers called it among themselves) to which all of them were committed. Personal considerations could not be allowed to count. He had his own part of the work to do and must persevere to the end, no matter what it might cost him.

He left his room early and was very much surprised to find that Gabriel was down before him. Gabriel was the ninth of the brothers. He was nearly sixteen and he carried himself with great dignity.

Gabriel was sitting in the darkened salon of the apartment that the family occupied on their rare visits to Longueuil and was rattling the dice on the trictrac board with an impatient hand.

"You're up early," said Jean-Baptiste.

"I couldn't sleep. I don't think I slept one minute all night. Do you want to play me a game?" He changed his mind immediately on that point. "No, you always beat me. Charles says you're the clever one of the family. He's always saying things like that, drawing comparisons and finding fault."

"Is Claude-Elizabeth up?"

Gabriel nodded. "She's in her room, writing letters." The ninth brother gave the dice an impatient flip. "Now why does Claude-Elizabeth go to such trouble to write letters to people? Does she forget she was lady in waiting to Madame de France[1] before Charles saw her and brought her back? Why should she write letters?" He scowled importantly. "Of course it's proper for people to write to *her*."

Jean-Baptiste decided to give the young man a piece of advice. "You should never say things like that, Gabriel. I've been keeping an eye on you lately and I must tell you now that you're much too proud. You never care what you say or how much you hurt people's feelings."

"St. John-before-the-Latin-Gate!" exclaimed Gabriel. He opened his mouth and emitted a resounding guffaw. "You're daring to lecture me, you bookworm! So! You're the sagacious one, the Ulysses of the family! To me you would look perfect in the white cap of the Captain of the Head." After this reference to sanitary arrangements on seagoing vessels, he broke off and with the most complete friendliness gave his brother a clump on the back. "Have you heard the news? Pierre is coming here today!"

The face of the Sieur de Bienville became suffused with joy. "I heard a hint of it last night!" he exclaimed. "Charles told me of the rumor he'd heard in Montreal that Pierre was due to arrive. It seemed too good to be true. Gabriel, are you sure about it?"

The younger brother nodded excitedly. "A messenger came with the news before daybreak. Pierre got to Montreal at midnight. He was going to get a few hours' sleep before crossing the river." He indulged in a dance step, twirling one toe high in the air. "Jean-Baptiste! He has conquered Newfoundland! Every village in the Isle of Fogs had surrendered before he left. All the church bells in Montreal will be ringing now to announce the victory. *Donc-donc!* How I wish I was there! The streets will be jammed with people and all the women will be out in their best and the taverns will be filled——"

A sudden hurry took possession of Jean-Baptiste. "I must see Claude-Elizabeth at once," he said.

[1]The eldest daughter of King Louis XIV.

Gabriel paused in his gyrations. "I can't understand why the wife of the Seigneur of Longueuil, with a great man from France in the house as a guest, and Pierre coming this morning, should be staying in her room to write letters. Well, my wise Jean-Baptiste, run along and talk to her. She'll be glad to see you. She seems to like you." After a pause he added, "We all have our tastes."

The Sieur de Bienville walked up a handsome stone staircase to the second floor. His knock on the door of his sister-in-law's bedroom was answered by a prompt and pleasant "Come in." Nevertheless he turned the knob with some hesitation and did not at first venture to put a foot inside.

Claude-Elizabeth, the wife of the seigneur, was so completely French in the eyes of the family (although she had been sent out from France as a girl to attend the Filles de la Congrégation) that they were always a little diffident in their relations with her. Jean-Baptiste had never been inside this much discussed room, which was furnished entirely with beautiful things from Paris. He had seen some of them when they arrived and were taken out of their crates but they had not seemed as fine then. This room, he decided, glancing about him with a feeling of awe, must be the most perfect thing in the world. Certainly there could be nothing finer than the low ivory-colored bed with scenes painted on the headboard (no gloomy four-poster with cobwebs on the tester for the chatelaine of Longueuil) or the commode of the same shade which she used as a dressing table and which sparkled with costly toilet articles. The room was carpeted softly and luxuriantly and there were hangings of lutestring, a glossy silk material, at all the windows. He was surprised to see the curtains because he knew that the windows were filled with what was called "jealous glass." It admitted light but made it impossible for anyone to see into the room.

"Well, Jean-Baptiste?" said his sister-in-law, turning her head to look at him.

"Claude-Elizabeth," he said in a hesitant tone, "I'm hoping you'll say a word to Charles for me."

She smiled at him affectionately. "I'll do anything I can for you but I'm afraid it will be of no use to speak to Charles. It's about the girl, of course——"

He interrupted, shaking his head dismally. "No, not that. That's all settled. I'm not to see her again. I thought you knew."

"I've had no chance to talk with Charles since this"—she dropped her voice—"this *dreadful person* came. Jean-Baptiste, this Monsieur de Mariat makes my flesh creep." She reached out a hand and patted his arm. "I'm *very* sorry about this sad ending to your romance. But I must tell you that I think Charles was right about it. I'm glad you're being so sensible."

"I can claim no credit for common sense." A flush spread over his thin, sensitive face. "Marie made the decision. She wanted to go back to France so much that nothing else counted. She talked to Charles and—and made her own terms." He had been keeping his head bent but now he looked up and 'she saw that his face wore a new expression, one of determination. "Since this has happened to me I should be allowed some say as to what I'm to do now. I must go this time to Mort Bay² with Pierre. It may be the last chance to have a hand in the fighting. Everywhere now you hear it said that the King will soon make peace with the English. I *must* go this time! I must!"

His sister-in-law had gone on scratching at the paper in front of her as they talked. Now she swung around in her chair, surprised at his sudden vehemence. Her dark eyes regarded him with grave concern.

"There are two reasons why Charles doesn't think you should go," she said. "And they sound like *very* good reasons to me. In the first place you're not overly strong. To fight under Pierre—well, it's not work for boys."

The eighth brother began to argue his case in an eager voice. "I've had my term in the navy. I'm stronger than any of you think. I've been training myself all year—running, swimming, fencing. I could stand a campaign under Pierre."

"But Charles says you're better fitted for more important things. You are a scholar, Jean-Baptiste, and there will be so much for you to do that none of the others can. I suppose it would have something to do with administration. Your older brothers feel they can't risk you, Jean-Baptiste."

A change came over the boy. The diffidence with which he had begun the conversation left him completely. He began to speak clearly and vigorously.

"Claude-Elizabeth, you probably have heard of a man in Montreal named Laurent Guillet. He's a merchant in hides and leather. Laurent Guillet is the unhappiest man in all of New France. I'm mentioning him because I don't want to find myself another Laurent Guillet later on.

"It was this way. When Adam Dollard saw the chance to save Montreal by going out to meet the Iroquois at the Long Sault, Laurent Guillet was one of the first to volunteer. But he didn't go. He got the smallpox and he was unconscious when the party left. By the time he recovered, Adam Dollard and all his men were dead. But they had saved the country! He felt so badly that he began to call himself the Man Who Stayed Home. Everyone knew he had meant to go and naturally no one blamed him—but that name stuck to him. He's an old man now but he's been called it ever since. . . . None of the Le Moynes have ever stayed home! When there's been fighting to do, anywhere, on land or water, they've taken the lead. Am I to be the first to stay home?"

²A term sometimes applied to Hudson's Bay by the French who resented the name bestowed on it by the English.

Claude-Elizabeth, who was blessed with understanding, made no effort to meet this argument. She regarded him solicitously for several moments and then said she would speak to her husband. "You're being wise about the girl and very brave about this other matter," she said. "You must be allowed to go with Pierre. I can see that. You must have a chance to win your spurs like the rest. I'll have a word with Charles. Run along now, dear boy, and don't worry about it any more."

Jean-Baptiste took one of her hands and kissed it fervently. "You're wonderful, Claude-Elizabeth!" he exclaimed. "I've always looked up to you and admired you. I think I fell in love with Marie because she looked like you—when you were younger."

"Thanks for the modified compliment," she said, smiling at him. "I'm glad you like me. Some of the others don't. Gabriel always looks at me as though he considers me completely worthless. He's very young and brash but he frightens me." She gave his shoulder a pat and turned back to her correspondence. When he reached the door, however, she looked up again. "Were you very much in love with your Marie, Jean-Baptiste?"

He became instantly again the uncertain hobbledehoy who had entered the room. He blushed and stammered as he replied: "Yes, Claude-Elizabeth. Charles says I'll get over it but I—I'm sure I never shall."

"You will, my dear Jean-Baptiste. Everyone does. You see, there are very few people who haven't made a great renunciation at some time in their lives. It will surprise you how quickly this wound will heal."

Gabriel was still loitering about downstairs. "You were a long time," he said accusingly. "If I didn't know what a frozen stump of a fellow you are, all brains and book learning, I might think you were making love to your brother's wife." He began to shuffle his feet excitedly. "We're getting ready to give Pierre a big reception. Twelve-and-One-More is preparing food for a hundred people. Charles, that prigging miser, will have to dig down into his purse to pay for this. There will be a mass on the common because the chapel holds so few. Charles, the old moneybags, ought to build a larger chapel."

Jean-Baptiste nodded his head with equal delight in the prospects. "Pierre will be pleased. He likes it when people pay him attention. Won't it be grand, Gabriel, to see him like this, coming back a victor and with a laurel wreath in his hair!"

"What's that, poetry?" demanded Gabriel contemptuously.

II

Jean-Baptiste breakfasted pensively but enormously on a fried fish, right out of the river, a crusty loaf of bread, and white wine diluted generously with water. Then he went to the smithy, one of the huddle of wooden buildings within the château walls, and talked with Sooty-Arms, the name by which Jacques Descaries, the smith, was usually known. There was a mystery about Sooty-Arms which no one had ever solved satisfactorily. It was suspected that he had been a man of good birth and an officer in the royal army of Flanders, and that some great tragedy had upset his life. He was a silent man who lived sparsely and always seemed interested in the horizon.

They were comparing D'Iberville with the royal marshals of the day when a message reached Jean-Baptiste that the seigneur desired his presence. He got eagerly to his feet. "Claude-Elizabeth has spoken to him already," he thought.

The seigneur's room was in the northeast tower and was reached by a winding stairway cut into the stone of the wall. It had many advantages. It was large and airy, with windows facing in all directions, and it afforded a view of the great cross on the crest of the mountain as well as of the family island of Ste. Hélène. Here Charles le Moyne had collected reminders of his father. He had felt, when he began on the erection of this imposing structure, that it was to be a monument to the memory of the great man who had laid the foundations of the family grandeur and who was still called by everyone at Longueuil Old M'sieur Charles. Less sentimental in all other respects than the rest of the brothers, the head of the family had a feeling for his father which amounted to idolatry. There was peace as well as satisfaction for him in having about him some of the first seigneur's possessions.

The roughhewn beams of red pine on the ceiling had been brought from the first Le Moyne store in Montreal. There was a black walnut corner cupboard with sixteen small panes of glass, none of them so much as cracked, which had been a source of family pride when they lived on St. Joseph Street. The silver-hilted sword of Old M'sieur Charles hung on a wall with a silver cord.

Beside the sword was a hat which had belonged to the old man. It was of beaver and it was out of shape, which was not surprising in a hat which had known the icy spray of the river rapids, the smoke of Indian encampments, the bite of wind and storm. None of the older brothers (the youngest of them, beginning with Jean-Baptiste, did not remember their father very well, for he had brought sons into the world almost to the time of his death, twelve years before) could look at the old beaver without seeing his resolute face under it. They were even prone to believe that the hat projected itself into the discussions held in this room, its crown slipping over like a nod of approval or wrinkling itself in dissent. Even the three youngest had come to have this feeling about their father's hat and to regard it as a sort of family oracle.

When Jean-Baptiste entered, the seigneur looked as though he had been struggling with a decision on which the advice of the shabby hat of Old M'sieur Charles might have been helpful.

"Jean-Baptiste," he said, "I've been thinking about you. I've reached a conclusion which won't give me cause for regret later, I most earnestly hope."

The younger brother said to himself exultantly, "He's going to let me go."

The seigneur's mind might be made up but he seemed reluctant to commit himself. He rubbed a finger along the bridge of his nose and frowned.

"I'm going to let you go with Pierre," he said abruptly. "As you know, I've been against the idea. But—well, you're reaching a man's years, Jean-Baptiste, and you feel strongly about this chance to show your mettle. I yield to your wishes, my boy." He stretched a hand across the desk and laid it on his brother's shoulder. "I give in. I can't see you unhappy, Jean-Baptiste."

It seemed to the boy that the hot rays of the morning sun which poured in through the east window had become celestial beams. He was to have his chance! He seized the seigneur's hand and shook it exuberantly. "Thank you, Charles, thank you! I'll always remember this! I'll always think of you as the best of brothers!"

The seigneur studied the smiling face in front of him before proceeding. "You must make me a promise. You must promise not to take unnecessary risks. I must be sure you won't—throw your life away as Louis did in the bay and François at Repentigny. There was no need for those splendid boys to prove their courage the way they did. They seemed to think that death couldn't touch them; even that it didn't matter. You mustn't court death, as they did. You are, after all, a Le Moyne. No son of Old M'sieur Charles could fail of having courage. Everyone knows that."

Jean-Baptiste hesitated over his reply. "I must never hold back from doing my full duty because of risks," he said. "But this much I do promise, that I won't do foolhardy things—as Louis and François may have done."

Charles snapped him up on this with the alacrity he sometimes displayed in commercial deals. "That's all I ask. Always obey orders but never walk into the mouth of cannon or stand up under fire. To die may be glorious but victories are won by surviving." He nodded his head vigorously. "I happen to be quite fond of you, my boy. You've always seemed to me like a son as well as a brother. I don't want to lose you."

"I mean to keep my promise, Charles."

"You must never forget it." The tone of the seigneur had become urgent, even a shade peremptory. "I'm going to need you later. For the most important kind of work, Jean-Baptiste—work which you alone of the younger ones can do. You have gifts which will make you a great man, if you use them. I've said this to you before but I want to impress it on you again, now that you're to serve with Pierre. I see a shining future for you. Who knows, you may someday be governor of New France!"

"If any of us becomes governor, it will be you, Charles."

The older brother shook his head. "The mind of Versailles won't change soon enough for that. The old King is set against putting anyone of Canadian birth in a high post. A change of policy will come about but it's more likely to be in your time than in mine." He leaned back in his chair. "And now there's another matter, my boy. I have your promise about this girl, and I know you'll keep it. Always remember this, that you must marry well. You must ally yourself with one of the great families of France. Oh, it's not impossible! The name of Le Moyne is beginning to mean a great deal. Your wife, when you take one, must bring you wealth and high connections."

Jean-Baptiste was plunged back into his earlier mood of melancholy by this reopening of a sore subject. "I'm never going to marry, Charles," he said. Then he nodded his head with a suggestion of determination. "Can't we make a bargain between us never to—to mention the subject again? All I want to think of now is that I have some fighting to do!"

III

Because of the heat Old Kirkinhead had not started for work at his usual early hour. He was sitting at his breakfast, still in his cotton nightgown and with the cap of braided velvet still perching on the top of his head. Philippe had not gone to work either, having the household chores to attend to before starting on the serious duties of the day. He had brought water from the well and had carried in a day's supply of kindling wood. His voice could now be heard through the rear window, admonishing Blanchefleur, the goat, to get under way for the pasture with her latest family. "Must I haul you with a rope, old Stubbornness?" he was demanding. "Must I lay a stick across your rump to make you behave?"

Old Kirkinhead rose from the table and rubbed the side of his hand across his mouth. "Never has there been such a stupid one!" he muttered. "That boy was nearly a year old. Has he no memories at all? No hints to help me find which family he belonged to? That boy, he's the head of an ox!"

"No one remembers anything as young as that," protested Cécile, whose hands were deep in dough.

"I do!" snapped her father, his hot brown eyes fairly swimming in anger. "I could tell you hundreds of things which happened to me before I was a year old. I could tell you about my first bath."

His daughter said under her breath, "He could tell me about all his baths without taking up much time."

The old builder scuffled over to the door of the inner room. He was still muttering. "Can't he remember a single name? Can't he as much as describe a face? That boy, he's a silly *badaud* who doesn't care if he comes into property or not!"

The inner room held the evidence of a curious folly in which he had indulged himself all his life. He was a collector, a human raven who picked up everything old and useless. He never went out of the house without bringing something home—a flint, a discarded piece of sailcloth, a rusty hinge, a handful of dog nails. Whenever there was an auction in Montreal he would be found on the front bench, snapping his fingers, arguing with the auctioneer, bidding a sol here and a sol there. He always returned with his mule cart piled up with frayed whips and forks lacking tines and bells without clappers. He was convinced that he would be able to sell everything he picked up at a big profit but, needless to state perhaps, he never did.

One side of the room, from corner to corner and right up to the black larch beams of the ceiling, was filled with the fruits of his scavengering. There was a rope strung from wall to wall on which hung a collection of old hats: mangy caps of coonskin and otter, three-cornered hats called *claques* which had once adorned proud heads but would have been scorned by a city beggar in their present state, *tapabords* and old slouches of felt with tawdry plumes. There were trunks with open tops from which leaked the most incongruous trash. Old Kirkinhead's motive had always been to make a profit on his finds but it was curious how uneasy he became when anyone professed a desire to look over the stock with an eye to purchases. This reluctance of his had not gone unnoticed and it had fed the belief generally held that the builder was not above taking things which did not belong to him.

The old man was reaching for his clothes with the intention of dressing for the day's labors when he heard a feminine voice at the front door, crying, Cécile! Cécile!"

"That wife of Carré's again!" he muttered in a tone of disgust. "Why doesn't she stay home and do her work? If she was *my* wife I would give her a good beating every day of her life."

The high-pitched voice of young Madame Carré reached him again. "Drop what you're doing, Cécile! Get dressed at once. Pierre is coming to Longueuil this morning and everyone's to be at the château to give him a welcome. Yes, yes, the Sieur d'Iberville! Our great hero himself, back from the fighting. Oh, I love him, he has such a wonderful laugh and those great blue eyes which look straight through you! You must put on your best things, Cécile. I'm going to wear——"

Old Kirkenhead appeared in the door of his room. "What's this?" he demanded. "M'sieur Pierre is coming?"

Madame Carré, who was plump and pert, winked at the daughter.

"What an old dog it is! Does he wear that cap to bed? How can he sleep in it without getting notions——" She winked at him with a lively black eye. "Hurry, neighbor. I'm counting on you as my escort because Jules will be busy for another hour."

"And I," cried Old Kirkinhead, "will be busy all day! I must get to the mill and see to it that none of my lazy fellows hear of this and go running off to gape at M'sieur Pierre. I won't have it! I don't pay them to go running off like this because someone comes to the château, even if it is M'sieur Pierre."

He disappeared and for several minutes could be heard talking to himself as he dressed in frantic haste. When he returned to the outer room, which combined the functions of kitchen, dining room, and salon, the neighbor's wife had gone.

"That hussy, that vixen, that silly piece!" he spluttered. "Gadding about and putting notions in people's heads. 'Get yourself dressed for the reception, Cécile! Put on your best things, Cécile!' Her husband should take her over his knee and warm her cul with an ax handle!" He peered at his daughter, who was bending above the mixing bowl. "No running off, mind you. There's plenty to keep you busy here." He paused as a sudden horrified suspicion took possession of him. "Is that a cake you're making? And with an egg?"

"Yes, it's a cake, Father. My Prosper likes cake and I'm making one for his supper. And there are two eggs in it, if you want to know."

"You fool!" cried the old man furiously. "Don't you realize, brainless one, that everything I have will come to you in the end? When you put eggs in a cake they come right out of your own pocket, you great goose!"

His daughter indulged in a feeble giggle. "These eggs didn't come out of my pocket, Father. They came right out of the nest."

"I've nothing left to live for!" shouted the old man, throwing both arms above his head. "I have a daughter who throws my money away, who tosses it about like a spendthrift. My son-in-law will have my business after I'm gone and he doesn't know enough to build a hog wallow! There's that boy who forgets everything just to keep me from getting my hands on another bit of land!"

His eyes were passionately angry in his wrinkled, sallow face but for once his daughter did not cringe from him. He had put on a gilet of green ferrandine which had once been good but was now rumpled and split in places and stained yellow under the arms. That the *chaussettes* covering his skinny legs were of wool might have been owing to forgetfulness of the season (if anyone could forget it was midsummer!) or a disinclination to change; but certain it was that they hung loosely and fell into untidy folds at the ankles. Again, however, he proved by his hat that a sense of pride still persisted in him. It was of green felt and it was expensive and new, and its wide brim was turned up in the extreme of fashion on three sides. Altogether it looked as much out of place with the rest of his attire as an ostrich feather in the tail of a goose.

Cécile began to laugh and the old man's eyes filled with tears of self-pity. "My own daughter makes fun of me!" he croaked. "I've become an object of derision—I, who once had genius in me! *Tiens,* there's no trace of the genius left. Could I build a cathedral today after spending my life putting up mousetraps like this hovel? Could I design graceful columns after forty years of planing off the seats of *secrets* so ladies won't get splinters in their fat white buttocks?"

There was a brass hook in one of the ceiling beams which was used for weighing and measuring. The builder, who was sinking deeper into despondency with each moment, looked up at it.

"They don't want me around any more!" he whispered huskily. "They want to be rid of me. They want my business and my money, little though it is. Someday I'll listen to the voices inside me and I'll put an end to my life. I'll hang myself—up there—like the criminal they think I am! Then," nodding with the melancholy satisfaction to be found in this form of speculation, *"then* they'll know how much they need me, how much they depend on me! They'll be sorry. But—it will be too late."

"Get along with you," said Cécile briskly. "I'm tired of hearing you talk about hanging yourself."

While all this went on there had been complete silence from the garden back of the little house where Philippe, supposedly, was still doing the morning chores. Old Kirkinhead became aware at this moment of the lack of sound and knew at once what it meant.

"He's gone!" he shouted. "He heard what that woman said and he's legging it for the château this very minute!"

He rushed out of the house, screaming at the top of his voice. "Come back, you good-for-nothing *badaud!* Come back or I'll attend to you with a seaming mallet!"

IV

If he heard the loud commands of his master the boy paid no attention. At the first mention of D'Iberville he had thought ecstatically: "He's coming! He's coming home at last! I'll be able to see him!" It had not occurred to him not to go. If the hero of New France honored his old home with a visit everyone should be there to cheer for him.

He made his way through the woods in a mood of intense excitement, fearful that he would be too late to witness the arrival of the great man. "My master will be angry," he said to himself. "I don't care if he is! I don't care what happens to me. I must see M'sieur Pierre."

He had selected the cover of the trees rather than trusting himself on the white target of the river road, this being a form of caution which came instinctively to all sons of New France. The bold measures of the old governor, the Comte de Frontenac, had taught the Iroquois a lesson and there had been no raids as far north as this for several years. Still they were such sly and daring enemies that no Canadian believed he had heard for the last time the shrill and spine-tingling cry of *"Cassee Koues!"* with which the warriors from the land of the Long House went into battle.

As he made his way through the trees, where the heat was even more oppressive, the boy's thoughts went back to the last occasion when he had seen the Sieur d'Iberville. It had been three years before and on a day almost as warm as this. Several of the Le Moynes were accompanying him on the expedition he was leading to Hudson's Bay and all of Longueuil had turned out to see them leave. There had been praying and cheering, and much weeping on the part of the ladies; because, of course, many of the young men from the seigneurie were going with them.

He, Philippe, had climbed into a tree at the edge of the clearing, the better to see. His eyes had been so full of the great leader that he had hardly noticed the others. This had been a pity, as he realized later, for one of the brothers had not come back, M'sieur Louis who was called the Sieur de Châteauguay and was then no older than eighteen years. Philippe began to think now of the gallant way this boy had died, charging up to the English fort and paying no heed to the bullets until one lodged in his throat. "That brave Louis!" said Philippe to himself. "He was D'Iberville's favorite brother and no one was ever finer." He began to think, as he had often done before, that he would like that kind of death for himself. How splendid it would be to look down from up there in the sky and hear people talking about you and saying how brave you had been!

"I wish *I* was a Le Moyne!" he said aloud.

He stopped dead at that, realizing that he should know better than to entertain such thoughts, even in the inner recesses of his mind. The Le Moynes were a great and powerful and wealthy family. Their greatness did not come from any inheritance of aristocratic blood. Old M'sieur Charles, the father who had died full of honor more than ten years before, had been the son of an innkeeper of Dieppe. The family was remarkable because all of the ten sons, by some miracle, had seemed to come from the same mold, all sharing the qualities of their sire—courage, coolness, resource, the highest of ideals. Philippe had heard someone speak of them as fabulous. He had no idea what the word meant but there was something about the sound which suited it to the Le Moynes.

Standing motionless, with a hand pressed against the trunk of a tree, he said to himself: "They would be ashamed to have a puny bag of bones like me one of them." He knew all his own faults perfectly well because they were dinned into his ears from morning to night. He sighed and said aloud, "I'm where I belong and I must give up such foolish thoughts."

Thinking of his shortcomings brought the boy to an abrupt realization that he was afraid. This was not surprising. There was no living soul within a quarter mile of where he stood and an ominous quiet had settled down over the forest. He strained to catch any sound of the snapping of twigs under savage feet and he expected every moment to see painted faces staring at him from behind the trunks of trees. He jumped when a bird piped up above him, sure that it was the first note of the terrible Iroquois battle cry.

Then he pulled himself together and said, "I'm not a Le Moyne but I must try to act like one." He refused to hurry after that and even essayed to whistle *"Rossignolet Sauvage,"* the first tune which came into his head. It was with a sense of intense relief that finally he saw light ahead and knew that he had reached the edge of the common of Longueuil. If he had been in any danger it was over.

Never had the château looked grander or more impressive. Standing in the middle of the common, its towers seemed to stretch up higher than ever before. The cluster of roofs showing above the wall had a city-like density. The sculptured figures in the chapel niches gave an air of grandeur as well as sanctity to the pile. The sun glinted on metal from the top of one of the corner towers and Philippe knew that it came from the musket of a guard stationed there. This was a symbol of the security he had reached.

Twelve-and-One-More, the baker of Longueuil and the cook of the château (no one ever called him by his name, which was François Dandin), was working at the outside oven. There was an oven inside, of course, built in the cellar at the base of one of the huge chimneys, and this was large enough to supply all the needs of the household. In planning the château, however, Charles Le Moyne had been lavish about everything. The outside oven, which was raised on columns of stone and had double doors of cast iron, was for emergency use. The fact that the baker was tending it himself was proof of the extent of the preparations being made for the day.

Twelve-and-One-More was a giant, standing an even seven feet without his shoes and weighing some fabulous number of pounds. He had an immense round head with bristling black hair and a set of features as cruel and malignant as the mask of an Eastern magician. His appearance, however, was entirely misleading. The baker of Longueuil was as gentle as most men of abnormal size. His voice was thin and friendly and he was often seen with birds perched on his shoulders.

He looked up from raking at the coals under the oven when Philippe drew near. "It's my small friend," he said. "I expected you today. You have that piece of carving you promised me, no?"

The boy shook his head. "I had the figure finished, M'sieur Twelve-and-One-More, a soldier with long mustaches and a very fierce expression. I think it was good. But my master found it and said he would see how much it would bring in Montreal. I haven't heard a word about it since."

The cook said in his treble voice: "He has sold it, that old Kirkinhead, that clutch-purse! He has hidden the money away. He's a very bad man, your master. Whenever I see him I think how easy it would be, and how very pleasant, to take him in my hands and squeeze all the meanness out of him. I would like to do it because of the way he treats you, my small friend Philippe."

"I'll carve another for you, M'sieur Twelve-and-One-More," promised the boy.

The baker said "Good!" and then stooped over to rake at the fire. "When M'sieur Pierre gets here," he added, "he'll find Twelve-and-One-More hasn't forgotten what he likes. Three dozen loaves I'm baking and enough cake to satisfy every sweet tooth in Longueuil. Tonight for the supper *en famille*"—he straightened up and nodded his head importantly—"there will be a bisque of pigeons and cockscombs. There will be my *salade Longueuil*—ah, my small friend, what a *salade!*—and a pasty with every kind of game in it as well as two dozen juicy young squirrels. For the dessert *crêpes de Tante Marie*. My small friend, they will know tonight that I'm not only the biggest man in New France but the best cook."

The boy was noticing that tenants and their families were arriving already by paths through the woods. The sound of voices reached them from all directions and there was a creak of wheels on the Chambly Road. A male voice was singing somewhere:

> *"La mère étant sur les carreaux*
> *A vu venir son fils Renaud."*

"Everyone will be here," said the cook. "Except that master of yours and his great ox of a son-in-law. It will be a busy day for me. There's a whole steer roasting on a spit in the courtyard. Every pot I could get my hands on is filled with hens. *Mais voilà!* I like to see people fill their bellies, the good St. Joseph knows I do. I like to see them dressed up and having a good time. Keep your eyes open, my friend Philippe, and you'll see some gay costumes today."

He opened the door of the oven. His long scoop went far back into the interior and came out with a square of cake resting on the end. The most delightful odor which had ever assailed Philippe's nostrils filled the air. With a pleased wink Twelve-and-One-More broke off a large piece and then divided this in halves. He kept one half for himself and handed the other to the boy.

"Eat it, my small friend," he said. "I'll wager all the coins in my purse you've never tasted anything like it before."

He had made a safe boast. The cake was filled with almond paste, which was completely strange to Philippe's palate. In addition it was filled with unusual spices and there were so many fat raisins in it that they threatened to pop out at the slightest pressure of the hand. Philippe had never tasted anything which could be compared to this divine food.

The cook watched him with a shake of the head. The boy's face was thin and his eyes had a withdrawn look which was disturbing in one so young. It was clear that he was finding it easier to live within the four walls of his own mind. "That Old Kirkinhead!" said Twelve-and-One-More to himself. "He's starving this poor little fellow."

"Is it, Philippe," he asked finally, "that your master is sparing with the food?"

"No, m'sieur," protested the boy. "I have plenty to eat."

"I'm sure he doesn't understand the appetites of growing boys. You're much too thin, my Philippe. And that old cheese nipper makes you do the work of a man." He broke off another slab and divided it between them. Feeding his own share into his great gristmill of a mouth, he continued to air his unfavorable opinion of the builder. "He will be the only one to keep his men at work today. He has no decency of feeling, that dried-up pod of a man. He forgets everything M'sieur Pierre has done for us." The trend of his thoughts having been diverted to the exploits of D'Iberville, he became easier in mood. "It's hard to believe that such a great man was born and grew up right here. I remember when he was a rough little fellow with a quick word and a laugh and a blow always on tap. You, Philippe, are not like your master, you have a heart inside you; and so you can see it as a miracle, as I do, that this rough-and-tumble boy, this Pierre le Moyne, is now the greatest fighter on land and on sea in the whole world. It makes one think deeply on God's purpose." He brushed the crumbs from his mouth. "And now I must return to my work. I'll see you later, my small Philippe."

CHAPTER III

WHILE the people of Longueuil were gathering to welcome D'Iberville the seigneur sat in his tower room with Joseph de Mariat. It was easy to see that Charles le Moyne felt some resentment at the confidence of his visitor's manner, which came very close to condescension. He had been polite and complimentary but he had been on his guard. He had seldom taken his eyes from the large white face in which cupidity and guile lurked behind an outward suggestion of amiability.

The man from France extended a gold snuffbox. It was a handsome and costly specimen with a pearl-embroidered miniature of the King on the lid. Its owner raised his eyebrows when the seigneur refused. "It's the very best from Brazil. You never take snuff? Odd. Odd, indeed."

"We're far removed from the luxuries of the world. We have simple habits, m'sieur."

The visitor regarded the box with an eye of great pride. "A gift-from His Majesty," he said. "I prize it so much I never trust it out of my hands, M'sieur le Baron."

His small shrewd eyes were fixed intently on his host as he said this. When the latter reacted to the form of salutation with a start of surprise he burst into a laugh which caused his fat sides to quiver. "Your pardon, if you please, for permitting my tongue, over which I generally have complete control, to wax prophetic. Still, my good friend Charles, if you will allow me to call you that, it was an understandable slip. I've a reputation at court as a prophet and I'm prepared to stake it on this: you will soon be the Baron of Longueuil, perhaps within a year. It's written in—in the political stars."

His host's face flushed with excitement. No longer content with the ennoblement of the family, which had come in his father's time, he felt that the Le Moynes had earned something more. This first indication that his efforts to secure a title seemed likely to succeed afforded him the most intense satisfaction.

"I shall be very happy, my good friend Joseph, if time proves you to be right in this matter," he said.

De Mariat began to indulge in a habit of his, when engaged in conversation, of sharpening a quill point (which tended to make timorous people uneasy as it suggested he was about to set down dangerous evidence or draw up some damning legal document), taking great pains to get it sharp and even. Without looking up, he asked, "You would like this title very much, my good Charles?" Not waiting for an answer, he went on. "Brush all doubts from your mind. The King has promised. It's his way to give his word and then delay in the fulfilling of it. A caprice of greatness, you understand. Although the title will be yours, it will come in his own good time. Six months, nine, a year perhaps. It may be that when the news of D'Iberville's victories reaches him he will have the papers drawn at once. The royal ear catches and prizes every whisper of glory for France and himself." He looked up and tapped his thumb with the quill. "I had a double purpose in coming to New France. To acquire a full understanding of the fur trade. And to propose an alliance with you, Charles le Moyne."

The seigneur had sensed what was in his visitor's mind from the first moment of his arrival and he had given much thought in advance to the expected suggestion. He knew that De Mariat, although he held no ministry, wielded power in the inner council at Versailles. Of all the royal officials with whom he dealt, De Mariat was the most prompt and satisfactory. He would be a valuable ally; on that score the seigneur had no doubts at all. But he was ambitious, greedy, an opportunist, not to be trusted entirely. It was a trying situation to face.

As their eyes met and held, for the first time since the discussion began, Charles le Moyne said to himself: "But, after all, there's no one I can trust at Versailles. They're all selfish and unscrupulous. This man can be depended on, at least, to carry through his part of our plans. He doesn't allow letters to gather dust on his desk. He gets results."

Finding that he had thus in a few seconds come closer to reaching a decision than he had been able to do the night before after hours of careful thought, the Seigneur of Longueuil leaned forward across the desk.

"I may tell you," he said, "that the same idea has been in my own mind. But before we can come to any agreement you must know what we're planning to do. It's an ambitious idea. It may yield us more credit than wealth. And it may not be to your liking, m'sieur."

The man from France fitted his penknife back into its leather sheaf. "Tell me about it, then," he said.

"First, a question. Does it surprise you that of ten brothers not one has offered himself for service in the Church?"

"It is—somewhat unusual."

"It was not because of any lack of religious feeling. That I assure you. It was because we are men of action. We knew we could better serve our heavenly Father in other ways. I want you to understand that with us our duty to the Church and to the King comes before any thought of reward for ourselves."

Joseph de Mariat inclined his head to express his understanding of this.

"We Canadians see the dangers of our situation clearly. And even more clearly we see the great destiny which lies ahead of us. If we can grasp it, m'sieur, or rather *if we are permitted to grasp it*. The seaboard lands can't be taken away from the English but all the rest of this great continent must be ours. There's a way to win it. La Salle knew what that way was but he was hampered by neglect and carelessness. La Salle is dead. It's for us to finish what he began, the men of New France, and most particularly the family of Le Moyne. There are seven of us left. Can seven Le Moynes finish what one La Salle began? I think so, m'sieur."

The top of the desk was covered with articles of silver. The seigneur was a zealous patron of native art and he liked to have a few specimens about him. The collection before him now included a boldly executed silver cup of a singular purity of design, a small *écuelle* with a thimble handle which could be used as a dram cup, and a handsome platter on which the Le Moyne crest had been raised. All these pieces were the work of a young silversmith of Quebec, one of the graduates of the school Bishop Laval had established at Cap Tourmente.

Charles le Moyne was so absorbed in what he was saying that, for the first time perhaps, he was completely unaware of these prized items from his collection. When his hand touched the cup by mistake, and knocked it over, he did not realize what had happened.

"Much of what I'm going to say is an old story to you," he went on. "But I must say it again. If we can take the Mississippi into our control, with a great port at its mouth and with forts placed at strategic points, we can lock the English in between the river and the sea. But no time is to be lost. The English are pouring across the sea. They outnumber us already. Say what you like about them, they make good settlers, these sons of shopkeepers. They're clearing the land, building towns, spreading out like floodwater when a dam bursts." He paused to study the face across the desk from him, wondering how frank he could afford to be. "We mustn't mince words, my friend Joseph. Our King, generous though he is, hasn't the right conception of this problem. He still restricts the number of settlers allowed to come out. He hampers us with laws. He wants to dictate to us how we are to live and work—even how we are to die."

"His Majesty," declared De Mariat with a throaty chuckle, "would fall into a great fury if he heard you say that. But rest easy, my good Charles. I am no talebearer. His Majesty aims to make New France the ideal feudal state. He doesn't want you to think. He believes you Canadians should be content to stand on a rampart and hold a musket, and in your off hours cultivate a garden patch."

"Here is the difference, as I see it," declared Le Moyne. "The English decided from the start that America was to become a country for white men. We plan to keep it a country for red men—with settlements here and there from which Frenchmen may control them and save their souls."

"I've never heard it put that way before," said De Mariat. "But I believe, my good Charles, that you have stated the two policies accurately."

Watching the face of his companion closely, Le Moyne said, "It's a policy nevertheless which won't change until—until a very sad event transpires at Versailles."

There was a longer pause, the two men nodding slowly to each other in somber agreement. "Let us then talk about this openly and frankly," said Le Moyne finally. "If we're to make any move at all we must do it without delay. As there's no chance to match the English in numbers, we must pit against the inexorable growth of our enemies the qualities in which we excel—our vision, our daring!"

"Yes!" exclaimed De Mariat, whose part would be to sit at a desk and write letters and keep the threads of petty intrigue in his hands. "St. Christophe, yes! We have imagination, we have verve, we have a—a sense of destiny!"

"There's a great empire to be won," declared Le Moyne, not pausing to think what it would mean in terms of hardship and suffering and bloodshed to the men who, like the Le Moynes, must see to the winning of it. His eyes began to gleam with a trace of fanaticism which surprised his companion, who knew him as a keen man of affairs and the builder of a fortune under difficult circumstances. "Never in the history of the world has there been such an opportunity! Here we have a continent many times larger than all of Europe, perhaps greater than all the rest of the world put together. It teems with riches—fur and fish and, somewhere, gold. It's a greater opportunity, Joseph de Mariat, than you have ever realized." He paused and brought his eyes back to a scrutiny of his guest's face. "You've asked to be a partner. What can you bring to such an alliance?"

The man from Versailles straightened up in his chair. His manner became brisk. "I must tell you first that I'll never be a member of the ministry as long as the King lives. The old woman[1] will see to that. I'm not an appointee of hers and so she regards me as a potential enemy. She laughs at the size of me and calls me *ce petit Mariat*. Sometimes she calls me *ce ladre-là*, even to my face. There's an advantage in having her call me a skunk. Those she likes are invited to talk to the King in her apartments. They meet there in the mornings and evenings. She listens, smiles, puts in her opinion. The decisions seem to be made by the King but this I

[1]Madame de Maintenon, the King's mistress and later his unacknowledged wife.

tell you, they come from the old witch herself. Now I, *ce petit Mariat,* am in a much better position. I have an alliance with the Pen.[2] I sit at a desk at the center of things. Letters pass through my hands, often before they reach the ministers. His Benign Majesty passes that desk several times a day. Always he stops and talks to me. Matters are settled between us— quick! Like that! Matters of which the old woman never hears. Some- times I think I have more influence over him than anyone. My good Charles, I am a paradox. I am nothing, I am everything!" He smiled triumphantly. "What can I bring to the alliance? I will tell you. A chance to fill the ears of His Majesty with your accomplishments and your needs. The certainty that I can bring all matters to immediate consideration. The chance to influence him favorably about supplies and ships and soldiers. And"—he drew up one corner of his face in a wink—"an ear to hear what's being said and done, to learn of opposition early. I offer you, my good Charles, the most useful pair of ears in all of France, a tongue which has learned how to persuade the King to any action, and a brain. The best brain in Versailles, as I have no hesitation in proclaiming."

The two men, as though by an unspoken agreement, allowed them- selves to sink back into their chairs. For several moments they studied each other without a word being said. Then they smiled and nodded their heads. Le Moyne's smile was a wry one, for he still felt a reluctance to this arrangement which necessity was forcing on him.

"Then it's agreed?" demanded De Mariat.

"It's agreed."

The King's officer set to work again on the point of the quill but kept his eyes to their task of watching the Seigneur of Longueuil. "Shall we discuss terms now?"

The seigneur shook his head. "Let the details wait for our next talk. There will be no difficulty about the terms, I assure you. Today there are other matters to be settled which are more pressing."

"Very well. We'll do things your way."

"We have so much to do and so little time left. D'Iberville will leave again in a few days to meet the ships coming from France, and then he sails to attack the English in Hudson's Bay. When the conquest of the bay has been accomplished, a second fleet must be ready to seize the mouth of the Mississippi. If this program is to move forward without hitch we must have every move planned in advance."

De Mariat continued to scrape away at the pen point. "It's clear," he said, "that you've never been put to the necessity of getting the King's consent to anything. This was what he said when the question of the

[2]Louis XIV had a secretary who could imitate the royal handwriting and who attended to all his correspondence. The Pen, as this indispensable servant was called, exerted an influence over the King which even Madame de Maintenon could not shake.

Mississippi was last broached: 'Haven't I supplied ships for the Hudson's Bay? Must I promise more before we know the results of the first? Am I made of ships?' There is this to be said, he is hard pressed for funds at the moment. . . . Now allow me to explain how best it can be done. When D'Iberville has captured Fort Nelson he must sail at once to France and make the request for more ships himself." The large man leaned back in his chair and crossed one gross leg over the other. "You see? It is perfect! The hero of New France, with the laurels of victory on his brow, comes to lay another conquest at the feet of his King and begs a chance to prove his devotion in another field. It's the kind of thing our far from modest monarch has never been able to resist."

The seigneur had listened with a startled air. "But have you thought what this would mean? If my brother is fortunate enough to finish the campaign before the ice closes the bay for the winter, he would have to turn his ships eastward as soon as the fighting was over. Can you conceive of the hardships? What would he do with his wounded? Leave them at Fort Nelson for the winter or carry them across the Atlantic? Either way they would die like flies."

The court official raised his brows. "You know the danger of delay," was his only comment.

Charles le Moyne pondered the matter with a worried frown. "We must discuss this with Pierre. After all, it's for him to decide."

De Mariat uncrossed his legs and got to his feet, thus calling attention to the fact that the canions on the ends of his breeches were so expertly tailored that they concealed the garters which held up his hose. This was a nicety the tailors of New France had not yet mastered. He was so richly attired, in fact, that the seigneur had been in a state of amazement ever since his arrival the evening before. "And yet to judge this man a fop," said the latter to himself, "would be a very serious mistake. He has spun a web at court and sits in the center of it like a watchful spider."

The visitor cleared his throat. "My grandfather," he declared, "was a poverty-stricken merchant in Marseille. Your grandfather, my dear Charles, was an innkeeper at Dieppe."

"That is true. My father was a remarkable man and I take pride in what he accomplished."

"There's an interesting speculation for us to share. Someday the grandson of the Dieppe innkeeper may be the greatest man in America. Someday the grandson of the ship chandler of Marseille may be . . ." He paused and shook his head. "No, I mustn't put into words the full scope of my ambitions. This much I'll say, I aim high." He reached out one of his great soft hands and placed it on the seigneur's shoulder. "My very good Charles, what a splendid thing it would be if we could bind our interests more closely together by a matrimonial alliance. My fine little son is six years old. Now if you had a daughter . . ."

The seigneur answered with a haste which might have suggested a sense of relief. "No, m'sieur. My only daughter has espoused Holy Church. She is with the order of the Augustines in Quebec."

"But your wife—a woman of singular charm, my good Charles—might still supply the deficiency. Let us keep it in mind. I take the greatest pride in my small Auguste. You should have observed him killing ants, the little rascal, when he was less than a year old. With the heel of an old shoe. The sight of blood always made him fairly dance with excitement. Does that mean he will be a soldier? And what an instinct he has for acquisition! Before he was three he had filled the space under his bed with things which had caught his fancy. When anything was missed, one knew exactly where to look. Ah, what a promising boy!" He removed his hand from his host's shoulder. "Keep what I've said in mind, Charles, keep it in mind."

II

While Charles and the man from France discussed the future the two youngest brothers had been circulating among the guests. Gabriel made no effort to conceal the fact that he was annoyed at the way the tenants and their families were invading the interior of the château. He called the attention of Little Antoine, the baby of the family, who would be fourteen in a few days and was already close to six feet tall, to the fact that they had taken possession of the *puits-de-margelle* in the center of the grass plot and were hauling up buckets of water from it to quench their thirst and lave their faces.

"Something should be done about this," he grumbled.

Little Antoine did not share his brother's feeling. "I see nothing wrong in what they're doing," he declared. "They're here to welcome Pierre and they are guests of the house. Pierre will thump all of them on the back and call them by their first names. They'll worship him more than ever. See how happy they are, D'Assigny," giving Gabriel his title, a formality on which the latter sternly and unbendingly insisted. "They are all dressed up for the occasion."

They were indeed all dressed up. The men were wearing their long-tailed blue coats, which marked them as being of the Montreal district (in Quebec men wore red and in Three Rivers white), and they had hats of straw instead of the habitual brimless bonnets of their working days. The women were even more festive. Their usual cloth bodices and short skirts had been replaced by light gowns of gay colors with Basque bodices. Their hair showed signs of the hasty use of curling irons and on the cheeks of all the young women could be detected a furtive dash of rouge.

"Why do they ape their betters in this way?" demanded Gabriel in an indignant undertone.

He himself had spared no pains to look well for the occasion. He had donned a long coat (not for him the old-fashioned *pourpoint* or doublet) of light blue with turned-up cuffs. Under it he wore *brelettes,* as the first suspenders were called, of a violent purple shade, to hold his buff breeches in place. His hat was made of goat-hair felt, with ribbon around the brim, a kind which had been all the rage in Paris for some years and had at last reached the colony. He kept his hand on his hip in the approved manner as he scornfully surveyed the people milling about the central yard. On the point of indulging in more criticism, his eyes (which were quite handsome and could be good-natured when he forgot how important it was to be a Le Moyne) lighted up suddenly and his upper lip curled in amusement.

"Look at Babette Carré!" he said to his brother with a splutter of amusement. "That little *dondon* has certainly grown herself a well-rounded behind! Look at the swing she gives herself. *Donc-donc!* She even has a beauty patch at the corner of her eye. That's called *enflammé,* but of course you're too young to know about such things."

Little Antoine took no interest whatever in such matters. "Have you heard, D'Assigny," he asked, "that Jean-Baptiste's widow is being sent back to France?"

Gabriel swung around with a gleam of the most intense interest in his eyes. "St. Fiacre!" he exclaimed. "I can see the work of the Machiavellian head of the family in this. Charles, the archconniver, has been up to his tricks. But tell me, Antoine, how does the Ulysses of the family, the wise and talented Jean-Baptiste, take it?"

The youngest member of the family was taking the news in a more sympathetic frame of mind. "I'm afraid he's very unhappy about it. And yet I saw him just a few minutes ago and he didn't seem to be concerned then. I heard a great noise coming from that empty room in the southeast tower and I thought a quarrel was going on. I ran up the stairs to see what it was. It was Jean-Baptiste, and he was all alone! He had taken Father's sword—the one with the silver hilt, no less—and he was making passes at the wall. He'd stripped off everything but his shirt and hose and he was jumping about as though he had a dozen Indians in front of him."

Gabriel's face became very angry. "I understand about this——" he began.

"I asked him what he was doing and he stopped and said he was getting his hand in. He seemed excited about something."

"I know what he was excited about!" exclaimed Gabriel sharply. "Charles has given in. He's promised De Bienville he can go on this expedition. It's to make up to him for losing his lovely young widow. That's it, or may my scalp hang at an Iroquois belt! And what did Charles say to me when I told him I wanted to go? He said—and I'm giving you his exact words—he said I was a mere boy!"

"I'm glad Jean-Baptiste is to go with Pierre," said Antoine. "His heart has been set on it ever since he came back from the navy."

"There's Old Moneybags now," said Gabriel in a sulky tone. "Apparently he's through conspiring for this and that with the great Monsieur de Mariat. I wonder what they were talking about so long? Antoine, who's that little shive Charles is talking to?"

"That's Philippe. The builder's apprentice. He's a nice boy."

"But why is Charles talking to *him?* Is he just playing the gracious seigneur and having a kind word to say to each and every one? Let's go over, Little Antoine."

When the two younger brothers arrived within earshot Charles was asking, "Won't your master be here today?"

The boy shook his head uneasily. "He felt he shouldn't spare the time, M'sieur Charles. We're behind with the sawmill."

The seigneur looked surprised and very much displeased. "Do you mean it won't be finished at the promised time?"

Philippe swallowed nervously. "It's not for me to say, M'sieur Charles. But—there's no chance of that."

Charles le Moyne flushed angrily. "Then I'm not surprised the old *poltron* was afraid to show his face here. Well, I'll pay a visit to this elusive M'sieur Girard and I doubt if he'll ever forget the things I'll say to him!"

The boy swallowed again, with mounting nervousness. "If you saw my master he might tell you the mill would be finished on time. But, M'sieur Charles, that's impossible."

"Then why would your master say so?"

"Because he——" The boy stopped. He was far beyond his depth now and reluctant to go further. Then he flushed and said in a resolute tone: "He will be angry enough to skin me alive for saying this but—it's the truth, M'sieur Charles, that my master's afraid of you. When he talks to you he always says, 'Yes, M'sieur Charles, yes, M'sieur Charles,' when what he should be saying is, 'No, M'sieur Charles.' He would say the mill would be finished on time because he wouldn't want you to be disappointed."

The seigneur began to laugh. "Why in the name of the good St. Joseph won't it be finished?"

"Because, m'sieur, you're not often at the château. Advantage is taken of my master. Always there are things for him to do. He must fix this, he must drop everything and do something else. And then the supplies we need never come."

"Is it my fault that what we write for does not always come out in the ships?"

"No, M'sieur Charles, but it isn't my master's fault that he can't finish the mill without them."

Charles shook his head. "You should be training for a lawyer instead of a carpenter. How well you plead the cause of that master of yours!" His manner changed suddenly and he started to frown. "I should go to that doddering old rack of senility and give him the dandling he deserves but because you've spoken up so manfully for him I'll be patient with him. At the same time you've set a toad of remorse hopping in my own conscience. I *should* be here oftener. There's a saying in Normandy, 'When the owner's away, the crops are poor.'" He looked down at Philippe and smiled. "Do you like the building trade?"

"Yes, M'sieur Charles. But I'm afraid I learn very slowly. My master isn't pleased with me."

"Don't allow that to disturb you. Your master has been dissatisfied all his life. The world is a persimmon and it has set his teeth on edge. And now, Philippe, you may tell your master this. There will be no more demands on his time from my servants here. I shall endeavor to locate supplies for him in Montreal. I'll give him a month more to finish the mill and if he doesn't succeed he had better pick out a high tree to hang himself on!"

"I will tell him, M'sieur Charles."

"Tell him this also, that if he blames you for letting me have the truth, or because you left your work today, he had better find that tall tree. You must stay all day, Philippe, on my special invitation."

The two younger brothers, who had hovered on the edge of the conversation, began to follow the seigneur to another part of the grounds. "Charles," said Gabriel, "that's a very impudent boy."

Charles stopped and smiled at the dignified young Sieur d'Assigny. "Is that your considered opinion, Gabriel? You're such a good judge that I like to know what you think."

This pleased Gabriel very much. "He has no right to be here without his master's consent," he stated. "And he talked to you like an equal. He needs to be taught some lessons, that one."

The seigneur then asked the youngest of the family, "And what do you think, Antoine?"

Antoine spoke up stoutly. "I like Philippe. And I think it was brave of him to speak to you like that."

The seigneur nodded his head emphatically. "That's what I hoped you would say. Gabriel, you're quite wrong about this boy. He's a good boy. He showed spirit and a great deal of intelligence. I'm going to keep an eye on that young fellow from now on."

CHAPTER IV

THE FLOTILLA was now in full sight.

The four canoes on their way up the river were filled with men in blue coats who sang and laughed and made the echoes ring about them, their paddles moving in perfect rhythm. When it is considered that in the first of the four sat Pierre le Moyne, Sieur d'Iberville, it becomes easy to understand that the blood of the watchers tingled with excitement and exultation.

They forgot the heat as they crowded to the water's edge. They jumped up and down, and waved their arms, and shouted a welcome to the man who had won so many battles for them; the man who had once accomplished the incredible feat of leading an expedition through the dense forest all the way to Hudson's Bay and had captured all the English forts except the one he now proposed to attack, who was equally at home on quarterdeck or forest trail, who had never been beaten and never conceivably could be beaten, the unique, colorful, lovable, gloriously great M'sieur Pierre of Longueuil.

Philippe had struggled and pushed his way through the crowd until he stood at the edge of the *mouille-pieds* (a term used thereabouts for wharfs which meant "wet feet") where the seigneur waited for his famous brother with a small group made up of the members of the family and Joseph de Mariat. He was so close to this privileged few that he could hear everything said. Needless to state, he listened and watched with the most intense interest.

He heard the seigneur deliver a long speech for the benefit of De Mariat on the greatness of D'Iberville. "Pierre is no ordinary mortal. He's more like a god of battle out of the Norse legends. He fights in a mist, in a furious white heat, and with an unconquerable will to win. He sees everything, nevertheless, and can direct the movements of his men and all his ships as coolly as though he stood off to one side. He is—well, all I can say is that he's D'Iberville. There has never been another like him." There was a pause and then the seigneur asked, "Have you met him on any of his visits to France?"

Philippe heard a deep voice answer, "The honor of setting eye for the first time on this new Bayard you've contributed for the glory of France is mine at this moment."

The boy, finding himself unable to see anything at all, began a still more determined struggle for a better position. The result of his efforts was a narrow space between two backs through which he could watch the four canoes turning into the landing place. At the same time he could hear the seigneur giving further light on the character of D'Iberville.

"You're going to see him in his most human phase, my friend Joseph. He always goes about like a comet with a long tail. Who but the great D'Iberville would arrive like this, with four canoes packed with friends? He has—let me count—twenty-eight men and a dog with him. I'm ready to lay a wager I won't know any of them any better than I know that great *loup-garou* of a dog."

Philippe had already given eye to each man in the four long canoes. Most of them, he had decided, were "rabbits," the term used by the colonists for strangers. Many were soldiers or sailors. There were two Indians from the Hudson's Bay country. They were of the tribe of Gros Ventres (Big Bellies), although that name, which French traders had coined, seemed much out of place when applied to the spare-flanked and gravely dignified pair who sat in the first canoe with D'Iberville. The hardest one in the company to account for was a man in a black coat who had the dog on a chain leash. He looked as though his face had stiffened into a mold, and he was showing no interest at all in the noise and excitement of the arrival. The boy heard the seigneur endeavor to explain the presence of this individual. "There's always with Pierre at least one curious fellow like this. Usually he doesn't remember where he found them and always he gives them the quick boot. They never amuse him after the first few minutes."

The canoes were now so close that Philippe could make out the shining blue of D'Iberville's eye. The appearance of the hero thrilled him from head to foot. "He looks like a god!" he thought. He saw the great man raise a hand and wave as he shouted, "Hallo, my friends! Hallo, every-one!" In a few moments the first canoe came abreast of the landing place and the spectators backed to make room for the new arrivals, with the result that the boy was driven into a position where he could see nothing at all. However, he could hear D'Iberville issuing orders. "Easy, back there! One at a time. Draw up well under the bank. The current is de-ceptive." Philippe knew when he came ashore because his voice was close as he said, "You do me great honor, Charles, in having all my friends here to meet me."

The eager spirit of the boy could not abide that the great moments were

passing while he was unable to see a thing. In a kind of fury he began to
paw at the backs in front of him. Finally he achieved the desired result, he
had wedged himself between two indignant grownups and again had a
narrow space through which he could watch what was going on in the
center of the *mouille-pieds*. He could see the curling yellow hair and the
bold features of the great leader. Knowing this to be a moment he must
always remember, the boy searched out every detail avidly. He saw that
D'Iberville had changed a great deal after three years of continuous fighting. He was taller than the men about him and powerfully built. He was
handsomely attired (as boys like their heroes to be) in a plum-colored coat
with long tails and lace at the wrists, and a cascade of more lace at the
throat. His gray breeches fitted his well-shaped legs tightly. This was all
Philippe was allowed to see at the moment, for a bulky shoulder moved
into the gap and cut off his view. After that he had to be content with
hearing what was said.

"There was no summons," he heard the seigneur explain. "Everyone
flocked here when they knew you were coming. Even old Paul Loisel on
his crutches. Ah, my Pierrot, you've won for us again! How we thrilled at
the news!"

"Yes, things move," came the voice of D'Iberville. "We have Newfoundland now. The bay next—before the first snow flies, I pray. And then, my
brother, the important steps begin." His voice fell to a pensive note. "I
wish this next campaign was over and done with! I confess to a weariness
for the ice and fogs of Mort Bay."

"I don't see Paul. Didn't he come with you?"

This reference was to the Sieur de Maricourt, fourth of the brothers.
Although he had played his part in all the campaigns of the past twenty
years, Paul was chiefly noted for his skill in dealing with the Indians. In
this respect he took after their father. Old M'sieur Charles had spoken
several Indian languages and had been indispensable on all missions to the
savages.

D'Iberville answered: "M'sieur Taouistaouisse[1] was too busy to come
this morning. You must remember, Charles, that Paul has been with me
in Newfoundland from the start and hasn't seen his wife in a year. I
haven't seen mine either and I won't until I get back to France."

"How fortunate that Marie-Thérèse will be in Paris when you arrive
there this fall."

It was clear from the tone in which D'Iberville responded that he had
been taken by surprise. "This fall? I had not planned——"

Charles said in a hurried voice, "This is Monsieur de Mariat, who has
come all the way from Versailles to lend us his help and the benefit of his
advice."

[1]Little-Bird-Always-in-Motion, a name given to De Maricourt by the Onondaga
tribe.

Someone turned at this point and a wide enough gap opened for Philippe to see all that happened from that moment on. He saw D'Iberville take the plump white hand of the visitor in his own lean palm. "We need all the help and advice we can get," he declared, "and so Monsieur de Mariat is very welcome. There are so many things to be settled. We must all get our feet under a table at once. I confess that an uneasy bird sits on my shoulder."

"Do you anticipate stiff opposition in the bay?" asked De Mariat.

D'Iberville nodded gravely. "There's always stiff opposition when we meet the English. They are stout fighters. We should know that because the French and the English have been fighting for centuries." He nodded a second time. "Certain memories rouse a hate in me for the English but at all other times I admire them. They have produced some great men, some stout fighters. None greater, I think, than that glum fellow Cromwell, who taught the world that rulers have a responsibility to their subjects."

D'Iberville turned at this point and waved an arm to one of the Indians accompanying him. "And now, my brave Gip, you will oblige me, if you please."

The Indian answered in clear and perfect French, "At your command, my lord." He reached into the canoe and raised a large bundle in his arms. This he carried to D'Iberville.

"Presents!" cried the latter. "For you, Claudine," to his sister-in-law. "And for you, Charles. Presents, in fact, for everyone in the family and for everyone who lives in Longueuil. In this bundle," holding it up above him, "are mementos of a victory in which the men from Longueuil played a great part. It will be opened—after we have all had something to eat."

II

For a full hour thereafter Philippe followed his hero everywhere. He was amazed to find that the great captain had not forgotten a name and that he had a special message for each resident of Longueuil. D'Iberville shook hands and thumped backs from one end of the common to the other. The boy, never more than six feet in the rear, heard every word spoken and stored them away in his memory as something to be remembered always and treasured. The closeness of his attendance was finally noticed by M'sieur Pierre.

"Has my conscience taken human form to follow me about like this?" he demanded, facing around and confronting his shadow. He paused long enough to study the boy's face. "I think you must be Girard's apprentice. You've been growing while I've been away but I can never be mistaken in a face. You were found after the trouble at Lachine?"

"Yes, M'sieur Pierre," answered Philippe, trembling at being thus noticed.

"Your interest in me is flattering, of course, but it might be a trifle inconvenient under certain circumstances. For instance, at this exact moment." D'Iberville's eye had lighted on the plump figure of Babette Carré strolling by, her hands tucked jauntily into the horsehair *poupettes* attached to the front of her green dress. "I desire a moment's talk with an old acquaintance and our conversation can't be expected to interest you at all, my fine young friend. You will be kind enough, then, to grant me a few moments' respite?"

Philippe accepted the hint and took his departure. When the midday meal was served in the open, however, and the people of Longueuil seated themselves on the grass in ever widening circles about the great man, he considered himself no longer bound to keep his distance. He found a place for himself immediately on the edge of the bevy of ladies who surrounded the guest of honor. Here he could watch everything that went on and hear each word spoken. He never took his eyes from D'Iberville, observing the bold hook of the hero's nose, the fine arch of eyebrow, and the play of expression which kept the D'Iberville face in continuous animation. He observed also certain interesting details of the leader's attire: how he wore a chain of whinstone matrix about his neck with a birch-bark sheath to hold his table knife (guests in New France were never supplied with knives at table and so they always carried their own with them), and a ring on his finger which the boy was sure had been a gift from the King. It was, at any rate, a most remarkable ring with a huge gem which sparkled at each movement of the hand.

It did not take D'Iberville long to realize that his follower was back. "So, here you are again," he said. He addressed himself then to the members of his feminine guard of honor. "It's said that a man who sells his soul to the devil never casts a shadow from that day on. I call your attention to the proof that my soul is still my own. All day I've had two shadows—my own and this very persistent boy."

He saw to it, however, that Philippe got a full share of everything. The boy responded to his hospitable plying by consuming several thick slices of beef, just red enough and with sizzling brown fat on the outside, both drumsticks of a fat capon, innumerable slices of bread hot from the oven and soaked in gravy, and a great slab of *gâteau d'anis,* the justly famed aniseed cake of New France, the secret of which had come over with the first settlers in 1608. To wash it down he drank *vin de gadelles,* well diluted with water, with the voracity of one to whom such a beverage was a rare treat.

There was an interruption when the meal was nearly finished. The man with the dog, who had been sitting in a daze and refusing all proffers of food, came suddenly to life. He got to his feet, said to the dog, "Not a move out of you, William Longsword," and then drew a violin from the red indienne bag which he had carried over his shoulder. Looking in the direction of D'Iberville, he nodded his head and announced, "I am ready."

D'Iberville nodded back. "It is time, stranger," he said.

The stranger asked, "Can one play and sing when the mood is not right?" He proceeded to drape the bag over a small evergreen with a nod and a grin, it being the custom when a minstrel visited a tavern to attach the bag to the outside knob so that passers-by would know of his arrival.

Tucking the instrument under his chin, the minstrel swept the air with his bow and announced: "I am of a mood to sing the songs of Normandy. There are none better, my friends."

With the first sound which issued from the strings a silence fell on the company. The minstrel had come to life with a vengeance. His face reflected every mood of the music. His voice, a rich baritone, trolled out the ballads of Rolf and his sea rovers with a heartiness which set the listeners to swaying.

All of them had heard the music before but none of them had heard it rendered with such vibrance and spirit. They sat entranced, feeling in every chord the beat of life in that stern and hardy land from which they had sprung. The music sang to them of Senlac, of the rough and early days when Normans fought to hold the coast of Calvados and the granite slopes of Cotentin, of the Hundred Years' War and the Maid who had died at Rouen. It was not music for the ear alone, it went far deeper. It made the audience want to sing and laugh and weep, and all at the same time.

When the voice of the violin ceased to throb and hum and began instead to skip with the airs of less rugged days, D'Iberville felt at liberty to begin an explanation. "I heard him last night," he said to those around him. "He was singing in a waterside tavern and I knew at once that he was an artist. He gave us 'La Nourrice du Roi' with such supreme sweetness and taste that I knew I must bring him with me today. But when he joined us this morning he was in such a stupor that he wouldn't speak, let alone sing for us as we paddled up the river. I began to fear that the impulse on which I had acted had been a wrong one."

He now had so much of the attention of the company that the minstrel lowered his instrument and said, "You've heard me play, now give heed to the words of a great man."

"I was very much disturbed," went on D'Iberville. "I am a man of impulse, as many of you know. When I obey that first inner voice which tells me what to do everything comes out right. When I am facing the enemy and the voice says to me, 'Go in, go in, go in!' I attack with all the force I can muster without waiting for a second thought. When the voice says, 'Easy, my friend, they are too strong, you must make them come to you,' I know I should depend on guile and not on force. And so, when this stranger, who must sing sweetly enough to fill two bellies, his own and his dog's, refused to sing at all, I was afraid that perhaps that inner voice had lost the knack of truth." He indulged in a confident smile. "But now you have heard this friend of a few hours and I'm sure you agree it was right to bring so fine a singer to join in our celebration today. He has sung to us of the past so that we will continue resolute in what we must do in the future. I'm placing a silver coin in my hat and placing the hat on the ground. Any who so desire may now step forward and see that my coin does not lack for company."

The minstrel's face puckered up in a wry smile. "Music should be a free gift to all who care to pause and listen," he said. "But Mother Nature was shortsighted enough to supply musicians with bellies which have to be filled. I shall be happy to accept, on behalf of myself and my friend, William Longsword, any contributions you may care to make."

After dinner D'Iberville withdrew into the château in company with Charles and Joseph de Mariat. Some of the company stretched out and went to sleep, others sat about in groups and indulged in talk made desultory by the heat and the abundance of the wine and food. Finding himself at a loose end, Philippe sought out his friend the baker. Twelve-and-One-More was again making bread at the outside oven against the evening needs, and looking hotter and redder of face than before.

"St. Honorious!" he said to Philippe, wiping his brow on a huge forearm. "What eaters people are when it's not their own food they're cramming down their gullets. I've performed a miracle today, my small friend, a miracle of loaves and soups and beef and rissoles."

Philippe seated himself with crossed legs in front of the oven, hoping that the cook had no knowledge of his own share in the consumption of the food. It seemed to him wise to find another topic for conversation.

"I've often wondered, M'sieur Twelve-and-One-More, if you who are so large and strong are afraid of Indians like everyone else."

The cook paused in his labors. "I've never had any fear of them," he declared. "To me they're no better than wolves which find courage by running in packs. They shout to get up their courage and they stink in their war paint like dead fish cast up on a beach." He began to rake at the coals under the oven. "They nearly had me once. There were three of us, cutting logs off St. Lambert's Shore, and before we knew it the yelping devils were on us. Later we figured it out that there had been a dozen of them. I got my hands on two and I picked them up and knocked their heads together. They dropped like logs and I thought it certain their skulls had been cracked. The other savages thought so too and they didn't seem to have much liking for that kind of fighting. At any rate they stopped their *cass-cass-casseeing* and vanished into the woods. . . . No, my small friend, I can say truthfully that I've never lost a moment's sleep through fear of Indians."

"And were the two Indians dead, m'sieur?"

"No. They came to their senses soon after. We sent them to Quebec as prisoners."

"And what happened to them then?"

"The old comte ordered them to be roasted alive as a lesson to the torturing dogs that Frenchmen were to be left alone. I heard it said later that neither one of them let out as much as a whisper when the flames began to lick at their red hides."

"You must be the strongest man that ever lived," said the boy, looking admiringly at the structure of muscle and bone employed in the prosaic task of raking the fire. "You must be stronger even than M'sieur Dollier de Casson."

The cook straightened up. "It's said in the Holy Word that Samson was the strongest man," he admitted unwillingly. "It's wicked to dispute the Bible. But sometimes I think about this Samson—and I wonder."

"There was also Goliath," said the boy.

"Goliath!" the cook spoke the name in a tone of the deepest scorn. "I think very little of that one. If I had been the one to go out and meet him it would have been Goliath who needed the slingshot."

The boy seemed in complete agreement with this. He nodded energetically and said, "It would take a very big weapon to kill you, M'sieur Twelve-and-One-More."

"I think it would take a *very* big weapon. When one is as large as I am the layers of muscle are deep and hard. It might even be that it would take a cannon ball to kill me."

The boy was still casting back into his knowledge of the great giants of the past. "Then there was Og, the King of Bashan, who slept on an iron bed nine cubits long——" he began.

A shout sounded from above them. Philippe knew that it had come from one of the tower guards. Instinctively he threw himself on the ground.

"Indians!" cried the guard, beating excitedly on a piece of pipe. "On the Chambly Road!"

Philippe raised his head fearfully and glanced in the direction of the Chambly Road. A single naked figure had bounded out from the trees and was bending a bow. As soon as the arrow had been discharged the redskin turned and vanished into the forest. A second warning was sounded from the tower but it was doubtful if anyone heard it in the general panic. The boy, who had crept under the cover of the oven, could hear wild screams and much hasty scuffling as the people on the common rushed for the safety of the castle walls. He kept his head down, however, even when the cook joined in the scramble and called to him in treble urgency to follow.

Through the boy's mind the thought kept running, "They'll burn us at the stake if they catch us!" His teeth began to chatter. He said to himself, "I'll count ten and then it will be safe to get up and run." It was impossible to concentrate on counting, however. Remembering that it was a favorite Iroquois trick to tear out the fingernails of their victims first, he pressed his hands against his sides as though determined to hide them. Then he heard the voice of D'Iberville and this had a steadying effect on him. He raised himself on hands and knees, thinking, "M'sieur Pierre is here so there can be no danger."

D'Iberville came out slowly from the castle gates, looking about him at the frightened people. He had not paused to loosen his sword in its scabbard or to possess himself of a pistol. Philippe saw that the greatest of the Le Moynes was not at all alarmed but that he was very angry.

The voice of the conqueror of Newfoundland could be heard distinctly above the clamor. "Come! What's the meaning of all this running and bleating? Great St. Nicolas! Have you taken leave of your senses? This isn't an attack in force. There's no reason for fear." He held a hand above his eyes and stared intently down the Chambly Road. Turning about with an impatient shake of the head, he demanded: "Have you ever known the Iroquois to strike in broad daylight? Do they wait until we're gathered in force before attacking us? Would they send out a single warrior to give us warning like a herald in the old days? No, my friends, they would have sprung at us like wild beasts from the woods all around before we suspected them of being within a hundred miles of us!" He began to laugh in a high-pitched, scornful tone. "This warrior, who has shot his little arrow our way and vanished, was thumbing his nose at us. That's all!"

Philippe got quickly and shamefacedly to his feet. He saw now that all the Le Moyne brothers had followed D'Iberville out from the castle and they were treating the matter as a joke. He heard Gabriel saying in a disappointed voice, "There won't be any fighting today. And I had my mind set on getting some Indian hair for my belt!"

The boy said to himself, "I've acted like a coward! I, who wanted to be a Le Moyne!" He looked about him to see where the arrow had gone, supposing it had struck against the walls or had found its mark in the ground. Then, with a sudden sick feeling, he came to a stop.

The arrow had found its mark but not against the walls or in the ground. An inert body lay face down on the path between the oven and the castle gate. The feathers were sticking straight up from between the shoulder blades of the victim.

"God and St. Joseph have mercy on him!" exclaimed D'Iberville, who had caught sight of the body at the same time. He crossed himself hurriedly. "It's Twelve-and-One-More! My poor old friend!"

The arrow looked small in that huge expanse of back and certainly not capable of causing serious hurt. But Twelve-and-One-More had been wrong when he boasted to Philippe that it would take a very big weapon to bring him to grief. The Iroquois arrow had sufficed. Even to the tear-blurred eyes of the boy it was clear that the largest man and best cook in New France was dead.

CHAPTER V

FATHER MILLET, a retired Indian missionary who was living out the few remaining years of his life ministering to the spiritual needs of the little community, had watched the celebration during the day with a tolerant eye and had said nothing, even when a few men drank too much wine and became a little noisy. But when supper was over and there was talk of dancing on the green, he decided to intervene.

"There will be no dancing, my children," he declared in the hearing of all. "Must I remind you that girls are permitted to dance only with each other and in their own homes, with their mothers present?"

"But, Father, this is a special occasion," protested Handsome Hyacinth Dessain, the only bachelor on the seigneurie. Hyacinth was a fine dancer and did not want to lose such an excellent chance to display his skill.

"It's not special enough, my son, for us to allow the good old laws to be broken. And have you forgotten that we've suffered a loss this day?" Father Millet looked about at the disappointed faces. "Most sins are committed in the hours of darkness. I've come to look upon them, as our ancestors did, as belonging to the devil." Certainly the old man had seen enough deviltry perpetrated after dark in the Indian encampments where he had spent his life. "There's another of the good old laws which has fallen into disuse. Women must be in their homes by nine o'clock. It will be observed this night, my children. And as they cannot return through the woods alone, their husbands and fathers must accompany them."

A few voices were raised in dissent. The old laws, they pointed out, had not been applied in so many years that they had ceased to be laws. Even in Montreal, where the Sulpicians were inclined to be severe, people were allowed to sit as long as they pleased on the benches built at the front doors. Surely a stifling hot night was no time to revive a long forgotten regulation!

The old priest fingered the crucifix about his neck and said nothing more. There was no mistaking the message of his eyes, however, and gradually one family after another good-naturedly collected itself and moved off for home along the forest paths. The women carried lanterns and the men had their guns primed and loaded. By nine o'clock everyone had gone.

This lesson had such a profound effect that on the second evening all the women in the château had retired to their own quarters before the hour struck. A small group of men, however, had gathered outside the walls, where they hoped to have the advantage of any breeze. Inevitably they fell to discussing the death of their comrade.

"It's as I say," declared Sooty-Arms, the smith. "Twelve-and-One-More told us many times how he wanted things to be. He said it to me, he said it to you, he said it to everyone here. His father was a big man—though not to be mentioned in the same breath with our poor friend—and he was buried back in Normandy in a coffin of the hardest wood, bound with strips of iron. Twelve-and-One-More didn't want it said he'd failed to keep up family standards. If you ask the seigneur, you'll find he has funds for the purpose, which were paid in at so much a month. It was M'sieur Charles who gave the order to Girard for the coffin."

"That's all very well, my friend," protested the miller, "but haven't you heard what Old Kirkinhead says, that it will take another full day to make such a coffin? Have you given a thought to this heat? Twelve-and-One-More wanted a fine coffin, granted; but he also wanted to look his best. He was as vain as a peacock."

"Father Millet has set the time for five o'clock tomorrow," said the smith. "Why talk about it, then? The matter is settled." After making these remarks, however, Sooty-Arms experienced a change of opinion. He suddenly grinned and slapped one callused fist against the other. "We will tell no one," he declared, looking about him cautiously. "Not Father Millet, not M'sieur Charles, not—not Tante Seulette above all. We will take Twelve-and-One-More to the *glacière*. It's unfortunate that he must be lugged around like a quarter of beef but of this I'm sure: he would agree if he could speak to us. He would want to look right for his own funeral."

The others agreed at once and no time was lost in putting the plan into operation. The body was carried out from the chapel on a stretcher improvised from three pike handles and a discarded mattress, six of the men being needed to lift it. The *glacière* was not, strictly speaking, an icehouse at all but a well-shaded spot about two hundred yards from the château where the summer's supply of ice was kept under a thick covering of sawdust. It took such a long spell of tugging and hauling to raise the body of the dead man to a position on top of the pile that all the participants were breathless when they finally succeeded. They grouped themselves around the base and rested for several moments without a word being said.

Sooty-Arms glanced at the body finally and, feeling reassured, nodde
his head. "It's as though he was lying in state," he said in a whisper. "
remember once in Paris when——" He checked himself abruptly and di
not continue with what he had intended to tell.

The others seemed accustomed to his reticences. After a moment th
miller said: "What a pity it is! What a loss to Longueuil! In my opinio
Twelve-and-One-More was better known than any of the Le Moynes—
except, of course, M'sieur Pierre."

Sooty-Arms took it on himself to reply. "And a man with two head
would be more talked about than the Comte de Frontenac." He glance
about him. "Who's to stand watch?"

They had carried a single torch with them and it was now stuck i
the notch of a tree. The light thus supplied was too small to make clea
the hesitation which visited each face when this point was raised. For se
eral moments nothing was said and then a voice spoke up. "Let me sta
and watch."

The smith sat up straighter and looked about him. The voice, he pe
ceived, belonged to a boy who had followed them from the château an
was standing at one side. After a moment's scrutiny he recognized hin
"You're Old Kirkinhead's boy," he said. "What are you doing here at thi
hour?"

"My master sent me with a message for M'sieur Charles."

"And why do you want to stand watch?"

"He was my friend," said Philippe. "I think he would like it if
stayed."

The smith said brusquely, "And in half an hour you would come bac
squalling and say you were afraid to stay."

There was a pause and then Philippe said: "I would be afraid. Ye
m'sieur. But I wouldn't come running back because of it."

"I also was a friend of Twelve-and-One-More," said the smith. "Ca
I allow this boy to do more than I'm willing to in the name of friend
ship? It shall be this way, Philippe. We'll stand watch together, you an
I, and if we become frightened of noises in the dark or the fear that In
dians are still about, we'll sit close together and take comfort in eac
other's company."

The rest were only too glad to have matters settled in this way. Gun
were left with the two volunteers, the torch was extinguished, and th
party quietly withdrew to the shelter of the château. For the smith an
the boy the long vigil began.

II

It had been decided earlier in the evening that the members of th
family would remain at the château until after the funeral services wit

the exception of D'Iberville, who still had so much to attend to in Montreal that it would be necessary for him to depart immediately after a morning conference of the family. He found that he had many things to do in Longueuil also, in particular a conversation with De Mariat which lasted for hours. So much time was consumed in one way and another that it was quite late in the evening when he was able to attend to a matter which had been very much on his mind. He wanted to say a prayer beside the body of the unfortunate baker.

Acting on a hint from one of the château guards, D'Iberville made his way through the darkness to the *glacière*. An instinctive caution made him stop at the edge of the trees.

"Who is there?" he asked.

The smith answered, "We are keeping watch, M'sieur Pierre."

"St. Peter of Alcantara!" exclaimed D'Iberville. "This is a curious state of affairs. I was told you had the body here. Is that Jacques Descaries?" It was typical of the tact he employed in all his dealings that he did not address the smith as Sooty-Arms.

"Yes, I am Descaries. The builder's boy is sharing the watch with me."

"That boy again!" D'Iberville began to laugh. "Truly, I never expect to be alone in this life or the next. I'm sure he'll be right behind me when I pace my quarterdeck on Mort Bay. He'll be on my heels when I climb to the gate where St. Pierre divides the flocking souls." He began to make his way cautiously through the trees and the underbrush toward the ice pile which was serving Twelve-and-One-More as his bier. "This kind of thing, Philippe, isn't for a boy of your age."

Philippe repeated what he had said earlier. "He was my friend, M'sieur Pierre."

D'Iberville found this answer to his liking. "And that is a very good reason. It seems that you are a fellow of stout heart, my small Philippe." The interest he took in everyone about him manifested itself. "You were born at Lachine, I think."

"Yes, M'sieur Pierre."

"Your parents were killed in the massacre but you were saved."

"Yes, M'sieur Pierre. I was less than a year old. After the Iroquois had gone I was found under a tree at the edge of the village."

"I knew all the men of Lachine. Which was your father?"

"No one knows. You see, M'sieur Pierre, there were four boys of my age and I'm the only one of them alive. All the parents were killed or carried off and so there was no one left who could be sure which of the four I was."

"And nothing has been found out since?"

The boy answered in a low tone of voice. "No, m'sieur. Nothing has been found out."

"Then the name Philippe may not be your right one?"

"They didn't want to make a mistake and so they gave me the name of all four of the boys. I am Philippe-Christophe-Marcel-Amaury."

Despite the danger of their situation, D'Iberville began to laugh. "It much like hoisting a full head of sail on a kelp or a buss to give so man names to such a small boy. I assume you like Philippe best?"

"Yes, m'sieur. But my master wanted to call me Thomas because h says he will make an architect of me. He calls me that sometimes still Cécile was set on Philippe because she was in love once with a man o that name. But when any of them are angry at me they call me Amaury Why it should be so I can't say. And when there are visitors and they wan to be very polite, they always call me Christophe."

"And why is that?"

"I think the parents of the one who was christened Christophe wer of the best standing of the four. So it sounds a little better, they think."

D'Iberville laughed again. "You must have a difficult time, answerin to so many names. I think I shall make a soldier of you, my stout Phi lippe." He turned then in the direction of the smith, who had made n sound while the conversation was going on. "I've always been curiou about you, Jacques Descaries. I've heard what is said, of course, tha you had a reason for leaving France and that you occupied a differen station in life there."

"That is what is said about me." There was a pause and then th smith added, "It is true."

"I've a very strong suspicion you served in the French army."

"That also is true. I served through three campaigns in Flanders an one in Italy."

There was a new note of dignity in the smith's voice which caused hi questioner to proceed carefully. "It may very well be then that Jacque Descaries is not your real name."

"It may very well be."

D'Iberville remained silent for several moments. Then he began again "As you've had so much experience, I can't understand why you sta here as blacksmith instead of lending me your aid in the campaign ahead . . ."

"I'm fifty-eight years of age. I still have strength in my arms, enoug to carry on my trade. But could I hold my own in a campaign such a you will fight? I might be worse than useless, for on the march a party i no faster than its slowest member."

"That's quite true." D'Iberville nodded his head in the dark, mentall wiping the name of Jacques Descaries from his list of possible recruits "But what of the Mississippi venture? It may lead to some fighting bu it's more likely to provide as its main excitement the protection of a few shiploads of settlers. It's a land of sun and flowers and gentle winds. I might be a pleasant place for a man of fifty-eight."

Although he could not see in the darkness, D'Iberville was aware that the smith had given his head a negative shake. "That is small inducement, Sieur d'Iberville. My blood may be thin and there may be an occasional twinge of rheumatism in my joints but I've come to love the hardiness of this land of ours." All trace of the slovenly use of the language into which he had fallen was gone. He was speaking the tongue of the universities. "Is there anything to equal a crisp winter day when the snow has covered the trees and has piled up to the window sills or even higher, and the sun makes the snow glisten as though the beneficent God has showered diamonds on the earth? You spoke of gentle winds. I love the wind best when it comes straight from the north and howls through the trees. Is there any sound as lovely as sleigh bells on a frosty day? I couldn't be happy if I were no longer able to see the slow flight of whisky-jack and crossbill against a sky which is winter gray." It was apparent that he was indulging in more shakes of the head. "This land is in my blood, Sieur d'Iberville. I am going to die here."

D'Iberville had been staring intently in the direction from which the cultivated voice came. "There's much truth in what you say," he declared at the close. "This country, this beautiful New France, brings out all that is good in men. Consider the missionaries. If they stayed at home they would spend their lives as humble curés, striving to bring light into the sour minds of country clods. But they come here, they go out and live among the savages, where they are scorned, beaten, subjected to every hardship and indignity. They live on loathsome messes of half-cooked dog. And in the end, perhaps, they die heroically at the stake, their eyes filled with the glory of martyrdom!" He had been speaking rapidly and he now indulged in a pause for breath. "Consider Adam Dollard and his companions, and the little Madeleine de Verchères. Consider my father. If he had remained in Normandy he would have been an innkeeper all his life, bowing and scraping and humbling himself. But in this miraculous land he became a great man, wise and successful and noble. He could never have married as fine a woman as my mother if he had stayed in France."

"M'sieur Pierre," said the boy eagerly, "tell us how Old M'sieur Charles made the Iroquois let him go after he was taken prisoner."

The conqueror of Newfoundland seemed quite content to repeat this story which had become one of the favorite legends of the colony. "For years," he began, "the old women of the Long House had been gathering wood to burn Charles le Moyne at the stake, Akouessan, as they called him. They knew he was the one man they had most to fear. He was wise in their ways and wise also in the life of the forest. He could talk many Indian languages, and best of all their own. And then one day they caught him, and they started back down the Richelieu River to their own land. They were wild with excitement, you may be sure. As they paddled they whispered among themselves, grinning and tasting already the sweetness of their triumph. But after a time they were less happy about it. My father was talking to them, telling them of the disasters which would befall them if they killed him. His people would come in canoes which were taller than trees and with big guns which roared like thunder. The Indians tried to close their ears to what he was saying. They laughed and jabbered and joked about how they would put him to the torture. And all the time his voice went on, telling them the same thing over and over again. Finally they stopped talking and the energy seemed to have gone out of their arms.

"At the same time," went on D'Iberville, who had something of the poet in him, as all great fighting men and inspired leaders have, "another voice was speaking to them, a voice from the feeble bushes in their own minds. It kept saying: 'Heed what he is saying. Terrible vengeance will fall on the people of the Long House if this man is killed.' It became too much for them. They couldn't resist the two voices, that in their own minds and that of wise old Charles le Moyne. They held a council, whispering back and forth in the canoe, and then they turned it around and started back for the mouth of the river. They delivered my father over to a party of friendly Indians, begged his forgiveness, and then set off in the other direction, paddling furiously as though all the hob-thrusts of the woods and Matshi Skoueow herself were coming on the wind behind them!"

There was silence for a moment and then D'Iberville shook his head proudly. "From that you will know the kind of man my father was. And now tell me, how did you like the story?"

The boy answered, "It is one of the greatest stories I've ever heard, M'sieur Pierre."

D'Iberville had been sitting at one end of the ice cache. He got to his feet now and began beating the damp sawdust from the tails of his coat. "It's time to go. If anything happens during the night, fire a gun and I'll be with you in a trice. I sleep light."

He bent one knee beside the improvised bier and murmured a prayer for the soul of the dead man. "Farewell, François Dandin," he said at the finish. "You were a good man. You were both gentle and brave, my old friend. I shall always miss you."

CHAPTER VI

PAUL LE MOYNE, the fourth of the brothers, arrived at the château late that night. There were six of them, accordingly, to hear mass together at five o'clock the next morning. Father Millet joined them at the door of the chapel as they filed out. "Always remember, my sons," he said, "that you are special instruments of the Lord's will. He has selected you to carry out His purpose in this new land. It's truly a great responsibility which rests on your shoulders. You must never forget that devotion to the cause must come before everything, before pleasure or ease or personal desires, even before the responsibilities you bear as husbands and fathers."

"Yes, Father Millet," answered Charles. The others bowed with equal gravity and murmured, "Yes, Father Millet."

They turned in a body toward the stairs which led to the tower room. The three eldest walked arm in arm, Paul in the center. He was slender of build and a trifle shorter than the others. His features, which were small and finely cut, seemed out of place in the face of a woodsman.

"You're looking well, M'sieur Little-Bird-Always-in-Motion," said Charles, glancing down at the diplomat of the family. "I was inclined to fear the effect this last campaign might have on you."

Paul le Moyne laughed. "The rest of you," he said, "have been solicitous about me all my life. As far back as I can remember I've heard some of you asking, 'Can Paul stand this?' or 'Can he do that?' Sometimes I get angry about it. I'm as tough as any of the Le Moyne breed, as I've given you ample reason to know." He looked back over his shoulder at the three youngest members of the family. "I'm still amazed at the change in the boys. I swear that both Gabriel and Little Antoine have grown three inches since we've been away."

"Little Antoine," declared D'Iberville, "will be the tallest of all in the end." It developed later that he was right. Within a few years the baby of the family had outstripped them all in height although, much to his chagrin, he never succeeded in divorcing himself from the name his brothers had given him when he lay in his cradle of wild cherry wood (which each of them had occupied in turn), that of Little Antoine.

Charles seemed relieved that Paul had professed himself in such good health. "I've less of a feeling of guilt in what I must propose——" he began.

D'Iberville applied an affectionate pressure to Paul's arm. "I knew it," he said. "Charles the Taskmaster has some mission for you. And from the look on his face I judge it no simple matter."

"It is not indeed," affirmed the head of the family. "Not all the pelts from the Ottawa country are coming to us, Paul. We haven't discovered yet what route is being used but the fact remains that a large share of the trade is going to Beverwyck.[1] This can't continue. If we allow this raiding of our territory to go on, they'll soon be competing with us all over the north." He frowned uneasily. "I lay the problem in your lap, Paul. I can't solve it, sitting here in Montreal."

An equally serious expression had settled on Paul's face. "I thought we had them barred from the Ottawa for all time." He gave his head a determined shake. "I must visit my friendly chiefs and find what has been happening up there while I've been away."

"I hesitate to ask it of you so soon," said Charles. "But there's no denying that we may lose a large part of our trade if we don't act quickly. *Le diable est dedans.*"

"I'll go at once. All you will have to do," with a smile, "is make your peace—and mine—with Marie-Madeleine. In fact, I'll leave it to you, Charles, to break the news to her that I must leave her so soon again. She'll be very angry, I promise you." He added after a moment: "It will be no hardship for me. I like the woods. I've a very special liking for the Ottawa country. And—I like Indians."

D'Iberville's voice boomed out in protest. "You would like them less, my Paul, had you seen poor Twelve-and-One-More lying dead with that arrow in his back." He crossed himself. "I wept when I stood over the body of the gentle big looby. I swear they shall pay for his death!"

"I too wept," declared Charles. "Longueuil will never seem the same without Twelve-and-One-More."

Paul was the gentlest of all the brothers in most respects but he accepted the killing of the baker with a realistic attitude of mind impossible to the others. "What can you expect?" he asked. "The Indians don't want us here. They'll fight us to the end for the land which was once all theirs. If our young men had done what this small party of warriors did, we would hail them as heroes. They dropped arrows in half a dozen places. One went through the open door of Old Kirkinhead's house and pinned one of his ridiculous hats to the wall. Another landed in the courtyard at Chambly. It was their way of warning us that there's no thought

[1]Beverwyck had been the Dutch name for Albany and the French still used it.

of peace in their minds; and also a small token of contempt. By this time, no doubt, the party is well on its way down the Richelieu." He raised one of his slender white hands. "It was unfortunate that the baker got in the way of one of the arrows, Charles, but I refuse to fall into a froth of hate because they dared to give our complacent noses a tweak."

The glower of resentment had not left D'Iberville's face. "Play the philosopher as much as you like, my little Paul. I still swear that I'll never consider my old friend's death squared with them until a score of scalps have been ripped from their mangy skulls. *Pro pelle centum!*"

De Maricourt said quietly, "It seems to be a difference in viewpoint."

A long table had been moved into the tower room with an armchair at the head and five smaller ones at each side. The brothers went to their places without any question. Their father had occupied the chair at the head at all family conferences during his lifetime and it had never been used since. Charles took the seat to the right of it. The one next to him remained unoccupied as it had belonged to the second son Jacques, the Sieur de Ste. Hélène, who had died gallantly in the defense of Quebec against the English fleet nine years before. D'Iberville lowered himself into the third chair and Paul took the fourth. The last one on that side, which had belonged to François, killed while fighting the Oneidas at Repentigny, remained vacant.

Directly across the table from Charles was an empty seat but this was not due to death. It belonged to Joseph, the Sieur de Sérigny, who was bringing the ships out from France to keep the rendezvous with D'Iberville at Newfoundland. The second chair was empty also, however, the most tragic gap of all, for here the brave Louis had sat. He had thus been across the table from D'Iberville. The other members of the family could remember the nods and smiles of affection which had always been exchanged by the pair. As usual the sight of the empty space across from him caused the famous brother to subside at once into an unhappy silence.

The next three chairs were taken in order by Jean-Baptiste, Gabriel, and Antoine.

"It was our father's custom to begin with a prayer," said Charles, lowering his head. The others did the same and for several moments the room was filled with the low murmurs of its six occupants. The seigneur then leaned back in his chair and gazed in front of him with a somber air. "I call these meetings as seldom as possible," he said, "because they serve as reminders of the losses we've had. There are times, however, when it's absolutely necessary for us to put our heads together; and such is the case at the moment. We face today a problem of the utmost importance."

The seigneur broke off and raised some sheets of paper from in front of him. "But first I have financial reports for you. Our trading ventures have all turned out well; so well, in fact, that we would soon all be very rich men if we could go on without any interruption. Here I have the financial position of each of the inheritances set up for us and of the general fund in which we all hold shares. The general fund has become much larger than I thought possible on the last occasion when we were together in this room.

"The problem facing us today," he went on after clearing his throat, "is the need which has arisen for a large expenditure—in fact an enormous outlay of funds which may very well undo all the careful financial planning and building of the past ten years. It will eat up the general fund and cut more or less deeply into our personal inheritances. Pierre and I have discussed it at full length. We realize that we may jeopardize the prosperity of the Le Moyne family—but that it must be done!"

Silence fell on the room. Paul le Moyne's face gave no indication of his reaction to this unexpected news but it was clear that the younger brothers were surprised and excited.

Despite the earliness of the hour it was stiflingly hot in the room. All the windows had been thrown open but the curtains hung limply at the sides, without the slightest hint of a breeze to stir them.

"How unbearably hot it is!" exclaimed Paul suddenly. "Or perhaps the nature of your announcement, Charlot, has caused my temperature to rise in this way. I—I am disturbed, I confess. Are you trying to frighten us, brother?"

"No," answered Charles. "I'm in no way overestimating the risks."

The Seigneur of Longueuil placed his hands together on the table and studied them for several moments. "I am a man of business," he said finally. "I've been directly responsible for the handling of the family funds—and I may fairly say for the prosperity in which you've all shared. It shocks me to bring this question before you. My mind rebels at the taking of such—such monumental risks! It's against my nature." He spoke with deep feeling. His hands had become so tightly locked that the strain on the knuckles could be noticed. "But after long hours of consideration I see no other course open to us. You all heard what Father Millet said this morning. There is one consideration which must outweigh all matters of personal welfare and happiness." He turned abruptly to D'Iberville. "You go on with it, Pierre. It will save time if you explain the situation."

D'Iberville made it clear at once that he did not share the hesitations which weighed so heavily on the head of the house. He smiled around the circle of expectant faces with full confidence. To him the situation was quite simple. There was something to be done: why not, therefore, proceed to the doing of it without discussion or fear of consequences? He sat forward in his chair and began to speak in a brisk voice.

"We're to have the ships for the Mississippi venture. After talking with Monsieur de Mariat, I'm convinced the King will provide them. And so we must plan accordingly. The great chance we've looked forward to, the chance to shape a continent and hoist the fleur-de-lis over all the west, is to be ours! I think you'll agree that nothing must be allowed to stand in the way of our success."

The faces of the three younger brothers left no doubt that they were entirely in accord with this but Gabriel was the only one of the trio who dared interrupt. "Nothing, Pierre, nothing!" he cried excitedly. "We mustn't allow points of wealth and security to stand in the way."

"That's the spirit!" said D'Iberville appreciatively. Then he frowned as he began to speak of difficulties. "But the King's consent isn't the end of our troubles. Rather, it's the start. If we leave the fitting out of the ships to the ministers at Versailles and the naval contractors, we can be sure the expedition will be a failure!" His eyes began to glow belligerently. "Those thieves, those wretched prig-pennies, who deserve no better fate than to bless the world with their heels"—a slang expression for hanging—"would send us out with casks of foul water and rotting meat and biscuit crawling with weevil. The muskets would be rusty discards, the gunpowder no better than mealed niter with sulphur and charcoal instead of properly corned powder. There wouldn't be a pound of brass in our guns. There would be no proper implements for the settlers, no proper seed, no supplies.

"It's always been like this," he went on. "La Salle was given the shoddiest support, and he failed and died. Get this firmly in your minds, my brothers. The settlers they send us will be a poor lot—weaklings and culls and cropped-heads from the prisons. They'll die quickly if they have to depend on the supplies the government will give us."

He nodded his head vigorously. "Our efforts will end in failure if we don't load the ships with everything that will be needed—at our own expense."

Nothing more was said for a moment and then Charles took up the burden of explanation. "I have on this sheet an estimate of what the cost will be. The total is—colossal. It will exhaust our balances and strain our credit. I suggest that each of you look this sheet over before we discuss the matter any further."

Jean-Baptiste spoke up at once. "I, for one, have no need to look at the figures. All I require to know is that you, Charles and Pierre, are convinced that we must do this. I give my vote now. I agree to the plan."

Gabriel said in a voice which, consciously or not, was an imitation of D'Iberville: "I agree, of course. What do I care about money!" He cared a great deal but at the moment he did not believe so.

Antoine echoed his two older brothers. "I agree!" he cried, nodding his head and smiling.

Charles asked in a sober tone of voice, "Do you realize fully that your personal inheritances may be wiped out? That you may have to go into

the woods as traders, if things go wrong with us, or even open stores as
our father did?"

"We understand the risk," answered Jean-Baptiste, "and we're ready
to take it."

Charles looked across D'Iberville at Paul. Little-Bird-Always-in-Motion
was not living up to the name the Indians had given him. He was making no motion at all. His eyes were gazing straight ahead and it was clear
he was giving the problem the most intense consideration.

"Well, Paul?"

"It's a heavy gamble," declared the Sieur de Maricourt. "We may throw
all we possess into it and still share the fate of La Salle. All that we've
worked so hard to acquire may go at one cast of the dice. . . . Oh, I
agree. It's just that I can't voice my acquiescence with the enthusiasm
of the three starry-eyed knights-errant across the table. Like you, Charles,
I find this a duty which carries deep regrets with it." He paused and
sighed. "Well, I agree. Go as far as you like, Pierre. We can't conquer
the wilderness with empty hands. Credit my tardiness in speaking to
the natural regrets of a man who must cancel at once his order for imported black slate for the new wing of his house and who will undoubtedly have to sell some prized pieces of silver—if the consent of a certain
charming lady can be obtained to such a sacrifice."

"Bless you, Paul!" exclaimed Charles. "I knew you would be with us,
shoulder to shoulder. Is this another explanation I must make for you to
Marie-Madeleine?" He looked along the line of faces. "Then it is settled."

"It is settled," repeated D'Iberville. He drew a gusty sigh of satisfaction. "I thank you all from the bottom of my heart. Now I can sail for
Mort Bay with an easy mind, knowing that after we are through there
we can begin the task of winning a continent!"

The scraping of feet under the table announced the belief of the
younger members of the family that the meeting had come to an end. The
seigneur raised a restraining hand, saying that there were other matters
to discuss. He began to speak of minor concerns: the investments which
had been made with various companies of *coureurs de bois,* the matter of
repairs to the stores and warehouses, the hiring of crews for the river
boats. These points discussed and settled, he gathered the sheets in front
of him into an orderly pile.

"There are two personal matters," he stated. He turned somewhat
reluctantly in the direction of Gabriel. "I understand you've been gam-
bling lately, and losing more than you can afford. You've had to borrow
from—from some of your brothers. You've been getting into bad company. I'm sure the rest will agree with me that this must stop at once.
The name of Le Moyne must not be tarnished. And now, of course, you
won't be able to afford the losses."

Gabriel flushed angrily. It was clear that an insubordinate retort was on

he tip of his tongue. He thought better of it, however, and answered in
a suppressed tone, "Yes, Charles."

"Now we have a decision about the future of Antoine. It's my feeling
he should be trained in a knowledge of Indian ways and languages.
You'll be needing assistance, Paul. Antoine has an aptitude for it and he's
agreeable. Isn't that so, Antoine?"

"Yes, Charles," answered the boy eagerly.

"Antoine, in fact, has a great aptitude. He has a turn for languages.
He can even speak some English. You needn't snort, Pierre, it will be
useful to him and to us." The head of the family gave another questing
look up and down the line. "Well, then, I think the meeting is over."

Paul and the three boys left the room. As each passed, D'Iberville gave
him an energetic thump on the back, saying in a heartfelt voice, "Thank
you, thank you, thank you!"

Charles had remained beside the chair at the head of the table. His
eyes were filled with tears. "M'sieur Charles," he said, turning in the
direction of the hat on the wall, "you've had many reasons to be proud
of these fine sons of yours. But never more than now!"

II

The chatelaine of Longueuil was one of those fortunate women who
always seem cool and unflustered. As though in defiance of the heat, she
was wearing on her shoulders a shawl of lavender damask with an edging
of grebe skin, and her cheeks were fresh and there was not a hair out of
place on her head. When her husband joined her in the lower hall, however, she was confronting the housekeeper of the château with a look
compounded of vexation and dismay.

"Haven't I told you before, madame," Tante Seulette was saying, her
mouth drawn down at the corners in unrelenting disapproval, "that it's
impossible? There's a set order of work the servants must follow. They
sweep, they dust, they wash. Can they be set to washing when they should
be sweeping? Can the sun, madame, rise in the west instead of the east?
Madame, what you ask is quite out of the question. I've told you the
same thing many times."

"You have indeed." There was almost a despairing note in the voice
of the mistress. "Someday, perhaps, I'll make a request which you will
deign to grant. I was hoping this was the time. Truly, Tante Seulette,
it's important that our clothes be ready to take back to Montreal. We
leave in a very few days for Quebec——"

The housekeeper was a tall dragoon of a woman. She had been a King's
girl and had been placed on inspection in the third of the three chambers
in Quebec; but although the men who went to the third chamber were
so much in need of wives that they were not likely to balk at lack of

pulchritude, none had wanted her. The only one of all the King's girls to fail of selection, she had been nicknamed Mademoiselle Seulette (All Alone), which had been changed in time to Tante Seulette. No one at Longueuil could have told her real name.

"Madame," said Tante Seulette, drawing herself up to her full angular height, "it is impossible."

At this point an interruption was provided by a lively cricket of a boy who was perhaps two and a half years old. He appeared suddenly in the doorway and danced about like a little imp of Satan, crying at the housekeeper in a piping voice, "Sans Mari! Sans Mari!"

This reference to her husbandless condition sent Tante Seulette after him in a trice, shaking her apron at him and crying: "You, Bertrand! You little pest, you rascal, you very bad boy! I'll tell the seigneur about you."

A feminine voice from the far end of the hall called "Bertrand!" and the boy vanished in that direction after a pause to twiddle his fingers. Tante Seulette returned, her face blotched an angry red.

"She puts him up to it!" she exclaimed. "I know she does! She teaches him what to say to me."

Madame le Moyne, who had been finding it hard not to laugh, asked, "Who do you mean?"

"His mother. That Madame Malard, the miller's wife. A lot she has to be proud of when all she could catch was that sniffling old Malard! She married him for his property but, madame, you know the old saying, 'There are no pockets in a nightgown.'"

The seigneur, coming down the winding stone stairs, had seen what was going on. "I'll speak to that boy's father, Tante Seulette," he promised. "There seems to be nothing but trouble about children. I've spent the better part of a day trying to find a home for"—he turned toward his wife and added in a low tone—"the child of young Madame Halay. I've spoken to every couple in Longueuil and had the same answer each time. No one wants her."

His wife looked surprised and indignant as well. "But why not? Is it too much to ask when you do so much for them?"

The seigneur seemed reluctant to give the reason. "There were rumors about the mother. I'm convinced there was no truth to any of it but—the stories did get around. No one wants the child on that account."

"Perhaps there *was* some truth in the rumors."

"No. I had the best of authority for believing her innocent, as you know, sweet wife. But the strength of my conviction doesn't make it possible to find anyone willing to take the child."

"I wouldn't worry about it. You'll find foster parents for her in Montreal. There's no great haste in the matter surely."

"Ah, but there is! I want the mother to leave at once. She's anxious to

et back to France but naturally she won't leave until the child's future
as been assured." He dropped his voice to a whisper. "Don't you
ee? I don't want this woman staying in Montreal while Jean-Baptiste is
bout."

"Her permit is arranged?"

"Yes. I've seen to that. All that remains is to settle something about
he child."

While husband and wife talked Tante Seulette's eyes went back and
orth from one face to the other. She knew what they were discussing and
he seemed to be taking a deep and even excited interest.

"M'sieur Charles," she said finally.

"Yes, Tante Seulette?"

"This child. Is she healthy?"

"Quite healthy. A normal child in every way."

"Is she—is she a pretty child?"

"Strangely enough she isn't pretty at all. She doesn't seem to take after
her mother."

The answer seemed to provide the housekeeper with a great deal of
satisfaction. She nodded her head several times and even smiled, a rare
manifestation of feeling on her part. "M'sieur Charles," she asked in a
tone of surprising humility, "would you consider letting me take her?"

"You?" The seigneur was caught off guard. He glanced uncertainly at
his wife but received no help there, for Madame le Moyne had been
equally surprised.

"Yes, M'sieur Charles. I would be happy to take her. It would be—an
interest for me. I'm sure I could look after her without neglecting my
work."

"I'm quite sure of that," declared Charles le Moyne. "But I confess to
some doubts as to the wisdom of it."

"I know what's in your mind. You think me too hard. It's true I keep
after these lazy lumps and see to it they do their work or feel the weight
of my hand. We'd get nothing done here if I didn't. But, M'sieur Charles,
it would be different with the child. She would be safe from—from my
fits of temper. I promise it, I swear it." She looked at the master of the
house with a hint of appeal in her face. "No one else wants her. And she
isn't attractive. I feel drawn to her, M'sieur Charles. I'll raise her well.
I'll see to it that she grows up to be obedient and sensible and devout.
She won't become one of these flutterheads, these silly coquettes, who
think there's nothing in life but to win the admiration of men. Ah, no,
she won't become that kind at all!"

The seigneur looked questioningly at his wife. "Why not?" he asked.
"It is, after all, a solution."

Madame le Moyne hesitated. "I hoped a home could be found for her
elsewhere. Still, as you say, it is a solution." She was thinking that having

a child to care for might result in making the housekeeper herself more human. All other methods had failed. Tante Seulette was an inheritance from Old M'sieur Charles and her husband firmly refused to get rid of her. "If you want to arrange it this way, Charles, I see no reason why it shouldn't be done."

"Very well then. Tante Seulette, the child is yours." The seigneur spoke in a relieved tone of voice. "I'll have her sent across the river as soon as I return to Montreal."

The housekeeper did not smile but it was quite evident that she was well pleased. She began to make audible plans. "That bench bed we moved out to the carpentry shop when things were so crowded can be brought back to my room. I looked at it the other day and it's in good shape still. A scrubbing with soap and water is all it needs. As for clothes, madame, there are plenty of castoffs in that old press at the foot of the east stairs left by Ma'amselle Catherine when she was married. I'll cut them up and make them over for her if you will say the word."

"Of course, Tante Seulette, do whatever you believe necessary. But I don't like to think of the poor child having nothing but made-over clothes. I'll send you some new materials from Montreal."

"It won't be necessary, madame," said the housekeeper firmly. Her tone of voice left the impression that she wanted no help in the care of the child and no interference.

III

Charles le Moyne accompanied his famous brother to the southwest gate from which the path led to the *mouille-pieds*. They lingered under the stone arch and looked about them.

A tenant named Charron took advantage of their presence to bustle up with a piece of news. "Old Kirkinhead tried to hang himself this morning," he announced. "I was passing by his house and it was a very lucky thing indeed. I heard a sound like a chair falling over and I went to the door. *Palsambleu!* He was hanging from a hook in the ceiling! I cut the rope with my knife and down he went on the floor."

"How long had he been hanging?" asked Charles.

"A few seconds only, m'sieur. The rope hadn't even cut into his neck."

The seigneur indulged in a grunt of doubt. "It could have been a coincidence that he did it just as you were passing," he said, "but somehow I don't think it was. He's been threatening to hang himself for years."

The tenant nodded his head in sudden agreement. "Now that you mention it, I too remember the things he has been saying. And, M'sieur Charles, I thought as I approached the house that I saw him squinting out of the corner of a window. Of course I was sure I had been mistaken about it when I went in and found him swinging from the ceiling."

"If I had the time," growled D'Iberville, "I would go and teach that fellow a lesson."

"He'd left a letter for Cécile," went on Charron, enjoying his momentary importance. "He said they'd driven him to it and he knew they would regret it when they looked on his face in death."

"And how were things when you left?" asked the seigneur.

"He was eating a plate of soup. And he was grinning and winking and nodding at Cécile's back as though proud of himself." The witness was beginning to see the light. "That *badaud*, that great fool! Was it all a trick?"

"I think," said the seigneur, exchanging a glance with his brother, "that I must have a talk with Monsieur Girard."

"The foot," declared D'Iberville, "can be more eloquent than the tongue."

The witness was now completely convinced. "By St. Christophe, he saw me and waited until he could be sure I would rescue him! Much better it will be for him not to try it a second time when I'm the one to be there! If I catch him at it again I'll just stand in front of him and laugh in his face while he strangles to death. Is it to be expected that I'll make a habit of saving him?"

D'Iberville laughed. "When you see him again, tell him that the devil keeps pitchforks heated to give a rousing welcome to suicides." He shook his head. "It's indeed a misfortune that our stout little Philippe has to live in the house of this crackbrain."

The two brothers passed through the gate after the keeper dropped the chains. "May God and all the kind saints look down on you, M'sieur Pierre," said the keeper, "and bring you safely home."

D'Iberville had changed his plum-colored coat for a more comfortable *capot* of ratteen which flared out stiffly from the waist. He still had the birch-bark case around his neck but it was empty. Having a tendency to carelessness in such matters, he had left many knives about the countryside. Charles noticed what had happened and said that he would have the missing article found and sent to Montreal.

When they had gone about halfway to the landing place they stopped and faced each other in silence for several moments.

"Well, Pierrot, we begin."

"Yes, Charles. The next two years at least will be both busy and bloody. I expect to be fighting all the time. And you, my shrewd elder brother, will be having a hard time of it providing me with the sinews of war."

"It won't be easy for any of us." The seigneur glanced back over his shoulder at the high walls of the château. "We must see to it, Pierre, that the strong places on the great river are strengthened so we can hold all the West for France."

D'Iberville began to quote from the First Book of Maccabees: " 'Then Simon built up the strongholds in Judea, and fenced them about with high towers, and great walls, and gates, and bars.' That's what you were about, my brother, when you built the high towers of Longueuil. They couldn't see what you were doing, the blind fools who criticized you. Now that we're all going to have empty pockets, I suppose they'll start at it again."

"It doesn't matter," said the seigneur easily. "Perhaps they'll begin to understand when we have forts along the Mississippi. I pay no attention to the talk of pinchpenny neighbors."

D'Iberville was looking at the walls of the château with an air of deep regret. Then he turned to the river and studied the deep cover of trees on the island of Ste. Hélène, which belonged to the family.

"I've always loved Longueuil," he said. "I should never come back here because it puts thoughts in my head. Always when I come I wonder if it's the last time. At this moment the presentiment is on me heavily. I never expect to see Longueuil again."

CHAPTER VII

LATER that day two men were seated in a tavern room in the lower town at Montreal. Jules Benoit, an unpleasant-looking individual with a touch of the king's evil on his cheek, was one of them, Joseph de Mariat the other. It was stiflingly hot in the room and both men had discarded their coats.

"Everyone knows your purpose in coming here, m'sieur," said Benoit, clasping his knees with fingers which seemed uneasy at his temerity in addressing thus the great visitor from France.

"Indeed." De Mariat was sharpening a quill point as usual and did not look up. "And what is it that everyone knows?"

"That you are here to find how the fur-trading laws are being broken. You are an officer of the King and you're gathering evidence." The *praticien* indulged in a bleak smile. "I'm not a trader, monsieur. I'm a humble man of the law. I've nothing to conceal from you—and so, nothing to fear."

De Mariat leaned forward in the direction of the window, in the hope of benefiting from any stray breeze. The move did him no good, however, for a high stone wall closed them off.

"What everyone in Montreal doesn't know," he said in his husky voice, "is that I've found out all I wanted to know. I know about the deals with the customs men at Quebec. I've inspected the secret compartments in the holds of ships which the accommodating inspectors *never* seem to find and which are so admirably suited to the storing of furs. I know about the fishing vessels which meet the ships off the Isle of Oléron and unload the furs so that the inspectors in Rochelle find nothing at all."

He finished the sharpening of the quill and examined it closely as though saying to himself, "And now I'm ready to write down what I know about you, my clever Jules Benoit, and that—ha-ha!—will be the end of *you*." He nodded his head then and said in a ruminating tone: "I know, moreover, that the profits are enormous. After paying the customs men for their blindness, and scraping off a little for the captains and mates of the ships, and paying through the nose to the crews of the fishing vessels, and tickling the sensitive palms of the officials at Rochelle— after all this, Master Tabellion, it's still possible for the merchants of New France to make as much as seven hundred per centum on their money." He nodded his head with great self-satisfaction. "I have every name in my notes, every figure, every little single damning detail. I can go back to France and blow the whole mercantile fabric of this fine colony into bits just like—*pouf!*—just like that!"

The man of the law cupped a hand behind his ear and said in the interrogatory tone of the deaf, "What did you say?"

"I suspect your deafness," declared De Mariat impatiently. "I'm sure you can hear everything you want to know. But I'll repeat myself to this extent. I have the evidence to throw all the fur merchants in Montreal into prison."

The lawyer nodded his head. "But naturally," he said, "you'll do nothing of the kind."

The King's officer laughed. "But naturally I'll do nothing of the kind. These regulations, which our wise King has so graciously decided to impose on the fur trade, are not to be taken too seriously. Oh, I shall make a report and show there have been infractions. There will have to be scapegoats. None of the crown officials will be involved nor any of the important traders. It's inconceivable that any mention could be made, for instance, of—well, shall we say, the great Le Moyne family? I've already made up my list. There's a trifling little trader or two, the mate of a ship, an inconsequential clerk at Quebec who was foolhardy enough to collect a few sols for himself. I engage they'll get off with nothing worse than fines." He spread out the palms of both hands. "It's all very regrettable but there's the law to be satisfied and the suspicions of the King to be assuaged."

Jules Benoit was entirely at home with this kind of talk. "The little men always make such safe targets," he said. "It's a great mistake to be one of the little men in the breaking of the law."

Any hint of amiability which might have been detected in the round face of the King's officer—it would have been small under the most favorable circumstances—faded away. He stared hard at Benoit, whose face, by way of contrast with his own massive countenance, was thin and sallow and completely dominated by a long and pointed nose.

"You understand," he said, "that ways must be found to compensate those responsible for this unexpected display of leniency. I shall need an agent here, someone to make collections, to exert pressure in quarters where it may be needed, to buy up seigneuries under certain circumstances. I've been making inquiries and the answers I received to my discreet questioning bring me to you. You, M'sieur Benoit, are the one man cut to my measure. You, if you so desire, can make yourself most useful to me and the—the others I represent in these matters. If you decide to serve me, the rewards will be far from inconsiderable."

"That is understood." Nothing in the tone employed by the lawyer gave any hint of the exultation he was feeling. "The rewards must be far from inconsiderable."

De Mariat leaned across the space between them until his face was not more than a foot from that of his companion. "A word of warning," he said.

Benoit gasped. All sense of satisfaction had taken hasty wings. He felt as though he had been immersed suddenly under the waters of the sea and had found himself staring into the menacing eye of an octopus.

De Mariat began to speak in a husky whisper. "You will be infinitely careful and discreet in everything. You will be faithful and you will obey every order without question or delay. You will never let as much as a single word I've said to you reach any other pair of ears. If you should play me false in any single detail, like the niggling son of a horseleech I think you may be, you will find we have unpleasant ways of dealing with little traitors. Very unpleasant ways indeed. The prisons of France and the criminal graveyards are full of little traitors, and rash little liars, and misguided little thieves."

Benoit felt as though he had at last attained the surface after a period during which breathing had been impossible. He swallowed several times and then said in a small voice, "You'll never have cause for complaint, monsieur."

De Mariat laughed easily. "We'll discuss details later." He reached into the embroidered pocket of his waistcoat and drew out a beautiful watch made in the form of a rosary. "As I thought, it's quite late. You will do well to remember everything I have said to you."

II

His servant followed De Mariat out into the street, carrying a valise on one shoulder. Behind them came two porters, each loaded down with a sizable portmanteau. The weather had been cool now for two days and a brisk breeze reached them from the river but the effort entailed in the downhill walk to the Quay des Barques was sufficient to cover the King's officer's face with perspiration.

"It's good we are starting back," said De Mariat, stopping and pointing to a pair of Indians on the other side of the street. One of them wore a small breechclout and the other had no vestige of clothing to mitigate his nakedness. "To a man of sense and taste the habits of this country are deplorable."

The town seemed to be filled with sound. The streets were crowded with people who talked and laughed and sang and from the lower town came the jubilant ringing of bells. De Mariat stopped before a tavern and asked the landlord, who was standing in the door, "Is this plaguy place enjoying a celebration of some kind?"

The boniface came forward, wiping his hands on the canvas apron tied about his middle. "Yes, m'sieur," he said, his eyes crackling with excitement. "D'Iberville leaves today. He goes to win us more victories. Is it any wonder, then, that we are noisy? That great M'sieur Pierre deserves a send-off worthy of the King himself."

De Mariat grunted and went on. The landlord winked at the two porters and said under his breath, "That prying, snooping nose of a pig!"

The servant lengthened his stride until he was close to his master's shoulder. "I have word for you," he said. "About the—the one you pointed out to me."

"You mean the . . . ?"

"Yes, master. The lady."

"Not so loud, simpleton! Do you think I want everyone in the town to know my affairs? Come closer. No, no, a full stride behind. Do you think I'm inviting you to share my bed and sup with my spoon? I can hear you now if you have to whisper."

"Master," said the servant, "she's the same one. The widow who's being sent back to France. She leaves today, master, and sails from Quebec on the same boat as you."

A gratified look took possession of the official's tallowy face. "How very convenient! If I had set the wheels to turning myself, the results couldn't have been more satisfactory." He glanced over his shoulder at the servant. "What else? You have more news for me. I can tell by the gleam in your eye, you sly fox."

"The lady has money," whispered the servant. "She had none before and was making a living as a seamstress. Now she's buying things in the stores. New hats and shawls and shoes, master. And veils and silks for dresses. It's being said about town . . ."

"Yes, yes! Speak up. These are not state secrets you're telling me. There's no need to hem and haw like a state envoy."

"It's said she's been given money to go away; it must be so, master, because she's spending with a free hand. It's said in the taverns that she intends to play the lady when she gets to Paris. Why else would she want such fine things as she's laying by?"

"And she has the official permit to return to France?"

"Yes, master. And it takes influence to get one. Influence in high places. These are points much discussed in the taverns."

De Mariat made no comment for several moments but continued to plod along, planting his splayed feet down firmly as though matters of world-wide importance hinged on each step.

"So!" he said to himself. "My good Charles is seeing to it that the pretty widow is removed out of reach of the young brother. Very wise of him! He doesn't want this pert little hen taking away one of his sturdy fighting cocks." He grunted with a sense of complete satisfaction and fumbled a small piece of silver out of a waistcoat pocket. He held this up and addressed the servant. "You've done well, François. So well that I suspect you consider yourself entitled to the reward I promised you. Do you see this coin? It's yours. Unless"—a hopeful gleam appeared in his eyes—"you prefer some other kind of payment. I will give you a promise instead that the next time you are guilty of an error I'll remit your punishment."

"The money, if you please, master."

His master was not pleased. He held out the coin on the palm of his hand with a look of the keenest regret. It was a small coin indeed and not worthy of so much ado at a change in its ownership. "Very well," said De Mariat, and tossed the money in the air. The servant had to jump out into the street to catch it and very nearly dropped the valise in doing so.

They had reached the waterfront by this time. The river barges, eight in all (the larger the number, the less danger there was of Indian attacks), which were to start for Quebec within the hour were anchored beyond the Pied du Courant and canoes were being used to take the passengers out to them. It was clear that D'Iberville had not yet put in an appearance, for there was an air of expectancy about the crowds which filled all the space leading to the wharves. While waiting for their hero to appear the onlookers were contenting themselves with a close scrutiny of the other passengers arriving to take their places in the canoes.

"Look, master!" The servant pointed in the direction of the chief target of the public gaze, a young woman standing at the head of the water-steps. She was dressed in a gray traveling cloak and in place of a hat was wearing a thin shawl of the same color over her head. She was accompanied by a middle-aged woman who appeared to be serving her in the capacity of maid, and an unusual number of bags were piled up on the cobblestones beside her.

"It's the one, master. See how they stare at her!"

Joseph de Mariat was staring himself, but in the opposite direction. His eyes had singled out a young man in a sober brown coat who stood well back of the crowd. The young man was staring, with an air of the most complete melancholy, at the young woman in the gray cloak.

De Mariat called the attention of his man to the unhappy onlooker. "Is that the one they call the Sieur de Bienville?" he asked in a whisper.

"Yes, master." The servant had accompanied his employer to Longueuil and had made good use of his time while there. "That's M'sieur Jean-Baptiste, the clever one. He's the eighth. He leaves next week."

De Mariat nodded his head. "You are lazy, François, and a great liar. Although I've never caught you with your fingers in my pockets, I suspect you of being a thief. But at the same time you have your good points. As a getter of information, useful and otherwise, you have no equal. . . . Does it seem to you that the Sieur de Bienville is consumed with grief over the departure of the young woman?"

François gave a quick glance at the pale countenance of the eighth member of the Le Moyne family. "Yes, master. He looks very sad."

There could be no mistake about that. The Sieur de Bienville was looking very sad.

Book Two

CHAPTER I

JEAN-BAPTISTE LE MOYNE, Sieur de Bienville, shouted, *"Détapez vos canons!"* and heard a rush of feet as the gun crew hurried to obey the order.

Already the fids had been stripped off and the trunnions had been thoroughly greased with tallow. The Chevalier de Ligondez, who shared the command of the upper battery with De Bienville, was seeing that blankets and sheets were soaked in water and placed behind each gun for use in case the decks took fire. There were a hundred such details to be attended to in preparing for action.

De Bienville walked to the nearest porthole and stared out. There was a blazing sun and the three English ships, which were tacking to starboard in an effort to reach the roadstead before Fort Nelson, were now clearly to be seen. The first in line was a heavy frigate (five hundred tons, at least, he figured) which probably carried as many as fifty guns and looked most deadly forbidding. A strong wind was blowing across Hudson's Bay but the three ships kept beautifully in line as they beat up against it. None of the strange things the French had met on the journey into this grim and almost landlocked sea—the high dark rampart of the straits, the drifting icebergs like tall islands afloat, the awesome play of lights in the skies at night, the silence, the desolation, the feeling that they had reached another world over which death brooded—none of this had affected him as much as the sight of these three hostile ships. The *Pélican* was alone, for the rest of the French squadron had been lost sight of in coming through the straits. It would be three to one and these were heavy odds, even with D'Iberville on the quarterdeck. Behind them was Fort Nelson with a garrison thirsting for the extermination of the French.

The Chevalier de Ligondez called over his shoulder as he hurried by, "How far off now?"

"In another half hour their guns will start to sing," answered De Bienville. He felt a tightness in the pit of his stomach and it was some consolation that his brother officer was as white as chalk in spite of his activity.

In a tone of reluctant admiration he added: "They handle well. It's the *Hampshire* in the lead. A tough nut to crack."

De Ligondez walked to the water cask, into which brandy had been poured (not to bolster up courage but to cut the saltiness of the water and prevent the men from getting colic), and helped himself to a drink. His hand shook and some of the water spilled on the binding strake at his feet.

"But we'll crack that nut, my bold Jean-Baptiste," he said. He was only sixteen and had never needed to shave, and it was no wonder that he found it hard to put the desired fullness and authority into his voice.

A few moments later the commander came striding down the *second pont* on a final round of inspection. The blue of the D'Iberville eye had turned to cold fire. He had dressed himself as for a court reception, with lace at his neck and wrists and a heavy gold chain hanging low on his waistcoat.

"Well, my children!" he called in his battle voice, which was a tone higher than normal. "The English are coming in. We may have to board them but I'm hoping that a dose of this medicine"—he tapped a finger on the nearest gun—"will prove a complete cure. The order, when it comes, will be *Pointez à couler bas!* See that you rake them from stem to stern. I've confidence in your gunnery, my children." He looked up and down the gun deck, his eyes flashing. "In another hour the surface of Mort Bay must be three inches deep with roast beef and boiled potatoes."

A roar of laughter went up from the men working over their guns. De Bienville saw with a tug of pride that his brother's presence had acted already as a tonic. It was always the way; a single glimpse of him, the sound of his voice, the daring and humor in what he said, and the most timid rabbit of a man was ready to charge singlehanded at the enemy.

"A word with you, Sieur de Bienville," said D'Iberville in his brother's ear a few moments later.

They stepped behind the dripping canvas which had been rigged up in front of the budge barrels of gunpowder to ward off sparks. The commander looked his young brother over and then clapped him commendingly on the back. "This will be your first smell of powder, Jean-Baptiste," he said. "You look cool enough. But then you're a Le Moyne, and what else would be expected of a son of Old M'sieur Charles? I know you'll acquit yourself well today and my only worry is whether you'll try too hard. Do you remember your promise to Charles?"

"Yes, Pierre—I mean, my captain."

"I want you to do your duty to the fullest but I don't want to find it necessary to carry back word of another tragedy like the death of my brave Louis." His teeth bared as he thought of the passing of his favorite brother in these same unfriendly and bitter waters some six years before. "You must be careful not to go out of your way to meet danger. That's all. Go back to your post—and may the kind Father"—he crossed himself—"and all the saints in paradise look down on you the next few hours, my little Jean-Baptiste!"

De Bienville hesitated and then said, "I want to ask a question, my captain." He looked shamefaced and was careful to keep his eyes lowered. "I've tried to ask you this a hundred times but—but somehow I've never been able to get it out. And now if I don't ask you, I may never have the chance again."

"Be quick about it then." It was plain that D'Iberville's mind had gone on to more important things.

"You knew what happened before we sailed, about my falling in love. She, Madame Halay, was on the *Ferrand* when it sailed from Quebec, a day before us. I saw her on deck and Monsieur de Mariat was beside her. It seemed to me she was in very good spirits. She seemed to laugh a great deal and there's no denying she was dressed with care. Did you hear it said around the town that she and De Mariat had been together a great deal in Quebec? I was told everyone was talking about it."

"I heard some of the talk." D'Iberville dropped a comforting hand on his brother's shoulder. "They were about together and De Mariat was behaving like a rampaging old goat. Jean-Baptiste, you must accept a word of advice. Put your little Madame Halay out of your mind. She's a pretty creature but she's gone out of your life and you can count it good luck that she has." His feet seemed to be drawing him away but he compelled himself to remain long enough to impart a further piece of advice. "Very soon now, my brother, you'll be seeing Paris and other parts of the great world through a man's eyes. And then, God willing it not otherwise, you'll go with me to the warm seas of the south. This you'll discover for yourself: that the world is full of beautiful women, each one more willing and lovely than the last. There are so many of them that a man's fancy can stray from one to another like a fly over a basket of ripe fruit. You'll forget your little widow in shorter time than it's going to take me to clean the English out of Mort Bay."

De Bienville knew there was sound sense in what his brother had said but he was certain, nevertheless, that he would never forget Marie. The world might be full of enticing women but for him the one memory would never fade. He walked the length of the gun deck with this thought in mind but it was only a partial absorption, for he was able to give the battery a close and expert scrutiny at the same time.

"The captain may order swivels mounted on the rail of the weather deck," said De Ligondez when they next met. "I wish he'd put me in command up there, because then I would see everything. Here we'll fight in a smother of stife and all we'll know will be what they shout down the scuttle to us."

De Bienville answered with fitting scorn. "This battery will win the battle for us. Not a few paltry popguns, spitting into the shrouds!"

They were almost of a height and, standing face to face, they appeared resolute and alert in spite of their youth. The balance of their conversation, however, would have destroyed that impression.

"Jean-Baptiste," whispered De Ligondez, "I hope I'm not going to be sick at my stomach. I'm starting to feel strange already. They say men often vomit when the fighting starts."

"The captain warned me about that. He said I should draw in my belt tight to hold the muscles in. He said it didn't matter—that many brave men had been taken sick in battle."

"But," with a doubtful shake of the head, "what would the men think? I don't want to look like a puking coward to them."

II

D'Iberville paced the quarterdeck, his brows knitted, his head turning as he walked so that he could keep the enemy ships in sight. They were approaching more slowly now. The *Hampshire* in the lead was still under mizzens, topsails, and mainsail but the two following, the *Dering* and the *Hudson's Bay,* were carrying topsails only.

The commander of the French ship had a problem to solve. The *Dering* and the *Hudson's Bay* were vessels chartered by the trading company and it was easy to guess that they carried supplies for the garrison at Fort Nelson. The usual course would be to attack the escorting warship and, after disposing of it ("If God and the good saints bless me with a victory"), to deal with the merchantmen later. But if he made for the *Hampshire* now, the two supply ships would slip by into the roadstead. The fort, reinforced and adequately supplied, would then be able to hold out against him indefinitely. Clearly, therefore, his first duty was to prevent their entry.

To make his decision still harder, D'Iberville realized that he was in a position to beat the *Hampshire* if he struck at once. Even by close-hauling under full sail, Captain Fletcher of the English ship could not hope to get to windward of the *Pélican* where the initiative would be in his hands. D'Iberville could see that Fletcher was mustering his men at their stations, under the impression that he was to be boarded. The Englishman had turned and committed his stern to the mercies of the wind. If the *Pélican* could strike now! D'Iberville saw victory in his grasp, and the orders to attack at once were on the tip of his tongue.

And then, with the rare degree of daring which belongs only to genius, he elected not to take advantage of his drifting opponent. He would attack the two merchantmen while the *Hampshire* was temporarily out of control; and rely on his skill to catch Fletcher at a disadvantage again after driving the supply ships off.

"Gouverne là!"

His command for steadiness was pure routine, for his crew was made up largely of picked men. But the next order exploded through the ship with the impact of an enemy volley. His officers stared at each other incredulously. They were going to leave the warship to flounder and attack the *Dering,* the second in the now disrupted line! Orders were orders, however, and both officers and men sprang to obey. There was a scurry up the shrouds and in a very few seconds new sail billowed out. Below decks the gunners stood tensely at their posts. The maneuver was executed so neatly that D'Iberville cried from the quarterdeck, "Now, my brave children, let the lightning strike!"

It did not take the English captain long to perceive that D'Iberville had outguessed him. Fletcher hastily clapped on sail and put about with the intention of gaining the wind and attacking the *Pélican* from the rear. But he was too late to help the *Dering.* At a distance of three hundred yards D'Iberville's command of *"Pointez à démâter* [Aim to dismast]!" sent a half broadside through the rigging of the merchantman. Down came the mainmast. The unfortunate *Dering,* too crippled for anything but flight and not much of that, limped off to the northeast as fast as it could go, giving up all thought for the time being of reaching Fort Nelson with the vital supplies which crammed its pregnant hold.

D'Iberville had to commit himself utterly now to his daring and unorthodox conception; or so it seemed. If he cracked on sail and raced ahead he might be able to put the *Hudson's Bay* out of commission also ("God put steadiness in my gunner's hands!") as he went tumultuously by. But if he failed to hurt the second merchantman sufficiently, the latter could then crack on sail in turn and dash to the roadstead and the relief of the fort. It would be a close thing. A toss of the dice, a riffle with fate!

But again! It is proof of genius to change a plan in the very act of execution when something happens to make improvisation profitable. Something *had* happened. Fletcher had steered to the south in an effort to win the wind and was now reaching past the *Pélican's* track.

D'Iberville ordered his ship about. He would accept the disadvantage of the leeward position in the hope of beating the Englishman quickly while he himself still remained between the merchantman and the roadstead.

It would be quick enough and decisive enough! D'Iberville called an order, *"Hissez en douceur!"* and the sails flailed out. The *Pélican* gathered momentum. It was plain to be seen now, even to the excited occupants of the deck of the *Hudson's Bay,* thus unceremoniously left behind, that the battle to follow would be a madness of raking broadsides, a clash of gladiators set to kill with one blow, a decision one way or the other in a matter of minutes.

"Master," said D'Iberville's servant at his elbow, "your coat."

The commander, without looking around, slipped out of his handsome coat and let it fall into the waiting hands. Then he swung the gold chain up over his head, for it was long enough to interfere with his sword arm, and consigned it to the same care. He kicked off his shoes, preferring the sureness of stockinged feet if it should come to boarding.

The servant, who was Longueuil-born, remained behind him without moving, his face pale over the fine satin of the burden in his arms. He remained through fear; not fear for himself but for his master.

"I will guard the coat with my life, M'sieur Pierre," he said. "Will you take some care of *yourself?*"

Never was naval clash more quickly or more decisively ended. Fletcher had turned to take in sail and the *Pélican* came up alongside. As they began to pass, yard to yard, the *Hampshire* covered the French ship from the wind and so the *Pélican* stood straight up in the water while the English sails slanted. From the shrouds of the *Hampshire* musket fire raked the rigging and the deck of D'Iberville's ship. The servant, watching with no show of emotion, thought the sound was like the pelt of hail through the thick woods around Longueuil. He heard cries from the canvas thicket above and knew that some of the bullets were finding human marks. He instinctively tensed when he perceived that the passage of the *Pélican* across the English ship had brought them end to end.

"Pointez à couler bas!"

D'Iberville raised an arm as he shouted the order. The command was relayed down the scuttles and the guns in both batteries roared instantly. At no more than yardarm range, they poured their lethal medicine into the enemy hull.

The English guns responded instantly. Perhaps, however, the impact had thrown them off the mark. Most of the broadside raked through the French rigging, cutting a mast, slicing the stays, and tearing gaping holes in the canvas. Some shots found the hull and holes were made dangerously close to the water line.

But the *Hampshire* had fared much worse. The one volley had cut great holes in the hull, and she reeled and shuddered as the water poured into her hold. No time, no chance, to return the blow in full measure! Her pumps broken, her steering gear gone, a mortal wound in her belly, the once gallant frigate fell back like a stunned gladiator. Within three lengths she began to show signs of foundering, her masts slanting drunkenly, her crew swarming up the shrouds like ants in anticipation of the going down of the ship.

"Master, your coat," said the servant.

Breathing hard in the triumph of the moment, D'Iberville slipped his arms into the openings and fitted his feet back into the expensively buckled shoes.

"Giles, this battle is won!"

"Of course, master." Then the servant turned abruptly, his feelings getting out of control, and ran to the cabin to give vent to them in private.

Within an hour it was over. The *Hampshire* had gone down, the *Hudson's Bay* had hoisted the white flag, the *Dering* had taken to its heels and vanished over the horizon.

D'Iberville said a prayer as he stood beside the rail and watched the boat he had lowered for the purpose endeavor to pick up survivors from the unfortunate warship. "I beg, O Lord," he said in a low tone, "that the men who have died this day meet forbearance at Thy hands. They were fighting men, more prone to giving and taking blows than the saying of prayers. They've met death suddenly, these brave fellows, without time to think of the state of their souls. Surely, O Lord, they deserve mercy at Thy hands as much as those who stay warmly at home and never risk themselves in the furtherance of Thy plans. Lord, receive gently these men of mine who lie dead below."

As it turned out there was no need for his fervent appeal. The ship's surgeon came up on deck for a brief moment of fresh air. His arms were red to the elbows and the commander approached him with a hesitation he would not have shown under any other circumstances. "M'sieur Jean," he asked, "what are our losses?"

The surgeon answered with unexpected cheerfulness. "Not a man dead, my captain. Seventeen are wounded but I hope to pull them all through. There'll be amputations, naturally. But should one mind consigning a few arms and legs to the waters of Mort Bay when not one Canadian soul has winged its way from this earth?"

D'Iberville still spoke in a hesitant tone. "And my officers? Are any of them among the wounded?"

The surgeon's air of good cheer did not diminish. "Of course, my captain. Good officers are always in the thickest, and these are good officers. The Chevalier de Ligondez has a splinter in his leg, Rouer de la Carbonnière a broken elbow." His manner became less assured. "The Sieur de Bienville——"

D'Iberville turned quickly. "He's hurt? Badly?"

"A flying fragment of shell. In his arm, most fortunately. It's not to be considered serious, my captain. But he was thrown across the gun deck and wasn't found at first. He lost considerable blood. But have no fear. I pledge my head that I'll have him on his feet soon and with no more lasting harm than a—well, a rather large scar."

CHAPTER II

THE French flag flew over Fort Nelson and there was, perhaps, a consciousness of this fact in the stride of D'Iberville as he emerged from the governor's quarters and walked across the yard. Aware that one of the garrison children was watching him from around a corner, he stopped, smiled broadly, and said in English, "Allo, my small oaten loaf." The child answered without a hint of a smile. "Allo."

The victor had the unpleasant task before him of visiting the infirmary and he felt the need of a little refreshment in advance. Accordingly he tapped a knuckle on the cookhouse door and called, "A glass of wine, if you please." An arm came through the door with a tankard at the end of it and a face above it which was English and gloomy and uncompromising. "There," said a voice which shared in all three qualities. "That's wine."

D'Iberville took a sip and said, "It's a good thing you told me, for otherwise I would have entertained doubts." After a second sparing gulp of the thin and sour mixture he went on, gesturing with the tankard: "My man, the French and the English have been fighting all through history. Sometimes we win, sometimes you. But this much I assert: the French have always beaten the English in the making of wine."

As he crossed the small space within the walls he glanced at the sky with the questing look of one who knows that history hinges on a turn of the weather. The sky was still clear and blue but there was a suggestion of steeliness which meant cold. There was enough breeze to keep the flag twisting and turning, and occasionally to bring a shower of leaves whirling in over the walls. As he watched, an enormous formation of wild geese came up over the tops of the stunted trees and wheeled with military precision over his head.

Now that the last days of migration had arrived, he realized that he could no longer delay his departure and expect to get through the straits before they froze over. He would have been away long before this if it had not been for the storm which swept down from the northeast on the day following the battle. It had struck with such violence that the *Pélican* had snapped her anchor cables and had been driven ashore. The ship had split along the middle of the keel and the hold had filled with water, and it had been with the greatest difficulty that the wounded had been taken ashore on rafts and floats. It had been apparent at once that the *Pélican* could not be repaired in time for the journey back to France and D'Iberville had decided to use the *Profond,* one of the smaller vessels which had fallen behind in the passage of the straits and had arrived several days after the engagement. The *Profond,* it developed, had sustained some damage on its own account. The work of refitting and victualing it had not yet been completed and would take perhaps another week to finish properly.

D'Iberville took another look at the sky and decided to get away at once.

A covered way which ran from the north bastion of the fort to a demi-bastion had been converted into a hospital for the wounded of both sides. D'Iberville entered gingerly, wondering again, as he had done on all his visits, why surgeons seemed to prefer working in gloom and isolation. He did not go far enough with the speculation to realize that it was not by choice they existed in gloomy corners of castles or in the cellars of taverns or in malodorous holes down in the bowels of ships. They took what was given them and made the best of it, probing and cutting and doctoring by the flickering light of torches and saving more of the victims than might have been expected under such grim circumstances.

He found himself standing in a dark anteroom and drawing into his nostrils a sickeningly lethal smell. This dank hole was used for the keeping of supplies and on the wall opposite him was a row of bags on hooks in which drugs and herbs were kept. With a resentful eye (being a man of supreme health, he had little patience with illness) he read some of the names: bishop's weed, turpeth, scammony, galingale, cumin, cassia, flea-bane, saxifrage, tamarind. "By St. Christophe!" he muttered. "I'll never let them put any of these noxious poisons into *my* stomach!"

He came to a sudden stop when he reached a space closed off with blankets which lay beyond the supply room. A scream had sounded from within, a mad scream, high and wild and scarcely human. He drew back one of the blankets with reluctant fingers and saw that the surgeon and his assistants were engaged in removing a leg from a naked sailor stretched out on a trestle. If it had not been that he recognized the patient he would have moved on hurriedly.

"Edouard!" he heard the surgeon say. "The *fer ardent* at once!"

A man who had been at work before a blaze on the hearth obeyed the summons by carrying across the room a bucket of coals on top of which lay a long pokerlike instrument with a white-hot tip. The surgeon wrapped his hand in several layers of canvas before taking the *fer ardent* by the handle. He then applied the molten tip to the bleeding stump of the leg, his arm moving vigorously up and down as he cauterized the exposed flesh. A smokelike vapor arose from the limb and the room was filled with the stench of burning flesh. The patient made no further sound. He had fainted away at the first searing impact of the metal.

The assistants straightened up and stepped back from the trestle, perspiration streaking down their faces. The surgeon barked, "Bandage it carefully. But not tightly, you bunglers! I'm not pleased when my stumps begin to mortify."

He came across to D'Iberville, mopping his face on one of the towels used in the operation. *"Voilà!* There's an end to a very satisfactory bit of tinkering with the human frame. It's hard work but I think well of myself when it's a matter of legs. I'm always at my best with legs."

"That was François Murot?"

"Yes, my captain. Fortunately he's of a strong constitution."

D'Iberville dampened his lips with the tip of his tongue. "Was it absolutely necessary to remove the leg?"

"My captain!" The surgeon spoke with dramatic conviction. "I swear to you that mortification would have set in quickly if the leg had not been removed."

"François Murot is a Longueuil man. His father's land was just beyond the mill and I saw him often when we were boys. I want nothing but the best treatment and care for this old friend. You will see to it?"

"I will see to it." The surgeon nodded energetically. "The best I could do for him was to work fast. I didn't lose a single second, my captain. I am very fast at legs."

"What chance has he of living, M'sieur Surgeon?"

"He'll live. I swear it. He's as strong as a bull, that one. Yes, he'll be hobbling around on one leg to a ripe old age. But, St. Laud of Angers, how he bled!"

II

Beyond the screen of blankets was an equally dark and fetid area filled so closely with cots that the attendants had to wedge themselves in between. All the cots were filled with sick and wounded men: leggers, boners, ribbers, feverers, improvers, and goers, to use the lingo of the infirmary. The Frenchmen who had been wounded in the battle were together at the end where the darkness was not quite so intense, the air slightly less noxious, and the space between the cots a few inches wider perhaps. D'Iberville made his way to this section and found his brother sitting up, his wounded arm enormous with bandages.

"Jean-Baptiste," he said, standing at the foot of the bed, "I've bad news for you. We sail with the turn of the tide tomorrow."

De Bienville beamed with delight. "That's the best of news! I've been praying for a chance to escape this foul hole."

"But you're not going. You must stay here and return home on the first ship out in the spring."

The young officer sat up straight in bed. He protested in a low voice, "What you are telling me, Pierre, is that I won't sail with you to the Mississippi."

D'Iberville nodded unwillingly. "It's unfortunate, little brother, but what else is to be done? You are unfit for the rigors ahead of those who sail with me tomorrow on the *Profond*. I must take a few of the prisoners and I'll need as much in the way of stores as can be packed in. We'll make this voyage like jack barrel in a net! And of course there's the danger that we'll be imprisoned in the ice and have to remain there for the duration of the winter. No, Jean-Baptiste, I can't think of taking you. It would be the same as signing your death warrant."

"I'll be strong enough!" protested the younger brother. "A few days of salt air and I'll be a well man. Ask the surgeon, Pierre. He'll tell you I'm well enough to go."

"But can I take you and none of the others?"

"Every man here is set on going and thinks himself well enough."

"It's the truth, M'sieur Pierre!" cried a Longueuil man a few cots down the line. "Take us all with you. Kind Mother in heaven, we want no more of this!"

It was apparent at once that the conversation had been followed all along the line. A chorus of voices chimed in, asserting their desire to sail on the *Profond* and their unwillingness to be left behind for eight months of confinement in an icebound fort. D'Iberville listened to them with an uneasy scowl.

"Do you know, you soft-skulled simpletons, that I sail for France and not Quebec?" he demanded.

They all knew it, and they made it clear that the destination did not affect their preference.

"There won't be room enough for the able-bodied men," protested the commander. "What would I do with a lot of broken hulks, needing medical attention and waiting on all the time? By St. Christophe, I believe that great idiot of a François, if he could talk, would say that *he* wants to sail tomorrow!" He glared about him. "Don't you know that half of you would be dead by the time we reached France?"

Several voices clamored at him. "We're sure to die here!" "You can't leave us in this hole!" "Give us a chance and we'll risk it!"

D'Iberville scowled angrily. "You crackbrains! How can I be sensible and leave you behind when you all talk like this? But how can I take you when I know that it means death for most of you? What am I to do?" He stamped his way to the entrance but paused there and looked back. "I'll leave it to the surgeon. I'll take any he says are well enough, and no others. There will be no appeal from his decisions."

From the smiles which greeted this announcement, it was clear that they did not fear the decisions of the surgeon.

CHAPTER III

THE King of France was much gratified by the conquest of Hudson's Bay and he had decided, moreover, to equip the Mississippi expedition. But the kingly mind had not yet properly connected the two things. When D'Iberville arrived in Paris and took up quarters with his brother, the Sieur de Bienville, in a tavern called La Bouteille Noire, he found to his astonishment and intense dismay that his appointment to the command was seriously in doubt. Others wanted the honor, some of them men who had never been to sea, and it looked probable that the wobbling choice of the Sun King would fall on one of these courtly incompetents. Joseph de Mariat shook his head darkly and said he had done his best. He was inclined to blame it on the Old Woman, which made the prospects seem very dim indeed.

D'Iberville, accordingly, had to spend the winter in an intensive lobby. He haunted the anterooms of Versailles and Marly, he talked to ministers and their assistants and to the mistresses of ministers and their assistants. He spent long hours watching the King sup with the ladies of his court (Louis XIV made it a rule not to have men seated at the table where he consumed his enormous meals) and sometimes received a nod in passing. He talked to everyone who would listen, arguing, expostulating, promising, begging. It was not until the spring that he was given any assurance that the honor he had so magnificently earned was to be his.

In the meantime the Sieur de Bienville had been left to his own devices. He had landed in France a skeleton, after the horrors of the sea voyage from Hudson's Bay, during which no day had passed, it seemed, without a body being consigned to the deep, lashed in a hammock. At Rochefort there had been proper food and medicines and a chance to rest. In as short a time as a week he had been able to walk along the waterfront by himself, his arm free of its bandages and sling. His appetite became ravenous. In a fortnight he had color again in his cheeks. In three weeks he had been well enough to accompany D'Iberville to Paris. Having nothing to do, he proceeded to make himself familiar with the wonder, the miracle, the Pandora's Box of danger, the monstrosity, the hatful of tricks which was Paris. His wanderings in the great city were invariably made in the company of a small, bright, sensitive, and indifferently washed urchin whose name was Blaise.

To understand how this came about, it is necessary to explain that La Bouteille Noire stood close to the quayside at a point where the fine buildings along the river were no more than a new ruching sewed to the edge of a very ragged and greasy collar. Immediately behind the stateliness of a single row of houses was a poor section, so densely populated that it could only be compared to a rabbit warren. The tavern stood at the entrance to one of the narrow, crooked streets, and all day long people passed in and out, pale, undernourished, ragged, furtive-eyed people. De Bienville spent all his time during the first few days of his arrival watching this shabby procession and, as a result, he made the acquaintance of Blaise.

The boy lived with his widowed mother and a sister younger than himself in the cellar of one of the timbered buildings which had lapsed into evil days and decay: in a small section of the cellar, to be exact, separated from the other tenants by moldy blankets on a line (which were taken down and used at night), a damp hole with water dribbling down the walls, an earthen floor, and one small window. Blaise and another boy, who was somewhat larger and answered to the name of Le Drôle, hung about the tavern in the hope of finding things to do—run errands, hold a horse's head, open a carriage door, carry in luggage. De Bienville had selected Blaise because he was smaller than his noisy, bullying rival and because he discovered that the family in the cellar depended entirely on what the boy could earn.

With Blaise to guide him he soon achieved a certain familiarity with Paris. He quickly learned to love the city and to fear it. The fear was for its poverty and its wickedness. In New France life was so simple that there was no want, no hunger, and very little wrongdoing. Paris not only taught him things about life he had never suspected but instilled in him ideas and purposes he had lacked when he set sail from that long cloister which ran the length of the St. Lawrence. The need for colonies took on urgency when he saw how overcrowded the cities of the Old World were, and how miserably the spawn of the slums lived.

One evening he decided that he would visit a theater. He was so eager for the venture that he fairly ran to the door of the tavern. "Blaise!" he called, staring out into the darkness to find his attendant. There was a sound of scuffling in the shadows and then Le Drôle emerged.

"My lord, take me tonight," he urged in the whining voice of the underworld. "Me, I'll show you the best places in the city. Is it a lady? Do you want to gamble, to see a play? This one, this little mother's brat, this pull-the-cordon, what does he know of the Paris a great gentleman like you should see?"

"I'm used to Blaise. I want him to go with me."

"Listen to me, my lord. Don't you know this boy's father swings in rust?"

De Bienville frowned at the ragamuffin, not understanding what he meant.

Le Drôle endeavored to make himself clearer. "Do you want to use a boy whose father does the wind dance?"

"It's the truth, m'sieur," said Blaise, coming forward from the darkness of the innyard. "I didn't tell you because—because it hurts to talk about it. My father, m'sieur, was hanged a month ago."

"He was a thief!" shrilled Le Drôle.

"He was a *chiffonnier*. My father, m'sieur, went out at nights with his basket to visit the dumps and to pick over what had been emptied in the streets and back yards. He made a living for us out of what he got that way. One morning, when he returned, he found he had picked up a hand-kerchief, quite a fine one, m'sieur. There was a ring wrapped up inside it, a gold ring. He didn't know where he had found it or who owned it and so—m'sieur, was it so very wrong to try and get money for it? They took him, and they said he was a thief, and they hanged him. Because it happened this ring had belonged to a very great lady."

"He's still in the chains!" cried Le Drôle. "The crows have picked out his eyes."

"Come, Blaise," said De Bienville, scowling angrily at the tattler. "We must hurry, I am going to a theater."

On the way to the Rue des Fosses, where the Comédie Française was located, he asked his companion many questions, finally coming to the one he had had in mind from the first. Would he, Blaise, like to live in a country where there was always enough to eat, where each family had a home of its own, where there was no thievery and so no hangings? To his surprise he found that Blaise entertained some doubts. Leave Paris? It was an upsetting thought. Paris, with all its cruelty to her children who lived on the bare edge of existence, was still the whole world to them, even such as poor Blaise. This new country, the boy asked, was it not bitterly cold and full of great dangers?

The Sieur de Bienville paid out fifteen sous for a seat in the pit and found himself entitled to a place on a bench with no back and a single layer of green baize as a covering. Around the pit was a first gallery with boxes on each side in which great ladies sat (some of them quite breath-takingly lovely) with glasses at their eyes. He was impressed to find that the pit was fashionable enough. At any rate there were well-dressed men all around him, passing snuffboxes back and forth and talking in the loud tones of those who regard themselves as above criticism.

The man beside him was carrying on a conversation with one who sat immediately in front. "It's not to be *Gabini* tonight," he was saying in a voice of deep umbrage. "There will be two drolls instead. Baron appears in one and La Duclon, my sweet sprunny, in the other. I take it as a personal affront, for only the thought of seeing *Gabini* brought me out. If I had paid for this seat—which I haven't, naturally, my presence being worth so much to them—I would demand satisfaction this instant."

"Still," demurred the man in front, "it will have its points. Baron and La Duclon in one evening!"

De Bienville was looking about him with intense interest. The curtain was down but there was an "apron" in full view, extending out into the pit, in fact, for at least thirty feet and equally wide. He was so intent on waiting for the curtain to rise that he failed to observe how closely the audience watched the occupants of one of the side boxes. It was the first box on the right and so looked down directly on the apron, a great advantage because it not only gave a close view but enabled its occupants to bask in the public eye. A man and a woman sat there and the audience was indulging in a great deal of speculation about them, whispering and laughing and even pointing. This was not surprising, for the woman was young and lovely, and dressed in such an extreme of fashion that every feminine eye in the place avidly studied each detail. She was wearing a figurette gown of Sèvres blue and it was apparent from the way her skirts billowed out that they were stiffened with *monte-la-haut* wires. She wore no hat but instead had dressed her hair high. A patch of the variety known as *effrontée*—because it was on the tip of her nose!—made her look saucy and thoroughly charming.

The man with her was a long-nosed, thick-lipped gallant who insisted on wearing his hat and who leaned forward on a cane to regard the house with an air of arrogance.

The curtain went up, slowly and creakily, and the actors, headed by the great Etienne Baron, proceeded to give the first of the drolls, a term applied to condensations of full-length plays. To do so they appeared on the apron. The stage hands had already assembled some props there—a couch, two chairs, a tapestried fire screen. Baron's rich baritone immediately exerted its spell and no one in the audience fell more completely a victim to it than De Bienville. He was so enthralled that he was scarcely aware of the mechanics by which the illusion of reality was sought, not noticing even when the actors stepped farther forward on the apron to begin a new scene while the attendants hastily raised behind them shutters, or flats as they were called in the profession. These flats concealed the old props from view and gave the suggestion of a new background. It was not until the first droll had been finished that he was able to bring himself back from the enchanted land which the playwright had conjured up and to take some notice of what was going on about him.

His eyes lighted then, for the first time, on the lady in the box.

It was Marie. He knew her instantly, in spite of the costliness of her costume and the manners of a great lady which she aped so successfully. He sat without moving for many minutes, drinking in her beauty, his mind a riot of conflicting emotions. One moment he wanted to rush to the box and carry her off, and later, if necessary, run the blade of his sword through the midriff of her companion. The next he would feel a sense of revulsion, realizing fully the manner of life she had adopted.

From where he sat it was impossible to see more of Marie's companion than the brim of his hat. In order to get a better look at him, De Bienville rose and circled around to the other side of the house. Here one could look straight up into the box across the now empty apron. He was surprised, and horrified, to find that the man with Marie was not Joseph de Mariat. Her companion was much younger, and the rankness of pride he showed in every move and gesture made it certain that he belonged in a much more exalted social circle.

This was so unexpected that the rejected lover from the colonies stood transfixed for a second time, staring up at the box in an unhappily complete disregard of everything else. Marie, it was now apparent, had deliberately brought herself to the market where beauty was most eagerly sought and most extravagantly paid for; and, obviously, was doing quite well. The disillusioned youth watched the smug face of her latest purchaser and thought how his spirits would leap to face this man of the court over a crisscrossing of steel. He did not glance at Marie a second time.

He made no effort to resume his seat (which was just as well, for someone had promptly taken possession of it) but walked out of the house, disregarding the rise of the curtain and almost unaware of the sweet chirp of La Duclon's voice and the bantering tone of her laughter in the opening scene of the second droll. Outside the theater he stood in an unhappy daze, blinking at the darkness and not knowing, or caring, where he should go next.

"M'sieur," said Blaise, emerging from the shadows, "I stayed to see you safely back."

"That was considerate of you, Blaise."

De Bienville was still finding it hard to regain control of himself. He followed his guide silently into what in daylight was the Rue des Fosses but at night was only one of the yawning pits of darkness in which danger lurked. The necessity for vigilance finally drove from his mind the bitter reflections created by the shattering of a romantic dream.

"Blaise," he said, picking his way carefully along the foul and slippery surface of the street, "this evening has been a turning point in my life. I've been shocked and hurt and disappointed and my pride has been trampled on. All the hope I had for happiness in this world has been taken away from me. From this moment on I'll devote myself entirely to duty. Perhaps," he continued, conceiving himself a lean and grizzled explorer returning some night to this same theater, after many years spent in conquering the New World, and seeing the audience rise to cheer his entry, "perhaps it's better this way. Instead of becoming a dull man, tied down to a houseful of children, I'll be able to accomplish something for France and Holy Church." He nodded to himself in the darkness. "Yes, it will be better this way. Much better, my small friend. What is happiness after all? A dream, a drag, a drug. Without it to hold me back, I may become—who knows what I may become?"

II

In the mood created by the conduct of Marie, De Bienville was thoroughly unhappy during the rest of his long stay in Paris. When warm weather came, and with it the announcement that D'Iberville was to have command of the expedition after all, he beseeched his brother to send him on at once to Rochefort, where he could make himself useful in the assembling of stores and the fitting out of the ships. D'Iberville agreed to this and sent him on with a party of departmental officials.

At Rochefort the younger brother made a prompt discovery, that there are two cures for the moping condition of mind which has been romanticized as a broken heart. The first is work, the second the acquaintance of another pretty woman.

He had so much work to do that his days were completely filled. Knowing that the supplies which came through the naval contractors would be criminally bad and that nothing could be done about it (for the contractors must be allowed to wax wealthy on the profits and every itching palm in the departments must be attended to), he gave himself entirely to the purchase of supplementary supplies with the family funds. He proved a hard buyer; and, in addition, not a barrel or crate went aboard that he had not opened and inspected. He tasted the dried fish and the salt pork, he examined the muskets and the powder, he tested the edges of the agricultural tools. He fought with contractors and argued with ship chandlers. He buried his nose in invoices and checked bills with the assiduity of a hound on a fading trail. The capacity with which Charles had credited him manifested itself in abundant degree. He saw to it that every sou of Le Moyne money was well laid out.

One morning he was chaffering with a dealer in marine goods who had a dingy little shop overlooking the harbor. The merchant's eyesight was bad and he found it hard to find any specific article from his stock. Finally he bawled out: "Stéphanie! Stéphanie, I need you!"

In answer to this summons a girl came down the steps from the living quarters back of the shop. She was a little thing and she moved so silently that De Bienville did not favor her with a glance until he heard her say, "Yes, Father, and what is it now?" Her voice was pitched in such a pleasantly low tone that he looked up. He realized then that she had a pretty gray eye and dark hair which curled attractively over a brow broad enough to give assurance of intelligence. Moreover she was neatly dressed and the little he could see of her ankle was quite promising.

He watched her as she straightened matters out with a competence which both surprised and pleased him. She was, he realized, the exact opposite of Marie in almost every respect. Perhaps this increased her appeal for him. At any rate he found himself wishing that he could see her again.

He discovered many reasons after that for returning to the little marine shop and on each occasion the bumbling old merchant had to summon his daughter. She would come in quietly, bow to the visitor, and say, "Good morning, m'sieur," and complete the transaction with efficiency and dispatch. After many such visits he took advantage one day of the father's being engaged elsewhere to ask the girl if she would care to spend some time with him outside the shop. She was bending over a sheet of prices and looked up with a startled suddenness, her gray eyes full of questions. Apparently she did not find in his eyes the answers she had hoped for. Her response, at any rate, was given in a low and not too happy tone. "Thank you, m'sieur, but it wouldn't be possible—or right."

That she had been thinking matters over was evident when he called again. She raised her eyes and smiled at him, and then dropped them quickly. "What you suggested, m'sieur," she said, "would be—would be pleasant, I think."

They met a number of times after that, and always under difficult circumstances. They would take walks along the waterfront, Stéphanie wearing a cloak with a hood which served the double purpose of keeping her hair protected from the damp spray and concealing her identity from the seafaring men they met. Always when they did this, however, she was uneasy, fearing that someone would see and recognize her. Once they stopped at a tavern in town when hunger overtook them but her prettiness attracted so much attention that they decided this had been a mistake. They fell finally into depending on visits which he paid to the shop when they knew her father would be absent.

Every minute he spent with her increased his realization of how different she was from Marie. She talked with unusual intelligence but she could be gay also and sometimes she chattered like a schoolgirl. What appealed to him most about her was her daintiness. He marveled continuously at the smallness of her feet. They were much smaller, he decided after measuring them carefully and tenderly both with and without a shoe, than those of his first love.

On both counts, therefore, the first stage of his cure had been completed when the time came for the expedition to sail for the south.

III

On the long journey across the Atlantic, De Bienville became less and less conscious of the blow fate had dealt him in the matter of Marie, and he thought a great deal about Stéphanie.

But even the daughter of the marine merchant occupied a small share of his memories after the ships had rounded the lower end of Florida and had put in at the Spanish port of Pensacola. There was a party of Indians encamped outside the fort and De Bienville paid an early visit to them, being curious to see how they compared with the northern tribesmen. It is doubtful if he carried away any serious impressions, as he found on arriving that the daughter of the chief was with the party. She was graceful and lovely, with soft black eyes and a nicely chiseled nose which crinkled up when she smiled. A red blanket was draped over one of her shoulders in such a way that an arm was bare, a dimpled arm of a warm copper color.

Before the visitors left, the Indians sang some songs and the chief's daughter, after wrapping a fringe of bark about her waist and filling both hands with white feathers, performed one of the tribal dances. It was a quiet dance at first, being confined largely to a graceful motion of the arms, but gradually it took on a faster tempo and the white feathers were tossed over her head one by one and the bark fringe began to weave and sway.

De Bienville watched the slender figure with fascinated interest. The girl threw an occasional glance his way and at the conclusion of the dance she paused beside him for a moment and said something in a voice as soft and pleasant as the twittering of birds.

A young Spanish officer had accompanied the French party and had sat beside De Bienville during the dance. He could speak French and he now said, "Her name is Hushi Buhaha, which means Mockingbird."

De Bienville answered, "She's the prettiest native girl I've ever seen."

"Most of them are pretty but, of course, none of them can compare with Hushi Buhaha."

"What did she say?"

"I don't know," said the Spaniard, heaving a sigh. "But I wish she had said it to me."

De Bienville did not see Hushi Buhaha again but he was sure that, had the opportunity for further contacts been allowed him, he would have found their lack of a shared tongue no great handicap. D'Iberville was right, he said to himself. The world was full of lovely women; and they were of all kinds, shapes, and colors, and they could be very exciting and stimulating.

CHAPTER IV

D'IBERVILLE'S voice rose to its battle pitch. "The Hid River!" he cried, raising an arm and pointing. He and his party had fallen into the habit of calling the Mississippi by the name the Spanish had coined for it after many futile attempts to discover where it emptied into the gulf. "The Hid River, I swear! We have found it!"

For many days the Frenchmen had been venturing in *biscayennes,* a type of fishing boat, along a forbidding and puzzling coast. They had proceeded slowly to avoid trouble in shoal water and swampy shallows. They had been both amazed and perturbed by rocks of strange shapes (which turned out to be petrified logs) which stood at the mouths of streams and bayous, like fantastic sirens inviting mariners to enter. They had almost, it must be admitted, lost hope.

But D'Iberville had known at once that their quest had been rewarded when he saw that the blue waters of the gulf were turning gray and that there was movement and turmoil on its hitherto casual surface. He had felt a quiver of anticipation, an almost intolerable suspense, as the *biscayenne* began to toss under him. Standing at the prow, he had watched the shore with a hand shading his eyes from the rays of the setting sun, certain that they were drawing near to the meeting of the waters. Here or hereabouts the mighty river completed its destiny by joining the sea.

And then he saw it, a break in the monotonous line of willow trees, a wide break marked by rocks placed like sentries, a break which opened out before the eyes like the first glimpse of the sea and through which a body of water, turgid and red and gray, moved steadily, relentlessly, inexorably into the gulf.

No one had any doubts. This was the Mississippi, the goal they had sought. It could be nothing else. No Frenchman had ever seen the great river without recognizing it at once. They stood up to look at it, crossing themselves reverently before giving vent to shouts of triumph.

D'Iberville was silent for a time, while the men about him indulged in excited speculations. Then he pointed again. "Here the great La Salle and the brave Tonti stood," he proclaimed. "What strange thoughts must have filled their minds! How small and helpless they must have felt, witnessing this miracle that nature has wrought!" His voice rose again to its highest pitch. "And we have unlocked the door which was closed when La Salle died. The Mississippi, from its headwaters to its mouth, belongs to France! Ours will be the destiny to hold it for all time against all aggression!"

And then he became the practical leader again, deciding on a spot above the mouth of the river where the boats could tie up for the night. It was not until he was convinced of the wisdom of his choice and he had seen that preparations for supper were under way that he sought out De Bienville. The latter had been placing sentries and was covered with mud up to his hips.

"Jean-Baptiste!" whispered the leader. "We've accomplished the miracle after all! The Le Moynes have done it!"

They faced each other for several moments in a silence which said more than any words they could have found. Then the leader of the expedition dropped a hand on his brother's shoulder. "If they could only be here to join in this triumph—Charles and Paul and Joseph, and the two boys!" he said. "And the three who have gone! What a moment, what a place, for a reunion of all the sons of Charles le Moyne!"

"They are here in spirit, Pierre."

D'Iberville nodded slowly, thinking perhaps of the death of Louis, the brave young brother whose place in his heart could never be taken by any-one. And then, with a suddenness which was typical of him, his mood changed, becoming sharp and brisk. "Tomorrow we begin the first jour-ney ever made by white men up the waters of the Mississippi. We must obtain the necessary proofs. And we must find and mark the spot for the great city and seaport which we are going to build."

II

A week later—it was March 9 in the year 1699—the toiling Frenchmen saw a wide curve ahead, one of many which they had passed on their slow passage up from the sea. At the head of the procession was a *chaloupe* (an oar-propelled vessel on the order of a longboat) and D'Iber-ville stood at the prow, watching the banks of the winding monster with an observant eye and discussing various points with De Bienville. The latter, it was clear, was in a state of delight over the new land. The first unfriendly impression had been exploded by the wonder of a March burst-ing on them with an enchantment of exotic foliage and an extravagance of flower and bloom such as they had never seen. He had not yet broken himself of the habit of exclaiming at each new discovery, "Is it possible?" or "Mother of God, look at that!"

It was apparent from their talk that they were already well immersed in the atmosphere of this tropical wonderland. They spoke easily of bayous and lagoons, and discussed the habits of cypress trees and red cedars, and instead of such familiar names as Huron and Iroquois they had words like Bayougoulas and Quinipissas continually on their tongues.

"We are still close to the waters of the gulf," said D'Iberville, "and it seems to me certain that somewhere along here the Indians have found an easy portage. If we can locate that we'll have the perfect site for our city."

De Bienville nodded his head to show that he had heard but his interest at the moment was given most clearly to a mass of color which had suddenly burst on their view, in which the white of bridal wreath and many unidentified blooms made a background for the blue of myrtle and the lush rose shades of camellia and the yellow of the jonquil.

"You have a liking for this, *hein?*" As D'Iberville spoke, he gave the younger man a thump on the back.

De Bienville nodded eagerly. "It's beyond belief! Yes, Pierre, I like it. It's so different from our own country and yet I think it's getting into my blood."

"I'm happy to hear you say that. Because, my Jean-Baptiste, I think you're going to see a lot of it." He looked down into the earnest face beside him. "You've changed a great deal since we sailed for Hudson's Bay. It's always that way: your first campaign makes a man of you or breaks you. I'm pleased to see that you're showing all the signs of having come into man's estate." He burst into abrupt laughter. "For which we may thank also the little mademoiselle at Rochefort about whom I have heard. You thought I didn't know about her? Ha, my Jean-Baptiste, it was the first thing I learned when I came there. I even went to the length of seeing her. A nice little thing. You've forgotten her, perhaps?"

"No, Pierre. I'm not as forgetful as that."

D'Iberville gave his head a satisfied nod. "But you will. And also you'll soon forget your widow now, and that will be a very good thing. That widow, ah, what a swath she's cutting in Paris!"

The *chaloupe* swung around the bend. Ahead stretched a wide channel through which the Mississippi rolled majestically. The land north of the bend was high and flat with low hills in the background.

"Something tells me that this part is worth investigating," said D'Iberville, studying the conformation of the land closely. Suddenly he raised a hand and pointed ashore. "See! The remains of an Indian hut. It's clear there's been some kind of a settlement here. Could this be the end of that portage I've been watching for?" He turned to a man on his other side. "What do you make of this, De Sauvole?"

The man seemed surprised at the question. "I make nothing of it," he replied. "The land drops off behind the banks and it's quite marshy and wild."

"Do you like it?"

De Sauvole answered casually. "It looks no different from anything we've passed on this interminable pull up the river. If you must have an answer, I don't like it at all."

D'Iberville was regarding his matter-of-fact lieutenant with a smile which suggested he was leading him on for a purpose. "You don't believe, then, that we should stop here and examine the possibilities of the place?"

De Sauvole laughed. "Good St. Christophe, no!"

D'Iberville turned to his brother. "De Bienville, what do you see?"

"Two hundred yards ahead of us," answered De Bienville, pointing ashore, "the banks are high. I think they are well above water level. That would make the best site for the Place d'Armes. The square should open on the river so that the cathedral could be built on the north end and command a view of the water. The barracks should be on that rise of ground off to the west. The gunpowder stores would be safely out of the way there. The business section should lie along the river and the residential section back of that. This terrain would lend itself to a square plan——"

"That's it!" cried D'Iberville. "You see what I do. Here we have the site for the great city we must build. It's an ideal situation, flat and easy to drain and, I think, with two roads to the sea. Here"—he waved an arm about him and his voice took on an oratorical roll—"we will build the greatest city in America, greater even than Montreal. It will be the Paris of the west, the French capital of the New World!"

They made a landing near the spot which De Bienville had selected as the likeliest location for the Place d'Armes. While the men set about building fires and cooking a meal of bear meat and sagamité (a curious dish of Indian corn), the leader of the expedition took his brother on a walk back from the riverbanks. They stopped only when the marshy condition made further advance difficult and the roar of a bull alligator warned them that they had trespassed far enough.

"Jean-Baptiste," said D'Iberville, "founding a colony isn't a simple matter. It's more than selecting a spot for the church and telling your helpers to lay out streets. It's a matter of long years of hard labor, of hardship and starvation and danger. I'm not the man for that kind of thing. I can't squat on my quarters in one place and wait for families to increase and gardens to grow while my hair turns gray and my bones begin to ache for the final girding in. I am a man of action." He paused and looked down the river as though he longed to be getting on to some new task now that the mouth of the river had been discovered. "I'm disposed, my little brother, to entrust the task of building this new colony to you. You shall be the Maisonneuve of Louisiana. If there's to be any glory in it, I leave it to you."

The way De Bienville's eyes kindled at this convinced D'Iberville that his selection would prove a wise one.

"I promise you," declared the younger brother solemnly, "that if you entrust this duty to me I shall gladly devote my whole life to it. What greater chance could I ask?" He paused and then turned to his brother with a question. "Have you noticed that all the cities in France are badly overcrowded?"

D'Iberville indulged in an indifferent nod. "If it weren't so we would have no colonies."

"They say it's the same all over Europe. The poor people are forced to live in dirty slums where their souls are starved as well as their bodies. And here, Pierre, we have a continent large enough to provide land for all the poor people of the world. Here every beggar could have a farm of his own. Fresh air, good food, plenty, for everyone. Pierre, we must hurry! We must open up this country so that all the starving people may have a chance to become good and prosperous citizens."

"Or starve to death in the trying," said D'Iberville with a hint of dryness in his voice. "The difficulty is to make these poor people of yours give up their foul dens in the cities. They don't seem to yearn for a pastoral life, my little crusader, and their mouths pucker at the thought of a diet of milk and honey. . . . Still, with all this zeal you're showing, I'm more convinced than ever that you are the man to command ashore. The task, therefore, shall be yours. As for me, I plan to put out to sea again as soon as I dare. I think the time has come to patrol the Spanish Main and pick a fight with any enemies of the King I may chance to meet!"

Book Three

CHAPTER I

FÉLICITÉ always remembered her childhood as a gray period, filled with laws and restrictions imposed by a stern and heavy-handed old woman known as Tante Seulette. She was not allowed outside the walls of the château. Tante Seulette made it clear to her from the first that danger lay beyond the gates and that disobedient little girls who ventured out would be caught by red-skinned monsters and either killed or carried off as slaves. For the imaginative child, this was nothing short of a tragedy. The outside world looked so green and lovely and enticing that she would linger by the gates for a glimpse of it when arrivals or departures necessitated the swinging back of a metal-sheeted door. She was sure the woods were filled with flowers and that the pleasure of gathering them would make up for the dangers.

There was something else, however, which weighed still more heavily on her spirits. She was not allowed to play with other children. Tante Seulette told her at least once a day that she would be punished severely if she so much as spoke to any of them. Later she realized that Tante Seulette was striving to create a little world in which the two of them could live alone. Félicité was hers, and she did not want to share her. Also, perhaps, she was afraid that the girl would grow away from her if allowed to make friends. None of this, of course, was clear to Félicité at the time; and so she lived her lonely life with the conviction that she was a prisoner and that heavy bars stood between her and a world which seemed beautiful and exciting.

She had a retentive memory and never seemed to forget anything which happened around her. Her earliest recollection was of lying in bed and watching a light high above her. There was nothing else to the memory, no sound or action. She often thought of it as she grew older and wondered what that strong, unblinking light could have been. It had not been the sun or the stars; of that she was certain. She never mentioned it to anyone, believing that the memory belonged to her and would lose some-

hing if it were shared. One day, however, when she was perhaps as much
as six or seven years old, she began to question her grim old guardian
about it.

"Tante Seulette, did I always sleep in this bench bed?"

"Always."

"Even when I was the merest infant?"

The old woman snorted. "And what are you now, may I ask? The
merest infant! If you think yourself so grown up why aren't you of more
help to me?" Her tone of voice became less severe. "From the first day
you were put in my care you slept in that bed. You were just a year old at
the time."

The girl's attention was distracted by this reference to her infancy.
"Tante Seulette, was I a nice baby?"

"Well—I'm not sure. You weren't healthy and you cried a great deal.
You were so long teething that I began to think you would be a grown
woman before you got them all."

"Was I—was I a pretty baby?"

"You were *not!*" Tante Seulette answered aggressively as though she
wanted the girl to have no illusions on that score.

There was a long pause. "But, Tante Seulette, my mother was *very*
pretty. Won't I grow like her? A little, perhaps?"

"I hope not! I certainly hope not! Get this in your head, child, there
are more important things in this life than being pretty and attracting the
attention of men." The old woman shook her head grimly. "Some girls
think of nothing else but primping and getting ribbons for their hair.
Don't let me catch you turning into *that* kind of a girl. In the end they're
always sorry."

There was a still longer pause. Félicité seemed to have lost interest in
the inquiry she had intended to make. She seated herself on the edge of
a chair and looked up at the housekeeper as though hoping to read in her
expression some extenuation of the harsh finality of her words. What she
saw gave no such promise.

Finally she got up and looked listlessly at the bench bed in its usual
corner. It was closed up to serve its daytime function of a seat and, as was
the rule with everything belonging to Tante Seulette, it looked plain and
severely useful. Even the slip of ratteen draped over the top of it was of a
dull brown color.

"Where did it stand when I slept in it?"

The housekeeper, whose fingers had never been idle in all Félicité's
recollection of her, was counting pillow slips. She frowned and shook her
head. "What a time to ask questions! Now I'll have to start all over again.
. . . The bench bed has never been moved so much as an inch. There it
stood when you slept in it, child. There it stands today. I'm not one to
change things about."

The girl unlatched the lid and turned it over until it rested on the floor She stepped in and stretched herself out at full length. It proved a close fit (Tante Seulette said her legs were galloping while the rest of her grew at a jog trot) but by raising her knees an inch or so she managed it. Then she turned her head and stared intently out of the window.

"It came from M'sieur Charles's room," she said finally. "It must have come from there because it's the only window I can see."

"Whatever are you talking about?"

"A light I saw. A long time ago, when I was a very small girl. I saw it when I was lying in this bench bed, and I watched it for hours."

Tante Seulette forgot the task on which she was engaged. Her hands dropped in her lap and she looked at the girl with an aroused interest. "How long ago was it that you saw this light?"

"I don't know but it was many, many years."

"There *was* one night when M'sieur Charles was here and kept the candles burning in his room all night. Ah, how frightened we were! How we prayed to the Holy Mother! Word had gone around that M'sieur Charles and all the members of the family were ruined, they had spent so much on the ships."

She laid aside her work then and began to talk. From the very first she had made the child an audience, talking to her as though she were capable of taking an adult interest in things. Félicité would sit and watch her with her large eyes (never as a girl was she quite able to grow up to her eyes) and even fell into the habit of nodding and smiling as though she understood what it was all about. The hour between supper and the girl's going to bed was always spent in this way, the old woman knitting and talking and the child sitting on a cushion on the floor with no more than an occasional glance at a sad-faced doll which was her only plaything.

The housekeeper was now launched on a congenial topic (she loved to talk about trouble) and for once Félicité listened with the greatest attention.

"The stories had reached us here, you may be sure. People had even come across the river for no other purpose than to tell us the Le Moyne family was due for a fall. They said the seigneurie would have to be sold and that M'sieur Charles had already offered Ste. Hélène's Island to that M'sieur Benoit in Montreal. They came over together that day and when we saw that he, M'sieur Benoit, was with the master, we were prepared for the worst. He was worse than hounds which bay for the dying, that one. It was whispered in Montreal—no one dared to really speak about it —that great power had been put in his hands by men in France and that he collected money from everyone in the fur trade. He had taken over seigneuries when their owners got into trouble, and made a fat profit. Ah, that man! When the seigneur went up to his room, this Benoit, this horseleech, began to pry into everything. He went through my kitchens and the wine cellars and I could see him nodding his head and doing sums in his mind—I never left him alone for a minute!—and I knew he was setting a value on the place. He even dared to open the *panetières* [small cupboards suspended on pantry walls for flour and sugar and salt] and poked his long nose in to see what they held. He went to the root house—with me right on his heels—and he climbed up the ladder to the stable lofts. We all knew what he was about and we would have put poison in his wine when he sat down to supper by himself—if we'd dared."

Tante Seulette was enjoying the chance to draw on her recollections of one of the tense moments in the history of the château. "Our poor M'sieur Charles had gone to his room with orders he was not to be disturbed. When Damase carried up some supper on a tray, he refused to open the door. We knew he was sitting there and planning and figuring. We all sat up for hours and watched the light in his window, wondering if there would be bad news for us in the morning. We were sure he would tell us there would be a new seigneur. But he left early, taking that M'sieur Benoit with him, and without saying a word to anyone."

Félicité, who had listened attentively to every word, looked up and asked, "And what happened then, Tante Seulette?"

The old woman bobbed her head triumphantly. "Nothing happened. Our M'sieur Charles is a great man and all the lawyers in the world couldn't get the better of *him*. He had found ways of paying off the debts. He didn't sell as much as an arpent of land. The very next time he came here he was full of smiles and very friendly with everyone. Always remember this, my child, it isn't M'sieur Charles who commands the ships but without him there wouldn't be any ships." She paused and wrinkled up her brow in a difficult calculation. "But that couldn't have been the time you saw the light, Félicité. You weren't more than a year and a half old then and it stands to reason no one remembers things *that* young."

"But it was the time, Tante Seulette. It *was!* I'm certain of it."

II

From the time she was four years old Félicité remembered everything that happened to her. She could describe in full detail what occurred one evening in early summer when preparations for supper were going ahead in the kitchen and people were bustling about and voices were cheerful. She had been told to keep out of the way and had selected the corner nearest the larger of the two fireplaces where she could watch Damase keep in motion the side wheel turning the spit. Damase, who had a hump on his back, was in one of his moods.

"Sc'aun!" he said, imitating the metallic sound of the turning bars. He had a harelip and it was very hard to make out what he said. Félicité was

one of the few who could understand him. "Wha kin-ork is this for man Dos turn wheels i' F'ance."

"I think too, M'sieur Damase," said Félicité, "that it would be better to have dogs turn the wheels. It would be funny to watch, wouldn't it?"

Before Damase could add anything to the discussion the girl became aware of a pair of eyes looking at her from the landing of the stone stairs which led down to the kitchen. With dismay and alarm she realized that it was Bertrand, the miller's boy, and that he had her black-and-white kitten Dauphin tucked under one arm.

"Is this your cat, M'amselle Stay-by-Yourself?" demanded the boy.

"Yes, it's mine!" she said, jumping up and running to the foot of the stairs. "Give him to me at once! You're hurting him!"

"I'm going to hurt him worse than this." The boy had green eyes which seemed to gleam in the darkness of the stairway like those of wild animals at night. "Do you know what I do with cats? I kill them. I throw them in boiling water. I beat their heads between stones. That's the kind of thing I do to cats."

Félicité had been looking about her desperately and now her eye lighted on a shovel leaning against the wall within easy reach. She picked it up and brandished it over her head.

"You give Dauphin back to me," she cried, "or I'll kill you with this shovel!"

"You're just a girl and you couldn't kill an ant," said Bertrand, grinning at her. He snuffled and drew a finger under the tip of his nose. "What silly kind of name is that for a cat? Only a girl would call a cat Dauphin." He grasped the tail of the unfortunate pet in one hand and made a move as though to swing it over his head. "I torture cats with silly names like that!"

Félicité moved fast to save her pet. She sprang up the steps and gave the shovel a swing which just missed his head but landed with good effect on one of his shoulders. Master Bertrand dropped the cat and retreated up the steps, screaming at the top of his lungs that Félicité was going to kill him. The girl picked up Dauphin, who snuggled his head against her, and called after her enemy, "And that's what I do to boys who hurt cats!"

The delighted laughter of Damase over this episode had hardly subsided when there was a sound above of a slamming door, followed by much loud and excited talk. Félicité was on the point of hiding, thinking that the boy's parents were coming to demand her punishment, when she heard Tante Seulette from the pantry say, "The messenger from across the river is here." That was a different matter. Félicité ran to the pantry and sidled up as close to the old housekeeper as she dared; and so was able to hear everything that was said.

The curiosity of the château staff could easily be understood. Around the hour of noon they had been drawn to the shore by a spectacle they had

een watching and waiting for, a flotilla of flatboats and canoes on its way
o Montreal. The first boat carried the fleur-de-lis on a pole at the prow
nd so the watchers knew that the first ships of the year had arrived from
'rance and that these boats carried the long expected supplies and mail.
'élicité had watched from one of the corner towers where Handsome
Hyacinth Dessain happened to be on guard. He had nodded his head and
emarked, "There will be news from the south, from M'sieur Pierre."

He had looked gloomy, however, for a reason which no child of four
ould have understood. There would be news from France and if the old
King had already ended the short peace with the English it would be very
ad news indeed. It had been known that trouble was brewing over who
vould be the next King of Spain and all through the winter the apprehen-
ive colonists had been wondering why Frenchmen and Englishmen
hould be expected to start killing one another again over anything as un-
mportant as that. They did not want the forests filled with screeching
roquois because the new ruler at Madrid spoke French instead of Ger-
nan, or the other way about.

"There will be a law to make us fight," declared Dessain. This started
him off on a grumbling spree about the laws and Félicité was unable to
understand a word about it although she often heard such complaining.
The colonists resented the seemingly endless regulations which dictated
what they might do and what they might not do. They could not sell their
produce for resale, they could not trade or sell skins, they could keep only
so much wheat for their own needs and turn the rest in at a fixed price,
they could not weave cloth, they must have their chimneys cleaned once
a month; there seemed to be a law for everything from the time they got
up until they went back to bed. The old King felt that the people of New
France belonged to him body and soul because they had been sent out on
his bounty (and uncertain bounty it had been until they were able to support themselves on what they raised) and that he must be obeyed as un-
questioningly as a child obeys the will of a father.

And now the messenger had arrived at the château at last. The sounds
from above continued to grow in volume. Everyone was talking at once.
A single word could be made out above the din, repeated over and over
again, the word "baron."

"What's all this talk of barons?" demanded Tante Seulette. Unable any
longer to control her curiosity, she started for the stairs. She was no more
than halfway across the great arched space of the kitchen than a head
appeared in the gloom of the stairway and an excited voice cried, "M'sieur
Charles has been made a baron!"

Tante Seulette never questioned bad news but it was impossible for her
to accept any good tidings without an instantaneous reaction of disbelief.
"It's a lie!" she said to the bringer of the tidings who was one of the
grooms. "Don't stand there grinning at us, you great head of a calf, and

telling us such stories! He deserves a title, our good M'sieur Charles, and no one can dispute that. But they'll see to it that he never gets one." *They* figured continually in her conversation, a shadowy band of conspirators whose influence was always malignant. "It's a lie, Delbert! You may take your lies and your silly face elsewhere."

"It's not a lie," protested the groom. "M'sieur Charles has the papers —and they're straight from the King himself. All Montreal is talking about it."

The housekeeper plumped herself down in a chair. With her knees spread so far apart that the plain gray cloth was stretched tight, she glared at the man. "It's too good to believe!" she asserted.

"But I tell you that M'sieur Charles——" The groom stopped and grinned foolishly. "I mean, M'sieur le Baron de Longueuil has sent word that we're to have the best wine in the cellars tonight to drink his health. Wine from France, Tante Seulette, not homemade stuff. Not even the Montreuil. The old burgundy, he said."

The housekeeper became convinced at this point. She got to her feet with an air of determination. "The burgundy! I'll not have it emptied down the greedy gullets of a pack of good-for-nothings. *Peste!* I think I know better than that." She turned abruptly on the two kitchen maids who had been standing beside her with their mouths gaping open like the beaks of fledglings. "You two geese! If this is true, it means we'll have to embroider a new crest on every bit of linen in the place. Every pair of fingers in this house will be worked to the bone." There was a touch of relish in her voice as she spoke of the work entailed in their master's promotion. "A baron is entitled to have another stage on all the cupboards in the house. Someone tell *that* to Old Kirkinhead. That will keep him busy."

III

The next morning Philippe was building a frame arch in front of the main gate. He had grown almost to man's height in the three years, in which respect he had been outstripped only by Little Antoine. The baby of the Le Moyne family, who was standing at one side and talking as Philippe worked, had shot up almost to six feet. Their talk was all of the great news from the south, of the rediscovery of the mouth of the Mississippi and of the plans for establishing a colony there. Most particularly they talked of D'Iberville's return to France, leaving De Bienville in charge.

Little Antoine said wistfully: "What a great stroke of luck for Jean-Baptiste! My brother Charles has a letter from D'Iberville in which he says Jean-Baptiste has done wonderfully well. He says he has a cool head and a strong will. He keeps his men in line and yet has no trouble with hem. Charles is delighted because he always said Jean-Baptiste would make his mark."

Philippe asked, "Is he having trouble with Indians?"

The youngest Le Moyne shook his head. "We're at peace with England and Spain so the Indians aren't troublesome. If they had been D'Iberville would have stayed and sent someone else back to talk with the King about supplies. D'Iberville says a great empire can be established there, even if it is a wet place like one hears of Venice. He's begging Charles to send him more people—good farmers and mechanics, and their wives. He says the people sent out from France don't know a hoe from a boat hook. And, of course, D'Iberville is clamoring for more supplies. He says they'll starve if they depend on what's sent out from France. Poor Charles! His hair is turning gray with the strain of finding so much money."

Philippe asked eagerly, "Did you say M'sieur Pierre wants mechanics?"

Little Antoine nodded. "Yes. But you mustn't get your hopes up. I don't think Charles could spare you."

Although this conversation is being set down in full, no one listening to the youthful pair would have had any conception of what they were saying. They were speaking in a language which an Iroquois brave would perhaps have recognized as his own but interspersing the Indian words with French when the limitations of the speech of the Long House (or their own shortcomings, more likely) made it impossible to convey their meaning in any other way. The explanation for this lay in the liking which Little Antoine had conceived for the builder's apprentice and which had caused him to insist that he would be able to master Indian talk better if he had companionship in the study. Philippe had, therefore, shared his studies in such time as he had to spare. Between them they had become proficient in the tongue of the Six Nations and could converse still better in Huron.

"Why shouldn't I go?" Philippe spoke with such sudden vehemence that his voice changed to a high treble note. "I'm a good mechanic. I could be very useful. There must be a lot of building going on."

Little Antoine shook his head. "But Charles is full of plans for Longueuil. He wants houses for new settlers, an addition to the mill, a church. You know he can't depend on M'sieur Girard any longer and he says Prosper will never know a thing about building. He relies on you."

Philippe was both pleased and depressed by this; pleased because of the seigneur's good opinion of him and depressed because he wanted, in common with all the new generation at Longueuil, to share in this latest and greatest of the Le Moyne adventures.

"Are you going?" he asked after a moment's silence.

Antoine nodded happily. "With the next party. I'm to travel by sea."

"And M'sieur Gabriel's going with the party down the river?"

"Yes. I'll get there as soon as Gabriel. *Donc-donc!* He'll be angry whe
he sees me."

Philippe continued to hammer on a lettered scroll in lath which read
"Glory to the Baron of Longueuil."

"If M'sieur Charles comes over," he said, "we'll set this afire so th
words can be read at a distance. If not, we'll train roses over it." He sus
pended work and sighed deeply as he looked at his companion. "I'd giv
ten years of my life to be going with you!"

Antoine's eye had lighted on something behind the arch. "It seems w
have company, Philippe."

The hammer stopped its busy tapping as Philippe looked. A small gir
in a very plain and unbecoming brown dress was crouching back of th
arch.

Little Antoine said in a whisper: "I think it's the child of the prett
widow. But it's certain she doesn't take after her mother." He stared a
the girl who had hung her head in confusion at being discovered. "An
what's your name?"

Without raising her head the child answered, "Félicitéannalay."

"It's a nice name. But isn't it true, Félicitéannalay, that you're not sup
posed to be outside the gates?"

A nod from the bowed head. "Yes, m'sieur."

"Then why have you disobeyed?"

Félicité did not reply at once, then she burst out impulsively and tear
fully with, "I don't know!" She gave way completely to tears and after
few moments repeated, "I don't know, m'sieur."

Philippe went down on one knee in front of her and held out a hand
kerchief. "Here, dry your eyes," he said. "There's nothing to cry about.
know what's the matter and why you came out here against orders
You've been kept in so long and you've wanted to see what it was like ou
here that you couldn't stand it any longer and so—out you came! Wasn'
that it, my small Félicité?"

She nodded again, more vigorously this time. "Yes, m'sieur."

"And now that you've been out and had a look at things"—that was
misstatement because so far she had looked at him only—"you're going t
be a good girl and go back inside. And you're not going to disobey Tant
Seulette any more. Isn't that it?"

Félicité stopped weeping. "Yes, m'sieur. I'll try to be a good girl."

A hail reached them from the direction of the landing place. Littl
Antoine turned and waved a hand. "There's Alcide. He's taking m
across. I must be on my way as I'm expected back in time for dinner
Farewell, my doughty Unighkillyrakow."

"Farewell, Mighty Chief of the Rushing Waters."

Philippe resumed his work but, as he measured and sawed and ham
mered, he kept an eye on the child. He had never seen her at close rang

before, although there had been a great deal of curiosity about her throughout the seigneurie. She was small for her age, he decided, and so pale and thin that she completely lacked charm.

"Tante Seulette is strict with you, *hein?*"

The child did not respond although by this time she had recovered completely from her weeping spell and was watching him intently with her unusual eyes. They were so large and of such an intense and unmistakable gray that they almost succeeded, but not quite, in lending a touch of beauty to her face.

"You aren't allowed to speak to other children?"

Félicité affirmed this with a nod.

"That seems a great pity. A very great pity. Would you like to play with the other children?"

"Oh, yes, m'sieur! There's a little girl just my age I would like to play with very much. She's very nice."

"Would that be Antoinette Dalray? Where have you seen her?"

"In chapel. She's a very pretty little girl." There was a wistful note in her voice as she paid this greatest of tributes to the other child from whose company she was barred. "She wears a pretty dress. I think it must be the prettiest dress in the world, m'sieur." The gray eyes grew even larger and rounder with wonder. "It's white and it has lace on it."

"I think you should have a white dress too and with lots of lace on it."

At this point they heard an unmistakable voice raised loudly inside the walls. Tante Seulette was calling: "Félicité-Ann! Where are you, child? Félicité-Ann!"

"She'll be very angry if she finds you here," said Philippe. He suspended work and regarded her with a worried frown. "I don't want to see you get into trouble, Félicité. Will she give you a beating?"

The little girl seemed to be accepting her danger with equanimity. She nodded and said: "She'll use her switch on me." She nodded again. "It'll be a lesson to me."

"Yes. I guess it would be a lesson to you. Still I would like to keep you out of trouble. I've an idea." He began to empty his heavy canvas tool bag. "Climb into this," he said, smiling and winking at her. "See, I'll carry you in over my shoulder and everyone will think the bag is filled with tools. You mustn't make a sound. If you speak or laugh, they'll think it's a funny lot of tools I've got with me today."

The child was so excited that she could not prevent herself from laughing as she burrowed down into the canvas bag. "I won't make a sound," she whispered, "but please hurry, m'sieur. It's very hot in here."

He found her more of a load than he had expected. He was growing fast and running much more to height than width and so was not strong. Still he managed to make his way through the gate without staggering and proceeded down into the center plot.

"Keep still!" he whispered suddenly. "Tante Seulette's looking at us and there's a suspicious gleam in her eye. If you move as much as an inch she'll be down on us."

A few moments later he said: "Well, we're out of that. She's turned her head and is looking in another direction. But here comes Bertrand. He's a sharp one. Not a sound or a move out of you this time, my small Félicité!"

Bertrand came up, swishing an old horsewhip about his head and emitting loud whistles. "What's in the bag, Philippe?" he demanded.

"What do you suppose? My tools, of course."

"I thought you had a dead fox in that bag. Are you sure it's only tools?" The boy's eyes began to kindle. "I killed a sick fox once. All by myself. It let out squeaks. Say, Philippe, let's suppose it *is* a fox and let me give one good cut at it with this fine whip of mine!"

Philippe scowled at the boy. "If you bother me any more, Bertrand, I'll put down this bag and I'll take that whip away from you and I'll give you a few good lashes for yourself!"

Bertrand gave a hoot of defiance but was sufficiently discreet to hurry along. From a safe distance he began to chant derisively: "Philippe-Christophe-Marcel-Amaury! Philippe-Christophe-Marcel-Amaury!"

Philippe carried his burden to the carpentry shop, which proved to be empty. He closed the door after him and then lowered the bag carefully to the sawdust-covered floor.

The child crawled out, giggling. "That was fun, M'sieur Philippe," she said. Then she suddenly turned quite serious. "That Bertrand is a very bad boy, m'sieur."

"But he's a sharp one. You must get out of here before he follows us. The back door opens on the passage to the smithy. You had better go in there and talk to M'sieur Descaries. And the next time Tante Seulette calls, answer her as though you've been in the smithy all the time."

She did not leave at once but reached up and put her hand in his. "The other one had a very fine coat, M'sieur Philippe," she whispered, "but I like you the best."

Philippe was taken completely by surprise. He could hardly believe his ears. That anyone could prefer him to a Le Moyne was so unexpected and unbelievable that he stared down at the child in silence for several moments. Even when he had recovered sufficient control of himself to speak he found that he was stammering.

"Well!" he said. "You—you are a strange little thing. I'm complimented by your good opinion of me. But when you get older you'll think differently about it."

CHAPTER II

THERE WAS snow on the sill of the *cabinet particulier* of the Baron of Longueuil and, as he talked to his visitor, he kept an eye on the falling flakes which threatened to increase this ermine trim before the day was out. The visitor was a merchant of the town, a colorless little man who, in spite of his physical insignificance, was injecting a sting into everything he said.

"This new fur company!" he spluttered. "It's a complete failure. It's a bubble"—he gestured with one hand—"which will soon burst. What have you to say about it, Charles le Moyne? Your pardon, I should say, M'sieur the Baron. Nothing? Very well, I'm here today to say this, that I shall withdraw from it."

"Many of us would prefer to withdraw," said the baron, still staring out of the window at the antics of the wind, which had taken to whirling clouds of snow about the spire of the Church of Bonsecours. "But how can we? The company was decided upon in the King's council and it was then handed over to us. We all had to take shares. Do you think we will be allowed to drop out of our own free will?" Charles swung around in his chair. "It's a sorry affair, Anatole. You know full well that when this very sick concern was turned over to us we had to assume all the stocks on hand—all the tens of thousands of rotting beaver skins in the warehouses and vaults. We were loaded with a debt we had done nothing to incur. Can you blame me, and the other officers you had a hand in appointing yourself, for this state of affairs?"

The room was cold. The baron, who had been accustoming himself to inadequate fires since the need for retrenchment had been felt, did not mind the discomfort. A glance at his visitor, however, made it clear that the latter was suffering from the chill of the office. The fire undeniably was small. Charles considered having it replenished but then changed his mind. He said to himself: "*Peste!* Why should I bother about this troublesome fellow? He'll leave all the sooner."

"Why can't the skins be sold for whatever they'll bring?" demande
the visitor, rubbing his hands together to restore the circulation. "That'
what I came to ask."

"It's easily answered, Anatole. The hatmakers of France refuse to buy
They say they're overstocked. I suspect they prefer to make hats of imita
tion beaver on which there's a better margin of profit."

"Then why don't we sell to Italy, to Germany, to Holland? I know
what you're going to say, Charles—that the King denies us the right t
trade with any country but France." The indignation of the little mer
chant led him into an indiscretion. He suddenly blazed out with, "Th
King seems set on ruining us!"

The Baron of Longueuil's manner changed at once. "It would be ver
unwise, Anatole, to say things like that to anyone else," he said sharply
"I advise a closer rein on that tongue of yours. . . . The situation isn'
as desperate as you seem to think. The company will be a failure but th
shareholders can keep their private affairs from becoming involved. Th
King turned the fur trade over to us with the best of intent. He didn'
realize that the regulations his ministers drew up would be so ruinous i
their effect. When this is made clear he will have them removed. H
won't put us," using a phrase applied to bankruptcy, "to the long sands."

"But will he come to our rescue in time?" The visitor was still far from
satisfied. "This Joseph de Mariat! He never fails to collect through tha
jackal of his. Why didn't he see that these ruinous clauses were kept ou
of the charter? I sometimes wonder about Joseph de Mariat. Is he act
ing in our interests as he claims?"

Charles le Moyne stroked his chin reflectively. "I," he said in a ton
little above a whisper, "sometimes wonder about Joseph de Mariat also.

When the indignant caller had gone the new baron sat for several mc
ments in reflection. Then he sighed and glanced about him as thoug
in appraisal of this prison in which he spent all of his days. The roon
was small and crowded. There were presses, bulging with papers, on al
the walls and it was easily to be seen that the desk belonged to a busy man
It was piled up with letters, some with official seals dangling from them
There was a row of freshly sharpened quills and a sandbox beside th
bottle of ink.

The mind of the baron must have been filled still with the matters h
and his visitor had been discussing, for it took the peal of the Sanctu
bell, sounding faintly through the snow-filled air, to rouse him. He drev
himself together then and looked down at the desk as though wonder
ing which of the many matters awaiting his attention should claim hin
first. Then he indulged in a smile which had something furtive about i
and walked across the room to one of the presses. He opened the doo
and thrust a hand behind the papers piled up inside.

When he stepped back he held in his hand a silver *aiguière*. This h placed on the desk and fell to studying with an air of the deepest absorption.

"Never have I seen a finer!" he whispered. "It's beautiful! What perfection of line!"

It was indeed beautiful, a flagon standing about sixteen inches high with a fleur-de-lis handle. The excitement of the collector of rare objects, which can mount to a positive fever, was noticeable in the baron's eye as he studied the lines of this chaste example of the silversmith's art. He touched a finger gently to the smooth surface of the *plein* and then allowed it to run down the graceful curve of the handle.

He was thinking that the young artist who had made this unusual flagon would someday be famous and that there would be many collectors competing for whatever they could find of his work. When that time arrived the piece in front of him would be almost priceless. "I must have it!" he said to himself. "No one will ever find out—and, if they do, they may talk as much as they like. I've been sticking to the agreement. I'll swear none of them have a shine on their clothes like this suit of mine. I've pinched every sol which has come into my hands for five years. Surely I'm entitled to one small extravagance!"

He replaced the silver, with obvious reluctance, in its place of concealment. As though in defiance of the edict of economy he had forced on all members of the family and which he himself had most rigorously observed, he said aloud in a tone of finality, "I shall buy it!"

From the open door of another room farther down the hall came the sound of pens racing and squeaking over paper as his two clerks took advantage of the little daylight left. The baron stopped on his way to the stairs and called: "A candle, my industrious children! There's no economy in straining the eyes in light like this."

II

The merchants of New France, being thrifty and without any desire to set themselves above their station in life, considered that the ground floor of a house belonged to trade. Here the shops were located, here the apprentices worked, here the ledgers were kept for the master to pore over when the shutters were up for the night. In the house owned by Charles le Moyne on the Rue St. Paul, however, a change had been made which reflected the improved status of the family. There was a vestibule, both spacious and light, from which a door opened into what had once been a shop but which was now used as a salon for the reception and entertainment of guests. This large room had been furnished lavishly by the baroness with furniture brought over from France at great expense.

Charles, remembering when the front of the house had been filled with bolts of cloth on shelves, and barrels of salt fish and molasses and knives

and baskets of beads, could never enter the salon without a slight sens
of uneasiness. The rich hangings of Rouen blue, the carpets into whic
the feet sank silently, the elaborately ornamented fauteuils, the crysta
chandelier with room for sixty candles (never more than half a doze
were ever lighted at one time now) presented such an amazing contras
that he had asked himself a dozen times, "What would Old M'sieu
Charles have said about this?"

When he came into the room on this late afternoon in early Januar
he found his wife seated close to the fire on a couch-and-squab (a da
couch of the kind called later a chaise longue) which had been move
forward. Although she had her knees tightly wrapped in a coverlet o
the same shade of blue as the hangings and had a heavy shawl about he
shoulders, the baroness still looked cold and unhappy.

"Charles, Charles!" she said, turning her head toward him as thoug
she dreaded to withdraw from the warmth of the fire by even as little a
that. "This dreadful winter! I'll never be accustomed to it if I live t
be as old as—as that very old man in the Bible. I'm afraid, my Charle
that I make a very poor Canadian."

"You should have gone to France with the children as I said at th
time." He had walked as close to the fire as he could, with the couch oc
cupying so much of the space, and was warming his hands at the blaze
"I sometimes think, Claude-Elizabeth, that you should never spend
winter here. You are a delicate bloom, my heart, and born for the sof
airs of the south. And now that we're at war again——"

"Do you think I would leave you alone? To work yourself to deatl
in cold and discomfort? No, thanks, Charles, I prefer it this way."

"You may be a bad Canadian," he said, smiling down at her, "but you
are a very good wife, my Claudine."

"If only *that* had worked as we thought it would!" sighed the baroness
glancing at a curious object of quite considerable size which stood on th
other side of the hearth. "Then there would have been one room at any
rate where I could be comfortable."

The article in question was a box stove, constructed after a German in
vention but with refining Gallic touches. Its outer surface, instead of be
ing made of ugly sheets of iron, was of squared tiles, each tile elaboratel
covered with designs in strong blue and yellow. It had a figure on top
which resembled a gargoyle fitted to a gigantic torso.

The theory on which it had been built was an ingenious one. The
stove covered an opening into the chimney and it was supposed to drav
into its interior all the heat which otherwise would have gone rushin
up the flue to be wasted on the outer air, and then to radiate it evenl
throughout the room. In performance, unfortunately, it had not matched
its promise. It seemed to draw in smoke instead of heat. Every time th
wind changed clouds of soot would issue from its doors and slots (i

was as full of openings as De Mariat's coat had been of buttons) and frequently there would be ominous rumblings and then all the doors would blow wide open and great clouds of smoke would pour forth.

The baron looked at the stove and frowned. He did not like failures. "I've had the opening into the chimney closed," he said. "You needn't be afraid of it any more. And I swear I'll find a mechanic yet who will know how to make it work."

"Then find him soon, my Charles. I was willing to spoil my lovely color scheme with this ugly object if it had kept us warm in winter. Now that it's turned out worse than useless, I want to get rid of it." Her attention veered abruptly to another subject. "It can't be true that letters have arrived. Georges said some came for you this morning but I knew he was mistaken."

"But letters did arrive nevertheless. By way of New York. The English settlers are human and, even if we are at war with them, they do us a favor sometimes. These letters reached us through our settlements in Acadia. They were brought overland on snowshoes by the Saint John River and up the Côte Sud to Quebec. All the mail received hasn't been distributed yet."

The baroness looked up eagerly. "What news is there?"

"Letters from both Pierre and Jean-Baptiste. They're having a bad time of it. Pierre says that half of the men who went with him originally are dead. He sends me a list of the Longueuil men who've died down there. It's distressingly long." The baron was staring into the fire intently. "Pierre has established another fort on the river. He's calling it Fort Iberville and he's put Jean-Baptiste in command. Jean-Baptiste writes that he's been down with fever five times and has lost twelve pounds. It's a heavy cost we're paying—and this is only the start." He sighed deeply and there was a long pause before he went on. "Jean-Baptiste writes they're expecting a shipload of King's girls soon and he's at his wit's end to provide quarters for them."

"I wish some other way could be found. These women they send out——"

"What other way would you suggest? Three of the best wives on the seigneurie were King's girls. . . . I had a letter from that woman. The mother of the child."

"Oh! That one." The baroness did not seem much interested but after a moment she asked, "Why did she write to you?"

"To ask about the child and to give an address in case we should have occasion to communicate with her. . . . The letter was on good paper, and she spoke of traveling and of buying in Paris shops. She's having some money sent out through Paris bankers for the use of the child later on."

"That makes everything clear. The lewd creature is the mistress
some rich man. Perhaps she has a number of protectors."

The baron shook his head. "No, she's not a looselatch. I'm convince
of that."

"I confess to a distaste for having my husband in correspondence wi
a woman of this kind." Having said this, the baroness relented to the e
tent of smiling. "Still, she's at a safe distance."

Charles seated himself on a conversation stool at the end of the couc
"It's time we did something about the child," he said. "From what
hear Tante Seulette guards her like a lioness with a single cub. She ha
even refused to let her go to the school that good old Father de Franch
ville has started. We must go to the château and talk to the old woma
about it."

"*We?* No, no, my Charles. *You.* I wouldn't venture across that terrib
river in this kind of weather. And you know that I'm afraid of yo
dreadful Tante Seulette."

The baron patted her hand affectionately. "My poor Claudine! I'll g
alone. You won't have to face the creature in her lair."

"I allowed her to get the upper hand at the start," said his wife. "It wa
a great mistake. Since then she has ruled with a rod of iron. I get chil
whenever I know I must talk to her. Being a man, you can't understan
how this dreadful person affects me." She stopped suddenly. A ne
thought had entered her mind. When she spoke again she had reverse
her position. "I'll risk the cold and go with you, Charles. This may l
the chance I've been waiting for."

Charles gave his head a puzzled shake. "I don't understand, Cla
dine . . ."

"Don't you see? We'll set her in her place in this matter of the chil
If we're firm enough about it she may realize then who is mistress. You'
be surprised, Charles, at the strong stand I'll take."

"That's the way to talk! We'll go at once. Tomorrow. A resolution c
this kind must be acted upon at once."

Then, wisely, he led the conversation into other channels. They talke
of their children, who had been sent to France before the war was r
sumed with the English, all except little Paul-Joseph, who had been tc
young to be separated from his mother. A servant came in and drew th
curtains across the windows, and then built up the fire until it blazed an
crackled. They began to feel more comfortable and cheerful of moo
Claude-Elizabeth had an occasional twinge from a malady to which a
the people of New France were subject, an inflammation of the foot, bi
this did not impair her new good humor. She sipped a glass of wine an
chatted over the affairs of the town. She was speaking rather wistfully c
the good luck of Marie-Thérèse, the wife of D'Iberville, who was in Par
and so had escaped the discomforts imposed by the new war, when

loud knock sounded on the door. A moment later the servant handed in some letters to the master of the household.

The baron examined the seals and then nodded briskly. "The balance of the mail," he said. "I see there's another note from Pierre. Will you forgive me if I read it at once?"

"Yes!" she said eagerly. "I'm as anxious as you are to hear the news of our——" She began to enumerate aloud. "Pierre, Joseph, Jean-Baptiste, Gabriel, Little Antoine. Our five brave warriors. I hope Jean-Baptiste's health is better. I don't like to hear of him losing so much weight."

Charles le Moyne broke the seal and began to read, holding the sheets close to the nearest candle. From the first moment his wife knew that the news was serious. His face turned pale. He read to the end, however, without making any comment. Then he got to his feet. His hands fumbled as he tried to fold the sheets and put them in a pocket of his coat.

"Charles!" cried his wife. "What is it? What dreadful thing has happened now?"

He walked slowly to one of the windows, carrying the letter in his hand. Throwing back the curtain, he stared out into the darkness of the Rue St. Paul.

"Charles! Don't keep me in suspense!"

He returned to the fire like a sleepwalker, his face devoid of all expression. Putting one elbow on the mantel, he rested his head on his hand.

"Claudine!" he said in a tragic whisper. "Gabriel is dead!"

"Oh no! I can't believe it!" Her voice broke. "He was just a boy, that poor little Gabriel! And he was so—so full of life and with such plans in his head. Surely, Charles, there's been some mistake. I can't believe it's true."

"There's no mistake," he muttered. "The poor boy died months ago. At St. Domingue."

"Was he—was he killed?"

"No. He died of the fever." The baron's voice rose suddenly to a high pitch. "It's always the fever! It has carried off so many of our men. Pierre says he had been behaving well. He had been brave and resolute and had distinguished himself a dozen times. He was going to make a great soldier. Perhaps another such as Pierre himself."

The baroness got to her feet and stood beside him, drawing one of his arms through hers. They both stared down into the flames, their faces pale and drawn.

"How he must have rebelled in his last moments!" said Charles finally. "Gabriel didn't want to die in this way, of a putrid fever in some mean little tavern. He was sure the future held great things for him. He was going to Paris later and he talked of cutting a figure at court."

"Charles, is it worth it? Must you go on like this? You and your

brothers are doing it all. Why should all the losses fall on the L
Moynes?"

He did not seem to hear her. "I've a feeling of guilt about Gabriel," h
said. "He always said I was hard on him, that I picked him out for speci;
discipline. He even said to me once that he was sure I disliked him. No
that he's dead, I'm beginning to wonder. Was I hard on him? I swea
to you, Claudine, I had no such intent. I saw he had faults which woul
have to be curbed. He was selfish and proud and inclined to fall into ba
company." He turned his eyes toward his wife for the first time since th
letter had arrived. She could see that he was badly shaken. "But I didn'
want to be hard on the boy. My poor Gabriel!"

"It's sad to think of him being buried so far away. How do we knov
what they did with him? I—I shudder to think about it!"

"The letter explains. There was a priest with him at the end. He—h
was buried as we would have wanted him to be. The body was wrappe
in red wool and the coffin was filled with herbs."

"He's the fourth to go," said Claude-Elizabeth. She repeated her ques
tion. "Charles, must you go on? Is it worth it?"

He heard her this time. A trace of life came back into his eyes. "Is i
worth it?" he cried. "My dear wife, we can't allow anything that hap
pens to—to shake our resolution. It's our duty to go on, to finish the wor
we've started. I'm sick at heart over the death of Gabriel but I—I an
sure we mustn't turn back. Already we've established permanent settle
ments. We've made it possible for France to claim the whole great em
pire west of the Mississippi. Go on? We must go on to the last coin in th
chest, to the last one of us! There are still six Le Moynes left. Isn't tha
enough?"

CHAPTER III

FÉLICITÉ walked out into the cold of the garden and glanced up at the sky. It had a gray threat of storm about it. Birds hovered in the eaves and sought shelter from the wind behind the towers of the château. She shook her head dismally and said to herself, "He won't come today."

Her days were divided into two kinds. First, there were the days when some duty brought Philippe to the château, and these were the good ones, filled with happiness and excitement and all manner of possibilities. Sometimes he stopped and spoke to her, sometimes he gave her a friendly pat on the head. Once, and this was the red-letter day of her life, he had brought her a small wooden horse he had carved especially for her. It was her most precious possession. She kept it on the sill of the window under which her bench bed was located and so she could always see it. Her eyes lighted on it as soon as she wakened, its ears pricked up and its head held high against the morning sun pouring in.

She seemed to know by instinct when he was coming and she would be at the southwest gate when he put in an appearance. She would stand quietly at one side and would say, without raising her head, "Good morning, M'sieur Philippe." Sometimes he was too busy to do more than give her a quick nod in passing. She understood this and tried not to be unhappy about it, remembering the ecstasy of the few occasions when he was not rushed and had been able to stop and talk to her. The conversations had always been one-sided, for she could not summon up the courage to make any remarks beyond, "Yes, M'sieur Philippe," but they lingered long in her mind.

Then there were the bleak days when he did not appear. These, unfortunately, were more frequent than those blessed by his presence. She managed to get through them somehow but her mind always showed a tendency to wander from her lessons and Tante Seulette would rap her knuckles sharply. Once, when she had been guilty of some particularly

stupid mistake, and her guardian had demanded to know where her wi
had wandered to, she had been caught off guard and had said, "I wa
thinking of Philippe."

"Who?" Tante Seulette had demanded in a sharp and surprised voic
"Philippe, please. The apprentice of the builder."

Her guardian sniffed scornfully. "That little *copeau!* And why, m'an
selle, should you be thinking of him when your mind should be on you
lessons?"

"He is nice to me. He carved me my horse."

The next morning the horse was not at his usual post when the su
wakened her. Tante Seulette supplied the only possible explanation fo
its disappearance. "One of these good-for-nothing maids has stolen it,
she declared. She taxed each servant in the place with the theft but the
all protested their innocence vehemently. "You can't believe a word the
say," had been the housekeeper's summing up of the case. The horse ha
never been found and Félicité had not dared tell Philippe of her loss, fea
ing that he would think she had been careless and had not sufficientl
valued his present.

A second study of the sky did nothing to reassure her and so Félicit
went indoors, walking with reluctant steps down the stairs to the roor
she shared with her guardian. To her amazement, she found that Tant
Seulette was still in bed. This had never happened before, for the grir
old housekeeper was never ill and more punctual than any clock in th
château.

"What is it?" cried the child, running over to the bed. "Are you—ar
you very ill? Is there anything to be done?"

"There is nothing to be done!" declared the housekeeper in her mos
severe tone. A red flannel bandage covered most of her face and ther
was a distinct odor in the room of *sirop de pavots.* "How I suffer! Thi
tooth, it is driving me mad!"

Félicité had a practical streak in her which now asserted itself. "Ther
should be the surgeon," she said. "I will have them send for him and
will have water heated and hot towels ready for him when he comes."

Tante Seulette's eyes imposed an immediate veto. "There will be n
doctor!" she declared. "And as for you, child, I don't want you here
making so much noise and bothering me with such ideas. There will b
no lessons today and instead you'll go to the salon and clean the knive
and forks. It will keep you out of mischief. Polish them until they shine!
she admonished sharply, largely because of habit. The girl, she knew
always obeyed orders quickly and thoroughly. The pain in her jaw
brought her back then to a realization of her own dismal plight. "René
tells me this is the best medicine in the world but it's not helping me yet
Holy Mother in heaven, spare me this pain! It must be that I'm going to
die!"

Félicité became frightened. "If you are going to die I must bring Father de Francheville," she said.

The housekeeper sat up straight in bed and shook an angry finger at her. "You are full of ideas!" she charged. "You will bring the doctor! You will bring the priest! When I want anyone I will tell you. Do you understand that? Now you will go and do the work I have set for you."

II

When Félicité reached the salon she found herself reluctant to enter it. All the curtains were closed tight across the windows and the room was as dark as night. Drawing back a corner of one curtain so that she would have enough light to set about her task, she discovered that there were black coverings on the floor and a great sable bow hanging on the chimney. A feeling of chill took possession of her, because she knew this had been done on account of the death of the young gentleman of the family. A messenger had crossed the river the evening before with the sad news about Monsieur Gabriel and everyone had fallen to weeping and praying.

She was certain at first that she would not be able to stay in the room alone. Every sound caused her to start and stare nervously about her. As she polished the cutlery from each of the small drawers along the table (there was one at each place), she kept saying to herself, "I wish Philippe was here, so I wouldn't be afraid!" After a few minutes, however, she became familiar with her terror and did not allow it to interfere with the performance of her task. As her fingers kept briskly at work she repeated to herself: "I must be brave! They'll laugh at me and say I'm a stupid goose! I mustn't let anyone know how frightened I am."

She was glad nevertheless when there was a diversion. A sound reached her ears, the jingle of sleigh bells. It came from the direction of the Chambly Road and Félicité knew at once what it meant. "The children are coming to school," she said aloud. Her voice sounded hollowly in the closed room and she looked about her with a renewal of her fears.

Father de Francheville held his classes in what had once been the guardroom, a long stone chamber on the opposite side of the enclosure, where muskets still hung on the walls and a budge barrel of gunpowder stood in one corner with a heavy tarpaulin over it. The children of the seigneurie walked to the château when the weather permitted but on mornings such as this it was necessary to send a sleigh out for them. Félicité had often seen it start, Handsome Hyacinth Dessain driving, a musket against his knee, Damase at the back holding another musket with an air of great self-importance. Each time she had gone to the old housekeeper with a suspicion of tears in her eyes and had asked if she should not now be attending the classes too. The answer never deviated.

"Am I not teaching you everything you'll need to know, ungratefu
girl?"

The child did not go to the window, knowing that it looked on th
inner enclosure, and would not yield a view of the arrival of the sleigl
load of noisy young students. She wondered if she could dare risk goin
down to the gate. For the first time in her recollection there was no Tan
Seulette about to keep an eye on her.

"But it would be just as wrong if she didn't know," she said to hersel

Then she gave her head a nod. She had made up her mind to risk th
displeasure of her guardian. She wiped the polish from her fingers an
then replaced the piece of chamois she had been using and the dish c
polish in a corner of the cupboard. This was done with proper care bu
as soon as she turned to leave the room, she began to run as fast as he
legs would go.

She did not go far. Bertrand was standing at the end of the corrido
and his eyes began to gleam as soon as he saw her. He came toward he
on tiptoe.

"*Psisssst!* Don't make a sound!" he whispered. "Do you want to sti
it up?"

Félicité stopped dead still. She wanted to ask him what he meant bu
could not bring herself to speak.

"The ghost!" said the boy in a still lower whisper. "*His* ghost. Don'
go making any sound unless you want it coming down here." It wa
clear he was delighted at the effect this was having on her. "Are you
afraid of ghosts? Of course you are. You're a girl, and girls are afraid
of everything. I'm not afraid of ghosts. I'm not afraid of anything!"

"What—what ghost is it?" asked Félicité, afraid to make a move o
any kind or to raise her eyes from the floor.

"I saw it!" The boy's eyes glistened with pride as he made this an
nouncement. "I was upstairs. I went by the room where there's a bunch
of black ribbons above the door. It's where *he* used to sleep. I saw *i
staring at me." The whites of his eyes showed in the excitement of nar
ration. "Don't *you* go seeing ghosts or you'll fall dead of fright. It looked
right at me. It was just like white smoke but it had eyes. But *I* wasn'
frightened. I turned my back on it and came on down here. I'm no
frightened of ghosts."

Félicité did not wait to hear any more. She began to run and did no
stop until she had reached the main hall and saw the man on the gate
looking at her in surprise. As she ran she had heard Bertrand suddenly
take to his heels and she knew by the sound of his footsteps that he wa
frightened also. He had been too graphic in his storytelling and had suc
ceeded in scaring himself.

Father de Francheville was at the gate when she arrived. He was an
apple-cheeked old man with all the kindness in the world showing in hi

yes. He was nearsighted and had to squint hard at her to discover who
he was.

"Good morning, daughter," he said, smiling down at her.

"Good morning, Father." She had not intended to say anything more
ut her interest in what the children of the seigneurie did led her into
dding, "I didn't think there would be school today, Father, with such
ery deep snow."

"But yes, daughter! A little snow can't be allowed to keep them from
heir lessons." He studied her intently from under puckered brows. "Chil-
ren don't grow up into useful men and women unless they have some
earning. I've been rather concerned about you, my child. Do you have
our lessons regularly?"

"Oh yes, Father."

"And you are well? You are happy?"

She nodded her head. "Yes, Father, I am well and happy."

The old priest said to himself: "There are times when it is better to
make the brave answer this child has given me than to speak out what
s really in the mind. She is a fine little girl and I don't think what she
as said will be recorded against her but rather that it will be written
own fairly in her favor."

The sleigh had arrived at the foot of the snow-packed ramp and the
hildren were climbing out with much chattering and laughter. They were
undled up to the ears against the cold but Félicité had no difficulty in
ecognizing each one of them.

"Ant'nette has a new scarf," she said to herself. She was intensely inter-
sted in the scarf and in the fact that it was knitted of red wool. Most
enerally scarves were made of dark blue. She decided that the red looked
very well on Antoinette.

The pupils were coming through the gate now, walking in orderly files
ecause they knew that the eyes of the old priest were on them and that
he believed in discipline. In spite of this, however, Antoinette held up the
rocession by stopping. She not only stopped but, to the great surprise of
everyone, she smiled at the lonely little girl watching them and said, "Allo,
Félicité." It was a warm and friendly smile and the same qualities were
n the tone of her voice.

Félicité felt her heart swell with gratitude and happiness, and pride as
well. She was so overcome, however, that she replied, "Allo," with the
greatest difficulty.

Her pleasure was short-lived. As the files moved on she became aware
that they were talking about something which had happened that morning. There had been an accident. Someone, it seemed, had climbed up on
the roof of the Carré house to clean off the ice and snow, and had fallen
off. Several of the children had witnessed the fall and were excitedly treble
about it.

When Félicité heard the name of the victim the walls of her small world came tumbling down about her. It was Philippe! Her heart seemed to stand still and she found herself thinking with an agonized intensity, "He may die! Perhaps he's dead now and I'll never see him again!" The stories she had heard of the man who had fallen off the walls of the château while it was being built, and had died, came into her mind. A panic took possession of her, and she would undoubtedly have indulged in a wild outburst of grief if she had not heard one of the children say that the victim had been carried home and put to bed. If this were true Philippe was still alive.

The feeling of panic left her and her mind became filled with one idea. She remembered Tante Seulette saying, "Rénee tells me this is the best medicine in the world." If Rénee, who was one of the maids and a very sensible woman, said it was the best medicine in the world, then surely it must be that. Perhaps if Philippe had some of it his life could be saved. The responsibility for saving him rested, then, with her.

The housekeeper was sound asleep when the child entered the small bedroom. Propped up on a mound of pillows, she was snoring sonorously, her cheeks a speckled red. That she had been able to fall asleep was the assurance Félicité required. She said to herself as she gathered up the bottle, "She doesn't need this medicine, and Philippe does."

Holding the bottle tightly in one hand, she tiptoed from the room. As soon as she reached the gate, which the watchman had conveniently deserted in quest of a warm drink, she began to run as hard as she could.

"I must get there in time!" she kept repeating to herself. "I *must!* I *must!*"

III

It was Cécile who answered the knock on the door. At first she could see nothing. A furious wind had sprung up, sweeping straight across the river and carrying a cargo of needle-pointed snow. It required all the strength the builder's daughter possessed to keep the door from blowing wide open and it was many seconds before she realized that the knocking had been done by a child.

"Mother Mary and all the blessed saints!" she cried, staring at the small, white-faced figure on the doorstep.

She did not recognize this unexpected visitor but it was clear that something had to be done quickly. She whisked Félicité up into her arms and carried her into the house, the door slamming loudly after her.

"Now who are you?" she asked. "And how did you get here all by yourself?"

Félicité was so cold that she could not move her lips. The pain in her hands had made her cry and, as the tears had frozen on her lids, she could not see very well.

"*Palsanguienne!*" cried Cécile. "Now I know you. You're the little Félicité from the château."

Félicité nodded her head weakly and managed to get out a very faint "Yes." Cécile carried her to a chair and sat her down. "You must not be too close to the fire yet," she admonished. "Mother Mary, how did you get here all alone like this? I'll have a bowl of soup for you in a few minutes. Your hands—ah, ah, just as I thought! You have the hot ache. Child, what has happened?"

Félicité was beginning to cry in real earnest. "He might have died if I hadn't brought him the medicine," she said. "It's the best in the world. Tante Seulette said so. Please, madame, is he—is he very badly hurt?"

The woman looked puzzled. "Who? Philippe? He's not badly hurt, not that one." She looked down at the small figure and shook her head in bewilderment. "Were you sent with this medicine?"

"No, madame, please. Tante Seulette was asleep. So I—I came by myself."

"It's a wonder you didn't freeze to death!" A smile took possession of Cécile's heavy features. "I would like to see Tante Seulette's face when she hears about this! How angry she'll be!"

Félicité's hands pained her so acutely that she had difficulty in producing the bottle from an inside pocket of her coat. Finally, however, she managed to get it out.

"This is the medicine, madame," she said. There was a hint of urgency in her voice. If the medicine was to be of any use it must be applied at once.

The builder's daughter took it into her hands and frowned as she made a puzzled inspection. Then she gave it a shake, took out the cork, and smelled the contents.

"Who told you about this?" she asked.

"Tante Seulette was taking it."

Cécile let out a screech of laughter. "Mother Mary, this is funny!" She laughed so hard that it was several moments before she could go on. "What ideas children get in their heads! This may be the best medicine in the world—but only for toothache! I can't wait for Prosper to get home so I can tell him."

Félicité's eyes brimmed over with tears. Had her long walk through the snow in the face of the cold, biting wind been of no use after all? Would Philippe get no benefit from the medicine? Trying to control the impulse to give way completely to tears, the girl succeeded in saying, "I thought he would need it, madame."

Cécile looked aggressively across the room. "Our great climber of roofs isn't suffering from toothache. He's had a shock and there are many bruises, and all the *sirop de pavots* in all the chemists' shops in Montreal won't help him to get back to work any faster." She became more solicitous as she saw how much to heart the girl was taking it. "Come, child, you needn't worry about what's happened. Philippe will be quite recovered in a few days. And it was very kind of you to think of bringing medicine for him. Are you beginning to feel better?"

"Yes, madame."

"And your hands, are they still aching?"

"Yes, madame, please. They still ache a little."

A querulous voice called from the inner room: "Cécile! Cécile! What's all this noise and confusion? And will you tell me why you think it necessary to keep the door open when the worst gale since Champlain landed is sweeping down on us?"

"The door isn't open, Father."

"There's a draft which will bring me to the grave. The door *is* open. Why do you say it isn't? And why is my good wood being wasted to heat the whole shore of the St. Lawrence?"

"It was open for a few seconds only. A visitor came."

The voice from the inner room rose to a still higher notch of annoyance. "A visitor? Why don't people stay home and burn their own fuel? Why am I expected to make the whole population of Longueuil comfortable?"

"Father! Be sensible. There's only one visitor. A child. What's more, she's the only visitor we've had here in three weeks."

"This place," came the now thoroughly aroused voice of Old Kirkinhead, "is getting exactly like the Louvre, where all the people of Paris go to get out of bad weather and to void themselves in dark corners."

Cécile threw her arms in the air and walked with an expression of disgust to the table near the fire where she had been engaged in preparing food. Realizing that it was her arrival which had stirred up all this furious talk, Félicité sat where she was and tried to appear as inconspicuous as possible. It was only when she heard Philippe call, "Come here, Félicité," that she presumed to look in his direction, although she had been conscious of his presence from the moment she entered.

She looked across the room and saw that he was propped up with pillows in a rough pine chair and that a blanket had been wrapped about his knees. There was a block of wood on the broad arm of the chair and he was chipping at it carefully with a short-bladed knife, an occupation at which he had been engaged for some time, as the pile of shavings on the floor attested.

She walked over to his corner, being careful to go on tiptoe through fear of stirring up further furious protests from the inner room. Philippe took her hands in his and chafed them gently. "Soon there'll be no pain

eft. It was very kind of you, and very brave too, to come all this way with
he medicine. I know it's going to do me a lot of good."

Félicité was so relieved that he was in no danger that at first she could
do nothing but stare at him. Then she regained her tongue. "I'm glad you
think so, M'sieur Philippe," she said.

"It may be exactly the medicine I need most. Hadn't you better sit
down? It will have to be on the floor, I'm afraid. I know I should offer
my chair to a visiting lady but it's hard for me to move as things are."

Félicité sat down without taking her eyes from his face. He was pale
but the industry of his hands could be accepted as proof that he had experienced no great harm in the fall. She was so happy about this that she
forgot the pain in her own hands. Cécile, keeping a wary eye on the open
door into the other room, walked across the floor with a plate in one hand.
It was filled with steaming soup into which she had dropped a knuckle
of mutton and other tender bits of meat. In the other hand she carried a
thick slice of bread.

"There, small one," she whispered, handing the plate to Félicité. "It
will do you good after such a long walk in the cold."

The child's nostrils curled with delight as the delicious odor of the food
assailed them. She became ravenously hungry at once. "Thank you,
madame, I am very hungry," she said; and then lost no time in demon-
strating that this was indeed the case.

An enraged voice spoke from the door. "What is this? Does my own
daughter think she's called upon to feed all the waifs in New France?
Must she feed this good soup, which I toil and plan and save to pay for,
to all the beggars of Montreal?"

Old Kirkinhead had pulled a pair of fustian trousers over his nightgown. As they were supported by a single cloth strap across one shoulder,
they hung about him in perilous bagginess. He had not been in too great
a hurry to investigate what was going on, however, to appear without his
velvet cap.

"I am old and my blood is thin!" he cried, fairly dancing with rage.
"But does my own daughter, flesh of my flesh, bone of my bone, give me
the soup which exhausted nature clamors for? No, she takes it out of my
very mouth and lavishes it on a complete stranger!"

His daughter said in a tone of rising exasperation: "It's not a stranger.
It's Félicité. And there's plenty of soup, Father, if you want some now."

"*Plenty* of soup, eh?" The old man pounced on this damning bit of
evidence. "How many times must I demand that you never have plenty
of anything? Send them away from the table with strength renewed but
a hole still in the belly—that's the motto for all sensible housewives."

"All we ever have here is plenty of meanness and bitter words," declared
Cécile, turning on him angrily. "But there *are* plenty of gold pieces hidden
about. That I can tell you."

The old man stopped his angry shuffling. He stood stock-still and regarded her with sudden alarm in his beady eyes. "I knew it! I'm being watched. My movements are spied on. I can't trust my own flesh and blood any more." His voice died down to a whisper. "It's all clear now. They want to be rid of me. Well, I won't wait for it to happen."

Cécile flounced back to the fire. "Are you going to hang yourself again, Father?" she demanded. "It's five times you've pretended to do it. Why not make it the even half dozen?" She stopped and faced about, hands on her hips. "Everybody laughs at you and your silly actions. They say you've lost your mind. Well, I'm beginning to think so too."

Old Kirkinhead made no response for several moments. His mouth had dropped open and he stared at his daughter as though unable to believe his ears. Then, slowly, his eyes began to fill with tears.

"You're hard on me!" he quavered. "As hard as alder." He intended to say more but changed his mind and shuffled into the other room, muttering to himself and sniffling.

Cécile resumed her duties with what seemed unnecessary violence. She slammed pans about and rattled spoons and made a great deal of noise about adding a log, a small one, to the fire. "That my father should be such an *allobroge!*" she said aloud.

From inside they heard a new sound, the tinkling of a spoon against glass. Cécile looked up questioningly from her work and her eyes met Philippe's. The latter threw the blanket off his knees and forced himself to a standing position. Despite the stiffness of his muscles he was in the inner room before the builder's daughter could get there. He could be heard running to the far end, exclaiming as he went, "No, no, master!"

"What is it this time?" asked Cécile, pausing in the door.

"Poison, I think. But I got it away from him in time." Then a doubt assailed him and he gave the old man a thump on the back which made him cough and brought tears into his eyes. "You didn't swallow any of it, did you?"

"No," quavered the old man. "You were too quick for me."

Cécile flounced into the room and stood over her father with the air of a court prosecutor. She picked up the glass and examined it. Then she looked at the bottle from which the poison had been poured. "Where did you get this, you—you *gonin?*" she demanded.

"In Montreal." The old man's voice was not steady but it would have been clear to any disinterested onlooker that he was enjoying the situation. His eyes shuttled back and forth with a barely concealed look of triumph. It was easy to imagine him saying to himself: "Now do you see! This is how I'll keep you on tenterhooks. I'll find new ways. I'll frighten you again—and again—and again!"

"Did you buy it at a chemist's?"

"Yes. At Lahoue's on the Rue St. Paul."

"Did you pay a lot of money for it?" There was sharp accusation in the daughter's voice.

Old Kirkinhead gave a shamefaced nod. This, clearly, was the one fly in the ointment; it had been necessary to pay out money in order to thus play on the terrors of his household.

Cécile picked up the bottle and walked to the hearth on which the feeblest of fires was barely managing to keep alive. She threw the contents of the bottle on the flames.

"There!" she exclaimed, facing about. "For once in your life, Father, you've been guilty of an extravagance. And it's been a complete waste. You had better go back to the rope; it doesn't cost you anything!"

In spite of the scorn being thus heaped on him, the old man settled back in his chair with an air of contentment. The curtain had dropped on another successful act and he had suffered no unpleasant consequences. Then the fine edge of his content dulled because the presence of Philippe meant a loss in terms of work accomplished. "Are you making use of the time you must spend indoors?" he demanded. "Are you studying tangent lines as I told you? Tell me this: if you had a choice of two kinds of wood, fir or oak, which would require the use of larger scantlings to carry the same weight?"

The boy, it was clear, did not know the answer to this one. "Fir?" he hazarded.

"Oak!" cried Old Kirkinhead. "Truly your head's more full of flint than the Crau of Arles. You, who climb roofs and get hurt so you must sit around in idleness and whittle useless figures out of my valuable frowey wood, you will never make a builder! I waste my time on you!" He turned on Cécile then and said in a tone of exaggerated politeness, "I would like a plate of that soup if it's not presumption on my part."

Cécile's anger had not abated. "Soup?" she exclaimed. "It's not soup you're going to get. It's an emetic and it's going to be so strong that you'll part with it both ways. Make up your mind to it, Father, you will be taught a lesson this time."

IV

Félicité burrowed down under the fur robes at the bottom of the sleigh and had to be wakened when they reached the château. The afternoon sun was sinking in the west and there was no suggestion of comfort about it. Instead it told of more cold coming, of a cold which would grip the earth that night and send all living creatures into hiding and cause the frozen ground to crack like pistol shots. She answered Handsome Hyacinth Dessain's hail by shedding the robes and standing up in the sleigh.

"Well! Here we are," said Dessain, guiding his team up the ramp. "I hope I don't have to start out again today. One child running away in weather like this is enough. But two—good St. Joseph, that is too much!"

As soon as they were inside the walls and the gates had clanged to, a groom came running from the stables. He dropped an affectionate hand on the ribs of one of the team. "It's a cold day to be out, my poor Bayard," he said. "No way at all, this, to treat an old horse. Well, I'll have you in your snug stall in no time at all and a measure of oats for you. You too, my Roland. *Peste!* I would like to hitch up some of these lazy people around here and take *them* out on a day like this! That would teach them!"

"Are you sure they are to be unhitched?" asked Dessain in a doubtful tone. "I've brought this one in safe and sound but what about the other?"

The groom, whose sympathies seemed to be given entirely to his horses, grunted and said, "It's all right, my handsome friend, the other one's found too."

"Good!" cried Dessain, his face lighting up with intense relief. "I am happy about that. A thorough little *badaud,* that Bertrand, and yet he amused me with his tricks and the boldness of him."

The groom looked across the backs of the horses at the speaker and grunted again. "Not so fast! The news isn't anything to make you feel as good as that. Come, Bayard! Come, Roland boy!"

The gatekeeper, having dropped the inside bars and chains into place, came over and tapped Dessain on the arm. "Take the girl into the office, Hyacinth," he said. "There's a fire there and she'll get a good warming before starting out again. The orders are from M'sieur Charles."

The driver looked surprised. "M'sieur Charles! When did he arrive?"

"An hour ago. What a day he picked to cross the river! He brought his lady with him and they're going back tonight." The guard shook his head as though he could not understand why anyone should want to get to town as badly as that. "Come back and I'll tell you what's happened."

The office was a small room to the right of the entrance. There was a good fire blazing on the hearth and Dessain saw to it that Félicité removed her wraps and ensconced herself comfortably before the flames. Then he said: "You're to stay here for a few minutes, my small one. I'm going now but I shall be back for you."

"M'sieur," said the girl in an anxious voice, "what is it about Bertrand?"

"That I don't know." Dessain nodded his head in a not too successful effort to appear cheerful. He looked down at the small figure crouching in front of the blaze. "You were a brave girl to think of taking medicine for Philippe. It will never be forgotten how you went there all by yourself and on a day like this. But, St. Joseph, what grief and trouble you've caused by getting that idea into your head!"

The guard had lighted his lantern and suspended it on a hook at one side of the gate and was jigging about to keep warm when Dessain returned. "And now," said the driver, "you will tell me what has happened. Is it about Bertrand?"

The guard nodded soberly. "They found him. His body was brought back half an hour ago."

"His body!" cried Dessain. He stared at the guard with incredulity which is the first reaction to tragic news. "He is dead?"

"As dead as Pierre Chesne. You remember the story of the boy who started out from Montreal to visit his uncle Jean Petit, here in Longueuil? He was just Bertrand's age and he walked up the river on a day exactly like this——"

"I know the story of Pierre Chesne! I wasn't much older than he was when it happened. But must you plague me about such things now? What happened to Bertrand?"

"I will give you the bare facts only, if you must have it that way." The guard spoke in an offended tone. "I've been on duty here all day. Soon after the excitement started because the girl had disappeared, and everybody was running about and Tante Seulette was crying—the first time, I swear, in her whole lifetime!—this Bertrand comes to me here. I was on guard at once, for he was always up to tricks. But not this time! He was frightened. He said to me, 'Where is this little girl?' and I said, 'She's gone but not, I swear, by this gate.' 'She's a nice little girl,' he said. 'I like her.' He went away then and pretty soon there was more excitement and Madame his mother comes running here and wringing her hands and wanting to know if I had let her little Bertrand out through this gate."

"And had you let him out?"

"I? Hyacinth, I swear that I never saw that boy from the moment he was here asking me questions until his mother came."

"Didn't you step into the office for a few minutes to get warm and leave this gate untended?"

"I swear," cried the guard, "that I was here all the time! That boy found some other way of getting out."

There was silence for a moment and then Dessain said: "He went to look for her. That's clear after what he said to you. I knew he had it in him, that small Bertrand. He was full of his tricks and a great nuisance at times to all of us but I was always sure there was a stoutness of heart in him. What a fine soldier he would have made when he grew up!" The driver shook his head sadly at the thought of such waste. "Where was the body found?"

"On the river. And this you will find hard to believe. It was at almost the exact spot where Pierre Chesne was found. That is very strange, don't you think? Is there, after all, an evil spirit which comes out at times like this?"

"Don't let Father de Francheville hear you talking such wickedness as that!" Dessain was becoming more depressed with each moment. "If I were you, and if I were not *quite* certain in my mind that I hadn't left my post for a hot posset, I would feel responsible for this dreadful thing! I would feel I had been the cause of that small Bertrand's death."

He would have had more to say but Father de Francheville came down the stairs which led from the family apartments at this moment, followed by the seigneur and his wife. The driver gave a quick bob of his head and vanished from sight.

Charles le Moyne and his wife had adopted the *grand deuil* in memory of the deceased Gabriel and were heavily bedecked in black. The baroness had a headdress of *étamine* which, though somber in its effect, became her quite well.

"Courage in grown people is so general that it can be taken for granted," the baron was saying. "But children are raised to shun danger as a matter of duty and to save themselves from pain and trouble. Boys who run to their mothers weeping over a small cut will turn into fine stout fellows later. Isn't it to be wondered at, then, that these two never hesitated over what they did, the girl going out into the storm to help a friend, the boy following her! What fine stock we have, Father!"

Father de Francheville nodded his bare head in response. The winds, which showed no signs of diminishing but still roared over the walls of the château, were tossing his scant silver locks about and making them stand on end. Brushing them down with a trembling hand, he said: "God has placed us here for a purpose and it is He who puts courage in our hearts, even in ones as young as these. Yes, M'sieur Charles, we may be proud of the stock we have in Canada but it's to the Divine Father we should address our thanks."

"I've just had a talk with the boy's father," said the baron. "This has been a sore blow for him. At his age he's not likely to have another son. I thought for a time that the mother would lose her mind." He glanced up at the small square of forbidding sky visible above the gate. "It will be a cold drive but Madame the Baroness longs for the warmth and comfort of her bedroom so much that she's determined to go. I'll return, Father, for the funeral."

When the baron entered the office he found Félicité in front of the fire and holding her eyelids open in an effort to avoid falling asleep. She came to with a start at the sound of his footsteps and jumped up hastily. He had never seen her before and at first he thought that he detected in her a fleeting resemblance to her mother. For her part, Félicité was so overcome at thus finding herself face to face with the sun around which the life of the seigneurie revolved that she quickly dropped her eyes. She had seen him several times, staring at him over balusters in the dark or running to catch a view of his back as he strode through the halls of the château. These hurried glimpses had made her think him a handsome and

wonderful being, an opinion which her first close look at him was tending
to confirm.

The baron drew a watch from a waistcoat pocket and squinted at its
face. It was a most unusual timepiece, as large around as a saucer and with
the new baronial coat of arms on the back. Félicité had never seen a watch
before and her attention shifted at once to this magical instrument about
which she had heard so much.

"It's late to be starting," said Charles le Moyne with a worried look. He
snapped the watch shut and dropped it back into his pocket. "Félicité,
you are going to Montreal with me. You're to live with me there and start
to school."

If he had said she was to be taken to live with the King of France she
could not have been more amazed. Her eyes opened wide and her lower
jaw dropped as though she wanted to say something but had lost all
power of speech.

"Will you like that?"

She managed to get out, "Yes. Oh yes, M'sieur Charles!"

"You're a brave girl." The baron turned his attention to her exclusively.
He saw now that she had grown into a wholesome-looking child but that
she was quite different from her mother: which was just as well, he said
to himself. "I have arranged to send you to school—to the Sisters of the
Congregation. They have more boarders than they want now and the
Superior has agreed to take you as a day pupil. It will be an excellent
arrangement. You will live in my house while you are at the school, and
you'll have the chance to get as much education as you can absorb."

Félicité knew of this school which existed in the great, busy town across
the river. It had been started by the saintly Marguerite Bourgeoys and the
pupils were the daughters of the best families. It had never entered her
head that she, who was not even allowed to attend Father de Francheville's
classes, might someday go there. She looked up at the baron with eyes
which had begun to shine with excited interest.

"Among other things," said the baron with a smile, "you will learn
there about medicines and which ones to use under all circumstances.
That may save you from any more dangerous trips like the one you took
today."

"M'sieur Charles, am I to go with you tonight?"

"Yes, child. We start in a very few minutes."

"But, m'sieur!" She looked up at him in consternation. "I must take my
clothes with me. They will have to be packed. I have a book, M'sieur
Charles, and a doll. And my cat, Dauphin."

"Everything has been seen to. The clothes and the book are packed.
The cat is on a leash. We are, in fact, ready to start now."

Félicité was still in some doubt as to what all this meant. "Is Tante
Seulette going with me?" she asked.

"No," answered the baron hastily. "She has her duties here and can't be spared. I have arranged everything with her."

"Then I must go now and say good-by."

He shook his head. "Tante Seulette is not feeling well," he explained. "She has locked her door and gone to bed."

"But, M'sieur Charles, Tante Seulette always sleeps with her door open. She wants to hear if anything goes wrong and if she's needed."

"Tonight she decided to lock her door. Perhaps it was because she was so ill."

"And I can't even speak to her through the door?"

"No, my child. You'll see her when you come back to pay a visit or if she should come to Montreal. She—she didn't want to see you tonight."

Félicité had an uncomfortable feeling that there was something behind this but she asked no further questions. She would have understood if she had heard a conversation between the baron and his wife on the way to Montreal. She had burrowed down as soon as the sleigh began to move, however, and in a very few minutes had fallen asleep with the cat curled up in her arms.

"Never in my life," said the baroness, "have I experienced anything like the way that terrible old woman carried on. She made me feel as though we were thieves and that we were stealing her only possession. Charles, the woman is mad! She frightened me so much that I'm trembling all over still."

His hand found hers under the heavy fur rug and pressed it understandingly. "You didn't show any fear. In fact, my sweet one, you stood up to her like a lion. I was very proud of you, my Claudine."

The baroness indulged in a rueful laugh. "Charles," she said in a contrite tone, "I'm a poor, weak creature. We won our point but—you'll laugh at me, I know, but the truth of the matter is—I'm more afraid of her than ever!"

She sighed deeply and, for extra warmth, slipped both hands into the small muff of black fur which was attached to her arm by a silk strap. "I'm such a baby, Charles!" she went on. "I never want to go back to that dark place again. I never feel safe there, not even with its high walls and towers and the guards on the gates. And now I'll never dare face that old woman, not as long as I live."

"Then you need never go back. I value your happiness above everything, my Claudine."

They drove on in silence. The wind had died down and the stars were out. Nothing could be heard but the crunch of hoofs and the sweet music of the sleigh bells. The baroness became less disturbed in mood. "It's a beautiful night," she said. "How glad I am that we decided to return! At times like this I love the life here and think I'll never want to go back to France."

The baron gave a satisfied nod. "You'll become a good Canadian yet. It's taken a long time but I can see all the signs in you." Then he asked, "What do you think of the child?"

"She's changing a great deal, and for the better. You remember I saw her a year ago. She looked odd then but now she's rather attractive."

"I think," said the baron, unaware that he was quoting what Félicité's mother had said on the one occasion when he saw her, "she's going to turn out well after all."

CHAPTER IV

FÉLICITÉ was in disgrace for the first time since she had come under the kindly care of the Sisters of the Congregation.

She had been a bright pupil and eager to learn everything and this had inclined the other girls to eye her askance. They had not been unfriendly, however, not at least until this morning when three of them occupying a bench just in front of her had begun to talk. She would probably have accepted what they said in silence if it had concerned her but instead they had been talking about the Le Moyne family.

"My father said at breakfast that six more men from Canada had died in the south," whispered one of the girls. "My father said the Le Moynes were wanting more Canadians to enlist for service on that river with the long and funny name."

"My father says that the Le Moynes don't care how many Canadians die just so long as they win glory for themselves," whispered one of the others. "He says he hopes the King will put a stop to it."

Félicité was so angry that she was afraid she was going to be sick. She wanted to shout out so all the classroom could hear that these three girls were sly little gossips and that their fathers, who did so much talking, were cowards who stayed safely at home while the brave Le Moynes died to win a new empire for France. She had become a fanatical believer in the family and everything concerning it. She worshiped M'sieur Charles. The other brothers, none of whom she had seen, had become heroes in her eyes, brave and legendary figures who were risking their lives in strange lands and on the sea.

She sat very still, her hands clasped tightly in her lap so she would not slap the faces of the girls sitting in front of her. She might have restrained herself if one of them had not started then on M'sieur Charles, saying that he was just a fur trader after all like everyone else and that he had no right to put on such airs since he had been made a baron.

This was too much. Félicité placed one foot against the back of the bench and gave a vigorous shove. The bench toppled over and its occupants went sprawling on the floor, revealing the fact that one of them, Hortense, was wearing shoes with red heels under her long skirts.

Sister Agathe was in charge of the class. She was very sweet and gentle and found herself at a loss in facing a crisis such as this. Leaving her desk, she walked down the aisle, saying in a small, protesting voice, "Good little girls, good little girls, what is this, what is this?" Félicité made no defense other than to declare that the trio had been saying things. What they had said she refused to tell. How could she? To repeat such untrue things would have been to give them wider circulation and she would have endured any punishment rather than do that.

She was, therefore, judged to be guilty and penalties were meted out which caused an unhappy flush to cover her face. She must stay in and do all the cleaning of the classroom for a week, she was relieved of her duties as demonstrator of the Numeration Box for the younger classes, permission was withdrawn for the start she was going to make on the reading of *Christian Thought*. Sister Agathe, in imposing the sentence, flushed unhappily and said, "I hope, Félicité, that there will never again be any cause for such severity with you."

Félicité answered stoutly, "Then they had better not say such things again, Sister."

When the classroom had become emptied of its occupants she proceeded stoically about her duties. She swept the floor, she picked up pieces of chalk and paper, she cleaned chalk marks off the board, and she replaced the blocks in the Numeration Box. She kept her head lowered as she did so, feeling that the humiliation she had suffered could never be lived down. As soon as she was through she rushed to the kitchen to see Sister St. Charles, who was in charge there. Sister St. Charles was a cousin of the Le Moynes and had always been very kind to her.

She was greeted with a look of deep concern. "Félicité!" said Sister St. Charles. "I am so sorry! The first black mark on your perfect record! Ah, my child, I wept when I heard what happened. I had been telling everyone that you were the perfect pupil, that you would never break a rule."

"I had to do it, Sister!" declared Félicité. "I had to!"

"Why didn't you tell Sister Agathe what the girls said?"

"Because I was asked to tell in class. I couldn't do that. But, please, I would like now to tell you."

Sister St. Charles listened to the story and at the finish her face, which ordinarily was pale, had turned an indignant red. "My child," she said, "what you did was wrong and so it was necessary for Sister Agathe to punish you. But, my Félicité"—her voice sank to a whisper—"I am proud of you! You must never let anyone speak so of the Le Moynes. Never! Those who speak ill of them will be punished as they deserve. Their punishment will be harder than yours, my child."

As she talked the sister was preparing a tray of food with a degree of care which seemed strange when one noticed that the tray was of battered pewter and the food of the plainest kind.

"If I were a man," declared Félicité fiercely, "I would enlist today to serve with them. I would go to the south or anywhere they needed me. What does it matter that so many have died? It's a privilege to die in such a cause! And have they forgotten that many of the brothers have died?"

Sister St. Charles went on with her task. After straining all the haricot beans from the soup, she placed some broken crusts of bread beside the bowl.

Félicité's mood changed as she watched. "Is it for the Recluse?" she asked in a rapt tone.

"Yes, it's for the Recluse." Sister St. Charles nodded. There was reverence in the slow movement of her hands as she raised the tray. "It's my turn to take this to the grille. I wish I could do it always!"

"Have you ever seen her?" asked Félicité in a whisper.

The sister shook her head. "You should know that none of us has ever seen her. Every evening I pray to the Holy Virgin that someday I should be allowed to—to hear the sound of her footstep or the rustle of her gown."

Jeanne le Ber, who was now known only as the Recluse, was a cousin also of the Le Moynes. Félicité had been told everything that was known about her, of her great beauty as a girl, of the life she had lived for fifteen years in her small rooms behind the Congregation chapel, communicating with the Sisters by note only, of the miracles she had wrought.

Sister St. Charles touched one of the crusts with a light forefinger. "She eats only what the servants leave," she said. Then, dropping her voice to a low whisper, she added: "Félicité, you are unhappy about what happened today. I want to make it up to you. See, you may carry the tray as far as the door! But you must be very, very careful and you must not tell any of the others!"

They walked together to the door, Félicité stepping slowly and carrying the frugal meal of the Recluse with the utmost reverence and care. At the door she surrendered the tray to its proper custodian.

"Thank you, Sister St. Charles," she said. "I'm very happy that you trusted it to me."

"Someday," said the sister, "your class will be taken to sit in the chapel when the Recluse comes down to pray. It's done once a year. No one is allowed to move or make a sound. No one in all these years has ever caught a glimpse of her dress or heard the fall of her foot. She comes and goes as quietly and secretly as an angel from heaven."

Félicité hesitated, feeling a desire to justify still further her behavior in class. "Sister St. Charles," she said, "I didn't tell on Hortense. She was wearing shoes with red heels. And you know it's against the rules."

Sister St. Charles smiled back at her as she carried the tray down the dark corridor. "It's a secret, then, between us," she said. "I'm glad you didn't tell, Félicité."

II

That evening a note was brought for the baron as he rose from the table. He read it, frowned, and called for his hat and cane. He smiled when he saw that it was Félicité who had brought them. "We're going for a walk, you and I, *ma pouponne,*" he said. "That is, if you have nothing else on that busy little mind of yours."

"Nothing, M'sieur Charles," she exclaimed. She acquired a hat in a shorter time than it had taken to find his and they started out together.

"It's a fine evening," said the baron as they walked down the Rue St. Paul, "but I fear that I'm on my way to hear the worst of news."

A few minutes' walk took them to a tavern which fronted on the water but with a yard opening on the street. Here he asked for Monsieur Jean Carrier.

"Yes, M'sieur the Baron." The landlord nodded his head in the direction of the stairs. "He's expecting you. And he must be in need of an extra mouth to swallow all the drink he's had sent up."

A head appeared over the balustrade as they started to climb the stairs and a warning voice from above said, "Off with your boots, Charles!"

The baron stopped. "Take off my boots!" he said. "Have you been drinking all the wine the landlord says he's sent up to you?"

There was an impatient note in the whisper from above. "When I ask you to come up with the least possible noise I have a reason for it. I don't want these drunken rascals of mine disturbed. They're sleeping now like babes in arms but if anything should waken them the devil will be on the town!"

Without more ado the baron took off his boots and carried them the rest of the way upstairs under his arm. Félicité tiptoed after him. They were escorted into a large bedroom with windows opening on the river.

"Sit down," said their host. He acted on his own advice by taking a chair beside the bed. He glowered uneasily at Félicité. "Who is this, Charles? One of your own?"

"This is my ward, Félicité Halay." The baron took advantage of the fact that she was gazing out on the activity of the waterfront to wink at Monsieur Carrier. Then he added in a whisper, "You must recall taking her mother to Quebec at the same time you took a certain genial gentleman from France."

"St. Julian Hospitaler, yes!" said Jean Carrier. "I thought it would be necessary to put a ring in the nose of that great lump of evil before I got them on board the ship for France. So this is the child. She seems bright enough."

"Yes, she's a smart one," whispered the baron. "I've become very fond of her. I often take her with me and I'm always delighted with the comments she makes." He inclined his head in the direction of his host to ask, "And now, my friend Jean, what is the news?"

"Bad!" said the King's messenger. He began suddenly to rumble and splutter. "Blundering coxcombs, mincing dance masters without an ounce of brains in their twittering heads——" He stopped suddenly and leveled a forefinger at the baron. "Charles! Are those Indian chiefs from the Ottawa still here?"

The baron nodded. "As you know, I had them come to discuss new trade agreements. Since my poor Paul died——"

He paused for a moment. The death of his brother early that March, the fifth to go, had been such a blow that he still found it hard to make any reference to De Maricourt without giving way to emotion. De Maricourt's death had been due to a fever he contracted on his last excursion into the woods.

"Since there's no longer a Little-Bird-Always-in-Motion to keep them in line, I invited the chiefs to pay us a visit. I wanted to make sure that none of the fur from the north fell into English hands. And I may tell you that the chiefs have been so impressed that they're ready to agree to everything I want."

"Pack them off!" exclaimed the King's messenger. "Get them away from here, paint, feathers, and all! Start them on their return by tomorrow morning without fail!" He stopped and motioned toward the door of a room back of his own. "The four boatmen I brought with me are in there, dead drunk. I saw to it that they swilled enough, with the help of a useful drop I put in the stuff. I knew they would start to talk as soon as they got out of my sight. Your red devils must be on their way before these blabberers of mine can tell what they know."

"It can be done," said the baron. "And now, my good Jean, what is it they know?"

"The war has taken a bad turn. We've been beaten, badly beaten! A pestilential Englishman named Marlborough has defeated the silly drillmaster that our King put in command of the French army. They fought at a place in Germany called Blenheim and the French army no longer exists. It's the worst defeat France has sustained since Pavia, perhaps even Azincourt." Carrier's face was red with humiliation and rage as he gave this information. "These perfumed favorites, these languishing loobies! . . . If your chiefs get wind of this they may have a change of heart. They may not want to ally themselves with a beaten nation."

The baron said hastily, "I'll load them with presents and get them off before your men are awake. They'll stick to their bargain with me if I

can get them away before they change their minds." He seemed adverse
to asking for details of the disaster. Finally he said: "A beaten nation,
Jean? Is it as bad as that?"

"It's a crushing defeat, Charles. Our general, this favorite of Versailles
with his well-rounded belly and his bird brain, let himself be surrounded
in such small space that he couldn't use his men at all." The angry flush
of his cheeks subsided slightly. He laid a hand on the baron's arm.
"Charles, if the English follow up their victory by getting control of the
sea lanes, will it involve you in difficulties?"

The baron indulged in a wry smile. "I've obligated myself to buy every
pelt produced in the north country. As a result of the visit of these chiefs,
I'll have so much fur on my hands that I must begin at once to build
new warehouses. I've just bought an iron mine above Quebec and ordered
two oceangoing ships in Rochefort. I've been picking up land here in
Montreal as an investment and I'm angling for further grants across the
river. If the English close us off from the rest of the world"—he gestured
dramatically—"I'll founder on the long sands with a resounding crash!"

"Some men," declared the King's messenger, watching his companion
shrewdly, "would be inclined to let the fickle redskins stay and hear about
our bad fortune. It might drive them into the hands of the English—and
relieve the strain."

"I considered it," confessed the baron. "But I think, my friend, that I'll
see to it they get away in time. We can't let the English get any hold on
the north, no matter what it may mean to us as individuals."

Carrier picked up a pipe from the table, packed it full of tobacco with
a quick thumb, and began to puff furiously. "Good!" he cried. "That is
man's talk. But perhaps, my brave Charles, we are taking too black a view
of this. It may be that the old King will come to his senses someday
and realize there's no need for France to lose battles. Not when there's
one Frenchman who always wins, on land or sea." He glanced questioningly at the baron. "Where is D'Iberville now?"

"He's somewhere in the outer isles of the Caribbean with a single ship.
From the letters I receive, I judge he's playing a lively game of *cache-
cache* with the English and Dutch. He strikes a blow in one place and
vanishes, and then turns up unexpectedly someplace else. He's keeping
them so busy they have no time to disturb our poor little colony at the
mouth of the river." The baron gave his head a shake. "D'Iberville has
won all his victories with small forces. The King will never entrust him
with a command except on this side of the ocean." Suddenly he sat up
very straight in his chair and the tendency of his nostrils to flare when he
was excited became quite pronounced. "It may be that holding the mouth
of the Mississippi for France will prove in the long run more important
than winning battles in this war in Europe."

III

Two thoughts were in Charles le Moyne's mind as they left the tavern. First, there would be a letter in Benoit's hands by this time, bearing on the disaster at Blenheim. De Mariat, steeped in departmental caution, preferred to convey anything of a confidential nature in a cipher to which he and Benoit alone held the key. It was a method which the Baron of Longueuil found inexpressibly humiliating, having no stomach for contact with De Mariat's jackal.

The second thought was that it was fortunate Claude-Elizabeth had been persuaded finally to take the baby and join the older children in France. No matter what might happen now, they were safe.

"Was the news very bad, M'sieur Charles?" asked Félicité. He had been walking so rapidly that she had found it hard to keep up and it was apparent from her voice that she was nearly out of breath.

He shortened his steps. "What did you hear?"

"Not a word. But, M'sieur Charles, I didn't have to hear. I could tell from the way you spoke and the way you looked at each other."

"You're a very clever little girl." He gave a despondent shake of the head. "Yes, my child, the news is very bad. We've been beaten by the English in Europe."

They were passing a tavern before which swung a lighted lantern. By the light thus provided he saw that she was finding it hard to believe what he had said.

"But, M'sieur Charles! I thought the French always beat the English."

"I wish I could tell you it was so, my child, but that would not be the truth. We've been fighting the English for many centuries and it's been a seesaw between us. There was one time—it was during the Hundred Years' War—when they beat us in many battles. We finally prevailed and drove them out of France but the result didn't leave us with any confidence that we could always win."

Félicité digested this unpalatable statement with some difficulty. Finally she brightened up and said, "But M'sieur Pierre always wins."

Never having married, Benoit lived in a single room over a shop on the Rue St. Vincent. The baron knew from previous visits that it was a deplorable habitation, cheaply furnished and musty from lack of housekeeping care (the notary was too stingy to pay for help), but it had never looked so uninviting as on this evening. The candle which Benoit carried to the door in answering their knock was the only one in the room. All it did was to reveal the unkempt figure of the lawyer in a short cotton nightgown and his tallowy face peering at them curiously.

"A great honor indeed has been paid me," said Benoit, bowing so low that the candle in his hand spluttered and threatened to go out. "Not only does the Baron of Longueuil pay me a visit but he brings his young ward with him." He squinted down at Félicité and nodded several times with approval. "A nice little girl she is. A *very* nice little girl."

He turned and motioned them to follow him into the room. The atmosphere inside was so close and unpleasant that Félicité's nostrils wrinkled with disgust. She looked up at the baron and whispered, "This is a nasty place, M'sieur Charles." He nodded back and whispered in reply, "He doesn't like to spend money for soap."

In front of the hearth was a table heaped up with unwashed dishes and an untidy pile of books and papers. The baron looked about him. "M'sieur Procureur," he said, "we have matters of a confidential nature to discuss. I suggest we put this young lady in that chair by the open window."

Benoit was growing more deaf all the time but he heard and nodded his head in approval. He led Félicité to the chair in question. "You will sit here like a good girl," he said, "and I will bring you a glass of wine. With some water in it, he, he! And perhaps I shall also bring you a sweet biscuit."

The idea of partaking of refreshments in this hideous room did not appeal to her. "No, thank you, m'sieur," she said promptly. "I'm not at all thirsty."

He sensed the grateful fact of a refusal and his face took on a pleased smile. "You are a wise young person indeed. Refreshments are not good for youthful stomachs as late as this."

Félicité watched him return to the other end of the room, her eyes wrinkled in a disbelief that any legs could be as spindling and hairy as the pair which showed beneath the hem of his nightgown. She shuddered.

Benoit seated himself at the table. A letter lay on a small space which had been cleared at one side and he touched it with a not too clean forefinger. "This is bad, M'sieur the Baron," he said. "This is very bad. A defeat which may have the most dire consequences."

The baron seated himself in a decrepit chair which sagged and creaked under his weight. "Apart from the consequences it may have, this defeat is a blow to the pride which I for one find hard to swallow!" he declared. "We're not accustomed to defeat here in Canada. They look down on us at Versailles but we succeed where they fail."

The lawyer had cupped a hand behind his ear. "I didn't hear what you said. It's too dark for me to follow the lips."

"Never mind then." The visitor spoke with an impatience he made no effort to conceal. "I was indulging my feelings to a degree which was probably unwise. Let's proceed to business." Speaking louder and taking care to accent all his words, he went on. "This letter is, of course, from a mutual acquaintance. He has been, I'm sure, most explicit in what he has written you."

Benoit heard this. "Quite explicit, Baron. He's convinced the Englis
will now turn their attention to winning command of the seas and tha
we may be cut off from France."

The worried frown on the baron's brow deepened. "What will happe
to the fur trade if this is true?"

"He says we must find other markets."

"Other markets? And does he say where these other markets are to b
found?"

"He does, of course. He thinks"—Benoit kept an observant eye on th
face of his visitor as he went on—"we may find ourselves with no alterna
tive but to trade with the English. They're hungry for fur. You've cas
your nets so expertly that there's been little left for them. They need pelt
for their own home market and they have as well the chance denied us
of supplying all of central and northern Europe."

"Do you realize fully what you are saying?" The baron's expression ha
become one of open belligerence. "The right to trade with the English wa
denied us in times of peace. It would be treason to trade with them whil
we're at war. Has this—this acquaintance of ours taken leave of hi
senses?"

Again the lawyer had failed to follow him. "What was it you said? Ah
Baron, this affliction of mine! You can't conceive the hardship it cause
me."

"And those who converse with you," snapped the baron. He repeatec
"Doesn't he realize that what he proposes is treasonable?"

Benoit spread out his hands in a deprecatory gesture. "M'sieur l
Moyne! You've always been a reasonable man, a man of wide affairs
You've never hesitated to disregard the laws——"

"The old laws only! The regulations which have become absurdly ou
of date. What we've been doing in the fur trade is known in France, anc
winked at. If we did any different we would have been bankrupt long
ago, all of us."

"Then why not go a step further? Our friend is taking a reasonabl
view of things. There will be no difficulty about it at all. The merchant
of Boston and New York will meet us more than halfway. You may de
pend on that, Baron; they are sharp fellows and never let little scruple
stand in the way of business. A point of rendezvous will be arranged—a
island conveniently off the coast. We'll sell, for gold only. Ha, it's a chanc
for a fortune! We mustn't let a squeamishness of the stomach hold u
back."

The visitor answered this with precision and care to be sure that h
made himself understood. "My commitments are heavy as you, of course
know. If trade with France becomes impossible I may find myself agair
in a very difficult position financially. But take this as my last word, Maste

Benoit: I would rather lose everything I possess than trade with the enemy!"

Benoit looked startled. He drew in his thin lips before making any comment. Finally he asked: "Could the colony in the south continue to exist without your support?"

"It could go on. But the poor fellows would have to survive under greater hardships than they suffer now." The baron was thinking that never in his life had he faced such a decision. His loyalty to the venture in the south must be brushed aside because he could not turn away from a still greater loyalty.

"But are we actually at war? Professional armies are fighting on the Continent but life in both countries goes on as though nothing was happening. The French people are not fighting the English people."

"The French people will be fighting the English here—and very soon!" exclaimed the baron. "It won't be long now before we sight English sails in the gulf and hear the Iroquois war cry outside the walls of Montreal! Your reasoning is specious, Master Procureur. I'm a loyal subject first and a trader second."

The unwashed hand went behind the ear in the familiar gesture. Unwilling to repeat what he had said, the baron reached out impatiently and drew a blank piece of paper from the pile on the table. Using a pencil from the same source, he scribbled on the sheet angrily and in large and emphatic letters:

NO! NO! NO! NO!

Benoit looked at it and shook his head as though all this was beyond his comprehension. "There will be plenty of others to trade with the English. Make up your mind to that. You're the great merchant prince of New France today. You may be nothing tomorrow."

The baron got to his feet. "My views on this matter will be conveyed to him direct."

"But, Baron!" exclaimed Benoit. "If you write him, you must use the utmost discretion. No direct references, I beseech you, nothing to which the finger of suspicion could point!"

Charles le Moyne flushed an angry red. "You little toad, hopping in dark legal dungeons! Do you presume to set yourself up as my mentor? Must I learn the first rules of ordinary discretion from you—I, who have built up the largest trade structure ever seen outside the boundaries of France?"

Benoit became properly apologetic at once. "I beg your pardon most humbly, Baron. It was a slip—a lapse. An offense which won't occur again, I assure you."

"I trust not." The baron raised his voice. "Come, Félicité. We leave now."

As the girl passed him on her way to the door Benoit smiled and nodded his head with approval of her. "Such fine fair hair! One sees fairness like this very seldom. Nice, isn't it, M'sieur Baron?"

Charles le Moyne contented himself with saying, "I'll write to this friend of ours tonight and make my position clear."

As the door closed Benoit smiled again. "And I shall write tonight also," he said to himself, "and make it clear to our friend how little he can depend on *you*. I think I shall make some suggestions too—suggestions which would surprise you very much, M'sieur le Moyne!" He continued to nod his head without any hint of ill will. "I think it may be necessary to bring our great merchant prince toppling over in a hurry."

CHAPTER V

FÉLICITÉ wakened early and remembered two things in the very first moment of consciousness: it was her tenth birthday, and Philippe, who had come over the day before on some errand for the baron, was staying in honor of the occasion.

She looked through the glazed linen covering (which was much worn) of her bedroom window and could see that the sun was shining brightly and that there was nothing but blue sky around the tower of the Church of Notre Dame de Bonsecours. "It's going to be a lovely day," she thought, feeling both happy and important, as children always do on their birthdays.

She proceeded to dress herself with great care, choosing her blue dress and taking pains to smooth all wrinkles out of her stockings. Her mood descended the scale a little when she was putting on her shoes, which were neat and almost new. She remembered that the Recluse wore shoes made of the husks of corn and it seemed wrong that she should have a pair as fine as this. Common sense came to her aid, however, and she said to herself that it would be wasteful for her to wear shoes like the Recluse, for she was active all day long and would wear them to shreds in a few hours.

Madame Leblanc was preparing breakfast in the kitchen and greeted her with a friendly "So, we are ten years old today, are we?"

Félicité nodded. "I'm growing up, Madame Leblanc, and it's *very* exciting."

The housekeeper was not one to take unalloyed pleasure out of anything. She said in a grumbling tone, "If your appetite keeps growing too, we'll all be worn to shadows cooking food for you."

The girl went out into the yard. The absence of clouds in the small area of sky visible above the high board fence made it certain that the day would be warm. It was the eighth of July. She inspected the bed of lupine and orange lilies in one corner of the yard with an outward show of inter-

est but her mind raced back to something the baron had said to her th
evening before. He had touched her hair and had commented on the colo
of it. "Your father," he had said, "must have been a Norman. In Nor
mandy one often sees hair as fair as this. It seems to come out in mos
families. The Le Moynes are dark but look at M'sieur Pierre! Have yo
ever seen such a crop of golden hair? Your mother, now, was dark. Sh
was a beautiful young woman; and so will you be, Félicité, but in quite
different way."

There could no longer be any doubt about it; the girl who had been s
plain when she was placed in Tante Seulette's care at the age of one wa
blossoming out. Her features, which had defied description before, ha
begun to take on form and to assemble themselves properly in an ova
shaped face. Her nose was straight and rather short and her brow wa
wide over intelligent gray eyes. The fact that her hair was bobbed an inc
below her ears made her of the type often compared to a boy page; a ver
much idealized conception of a boy page, without a doubt. She was ta
for her age and gave promise of trimness later.

Philippe peered into the yard through the back door and then cam
out to join her. "I hope," he said in a teasing tone, "that you put you
stockings on wrong side out this morning. You can't expect presents
you didn't."

Some of the pleasure went out of her face. "I didn't!" she said. "I forgo
all about it. How very unfortunate!"

Philippe grinned. "I thought you might forget. So, to make sure yo
wouldn't be completely disappointed, I brought you this."

He handed her a small wooden crucifix which he had carved for her. I
was a beautiful piece of work to come from such young and untraine
hands but if it had been ugly and misshapen she would have taken th
greatest delight in it. Her hand trembled as she took it. "He must like m
He must!" she said to herself. At last she had something to put in the *ti*
of her trussing chest, the secret receptacle which all girls used for the
most prized possessions. Up to the present it had remained empty.

She was sure the day could yield nothing more after this but it deve
oped that there were plenty of pleasant surprises in store for her. Sinc
his wife and family had gone to France the baron had returned to an ol
seigneurial custom and took his meals with the household staff. Breakfa
was served this morning in the dining salon and, as usual, Félicité sat o
his right. The best part of the arrangement was that Philippe was in
structed to seat himself beside her. He did so with some reluctance, givin
an uneasy glance about him and taking in the splendor of the room wit
its high-backed chairs, its gleaming silver and glass, its handsome o
paintings. He went through the meal for the most part in silence.

There was a bowl in the center of the table containing ten white ros
buds and each member of the staff repeated, on entering, the birthda

formula, "May the next year bring you health and happiness, Félicité."
The baron had a present for her (perhaps there was nothing in the old
superstition about the stockings after all), a string of brown beads, of real
amber, which had been brought out from France. And there were her
favorite dishes for breakfast. First there were Breton pancakes with honey,
and then, to her loudly expressed delight, a *tiaude de morue fraîche*. This
dish was a great favorite with the people of the Montreal district because
it was so hard to get. It consisted of alternate layers of fresh cod and bacon.
When the round silver platter containing this great dish was placed before
the baron an appetizing odor filled the room as evidence that the steaming
had been done to the final stage of perfection. The top layer of bacon had
been added at the last moment and so was brown and crisp and tempting.
There was a smacking of lips around the board and an exchange of smiles
which said, "Now here is something for which the ears must be pinned
back!"

At the end of the meal the baron got to his feet and gave a smiling
glance up and down the board. "It's going to be a warm day," he said,
"and it happens also to be a day of some small importance. It has occurred
to me that, under all the circumstances, we might suspend work and go to
Longueuil to celebrate."

This announcement was greeted with loud expressions of approval and
delight, all of the staff being Longueuil people, and Félicité lost no time in
running toward the stairs to get her hat. Watching her, the baron said to
himself that she had been most satisfactory in every way and that he had
never had reason to regret bringing her away from the château. He was
impatient of slowness in those about him and the fact that she did everything quickly had been a great point in her favor. When she rose in the
morning, the first up, he would hear her footsteps on the floor above and
in no time at all she would be racing down the stairs, calling to him,
"It's a *very* fine day, M'sieur Charles!" The servants reported that she was
careless about her room and that she left her clothes anywhere. Somehow this seemed a minor fault to him, perhaps because he never saw the
evidences of it, and also because she was invariably neat about herself.
Once he told her of these complaints and she looked a little blank and
said: "I didn't know I was doing it, M'sieur Charles. I guess it's just because I'm so anxious to start the day."

She was an excellent scholar, judging from the reports he had from the
Sisters. She read continually. One day he found her poring over a book
the baroness had sent him from France, an abstruse document dealing
with the Jansenist movement. He himself had abandoned it in despair
after the first few pages and so he had asked her, with a smile of amusement, "Do you understand that stuff?" She had looked up and given her
head a negative shake. "Oh no! I don't know much of what it's about.
But it's *reading*."

It had become understood between them that she was to sit with him for an hour each evening after supper before going to her studies. In winter they sat in front of the fire, in summer on the porch at the front door. This was, for her, the great event of the day. If he happened to be late she would be looking apprehensive and unhappy when he finally arrived. Their talk was entirely on an adult plane. They would discuss at length the perilous game D'Iberville was still playing in the islands of the Indies and she would display quite a store of knowledge of that romantic part of the world. They would often study a map of the Low Countries and speak hopefully of the campaigns being fought against the terrible Marlborough. She was beginning to know a great deal about the fur trade and the ins and outs of city business.

When she returned with her hat on her head and an eagerness to be started in every line of her he said, "Not so fast, if you please. I've a few things to attend to before we can go and there's an errand you can do for me. Do you know where Master Benoit lives?"

She nodded her head. "Yes, M'sieur Charles. I think everyone knows where Old——"

She stopped in confusion. That had been a narrow squeak! She had checked herself just in time, just as she was about to use one of the names the children of the town had coined for the disreputable man of the law. It had become quite a game to follow behind Benoit, dancing derisively and taking advantage of his deafness to shout such things as, "Who did you rob today, Old *Griffe* (Claw)?" He had been given all manner of curious names, the kind which originate in youthful minds, such as Master Chin-in-Boots, because he was always so gloomy, Old Buttock-Face, and Master Once-a-Year, an allusion to his bathing habits. She had a nickname for him which was all her own, M'sieur Pump-Handle, because he always tried to catch her alone when he came to the Le Moyne house and asked her questions by the dozen.

"Yes, I know where M'sieur Benoit lives."

"Then you may take a note to him for me. We'll be ready to go by the time you get back."

II

Monsieur Benoit came to the door in response to her knock, snuffling and rubbing a hand over his unshaved chin. One of the tails of his coat had been torn and was hanging down behind him.

"The very smart little girl is paying me a visit," he said, making an effort to appear facetious. "I hear a great deal about this little paragon. Well, come in, come in! To what do we owe this visit?"

She held the note out to him and then drew her hand back quickly.

noticing that his hands seemed to have become utter strangers to soap and water. The man of the law shuffled back to the chair by the window and began to read the letter. She watched him closely, remembering something the baron had said about him: "I'm inclined to think that Master Benoit is sorry the French navy has been able to protect all our ships going to France." It had seemed impossible that any Frenchman could be guilty of such disloyalty and she regarded him now with a fascinated contempt.

He read slowly, nodding his head and muttering. She could hear what he was saying but the words came out in sudden jerks and with frequent stops and so did not seem to carry any meaning. "So! He has begun to hear things. And to wonder about—ha, shrewd one, there are many things you don't know. . . . Ask anything you like, mighty merchant prince, but don't expect you'll be told. . . . I've been doing something about *you*, my great piler-up of millions."

He raised his head suddenly. Aware that she had been watching him, he carefully folded the letter and tucked it away in a pocket. This done, he proceeded to study her intently.

"You are growing fast," he said. "I think you're going to be a fine tall woman someday. And a handsome one too. I like tall and handsome women." He stopped suddenly. It was apparent that a thought had occurred to him and that it gave him much satisfaction. "An idea has come into my head, one which concerns you, my little dabchick, and which on that account pleases me very much. Ah, such a clever idea! I mustn't tell you what it is now. No, no, that would never do! But someday—yes, someday I'll tell you about it and I'm sure that you'll be grateful to me then. I see a way to provide a great future for you, my clever little girl, a way to make you a lady. In France, with all the money you need and, perhaps, a handsome young husband. Who knows? You might even go to the King's court and become a *very* great lady."

Félicité was both puzzled and frightened. "But, m'sieur," she said in an uneasy voice, "I'm quite sure I could never be a great lady."

He kept nodding his head and repeating: "Yes, yes! A great chance. And, ah, what a future for this clever little girl!"

She was becoming more alarmed every second by this strange behavior. Turning uneasily in the direction of the door, she asked, "May I go now, m'sieur?"

He brushed a hand over his partly bald head, on which perspiration had been allowed to dry. "You may go now," he said. "But you must never forget what I've said. Someday I'll remind you of this and when that time comes I'll tell you what I intend to do for you." He contrived to squeeze a smile from the sour ingredients which had gone into the making of his face. "And you may tell the Baron of Longueuil, my very reluctant partner, that you delivered his note to me. The contents have been carefully

considered. You mustn't mention this to him but I have a plan that cor
cerns him too. Ah, what a plan it is! He would be quite surprised if h
knew what I propose to do for him."

III

The visit she had paid to Monsieur Benoit was the first of several inc
dents which were to change her memories of this important day. Ther
was a long delay at the waterfront, where the baron was seized upon b
shipping assistants who had a multitude of matters for his attention. A
violent thunderstorm rolled up from the west and drove them for mor
than an hour into the shelter of a small room on the Quay des Barque
which smelled of tar and moldy biscuit. It was as a result long after th
usual dinner hour before they reached the château. In spite of the unex
pectedness of the visit, there were many tenants at the entrance and th
warmth of their greeting made up somewhat for the disappointment c
so late an arrival.

Félicité looked about for Tante Seulette but the housekeeper was no
among those at the gate. She did not see her, in fact, until her search too
her to the cool vaulted lower floor which was given over to househol
offices. Tante Seulette was standing in the door of the kitchen.

The old woman did not speak or smile and she paid no attention whe
the girl held out the murlin containing a bottle of special wine which sh
had brought as a present. The oddness of this behavior caused Félicité t
stumble in her greeting. "I'm—I'm very happy to see you, Tante. M'sieu
Charles brought me today because it's my birthday. My tenth. You re
membered that, didn't you—that today's my tenth birthday?"

"I remembered," said the housekeeper. She still did not smile. Her ex
pression, in fact, became more grim as she studied the appearance of he
former charge. "You've changed," she said at last. "You've changed a grea
deal. One would hardly know you."

In an eagerness to break the chill, Félicité began to talk rapidly. "Ye
Tante Seulette. I think I've changed a great deal. I've grown inches sinc
I saw you last. I think perhaps I'm going to be quite tall before I'r
through growing."

The old woman continued to stare at her. "You've improved in you
looks. I suppose it's that mother of yours coming out in you. If you thin
I'm pleased about it you're much mistaken. I can see now you're going t
take after your mother in many ways. You're going to be one of thes
creatures who think of nothing but men." She raised her hand in a ge
ture of renunciation. "You are a stranger to me now."

To Félicité's amazement, she turned at that and went back into th
kitchen, closing the door after her.

The child walked up the stairs slowly, still holding the unwanted gift i her hand. The baron was standing in the upper hall in conversation with one of the tenants and she went up to him, holding the basket out in front of her. "M'sieur Charles," she said, "she wouldn't take it. She wasn't glad to see me."

The baron said something under his breath which, in all certainty, was not complimentary to his old housekeeper. "Don't let it upset you, my small one," he said then. "She's a cantankerous old creature and no one can tell what she's going to do next. There will be plenty of others only too glad to take the wine. I have an idea about that." He turned to the tenant. "We'll give this to Old Kirkinhead. I hear he's in low health."

The tenant shook his head. "There's no sense, M'sieur Charles, in sending it to Old Kirkinhead. He couldn't drink it. He's far gone, that one. *Sacristi!* He doesn't even recognize his own daughter any more. He keeps asking who that woman is. And as for Prosper!" The man paused to enjoy a laugh at the son-in-law's expense. "He thinks Prosper is a man he had a bitter quarrel with years ago and he snarls every time he sets eyes on him. Once he shouted for a carving knife and said he would have the life of that *ladre!* Poor Prosper doesn't dare go into the room any more."

Félicité understood from this why Philippe had disappeared immediately on their arrival. He had gone to stay with his troublesome old master and, she was sure, would remain there all day. This would ruin her birthday for her but she was more sorry for him than she was for herself. "Poor Philippe!" she thought. "He never has a chance to enjoy himself."

The baron took the murlin from her. "I'm sorry to hear about my poor old friend," he said, shaking his head slowly. "How he would have enjoyed this wine in happier days! Well, Georges," handing the bottle to the tenant, "this is yours. You'll find it excellent, I think. Drink a health to—to all the Longueuil men in the south."

IV

A black cloud was blowing up from the west as Philippe issued from the fringe of woods and began to hurry across the common. When the clear note of a horn sounded from the nearest tower (the baron had not yet installed bells in the chapel although he often talked of it) he said to himself, "Now I'll not be able to speak to Father de Francheville until after compline."

The man on the gate asked, "How is your master?" and the boy shook his head as he replied: "I've come for the priest, Jules. He can't last the night."

Félicité, following immediately behind the baron down the flagged path to the chapel, saw him come through the gate and knew at once that he was in trouble. She sighed with realization of her inability to be of assistance. "He needs help," she thought. "And I'm only ten and there's noth-

ing I can do!" She paid no attention to the baron when he stretched ou
a hand, palm-up, and said, "Late-comers will be well drenched."

The kneeling congregation were saying the silent prayer *Aperi Domin*
when it became dark in the chapel. The candlelights dipped and flare
with the currents of air entering through the half-opened windows. The
could hear the tottering steps of an old man who acted as *sacristain;* an
could see, through laced fingers, that it was too late to get the window
closed.

There was a flash of lightning, so vivid that a gold monstrance stoo
out like a circle of fire, against the north wall. Almost immediately afte
came the thunder, a sonorous roll which caused some of the women t
place hands over their ears. The wind followed. They heard it on the wa
and eye sought eye with surprise and even terror, for there was somethin
unnatural about the sound of it. But no one was prepared for the way i
hurled itself at the château walls, engulfing everything in swirling cor
fusion.

All the candles gave one startled flare-up and then went out together.

For a moment there was a stunned silence. Then a woman screamed
It was strange that only one lost control of herself in the first moment, fo
fear had laid its hold on all of them. Everyone knew that a candle blow
out during service was a sign of death. What could be meant when all th
candles went out together? Was it a sign of many deaths? They migh
say to themselves that it was nothing more than an old superstition; bu
in each mind was the memory of that dreadful night when the Iroquoi
warriors attacked Lachine in a thunderstorm. Was history repeating i
self? Were war parties on their way? Had they struck already and did th
blowing out of the candles mean that many poor settlers had died? An
other scream broke the stillness.

This was too much. People sprang up and started in a frenzy for th
door.

The baron fought his way down the crowded aisle, saying, "Easy, easy
There's no cause for alarm." Reaching the oak-screened lobby of th
chapel, he proceeded to organize the distracted men and women, namin
those who were to stand guard at the gates and in the watchtowers, an
selecting the boldest to see that such people as had stayed at home cam
to the château at once. He himself chose with one companion to carry th
warning down the Chambly Road.

Félicité had been as frightened as the rest and had followed the baro
down the aisle with a hand on his coat. She found relief at once, howeve
in the calm face of Father de Francheville, who was trying to restore quie
among the women and children. She heard him say: "When the Lord de
cides that lives must end, He stretches out a hand. He has no need to send
winds to blow out candles in church as a warning, like a witch tappin
with a bony finger on a window in the dead of night."

One woman, weeping hysterically, said, "But, Father, it always follows. have seen it, oh, so often!"

Félicité had lost sight of Philippe but she saw him a few minutes later, tanding beside Father de Francheville and talking without any sign of panic or fear. The priest was listening and nodding his head. She got as lose to them as she could and heard Philippe saying, "He has no strength eft and his voice has become very thin. He hasn't long to live, Father, and ie keeps asking for you." The priest answered, "As soon as I can leave this poor, frightened flock I shall go with you, my son."

A more normal mood was taking possession of the people and shame-aced smiles were testifying to a return of sanity. The sky was clear in the vest and the storm clouds were passing rapidly. Nevertheless when one nan said, "The devils aren't loose yet," someone answered, "Perhaps hey're striking farther down the river." Under the surface, therefore, they vere not wholly convinced. The blowing out of the candles had not neant that the woods were full of screeching savages as on that dreadful night at Lachine, but it had a tragic meaning of some kind.

When even this feeling of doubt seemed to have passed and people were beginning to talk in normal tones, Father de Francheville motioned to Philippe. The latter joined him at once and they left by the main gate. A nan was dying and not even the fear that death might be waiting to strike in the woods could keep the staunch old priest from doing his duty.

Félicité spent two hours in one of the watchtowers, never taking her eyes from the section of woods where the Girard house was located. The torm had departed, muttering to itself, and a breeze was blowing up the river and causing a slight motion in the tops of the trees. A dozen times n the first half hour she asked the custodian of the tower the same ques-ions. Could he see any signs of trouble? Did he hear anything?

The guard was roused finally to a sharp rejoinder. "You keep asking if I see any trouble down there by the river. I have told you a dozen times hat I see nothing. I go further now and say that I see no trouble in any part of the woods, north, east, south, or west. You ask if I hear anything and I have answered, 'No, I hear nothing.' I still hear nothing. It will please me very much if you keep from asking these questions and also it will save you from being sent down where you belong."

Félicité said in an apologetic voice, "You see, m'sieur, I have friends in hat part of the woods along the river."

The guard motioned with both arms. "My small head of a cabbage," he said, "I have friends in every part of the woods. You fear for one family. I have fears for a dozen."

"Do you think the Indians are going to attack us?" she asked, not being easy in her mind yet.

"They may attack us or they may not. Who can read the mind of an Iroquois? But this much I may tell you, my little buzzing mosquito, they never attack in broad daylight. If we are going to hear from them, the screeching devils, it will be just at dawn. Now are there any more questions you want to ask me?"

"Yes," said Félicité in a small and worried voice. "There are many, m'sieur. But you don't like me to ask questions and so I won't bother you any more."

"That is good." The sentry drew a pipe from a coat pocket and began to fill the bowl carefully with tobacco. "Now I shall smoke in peace and not have to say, 'I see nothing, I hear nothing.'"

The child took some consolation from what he had said but it was not until a figure emerged from the woods in the fast gathering darkness that she felt any real sense of security.

"There," said the guard, pointing at the figure with the stem of his pipe, "is the good priest. He walks slowly and he doesn't look around and so it's clear that there are no Indians in the woods."

Félicité sighed deeply and happily. "Then they are safe!" she declared.

The guard nodded. "They are safe. All, I think, but one." He was studying the bent figure of Father de Francheville. "There is something about the good father. He isn't happy. His thoughts are far away. I think this has to do with Old Kirkinhead. I think, perhaps, he is dead!" He leaned forward over the wall. "Yes, that is it. He's talking to the seigneur. I can't hear what is being said but that doesn't matter. It is the duty of a sentry to watch and my eyes have become quicker to get at the truth than the sharpest pair of ears. Old Kirkinhead is dead."

He leaned his back against the parapet and puffed reflectively at his pipe. "You asked me if I saw signs of trouble over there. I saw none then but I see plenty now. Yes, there will be trouble. Cécile will get all the money and Philippe, who has never been paid a wage, will get nothing. Prosper will carry on the old man's business and soon there will be no business left. Cécile will know where the gold is hidden in the house but she won't tell Prosper. When the business is gone Prosper will beat her to make her tell. I sometimes think that a will can cause more trouble than a raid by Indians.

"And now you will see how stupid people are," he went on. "The good priest will tell them that Old Kirkinhead is dead and they will all say at once, 'There you have the proof. The going out of the candles was a sign of his death.'"

Félicité asked timidly, "And don't you think it was, m'sieur?"

"Me, I think not." The guard turned suddenly in her direction and began to speak in a controversial tone of voice. "Do you think our kind

Father in heaven and all the blessed saints would make a great storm like that and send a wind sweeping through the chapel to blow out all the candles just to let us know they were taking Old Kirkinhead? We knew he was going to die and it didn't seem to matter very much. Are they getting a great bargain in him? No, no, the coming of darkness in the chapel had another meaning. We'll be hearing what it meant soon enough."

He drew a few small coins from his pocket and began to clink them together. "If you were a man and had a liking for a wager, I would bet you that Cécile and Prosper, those two great hearts of gold, won't spare the old man one of his fine hats to be buried in."

CHAPTER VI

JOSEPH LE MOYNE, Sieur de Sérigny, the sixth of the brothers, looked at the health officer who had come out from Havana in an official boat to inspect the bodies of the three dead sailors and to pass on the symptoms which were confining D'Iberville to his cabin. De Sérigny was a disciplinarian of the strictest order, a quality which helped to make him second only to his great brother as a sea captain and which later would make him the most successful governor that the French port of Rochefort ever knew.

"Tell this timorous rogue," he said to the one member of the crew who spoke Spanish and who was acting as interpreter, "that he must arrange for the Sieur d'Iberville to be taken ashore at once." He gave a quick glance at the scuppers where the three bodies awaited burial, sealed up in canvas. "He must be saved from all further contact with this accursed disease."

The doctor and the sailor talked back and forth, with much gesturing and what seemed unnecessary emphasis. The cool eye of De Sérigny hardened as he watched. What was the matter with this mangy baboon of a doctor? Was he raising obstacles, this puny landlubber and simpleton? Didn't he know how important it was that D'Iberville should be restored to health quickly?

The interpreter turned finally and began to explain. "It's this way, M'sieur Lieutenant. This stupid ox does nothing but talk of something he calls *peste*——"

De Sérigny had been expecting this but to have his fears confirmed caused his pent-up feelings to explode in a furious tirade. Angry though he was, he kept his tongue from any mention of the plague, knowing that the first hint of the word would cause a panic in the crew. He directed all his rage, therefore, at the weakness, the stupidity, the venality of this ill-informed, ill-born, ill-looking fool, dotterel, and coward who by some ill chance had been made port health officer of Havana. "Tell him," he

tormed at the interpreter, "that our country and his are allies and that the
Sieur d'Iberville is the only man who can win battles for us at sea. Tell
him that his harbor regulations are of no importance when it's a question
of the recovery of this great hero who is suffering from nothing worse
than a headache and a slight tendency to vomit. Tell him it would be
better for ten thousand of these degenerate, prick-lugged mustees to die in
his flyblown hole than for anything to happen to this one great man——"

The doctor interrupted in halting French. "It is much to be hoped," he
said, his thin brown face livid with rage, "that the honorable officer will
enjoy an immediate foretaste of the torments of hell-fire! It is much to be
hoped he will die himself with great red spots on his hide——"

The temper of De Sérigny subsided at once. Since the man knew some
French after all, he could be made to see reason, an outcome which had
seemed impossible as long as the facts had to be strained through the
coarse mesh of the sailor's understanding.

"So, Señor Doctor, you speak some French! That is good. Now you and
I may talk like reasonable men and come to a proper solution. I beg your
pardon, Señor Doctor, for the things I said in my impatience with this son
of a mule. My remarks were directed at him and mustn't be thought to
imply any disrespect for you or the great people of this admirable city."

The doctor bowed. "Your apology is accepted for words spoken in an
impatience which can be understood."

They talked after that in an excess of politeness and with great care on
the part of each to understand exactly what the other was saying; and the
upshot of it was that the health officer agreed to lay the facts at once before
the city authorities. The man of medicine then bowed elaborately and
continued to utter compliments until he reached the boat at the foot of
the ladder. Settling himself in his seat, he called an impatient order to
cast off. The crew were quick to obey since they knew the meaning of
the word *"peste"* only too well.

"That maggoty French pig!" said the health officer to himself. "I hope
he catches it himself and dies in convulsions!" Recovering then some of
his better nature, he conceded that there had been some reason after all in
the Frenchman's contention. "It's true," he thought, "that the life of a
great leader must be preserved at any cost. All that one has heard of this
D'Iberville is good. I shall lay the case fairly before the *comandante*. If he
does not happen to be in one of his moods, when he is as impervious to
reason as the withered ear of a deaf mule, it may be possible to make some
arrangements for this great man who is so very sick."

The Sieur de Sérigny did not visit his brother immediately after the departure of the boat. His was a logical mind and he knew that D'Iberville
had contracted the disease by his solicitude in visiting the sick members of
his crew. It was in no sense fear which kept him from repairing to the
darkened cabin where his brother lay but an appreciation of what it would

mean if he were to get the fever also. He knew only too well that none of the officers under him were capable of assuming command.

He paced the quarterdeck impatiently, his face set in rigid lines. He could make out the towers of Morro Castle on the shore line and this seemed to add fuel to his bitterness.

"Not here!" he said to himself. "If my brother is to die it must be under the fleur-de-lis. Isn't it bad enough for the eagle to lie ill of a disease fit only for sparrows and twittering sand birds?" His hand on the rail showed white at the knuckles. "It can't be! God has made it clear that my brother is the instrument of the Divine Will in America. He won't be allowed to die of a putrid fever like a beggar in a spital house!"

It was early in July and desperately hot in the glazed sea outside the harbor. The cabin where D'Iberville lay was a large one with no fewer than three portholes. It was furnished elaborately: a bed clamped tight to the wall, a table which seated eight, an English secretary desk. The desk, which was made of mahogany cured under sea water until it had become a warm brown, had been taken from a prize ship and it had become his most valued possession. He never passed it without allowing his hand to run affectionately over its smooth surface and he had spent much time exploring it for secret drawers. Eight of them had come to light, one a velvet-lined compartment within a secret drawer. How he had laughed when he discovered this one. "What a careful, planning race!" he had said. Then he had added in a completely sober tone: "I sometimes think they plan their colonial ventures too well for the good of others!"

But the sick captain had no eyes for his cherished desk this blistering hot morning. He had been delirious for many hours. Though his fevered mind had taken him far away—back to boyhood days when he swam in the great river at Longueuil—he was conscious always of the splitting pain in his head and the heat which smoldered in his strong frame. He groaned incessantly and twisted about on the bed, threshing out with his arms as though striving to bring this cruel and treacherous opponent to grips.

Reason had returned at rare intervals. He would realize at once where he was and he would begin to issue orders in his thickened voice. Why did no one come in response? Why was he alone? Where was the faithful Giles who for so many years had waited on him hand and foot? He would struggle to get out of bed in order to find the answers to these questions. He knew, of course, that the ship was at anchor. Why, then, was everything so quiet on deck? Had there been a mutiny and had the crew left? Was he a prisoner on his own ship?

He was in one of his sane moments when the health officer came back with two assistants. All three men were wearing white masks over their faces and long white robes. Even their hands were carefully gloved. They looked like ghosts as they came into the darkened cabin and the sick fancy of the stricken captain turned them into creatures which had escaped out of his delirium.

"What's this?" he demanded, striving frantically to get up. "Who are you? Where is the Sieur de Sérigny?"

The officer said in his uncertain French: "You are sick, Señor Captain. We come to take you ashore where you will have comfort and better care."

De Sérigny's anxiety had triumphed over his sense of duty. He came into the cabin on the heels of the health officer and walked over to the side of the bed.

"My poor Pierrot!" he said, looking down at his brother. He was appalled by D'Iberville's drawn features and deathly color. "They are taking you to a cool *finca* outside Havana——"

"Havana? Is that where we are? Are you—are you sure, Joseph? It's strange that everything is so quiet. Always in Havana Harbor there is noise and much shouting and quarreling."

De Sérigny answered uneasily, "We're anchored outside the harbor, Pierre."

The sick man seized on the reason at once. "Are we quarantined? Joseph! Are you afraid to tell me? It's the plague, then." He squirmed and groaned with the pain in his head which had become intensified by the need to speak. "I was afraid of it. They had some of the symptoms, those poor fellows. Joseph, Joseph! Tell me, what has become of them? Are the poor fellows—dead?"

"You need have no concern about them, Pierre. They are doing well now. Did you hear me when I said you were to go ashore? They are here to take you at once."

D'Iberville had lost the power to hear. He muttered the word "Plague!" again. His reason deserted him and he fell back into delirium. He began to babble in his thick voice, a jumble of words meaning nothing.

The two medical assistants went to work at once. They tied a mask over his face and then lashed the mattress about him. In this manner he was carried out on deck and lowered over the side, where other hands took hold.

The crew lined the rail, watching in a grim silence. Many of them were Canadian-born, a few even came from Longueuil, and it was not to be wondered at that they cried openly and bitterly as they witnessed the departure of their great captain. He had driven them hard when necessary and had demanded the most from them, but he had always been just and even kind. They loved him for his greatness, for his warmth of character, for his ready wit and understanding and for his willingness to make himself one of them. They were ready to follow him anywhere, even to certain death.

They knew that some of them, if not all, would follow him on this grim journey he had started. It was no longer a secret that they carried the plague. In addition to those who had died the day before, there were five more down with it in the sick bay. Each man drew away uneasily as they lined the rail and watched the bark in which their sick commander lay as it bobbed and tossed over the choppy water.

De Sérigny issued a curt order from the quarterdeck and the bosun called: "Back to quarters! Lively, now! There's work to be done. This old lady's to be washed and scrubbed and painted!"

II

The house to which D'Iberville was taken had been hastily evacuated to receive him. The last loaded donkey cart, in fact, was turning onto the road as he was carried to the entrance in the mattress. The sick man was laid in a huge carved bed in a cool, high-ceilinged room. There was a painting on the plaster above him and whenever he regained any degree of consciousness he could make out angels looking sadly down at him as though they knew the danger he faced. There was an attendant in white who came in and out of the room but never spoke. D'Iberville thought it was a man but, because of the mask, could not be sure. All he ever got in answer to his questions was a movement of the head.

His condition became steadily worse. His breathing was rapid and labored and there was a growing pain in his chest. Sometimes he was so hot that he protested to the silent attendant at the folly of building fires under the beds of sick men in the middle of summer. Fortunately these spells would pass and he would have brief periods of relief.

Once he heard his brother's voice outside the door. There was a dispute going on, in carefully restrained tones. He realized, after a moment of painful attention, that De Sérigny was being denied the right to enter; and for the first time he knew that he was dangerously ill.

He was in possession of his reason when the health officer made his first visit. In a voice which he made coherent only by the greatest effort, he asked, "There is an epidemic of the plague?"

The officer hesitated and then nodded. "Yes, Señor Captain. It is a form of the plague. I think, bubonic."

"Am I going to get well?"

"I can make no predictions, señor. And no promises."

D'Iberville's mind achieved a moment of complete clarity. He looked at the white-masked officer with the frown he always wore when in his fighting mood. "Señor," he said, "I've been close to death many times. Once an Indian arrow plowed a furrow along my temple. Once I stood on the quarterdeck of my ship when a cannon ball went through the railing a foot from me, and I didn't suffer so much as a scratch. I've never

worn a mask and I've looked death in the eye; and never felt any fear."
He was panting with the exertion of speech. After waiting several moments to recover strength, he went on. "Do you think that I've escaped
such real dangers to die without my boots of a disease which feeds on
weak little brown-skinned men?" The veiled look left his eyes. Back of
them the familiar fire was beginning to glow. "Señor Officer, I am D'Iberville! Do you know that? Do you know I have much work still to do? I
will tell you this: I need no promises from you. I have this instead, the
knowledge that the good Father of all has need still of my services."

The strength he had summoned up began to quit him. In a husky voice
he added: "Did you hear me? I am D'Iberville! I have no intention of
dying, señor. Tomorrow I'll be much better. You will see. The day after
that I'll be on my feet. In a week's time I shall be out on the Main, looking
for enemy sail."

The next day he was not better. He was delirious most of the time, his
eyes were red, his tongue was so swollen that it was hard for him to make
any sound. The health officer did not appear and the attendant seemed to
think it sufficient if he put his head in at the door at long intervals. The
curtains had been drawn across the windows but it seemed to the sufferer,
in whom the fever had mounted to its highest point, that none of the heat
of the day was being kept out.

His confidence had been shaken. He tried to address his Maker aloud
but the condition of his tongue made speech impossible and so he had to
formulate his appeal in his mind. "Kind Father, I appeal to You," ran his
thoughts. "I beg of You the chance to finish my work. I have only begun.
Oh, gracious Lord, there's so much still to do! There's the colony on the
river to strengthen and to establish for all time as French. There's the west
to be held, the passage to India still to be found, and trade routes to the
east to be opened. I see everything so clearly and I have in me the power
to do all this, as Thou knowest who gave it to me. Am I to be wasted, cut
off so strangely, so needlessly, in this way?" A feeling of despair was
mounting in his mind and now a panic gripped him. "Oh, God, I can't
die, I can't die!"

On the second day he was so weak that he knew he would never again
put out on the Main, looking for enemy sail. He was going to die.

This knowledge brought resignation and he prayed long and earnestly
for the remission of his sins. When the day was half gone he fell into a
state of coma and, when consciousness came back to him, the curtains
were blowing a little with an evening breeze and he caught a glimpse of
stars in the sky.

His mind was clearer than it had been for several days and he began to
marshal the instructions he must leave to those who would carry on the
work. If only Charles and Joseph and Jean-Baptiste were here so he could
talk to them! It would be so easy then to tell them the things he had left

undone (there were so many!) and which must now be taken in hand. It would not be hard to strengthen their faith, to make sure they would never slacken in their efforts. Jean-Baptiste must be told that someday a city was to be founded at the bend of the river which had impressed them both so much. That, above everything else, stayed in his mind. The French needed a capital for their new empire of the west, and this was the perfect site. Jean-Baptiste! Jean-Baptiste! Would he remember his instructions?

Why didn't someone come? Where was the health officer? Were they still preventing Joseph from seeing him? Was he to be allowed to die alone, unshriven, and with so much vital information stored up in his mind? He tried to cry out but no sound came from his lips.

A terrifying thought took possession of him. If they did come he would not be able to speak. His hand was too weak to hold a pen. There was nothing he could do.

While still alive, he had become the prisoner of death.

It was late in the evening when the attendant entered the room, followed by a figure in a black cassock. The dying man was unable to do more than move a hand in response to the questions of the priest.

III

The port officer carried the news to De Sérigny. "There was no chance for him," he said, shaking his head. "I knew it when we took him ashore. The plague, it is not to be gainsaid. This much we can do for you and for the great captain who is gone. The body can be placed in a leaden coffin and later we will be permitted to bury him in one of the churches."

De Sérigny, unable to speak, nodded in response.

The officer continued, motioning with his hand in the direction of the scuppers where more figures were wrapped in canvas in readiness to be consigned to the water. "We can do nothing more for you here. Obey all my instructions and the spread of the disease may be checked. But this I predict at the very least: you'll find yourself with a short crew when you're through with it."

"I'm reconciled to that." De Sérigny was finding it hard to speak without giving way to his emotion. "I—I thank you for what you did, señor. Did he—did he send any last messages?"

The officer shook his head. "No, señor, no messages at all."

CHAPTER VII

THE NEWS of D'Iberville's death did not reach Montreal until the fall. It came, in fact, on the day after La Grosse Gerbe had been celebrated at Longueuil and Babette Carré had won the blue pompon for the most original costume.

The Baron of Longueuil was one of the last to hear it. He had been at the parade ground just inside the Porte Lachine, a stretch of flat dry land with no more than a scattering of trees and underbrush. Ordinarily this bit of common, located so conveniently under the town walls, was given over to boys, to much noise and confusion after school hours, to games such as *ostes-moi* and local versions of scalp-the-last and bob-and-mow. The baron had been placed in charge of the defense of the town against the possibility of English attack, and had decreed that all male citizens should drill in squads. He had selected the approach to the Porte as the best spot for the purpose.

On this particular day he had been in a preoccupied mood, for no reason he could have named himself, and he finally reached the conclusion that his presence was more necessary elsewhere. He turned his back on the awkward squads gyrating on the common.

The first intimation that something was wrong came to him when he approached the point of intersection of the Rue St. Joseph with the Rue St. Paul. He always paused here. The house in which he had been born, and where in rapid succession all the oldest sons of the family of Le Moyne including D'Iberville had followed him into the world, stood here and he never failed to give it a glance in passing.

As he crossed the intersection he was surprised to see that a man had stationed himself in the middle of the road and was staring up at the house with a curious intentness.

"Now what is Prévost doing there?" he asked himself, recognizing the man at once.

Pierre Prévost, who served as night watch, was a small individual of the same age as D'Iberville, and as a boy he had followed the latter around like a faithful dog. This might have served as a clue if the baron had been in any position to draw conclusions. He remained in the dark, however, even after noticing that tears were streaming down the cheeks of the little man.

"What is it, Pierre?" asked the baron.

The other did not hear him. At any rate he made no response and the tears continued to pour down his face. The baron repeated his question with no greater success and then gave it up with a shrug of the shoulders. "If I didn't know that Marie rules him with an iron hand," he thought, "I would believe that poor Pierre is drunk."

He kept thinking of the curious behavior of the little man as he continued on his way down the Rue St. Paul and it was then he began to realize that a strange mood had taken possession of many others as well as gentle Pierre Prévost. Something had happened to the town. The streets were oddly quiet and the churches were crowded. It seemed to him that those he passed on the streets were embarrassed at the necessity of meeting his eye. They shuffled by hurriedly and he was sure he could detect in all of them a suggestion of solicitude.

He had part of the answer as soon as he entered his house. The lower hall was crowded. All the members of the household staff were there as well as many of his best friends and acquaintances. They had been talking freely as he came to the door but at his entrance a complete silence fell.

Charles le Moyne stood in the doorway and looked about him silently. He could see Félicité near the kitchen door, looking white-faced and unhappy. She was standing between the cook (who could be recognized only by the flour on her arms, for she had thrown her apron over her face) and a small and dirty gnome who quite obviously was one of the town chimney sweeps. Even the black face of the sweep was streaked with tears.

"Well?" said the baron. After a moment he added, "Which one is it this time?"

Charles Guilmot, a friend who happened to be staying in the house at the time, handed him a letter. "Charles," he said, "you will find here without a doubt the same sad word which has reached us from—from other sources."

The baron looked at the letter and recognized the handwriting of the Sieur de Sérigny. He knew at once what it contained. Everything had drawn close together to form a recognizable picture—the grief of Prévost, the strained attitude of people on the streets, and now the fact that it was Joseph who wrote him. He did not need to be told anything more. He turned silently and walked to the stair, keeping his eyes lowered. When he reached the floor above they heard him go into his cabinet and close the door.

II

Philippe had been one of the spectators but he had kept an eye on Félicité only. He walked over to her now and placed a guiding hand on her elbow. "M'sieur Charles won't want me to go on with my hammering in the addition," he said. "And I can see that you're on the point of bursting into loud wails. He won't want that either. Let's go out to the *cour* where we won't disturb him."

There was a plum tree in the yard, filled with late fruit, and they ensconced themselves on the grass under it. The fence was too high to allow them any view of the river but over its top they could see vivid blue sky and the wooden tower of Bonsecours.

They talked of many things and finally came to a matter which was to affect their whole lives, to send both of them on a long journey across the sea, and to cause them much suffering and unhappiness.

Félicité began it. She had seated herself on the grass tailor fashion and was gathering into her hands some dried heads of clover. Looking up with sudden intentness, she said, "Six of them are gone, Philippe."

He gave a somber nod. "It seems impossible. About M'sieur Pierre. He wasn't like a man, he was a god. To me he was so much a god that I was sure he would never die."

"Will there be enough of them now?" she asked. "To do the work that's still to be done? I hear things that M'sieur Charles says and so I know what has been planned. With so many of them dead . . ." She paused and then went on impulsively, "Doesn't it seem to you, Philippe, that they will need a great deal of help now? That all of us, even a girl like me, should be ready to help in any way at all?"

Philippe looked at her with a rather uneasy air. "What do you think you could do?" he asked.

"I don't know. Very little, I suppose. But—but, Philippe, I would be willing to do anything they might ask."

Philippe's face became clouded with a frown. "I pray every day," he said, "that I'll be allowed to go out with them. I didn't think I would be able to stand it when Antoine left for the south and M'sieur Charles wouldn't let me go. We were friends, Antoine and I, even though he was a Le Moyne and I was a carpenter's apprentice. I've spoken to M'sieur Charles a dozen times about it since and his answer is always the same—that I'm needed here and can't be spared." His voice rose. "Does he think I'm a coward? Does he think I'm fit for nothing but to plane boards and drive nails?"

Félicité's manner changed. There was nothing of the child of ten in the way she looked at him. "He's right," she said. "There wouldn't have been anything for you to do if you'd gone with M'sieur Antoine. All they needed were men who could dig trenches and stand sentry. When the time comes to build the town M'sieur Charles talks about, he'll let you go. You'll be needed then. You ought to be as glad"—she hesitated and a trace of a blush showed on her cheeks—"as glad as I am—that you weren't one of those who went first and died down there."

He had been leaning on an arm and looking out over the top of the fence. Now he swung around and looked at her with surprise. "I never thought of it that way before," he said. "Perhaps you're right about it. I should have known M'sieur Charles had a good reason for keeping me here." He continued to study her. "You talk like a lawyer, Félicité. M'sieur Charles tells everyone how clever you are. I can see he's right."

She was not sure that she liked this. There was constraint as well as admiration in the way he had spoken and she knew instinctively that this would not do. She hastened to set herself right. "It's because I hear M'sieur Charles explain about things. He talks to me all the time. He says now that they'll found a city on the Mississippi in a few years and I'm sure you'll be allowed to go then." She was watching him as she spoke and saying to herself with an emotional intensity she had never experienced before: "It mustn't be until I'm old enough to go with him! Holy Mother Mary, hear my prayer. Don't let him go yet! Don't let him go yet!"

III

The baron did not leave his room at all that day. An unbroken silence met the summons to supper. When the cook carried a tray to his door he shouted at her, in a muffled but passionate tone, "Go away! Go away!"

It was the same thing the next morning. He could be heard pacing about the room but he ignored the calls to breakfast and dinner. By this time the household was in a state of alarm. "Poor M'sieur Charles!" wailed the cook. "He's always been such a good eater and now he must be as empty as St. Benet's boots! And I've such a fine ragout for him!"

They were much relieved when the Superior of the Seminary arrived. Dollier de Casson came into the darkened hallway and shook his head at them when he saw that every pair of eyes in the house was red from weeping.

"It's natural for you to mourn the passing of our great leader, who was a good friend to all of you," he said. "But are you forgetting that it was the Lord's will? It's not for us to question His ways nor His judgment." He nodded his gray head at them vigorously. "When your master comes down he should not see eyes red with tears and heads bent in sorrow. He must find you going about your tasks with a good will. He must not be reminded everywhere he looks of this loss which has fallen so heavily on him."

His eyes darted over the company and came to rest on Félicité. "So, you are the little girl," he said, putting a hand under her chin and raising her face so he could study it. "I was happy, my daughter, when it was decided you were to come and be taught by the Sisters of the Congregation. Do you like it here?"

"I like it very much, m'sieur."

"Do you hear from your mother?"

The girl nodded her head with pride. "Yes, m'sieur. My mother writes letters from Paris. There have been three and the last one was addressed to me because she knew I was at school and could read. Twice," with an important nod, "there was money for me."

His brows drew together at this and she realized that, for some reason she could not understand, he was not entirely pleased. He contented himself with saying, "It is good she thinks of you," and then went on to speak of her record at school. "The Sisters tell me you are a good scholar and an obedient girl. I am proud of you."

Turning about and leaning heavily on a cane, he walked to the foot of the stairs. "I will go up without being announced. It will be easier for him that way."

He was not making it easier for himself. They could hear him stumble many times and pause for breath. But when the cook protested from the foot of the stairs that he must not go any farther he answered with a touch almost of impatience. "We must respect his sorrows, my children. He is so overcome with grief he doesn't want to show his face. I must go to him."

It was an hour before Dollier de Casson returned to the ground floor. The staff had gone about their work in the meantime but they flocked back into the entry hall at the sound of his footsteps. He looked at them closely and then shook his head with approval.

"That is better. I see, my children, that you have heeded my words. When he comes down he must see you just like this." He raised a hand to bless them. "No mortal man may read the purpose of our heavenly Father but we can be sure that He had a reason in letting D'Iberville die. We have a memory now to which we may look up in the dark days ahead of us." He turned and walked slowly toward the door. Before leaving, he glanced back and shook his head sadly. "But we shall never see the like of our great champion again, my children!"

It was not until the next morning that the baron made his appearance. He came down to breakfast and took his place at the head of the table, saying no more than "Good morning." He glanced about the room to see if the customary things had been done. Nothing had been overlooked. There was black at the windows and over the hearth. Everything had been removed from the top of the sideboard: his favorite candlesticks, which were two feet high, the silver salt cellars, the porringers, the *écuelle* with strap-work handles, the pap bowl with the gull badge. Plain dishes had replaced the usual service on the table.

At first he took little interest in the food but gradually his appetite began to assert itself. His hollowness, on which the cook had commented, was forcing him against his will to concern itself again in normal things.

He talked only to Félicité and at first it was all about business matters, the letters which had come, the messages received. When he had finished his meal, however, his manner changed. His expression became set and grave.

He looked slowly about the room. "Six of my brothers are dead!" he declared. "The one on whose strength we always relied has been taken. It won't be easy for those of us who remain to carry on the work. Four left out of ten! Joseph in France, Jean-Baptiste in Louisiana, and Little Antoine in Guiana. And I, at home."

He got to his feet. It had been his intention to leave the room but he hesitated, looked about him, and then addressed Félicité.

"What is the date of your birthday?"

"July eighth, M'sieur Charles."

"That was the day when the storm came at Longueuil. We remember it by that. The letter from my brother, the Sieur de Sérigny, gave me the date of the death of—of D'Iberville, and the time of day. He died on July eighth and at the exact moment that the lights in the chapel went out!"

CHAPTER VIII

THERE WAS a tap on the door and the voice of Félicité called cheerfully, "It's six o'clock, M'sieur Charles!"

The baroness burrowed her head deeper into the pillows. "Six o'clock!" she moaned. "Charles, I *can't* get up to have breakfast with you! . . . Isn't that child getting a little officious? She's been so busy about everything since she finished school."

The baron paid no attention to her half-asleep complaint. He sat up in bed and whisked off his nightcap. He did not need to see that the windows were frosted to the top in order to know that the weather had turned bitterly cold. He hesitated before plunging out on the floor but, once there, he dressed with furious haste. It was not until he had wriggled into his coat that he made any comment.

"I've told her to waken me at six. There's so much to be done these days that I shouldn't go to bed at all."

"*Must* you be so Spartan? You make me feel completely useless. And that child, getting up in time to call you and being so cheerful about it, makes me even more ashamed of myself."

The baron laughed as his cold fingers fumbled with the buttons of his coat. "Just by being here, my heart, you make it easy for me to carry this heavy load of work and worry." He immersed his face in a bowl of water and spluttered at the coldness of it. "I've been keeping it from you but—it's certain now that the English will strike at us as soon as the ice goes out on the rivers. Our advices are that they'll attack us here in Montreal."

He observed how she seemed to cower at this reminder of the danger in which they lived continuously and was sorry it had been necessary to tell her. With affectionate solicitude he thought of the way she had disobeyed orders and had sailed to rejoin him, leaving the children behind in France.

"We'll be ready for them, Claudine, when they come. I'm giving most of my time to preparations."

"I really believe," said the baroness reproachfully, "that you're glad about it."

He had been on the point of leaving the room but at this he walked over and stood beside the heavily curtained bed. "Yes, Claudine, I *am* glad. I confess it. It has irked me that people think I'm nothing but a man of business. They forget I fought in France and in two campaigns here as well as at Lachine, where I got this bad arm. I might have been as good a soldier as any of them—except Pierre, of course—if I hadn't been the eldest son, with all the responsibility on my shoulders." He drew himself up. "And now that the defense of Montreal has been entrusted to me, I'll have the chance to prove it. Are you surprised that I find the prospect stimulating?"

His wife's voice had a suggestion of tears in it. "Why must this dreadful war go on and on and on!"

Félicité was already at breakfast when he reached the dining salon. There was cheer in the warmth of the fire on the hearth and an equal degree of it in the smile with which she greeted him. A pile of papers lay beside his plate and she gave it a pat with her hand. "We're going to have a busy day. And, oh, M'sieur Charles, it was unfortunate you had to go out for supper last night. Monsieur Hertel called about the land."

The cook brought in a loaf of bread, hot from the oven, and made the sign of the cross over it with her knife before cutting off slices for them. The baron took a piece and began to eat it thoughtfully, with an occasional sip from his cup of chocolate.

"You talked to Monsieur Hertel?"

"Yes. He wants now to sell the whole fief of Beloeil instead of the part he offered first. Do you suppose it's because the land fronts on the Richelieu where the English will come?"

"That consideration has helped him make up his mind." The baron indulged in a smile. "It's in an exposed location but I want it. I want to round out our holdings in all directions. What price is my old friend asking?"

"Too much, M'sieur Charles." The businesslike manner of the girl sat oddly on her. She should have been interested in clothes and beaux and the next dance; but here she was, her gray eyes intent and thoughtful, concerned only with the asking price for a two-league strip of land along the Richelieu River. "He wants a thousand livres for the land and another hundred for the *droit de quint.*"

"Much too high!" The baron looked suddenly angry and resentful. "They seem to think the Le Moyne money is inexhaustible. How they come at us, how they add up their bills! But we get around it, don't we? We're sharp, you and I, my small one."

She started to smile but another reminder of the previous evening drove the pleased expression away. As the cook had returned with a platter of broiled fish, she spoke cautiously. "*He* was here also."

"Do you mean——"

The cook left the room, closing the door after her. Félicité said, "Monsieur Benoit, of course."

The baron lost at once all interest in his breakfast. "The thought of that man takes away my appetite. I'm sorry you had to see him. I suppose he asked you a hundred questions?"

The girl nodded. "But he gets no satisfaction out of me any more. I've found the way to deal with him. I begin to talk quickly and I nod my head at him. He thinks I'm telling him something important and he can't hear a word of it. That makes him frantic. He waves his arms at me and says, 'Come! Hold! Not so fast, I implore you. My good girl, have regard for my infirmity.' I go right on and he never does find out what I've been saying." Her voice took on a belligerent note. "It's just as well, M'sieur Charles, for what I'm saying wouldn't please old Chin-in-Boots at all."

"Did he tell you why he called?"

"He hinted at it. As far as I could make out of his muttering and head shaking, M'sieur de Mariat has sustained some heavy losses."

"Again!" cried the baron. He put his cup down on the table with such violence that Félicité expected it to fly into pieces. "Must the hat be passed for him a second time? I think it's nothing but an excuse to get more money out of us. This time I shall refuse."

The girl pretended to be absorbed in eating and did not look up for several moments. What she was concerned about actually was a doubt of the wisdom of mentioning a deduction of her own. Finally she said, "M'sieur Charles, I—I think he expects you to refuse."

"He might readily enough expect a refusal after what I said to him the first time."

"He expects it and he—he has a weapon to use in bringing you around."

"A weapon?" The baron had no more interest in breakfast. He turned in his chair and regarded her with a frown. "What do you mean?"

"It may be no more than a guess but I know that it's true. There's no proof I can give you. He made no threats and he didn't say a word I can repeat. And yet—M'sieur Charles, there was a hint back of everything he said. There was a threat in his manner." She suddenly lost her grown-up air and looked at him like a child who sees trouble ahead and is ready to break into tears. "M'sieur Charles, I'm afraid of him! He's an evil man!"

The baron was annoyed rather than disturbed by what she had said. "Do you think he's found some secret in my past to hold over me? I as-

sure you I've nothing on my conscience. Until Monsieur Benoit lets his
terrible secret out of the bag, I'm not going to lose any sleep over it." He
took up the first letter on the pile. "Have you looked at these?"

She nodded. "Yes. There's nothing pressing in the lot. I can attend
to most of them for you."

"Good! I find that I'm developing quite a dislike for detail. I'm only
too glad to leave it in your hands." He looked up as a sudden thought
occurred to him. "Sometime this morning you must see Philippe. Tell
him that, war or no war, I want that addition built on the warehouses on
the Quay des Canots. Please don't forget it, my small one."

Forget it! Félicité indulged in an inner laugh. She was happy to have
a reason for seeing Philippe, a real reason in the way of duty, instead of
the excuses she so often invented. This, she said to herself, was going to
be a pleasant day.

She got to her feet and with a quick pat shook into place the *considérations* she was wearing. These were panniers over the skirt which
fashion had long before decreed in France for morning wear and which
had just recently become the practice in the colony. To be allowed
considérations was the first acknowledgment that the days of girlhood
were over.

"I'll see Philippe as soon as I'm through with the letters," she said.

II

At one side of the busy establishment of René Fezeret, the armorer
and silversmith, there was a narrow lane. Above this, on a neatly carved
board stretching from building to building, was a sign which read:

PHILIPPE GIRARD ET CIE.

When Félicité turned in here, accompanied by Lisa, one of the maids,
she was aware that her heart was beating fast. It was always this way
when she knew that she was going to see him, particularly since he had
become a tall and serious-minded man and had set up in business in
Montreal for himself.

He was doing quite well. It would have been a curious thing if he had
failed of success, for the baron was his silent partner and saw to it, with
Félicité to remind him constantly, that the concern kept busy. Félicité
had superintended every detail, even to the extent of purchasing the
books and making the first entries in them in her neat handwriting. He
had relied on her for everything, except one thing, the selection of the
clothes which he was to wear as a man of affairs. This had been a matter
which he kept a secret between himself and the tailor but he had made
an excuse the first time of wearing them to visit the Le Moyne house
so she could see him in his new glory. The coat was blue, of course, and

a most handsome one indeed, with buckram lining in the tails to make them stand out in the fashionable way. On the tailor's advice he wore his cravat tied in the steinkirk manner, a careless knotting of the linen (which got its name from a battle where the French officers had been taken by surprise and had been forced to dress hurriedly before sallying out to fight), and he had rolled his stockings up over his knees to cover the ends of his breeches. All this was strictly *de rigueur* but he had not been so fortunate in one important respect. Félicité's heart had sunk when she saw how far the tailor had gone in the matter of buttons.

She had tried not to hurt his feelings but something in her expression gave it away. He stopped his prideful pacing and looked at her with a disturbed frown.

"What's wrong with it?" he had asked. "Is it the coat?"

"Oh no, Philippe. The coat is a splendid coat. It's truly a miracle of well-fitting."

"The waistcoat, then?"

"No, no! It's so nice and long and the pattern is beyond compare."

"The—the breeches?"

"The breeches are perfect." She was afraid by this time that his feelings were going to be seriously hurt. "It's not a matter a lady should mention but you look *very* well in the breeches."

"Then," he asked in a despondent tone, "what is it? I know I've made some terrible mistake. It will be a kindness if you'll tell me."

"I swear there's no fault. Oh, perhaps there's a button or so too many. But what of that? It's a matter of no importance."

"So, that's it!" Philippe looked ruefully down the front of his coat. "Now that you've called my attention to it, I can see there *are* too many." His face looked red and unhappy. "I suppose I must expect to find that my taste is bad."

Félicité's heart sank. "Now I've hurt his feelings and he'll never get over it!" she thought. Then her common sense came to the rescue. "Still, it was better to let him find out before any outsiders could laugh at him. *That* he would never forget."

She touched the lapel of his coat and gave the problem of the buttons serious consideration. "Now let me see. There are fourteen on the coat. Perhaps it would be better to cut them down to—well, eight. Fortunately it's going to be possible to change them around without spoiling the style of the coat. On the pockets we'll make it three instead of five." To herself she was saying, "That tailor, that beast without taste, to do this to my poor Philippe!" "Now turn around. On the tails we can dispense with a few more and then, *parbleu,* you will be as correct as any great nobleman coming right out of the hands of the smartest tailor in Paris!"

But Philippe had not been deceived. He had known then that there was much for him to learn.

Félicité was thinking of this as she turned into the lane and walked under the sign. She said to herself: "Philippe is a quick one to learn. Since then he has found out everything for himself. He's as perfect in his manners now as M'sieur Charles himself."

The lane ended in a small rectangle of yard with a frame building two stories in height occupying one side of it. Here Philippe lived and carried on his trade. The ground floor was his shop and supply room, his living quarters were in the sharply pointed second story.

A pleasant odor of wood was noticeable as soon as the door was opened. Philippe was at the far end, hammering busily on a frame base which would become in time a gantry for the support of kegs of ale in a tavern cellar. To Félicité's left, as she stood in the doorway, was a towering pile of miscellaneous articles which represented the lifetime collection of Old Kirkinhead. The builder had left the lot to Philippe, saying in his will that someday it would make him a rich man. All it had done so far was to take up valuable space and Félicité had urged him many times to get rid of it.

Someone was stirring about in the pile, for suddenly there was a loud crash and the whole structure gave a heave. A cloud of dust rose from it. A moment later a head appeared above the pile. It was a curious head, fringed with a dusty mop of hair and untidy whiskers, and with a pair of eyes of differing sizes. The larger one had a fixed and glassy quality. This was Polycarpe Bonnet, who served Philippe in the capacity of assistant.

"Good morning, Carpe," said Félicité.

The assistant paid no attention to her, his gaze being fixed on his employer, who had dropped his work and was walking toward them. In a voice of froglike depth, which issued incongruously from his meager frame, he asked, "Are you suited with me, master, are you suited?"

"I don't pay you to waste your time in that pile of rubbish. *Sacristi!* Haven't I told you that often enough?"

"There's a fortune in it, master!" cried the assistant. "I'm sure of it. Hidden in there are things that'll make you rich. Give me the time and I'll find them for you. Bits of finery and plumes and glass and metal. Perhaps even jewelry. There's no telling what's to be found."

Philippe looked at Félicité and allowed the lid of one eye to drop a mere fraction of distance. "Carpe isn't interested in fortunes. All he's concerned about is women, big women, the bigger the better. If you offered him his choice of a fortune or a giantess as a wife, he'd take the giantess every time."

The assistant beamed with pride at hearing himself discussed in this way. "I like armfuls," he said. "If they're small they have sharp tongues. If they're thin they complain all the time. I like them tall and fat and as round in the middle as a bushel basket."

"Well, Carpe, you won't find any fat women in that pile of junk," said his master, "so I suggest you get back to work." He turned to Félicité. "It must be that M'sieur Charles has something special for me to do that you come out on a cold morning like this."

Félicité stated her errand. As she did so, she studied his face with anxious eyes. He had been working hard and it was beginning to show. He was thin and a little pale. She decided that a word of restraint was needed. "He's in a great hurry but you mustn't start the outside work while this cold weather lasts. You'll make yourself ill if you do."

"You're a managing little person, aren't you?"

She provided further proof of her capacity for management by going to a battered old pine desk which stood against the wall of the shop. It was piled high with letters and sheets of paper and memorandum slips. There was a layer of dust over all of it.

"Philippe!" she said accusingly. "How can you expect to keep your affairs straight this way? You have a proper set of books, a *grand livre* and a *livre de compte*. You should enter the items each day."

"But it's such a small business!" he protested. "Don't you think people would laugh if I started posting things up in a ledger? Anyway I can keep all the details in my head."

Félicité pointed a stern finger at him. "So! You can carry all the details in your head! But suppose, my careless M'sieur Philippe, you had a disagreement with a customer and went to law. You go before the *juge royal* and then what do you find? You find that memory is of no account. That judge, he wants papers, bills, receipts, agreements. He will shake his wig and say, 'I'm sorry, m'sieur, but I must give the verdict against you.'"

"But I've forgotten all you told me about keeping the books."

This was the chance she had been looking for. "I'll keep them for you until you learn. I'll come in each afternoon, and you'll give me the items to be posted. You'll soon be able to do it yourself."

She decided to take full advantage of the opening thus provided. Seating herself on a creaky stool, she swung around on it slowly. "Of course, when you're married," she said, "your wife will keep them for you. You'll be thinking of marriage soon?"

Philippe gave her one quick look and then glanced away. He cleared his throat uneasily. "Yes," he said finally. "I suppose I will. Sooner or later. St. Joseph, I was very sure about it once! I intended to marry early and I used to think"—he smiled self-consciously, keeping his eyes fixed on the sawdust floor—"I used to think I'd wait until you grew up. Wasn't that an idea for a simple fellow like me to have?" He added hastily, "I soon realized, of course, that it wouldn't do."

Félicité's heart was pounding. She also kept her eyes averted. "I'm very much flattered, Philippe," she said, "that you—that you thought of me."

He looked startled. "Not flattered! You might be amused. You've grown into such a fine young lady and M'sieur Charles thinks so much of you that he'll have plans about a husband for you. I saw long ago that I would have to give up the idea."

The shop was a dingy place, with dusty bits of machinery here and there and with shavings and cobwebs hanging from the beams. The windows were piled so high with sawdust that little light got through. But it seemed to Félicité that it had suddenly been transformed. Beams of celestial light were coming through the panes instead of the dull sun light of a cold winter morning. "He wanted to marry me!" The words kept running through her mind like a beautiful litany. "He still wants to marry me! I can see it."

"I don't think I'll be in any hurry about getting a wife," Philippe went on. "But perhaps I'll have to come to it someday."

Félicité said to herself: "Sooner than you think, my sweet Philippe my loved one! Much sooner than you think. Now that you've said this I can take the matter right into my own hands!"

It was probably not in her mind to say anything more at the moment on this all-important matter but in any event she did not have the op portunity. There was a loud knock at the door and Philippe answered it to find that his landlord, the armorer, was paying him a visit.

"Philippe!" cried Monsieur Fezeret, his eyes gleaming with excite ment. "They're coming! Word's arrived that the English are getting a fleet together to attack Quebec. At the same time an expedition will come up by way of Lake George and the Richelieu to attack Montreal."

Félicité's eyes turned from the face of the armorer to that of Philippe and she was dismayed to find that he looked eager and excited.

"Surely they won't move in this kind of weather," he said. "How did the news come?"

"I don't know. We have spies, of course, in Boston and New York, just as they have spies here. I suppose the word came through them. It's certain this time. They're coming!"

Philippe turned and ran for the open wooden steps which gave access to his living quarters above. He vanished in a few seconds and they could hear his quick footsteps on the floor above, crossing and recrossing the room. When he returned he was attired in a scout coat with hood at tached, trousers with fur along the seams, and heavy winter moccasins.

"It's come at last!" he said. "The chance I've been waiting for. M'sieur Charles agreed months ago that I'm to serve at Fort Chambly. At last I'm to be allowed to fight for my country!"

He looked at Félicité, his eyes sparkling. Then, swept away by a sense of triumph, he took her by the waist and swung her up into the air above his head. He held her suspended there for several moments and then lowered her to the floor.

"I'm a man at last!" he cried. "I'm not a carpenter, tinkering away at little chores while other men fight. I'm to be one of them."

When Félicité said nothing, her mind being too full of all the possible consequences of these alarming developments, he addressed himself to the armorer. "There will be a call for us this afternoon," he said, nodding his head and smiling. "And there'll be a call, m'sieur, for every weapon in your shop. You'll have a busy winter forging new stocks."

Monsieur Fezeret dropped snuff, of the very best variety from Brazil, on his thumb and drew it up fastidiously into his nostrils. "I'll be needing more assistance. If you're closing up, Philippe, I might make use of this fellow of yours. Come over here, my man, and let me get a good look at you."

Polycarpe came forward doubtfully. "I think perhaps I wouldn't suit you, m'sieur," he said.

"I've a way of making my helpers suit me," declared the armorer. "There's plenty of work done wherever I am. The sparks fly, the hammers ring, the sweat comes out on the brow! Oh, you'll suit me, my man."

"The sparks might fly livelier and the hammers ring louder, m'sieur, if you got another man."

"I'll always be right behind you with a heated ramrod," said the armorer cheerfully, "and when the sparks don't fly and the hammer doesn't ring the way I like it, I'll just touch that ramrod to the fleshiest part of your body. And after that you'll work hard enough to suit me."

"How very lucky it is that I can speak something of the Iroquois tongue," Philippe said to Félicité. "I'll be especially useful now. I've been spending my spare time with that old chief that the Sieur de Bienville sent up from the south and now I'm able to speak his lingo as well. At any rate I can make out what he says, and he seems to understand me." Then a more sober mood took possession of him. "The defenses at the fort are in need of repair so I may be sent over at once. I may not see you for a long time, Félicité."

To herself she said, "I may never see him again!" It required all her will power to keep her feelings from showing on her face.

"I must report at once." Philippe was in too exalted a mood to perceive how upset she was. He reached out suddenly, raised her hand to his lips, and kissed it. "When I come back I'll be able for the first time in my life to look everyone straight in the eye! You will think of me sometimes?"

"I will think of you sometimes." She blinked back the tears and smiled at him. "*Au revoir,* Philippe. You will come back a great hero."

When he had gone, followed by the armorer, she began to pray to herself. "Kind Mother in heaven, look down on him and bring him safely back! See that he doesn't throw his life away as so many of our brave men do. Above all, kind Mother, see that he isn't captured by the Iroquois!"

Polycarpe Bonnet had been watching her closely, and nodding and winking and achieving muscular contortions of his face which were intended to be consolatory. It was apparent now that the large eye was a glass one and that moreover it was a poor fit, for it rolled alarmingly in its socket. He had a long sharp nose and a jutting underjaw, between which his mouth seemed to lose itself.

"Take him, ma'amselle!" he said abruptly. "He's a rare one, that master of mine. *Moi-même,* I'm like most men, with an eye for every pretty face." He winked so energetically that the muscles of his face seemed to be playing tag. "This master of mine was born to be a good husband. You don't see many of that kind. If you'll have a word of advice from one who's never been suited in women, it's this: take him and marry him. You'll never regret it."

"But," cried Félicité, giving way to her tears, "how can I take him? He's gone away. He—he may never come back!"

CHAPTER IX

A FORTNIGHT later word came of the death of Tante Seulette. It was a shock because there had been no previous intimation of illness. She had, it appeared, gone to bed in her usual health and in an unusually sharp temper, and in the morning they found her dead. Félicité wanted to set out for the château at once but the baron refused to allow it. There was a blizzard blowing down from the north and the journey across the river would be too dangerous.

The girl had to be content with spending long hours in church and burning innumerable candles for the soul of the strange old woman. She was filled with a sense of guilt which only time could assuage. The fact that Tante Seulette had refused repeatedly to see her and had returned no answers to messages did not serve to lay the ghost in her mind.

The day after the funeral, the last day of March as it happened, the storm ceased and then almost immediately there was a change in the weather. The air became warm and the people of Montreal smiled as they met and said to each other, "By St. Joseph, we are going to have an early spring!" It came earlier even than they expected. One night there was a sound like a clap of thunder, followed by lesser rumblings and roarings. By morning the ice was well on the move.

That day a mounted messenger arrived from Quebec. He had started out with a heavy coat of bearskin and it was not to be wondered at that he was perspiring profusely when he rode in through the Porte St. Martin. He shouted as he rode through the streets and waved a paper above his head. He went straight to the Le Moyne house on the Rue St. Paul, for the baron was acting as governor of the city in the absence of Monsieur de Ramezay. The baron was out and so Félicité was the first to hear the news.

The messenger looked surprised when he was shown into the cabinet and found her sitting in the baron's chair with a pile of papers in front of her and wearing a completely preoccupied air. Then he recalled something that he had heard from the King's messenger years before, and he smiled and nodded his head.

"Jean Carrier told me about you. You came to see him with Charles le Moyne when you were a small girl. He remembered only that you sat in a corner and never took your eyes off his face, and that you looked very wise."

He was a young man, tall and strong and very dark; and bold, as one had to be to ride the frozen trails between the three cities of New France. His smile grew broader and he leaned down over the desk.

"You're much too handsome to be sitting at a desk and working over a lot of papers," he said.

She paid no attention to this but held up her hand for the letter. "What is it you bring?" she demanded.

"The best of news," said the messenger. "But should I tell it to you when you refuse me even as much as a kind smile after riding all these miles? That is a point which must be considered." Then he laughed loudly and tossed the letter he carried on the table. "When that's opened you'll find that the English have decided not to attack us—not, at least until the fall. The word comes direct from Boston and there's no reason to doubt it. If you care to drop a hint to the crowd who followed me here the word will spread over the town like the cowpox!"

Félicité sprang up with delight written all over her face. The last word from Chambly had been that there were no losses and that all members of the garrison were in good health. Philippe, then, was safe; safe, at least, until the fall, and anything might happen between now and then. The old King might even come to his senses and make peace with the English.

"Thank you, m'sieur!" she cried. "As the bearer of such good news you will be a hero to the people of Montreal. But first we must find the baron and put this letter in his hands. After that the church bells will ring and there will be a great celebration!"

"It's still my opinion," said the messenger, who was finding her even more attractive now that her eyes were sparkling and her cheeks were flushed, "it's my considered opinion that you are wasting your time in a dusty office filled with moldy papers. Ah, ma'amselle! That I might be the one to teach you better ways of keeping yourself occupied!"

II

Two days later the townspeople were massed along the waterfront to witness the return of the volunteers from Chambly. The *chaloupes* in which the crossing was made proved hard to handle in the flooding waters of the great river. It had been intended to land back of Normandin Island but the current swept them along to the extreme tip of La Canoterie Royale before they could make the shore. The anxious townspeople had to move along the waterfront in order to follow this tortuous crossing, hurrying first down the Rue Capitale and then spreading out over the snow-covered sweep of La Commune.

Félicité, excited and happy, was right in the van. She was wearing for the first time a new beaver coat and hat, the baron's latest *épingles*,[1] and the glow in her cheeks was due as much to pride as to the nip of the wind. The coat came almost to her ankles and it had leg-o'-mutton sleeves, drawn in snugly at the wrists and tied with small tails of the fur. The hat was three-cornered and it sported a jaunty pompon on top. Not all the dressmakers of Paris, meeting in a snipping, ripping, basting, and sewing convention could have fashioned anything more becoming. She was fully conscious of this and also of the fact that there were only four other beaver coats in the town.

Beside her tramped Polycarpe Bonnet. As his legs were unusually short, he found it hard to keep pace with her, and finally gave up the effort.

"Ma'amselle," he panted, coming to a stop, "is there any need for such a hurry?"

"So much need," she exclaimed, "that I wish I had wings!"

There was nothing to be done but follow. "I too," said Carpe, "am glad he's coming back. I've had enough of this new master, this devil with a prong, this driver who's never content with anything but a gallop! He wouldn't be suited with me if I worked twenty-four hours a day." He went on in a tone of complaint in which, nevertheless, it was possible to detect a hint of satisfaction. "And that's not all."

"What else have you to complain about?"

He gave her a wink with his good eye. "Women," he said. "You're young and you're innocent and this may not be suited to your ears—but I must tell you that things go on in this town! Ah, the winkings and the raising of eyebrows and the dropping of handkerchiefs and the rolling of hips! You meet them with a father or a husband or a brother and they walk right by you, and not as much as the flutter of a lash. But wait until their men are out of town! With so many away at Chambly, a man like me has no time left to himself at all."

He turned toward her and indulged in another wink of such broadness that his glass eye swiveled unsteadily. They were facing the river but any onlooker would have sworn he was staring at the mountain.

"I'm going to leave you as soon as they land," he whispered. "Some of the men coming back are husbands and fathers. After what's been going on, I wouldn't be able to look them straight in the eye!"

[1] The word *"épingles"* had come to have a special meaning in the colony, being applied to any gift to a woman. Departing guests gave *épingles* to the maidservants, and every transaction carried a small sum for the seller's wife which went by that name.

The boats were pulling in to the landing. Philippe was in the first and he saw her and waved an arm in greeting. But when the party had landed and he came over to speak to her, he became assailed suddenly by doubts.

"Is it really you?" he asked.

"Of course. Have you forgotten me already? They say it always happens when men go away to the wars."

He drew in a deep breath. "You're beautiful!" he said fervently.

Félicité answered, "It must be my new coat. Do you like it?" Inwardly she was in a turmoil. "At last he's really looking at me!" she thought. I had been an effort to keep her voice cool and casual. She was not sure she had succeeded. But, with him looking at her with his intense dark eyes did it matter?

"It's a very fine coat," he said. "But that has nothing to do with the way you look. You would look just as lovely in rags." He gazed down into the glowing eyes under the tricorne hat (she could not control her eyes as she had done her voice) and found himself carried away, spellbound. It was with the greatest effort that he regained the power of speech. "I don't understand it," he said. "You were a girl when I left. I was only a month ago and yet now I come back and find that you've become a woman."

"A month is such a long time," she said with a sigh. It was not at all an unhappy sigh. "And it can make such differences. You, Philippe, look pale and thin. You've been working too hard, I can see." Realizing that the golden moment might pass by if she distracted his attention, she asked, "And you really think that I've changed?"

Philippe's eyes had never left her face. He said again, "You're beautiful!" with even more feeling than before.

After that neither of them found it possible to say a word. They faced each other silently. There was no need for speech. They were telling each other with their eyes all that it was necessary for them to know. The milling about of the eager crowds, the excited greetings, the laughter, faded out of their consciousness.

"People are looking at us," breathed Félicité after a long time had passed. "I think we had better walk on."

They started off slowly, her hand under his arm. Quite unaware of the direction they were taking, they began to cross the untrodden snow which stretched from the rear of the Church of Bonsecours to the banks of the river. They were conscious of difficulty in raising their feet with each step but paid no attention to it until it became physically impossible to go any farther. By this time they were up to their knees in the snow. They stopped and stared at each other as though asking, "How did we get ourselves in this fix?" Félicité, still holding to his arm, began to laugh.

"People will think we're mad," she said.

"I *am* mad!" declared Philippe. He looked away from her but his eyes, which traveled up the wide stretch of the broiling river, saw nothing at all. "I've discovered in the last few minutes, Félicité, that I am in love with you!"

Now that he had thus come to the point of declaring himself, she found that she was perfectly cool, although up to that very moment she had been filled with conflicting emotions and had not known what she should say or do.

"Yes," she whispered, "you told me so before."

His eyes came back from the distance at that. He looked at her in amazement. "I told you!" he exclaimed.

Her head went back and she looked up into his eyes with the supreme happiness and confidence which the first moments of declared love beget. "Back there," she said. "With your eyes. You were telling me then that you love me and it—it made me very happy."

"Did they—my eyes, I mean—tell you anything else?"

"I believed they told me many things, Philippe."

"Did they say I was going to speak to M'sieur Charles at once, tonight, and ask his consent to our marriage?"

She answered in a dreamy voice. "Yes, Philippe, I am sure they said that too."

"And are you—are you willing to have me speak to him?"

"Yes," she whispered, "I am willing."

Philippe would have given an exultant leap into the air if he had not been so firmly anchored by the snow. As it was, he contented himself with saying: "You have said it! I'll never let you take those words back. You've said you are willing to marry me, that you—that you love me."

"Yes, Philippe." Her voice seemed to be coming from far away. "I do love you. I've loved you for a very long time. As long, I think, as I can remember."

Then, as is inevitable at such moments, he began to find himself filled with doubts. "M'sieur Charles may be very angry about it. He'll think me a poor suitor for you, my Félicité. And he'll be right. I *am* a poor suitor. You deserve someone much better than me. I have nothing to offer you except my love. My prospects are not good."

Félicité answered with a smile. "I am content and I am very happy."

"What if M'sieur Charles refuses his consent?"

Félicité gave a light laugh. "If M'sieur Charles says no to us I'll find some way to make him give in."

They turned then and began to plod their way back to the street. Félicité's hand dropped from his arm. "And now we must begin to talk about other things or everyone will know what has happened," she said. "Did you—did you see any Indians at the fort?"

"Not one. Not even a friendly Indian. But we were busy all the time. We completely overhauled the defenses of the fort. I had charge of the building of a new bastion." He was speaking in a casual tone but it was clear he was proud of having been given so much responsibility. "The fort could stand a siege now, even if all the warriors of the Long House came up the river against us."

"I'm glad the fort is so strong," said Félicité. "But I'm more glad still that the Indians aren't going to attack."

He shook his head in dissent. "How can we be sure? M'sieur Charles isn't taking any risks. We're going back soon. I expect to be at the fort all through the summer."

They had reached the street again and she had no chance to express her dismay at this announcement. A complete silence had fallen, for the banner which the Recluse had made with her own hands for the defending forces was being brought ashore. The youngest member of the company had been awarded the honor of carrying it. He was perhaps fifteen years old and so tall that he was able to keep it elevated so that everyone could see.

The head of the Blessed Virgin was on one side, and on the other the Recluse had embroidered the words of the prayer she had conceived:

> Our enemies rely on the power of their arms,
> And we on the powerful intercessions of Her whom we revere,
> And invoke as Queen of Angels.
> She is terrible as an army.
> And with Her assistance we will vanquish our enemies.

With one accord the people went down on their knees in the snow as the banner was carried past them. Some lowered their heads in prayer, others kept their eyes fixed on this visual manifestation of the intercession which had won them this respite from danger. None had any doubts on that score. The beautiful young woman who had entered the cell behind the altar of the Congrégation de Notre Dame sixteen years before, and on whom no human eye had since rested, had become a symbol of their faith.

When Félicité rose to her feet she found that Dollier de Casson was standing beside her. A full head above everyone, in spite of his stoop, he was keeping his eyes fixed on the proud back of the boy and the white banner curling slowly in the breeze. She saw that his eyes were filled with tears.

"When the voice of our blessed mademoiselle is heard through the grille, it seems very weak," he said in a tone little above a whisper. "We are beginning to fear that soon her long wait will be at an end. How long and how faithfully she has waited to be taken!"

The procession had passed on down the Rue St. Paul. The head of the

Sulpician order glanced at Félicité and smiled. "I see you seldom, my daughter," he said, "but I make a point of hearing about you often. I hear about the great help you are to your M'sieur Charles. That is good. He needs help, your M'sieur Charles, for truly a heavy burden has been laid on his shoulders."

He was watching her with affectionate concern as he spoke. His benevolence, in fact, seemed to wrap her about like a warm cloak.

"I try, monsieur, to do everything for him that I can."

"You have a wise head on your very young shoulders, my daughter. Do you know that your mother came to me when she was in need of counsel and that it was in part because of what I said that she left you here when she returned to France? Because of that I feel a double responsibility for you. I've been glad to see you grow up so healthy and happy." He glanced away from her then and let his eyes rest on Philippe. It seemed to her that he had divined their secret. "There will be a decision for you to make soon, I think, my daughter. It may prove hard. If the decision is too hard, I hope you'll come to me as your mother did. Perhaps our kind Father will lend me the understanding to be of help."

CHAPTER X

ENSCONCED behind the door of the salon which was open enough to command a view of the front entrance, Félicité saw Philippe enter that evening. He was wearing his best blue coat (the one which had caused so much trouble) and she could see that he was pale. He started up the stairs with the automatic stride of a man going to the gallows.

"What will he say?" she wondered to herself. "Will he be as firm about it as I told him he must? Ah, if I could only listen!" Then she indulged in a low laugh. "My poor Philippe, how frightened he looked! He will be glad when it's all over."

The talk upstairs proved longer than she had expected. Was Philippe not being firm with the baron after all? To occupy herself, she played a game of trictrac with the baroness and was too preoccupied to do anything else but win, which sent Claude-Elizabeth upstairs and to bed in a gently melancholy mood. A drone of voices still came from behind the closed door of the cabinet. Félicité was compelled to find other means of filling in the time. "What are they saying now?" ran her thoughts as she made her way to the kitchen. "Is it the dowry which is taking up so much time?"

She found the kitchen deserted and decided to take advantage of this chance to inspect the brass and copper utensils which hung on the walls in seemingly endless variety. They looked most imposing, these gleaming pots and pans, these casseroles and colanders of all sizes, these *brassières* and dripping pans. A quick glance at the rest of the equipment, however, revealed that there were blemishes. The tinderboxes, she found, had not known the touch of cloth and polish for much too long a time, and there was an aging mess of salad materials in the marble mortar. "I must see to *this!*" she said aloud.

At this moment she heard the front door close and, dropping the tinderbox which she was holding, she ran to the entrance hall. That Philippe had gone was clear to her at once, for the baron was standing alone at the head of the stairs, and he called down as soon as he saw her, "Will you come up, please, my small one?"

The first real doubt found its way into her mind. If the results of the interview had been favorable she would have been called in before Philippe left. Every second of the time which had elapsed since he arrived she had been waiting for the summons, picturing to herself the pleasantly dramatic look she would discover on the face of her guardian as a prelude to the joining of hands and the happiness in Philippe's eyes which would be her first proof that all had gone well.

As she climbed the stairs, in such a despondency as she had never before experienced, she said to herself: "He has said no. And now what am I to do about it?"

II

The baron did not come to the point with his usual dispatch. They sat across the desk from each other and he studied the tips of his fingers with an elaborately casual air. Finally he said, "I must confess that it was a surprise." When she made no response he added, "I was sure you would bring to—to matrimonial questions the same common sense you show in transacting business."

"But, M'sieur Charles! I love him!"

She was certain now that the interview had failed of its purpose. There was a desperate note in her voice.

"That," said the baron, "is what I've been told. I'm not finding any fault with you for falling in love. These fancies are natural enough when you're young. But I find it hard to understand why you haven't seen for yourself that such a match is impossible."

"But why? Why? I can't see any reason. I've loved Philippe from the first time I saw him. Every dream of happiness I've ever had has been bound up with him."

The baron's manner became less assured. His eyes dropped whenever they encountered hers and he pretended to be much concerned with the design of the new sander on the desk.

"Of course! Of course!" he said. "It's natural for girls to fall in love with nice young men. But, Félicité, they don't marry them."

"Please, M'sieur Charles! Look at me!" she pleaded. "This is so important for my happiness that we must understand each other completely. I want to know exactly what you are thinking and to make you see what's in my mind. I see no reason why it should be out of the question for me to marry Philippe. It's true that he's poor——"

The baron lifted a hand and gave an absent-minded twirl to one of the ends of his mustache. He said, quoting a proverb, " 'He who is born for a small loaf will never have a large one.' "

"That is wrong!" she cried. "This is a new world and fortunes can be made here. Why can't he be as successful as your father? As you, even?"

"As to that, it's a matter of temperament. Philippe is a fine young fellow and he has a great deal of ability. He has character and he's honest and he has skill in his trade. But at the same time he's quiet and unselfish and unassuming. Men who are quiet and unselfish and unassuming never make fortunes, my child. The best your Philippe could ever do would be to make a comfortable living for himself and his family. He'll always be a poor man."

"I've been told you thought differently about him when he stood up to you over the delay in finishing the new mill. He was only a boy then but he told you the truth. You were sure he had a bright future."

The baron nodded his head and smiled. "I remember it. It was on the day when Pierre came back from the conquest of Newfoundland. He *did* stand up to me and he told me some things I hadn't understood before." Having said this, however, he gave his head a shake. "It's hard to make the difference clear. Philippe is the kind of man who will make money for other people but not for himself."

"If that's so," said Félicité eagerly, "he needs a wife like me. Perhaps I've enough selfishness to supply his lack of it. And why do you think he's not good enough for me? I'm not an heiress. My family, about which I know nothing at all, can't have been any better than his." She paused and looked at him beseechingly. "You've always been so kind, M'sieur Charles, and now you're playing the cruel guardian after all. Why is it? Don't you like Philippe?"

"I like him, of course. I'm very fond of him and I admire him. He's a fine young man. He doesn't drink and never plays at romestick in the taverns. He's making himself into a solid citizen." The baron dropped the sander and spread both hands out in front of him. "My child, I'm not going to make the explanation that has been necessary, I expect, in every family since marriage became an institution and young people were foolish enough to fall in love. You know that the French people, being sound and logical, have a conception of matrimony which has been found the most satisfactory over the centuries, that marriages with us are on a basis of equality and suitability. You've heard all that many times."

"Yes. I've heard it many times. And I've never believed it."

"Young people seldom do, my child."

"No one believes in that system until they are old and have forgotten what love is." She leaned closer, her eyes bright with entreaty. "Sometimes love must be considered. When a girl has never thought of anyone else, when she has always loved one man—and so much!—when life would be nothing without him—surely then, M'sieur Charles, it's right to marry for love and for no other reason!"

The baron shook his head. "All love affairs are exactly like that. Always it's a grand passion which must override rules and tradition. Always! A thousand ardent lovers have pleaded their cases in those same words. But in the end, my Félicité, the grand passion fades, and it's the marriage made on a basis of common sense and mutual interests which goes on." He suddenly reached out and patted her hand. "It's hard, my small one, but you'll get over it in time. Everyone does."

She shook her head. "No! You may laugh but this—this *is* different."

"As I said before, I'm not going to din the usual explanation into your ears." The baron had lost the sense of reluctance and discomfort with which he had begun this talk. He had become as much in earnest as she was. "But there's a special explanation necessary in your case. I want to make this clear to you at the start: that if you don't want to do what I suggest I shall drop the matter at once and that I won't lose any of my affection for you because of it. That"—he smiled at her with so much proof of his feeling that she did not doubt he meant what he was saying— "is impossible. I've grown too fond of you to let anything change me where you are concerned. And in case you can't agree with me you may then marry your Philippe with my blessing."

She was listening and watching with an air of the most intense earnestness.

"There are four of us left. Four out of ten! You know, Félicité, how much remains to be done. Are we going to be capable of it? Sometimes I have doubts. Always nowadays I look at my mail with apprehension, fearing there is more bad news, that the ranks have been reduced still further. I'm getting more certain that we'll need all the help we can get. The stage has been reached where we can't stand any more losses, when we must add to the ranks instead."

She nodded her head solemnly. "Yes, M'sieur Charles. I know that."

"But haven't you known that I've come to regard you as a member of the family? You haven't the name but I think of you as a Le Moyne; and as a Le Moyne you may be called upon someday to play a full part. If you are willing."

"But what could I do?"

"I've nothing to suggest at this moment. You can't go out and fight Indians and you can't command a fort in the wilderness. But you have a great talent for administration and, if you did no more than what you're doing now for us, you would be playing a real and important part. There's always the possibility also of making a good marriage. You might someday bring wealth into the family, and make a connection for us which would be of great help. We will need both.

"But," he added with a vehemence which he had not displayed before, "you can't continue to help us if you marry now. Particularly if you marry a young man like Philippe with no connections and no prospects. You may think it possible but I say—no, no, no! You'll begin to have children and you'll settle down to a busy life of your own."

It was clear that the words of the baron had made a deep impression on her. She had become as firmly committed to the family ideals and aims as any of the surviving members. No amount of work ever seemed too much, no hours too long. But it had never occurred to her to think of herself as a member of the family, and as bound by the same need for unquestioning adherence which had sent so many of the brothers to their deaths, which had chained Jean-Baptiste through so many years of his youth to the hot swamplands of the south.

It was a new thought. She looked at him steadily, saying to herself: "He knows I want to play whatever part I may. What answer can I give him? Am I ready to tell him that I'll sacrifice happiness to duty?"

"M'sieur Charles," she said in a low tone, "I don't know what to tell you. I think I would die for the cause if it were necessary. But how can I give up a love that has been my whole life? Can I find any happiness——"

"There are many kinds of happiness, my child. Jacques and François and Louis were happy to give their lives in battle. Gabriel and Paul and Pierre have died in doing their duty and I'm sure, if they had known what was in store for them, they wouldn't have drawn back. They found happiness that way."

"I know! I've never doubted that all of them died willingly. Perhaps they were even happy to die. But they were strong, brave men."

"With some of us it's a case of being willing to live, of giving our whole lives to the cause." The baron's manner and voice showed that he knew himself to be on firm ground now. "Suggestions have reached me of matches for you. I've done nothing about them. To be frank, I'm against any idea of marriage for you yet. You are too valuable to tie yourself down to housework and childbearing. And so this attachment you've conceived for our young friend Philippe may serve a useful purpose. If you keep him in your heart you'll have no wish to marry any of the young gentlemen who will come seeking you. But not too much in your heart, my child, and not long enough to prevent him from marrying or to sway you when the chance for a great marriage presents itself. I want to see you a lady of high rank. I want you to add in that way to the stature of the family."

Félicité began to weep. "I must have time, M'sieur Charles. I can't make up my mind at once. And—and what did you say to my poor Philippe?"

"The same things I've said to you."

She was busy with her handkerchief. "What did *he* say?"

The baron took both of her hands in his and pressed them affectionately. "He seemed of the opinion that the decision would have to be yours."

III

Dollier de Casson's room was one of the smallest at the Seminary, little more than a cell in fact, and so his bed, which had to be of special size and strength, filled the greatest part of the space. It was a bare room also: a prie-dieu in one corner, a crucifix on the wall which faced him as he lay in bed, a tattered remnant of a military pennon on the wall above the bed and, therefore, not so continuously in his vision. When he joined the Sulpicians he had put his soldiering days, and most of the memories thereof, behind him; but it could only be assumed that the pennon, to which he had never been known to refer, had to do in some way with the days when he carried a sword for his country.

He had just been through one of his frequent bouts for the sanity of Georges Duchesne. Georges, a trader in the small goods used as barter for furs, had been captured many years before by a band of Indians and put to the torture. He had been rescued while the spark of life still lingered in his body and had been nursed back to health by his two devoted sons. The cure had been purely physical, however, and at intervals since he had fallen into spells of terror when reminded in some way of his hours at the stake. When this happened he would rush to a dark corner of his shop and cower down under a bear rug, and scream so loudly that people, gathering outside, would say, "Georges has a spell again!" It became the habit of the two sons, who were tall and silent men and unmarried, to take him by the arms and walk with him to the Seminary. Dollier de Casson had a way of grasping his hands and looking him straight in the eye while he talked in calm and reassuring tones of such commonplace things as the price of fur and the state of the weather. In a very few minutes the sick man would respond and gradually find his way back from the realm to which his terrors had drawn him.

The old priest always emerged in an exhausted condition from these tussles for the sanity of Georges Duchesne. On this occasion, as added reason, the old wound in his knee had begun to ache badly. He was lying on his narrow bed with closed eyes when Monsieur Ambrose came tiptoeing in and said, "Monsieur, Philippe Girard is here."

Dollier de Casson opened his eyes wearily. "Who did you say, monsieur?" he asked.

"The carpenter. The boy who was saved at Lachine but never got his land. Old Kirkinhead's boy."

The Superior sat up at once. He understood what had brought Philippe to him and he shook his head sadly as he said to the pudgy priest, "I've been expecting this poor young fellow. Bring him in to me here so there will be no interruptions to our talk. But first get a chair for him, if you will be so good."

When Philippe came in he looked as though he had been on a forced march for days or had just risen from a sickbed. He was pale and there were deep hollows under his eyes and he had not shaved. On leaving the Le Moyne house after his talk with the baron, Philippe had been in such an unhappy daze that he had started to walk, not knowing in what direction his feet took him nor caring. He had walked for hours, finding an outlet for the emotions which filled him in the sheer labor of forcing a way through the snow. Finally his mind had cleared sufficiently for him to realize that he had walked far on the frozen surface of the river in the direction of Longueuil.

"If I don't look out," he had muttered to himself, "I'll be lost like Pierre Chesne. They'll find my frozen body on the river."

In saying this he had brought himself to the further realization that he was not far from the spot where the body of the lost Pierre Chesne had been found and later that of Félicité's tormenter and admirer, Bertrand. He had stopped then and considered carefully which direction he should take in order to reach the château. His calculations had been sufficiently correct to bring him soon thereafter within sight of the high towers of Longueuil. After a short rest there and a mouthful of breakfast (with, for the first time in his life, a glass of brandy), he had started back for Montreal. Arriving there, in a state of weariness defying description, he plodded his way to the Seminary.

"Monsieur," he said, taking the chair which the little priest had brought for him, and sighing gratefully, "I've come to you for help."

"Yes, my son." The Superior nodded his head to him and smiled encouragingly. "It happens that I know what is in your mind. I talked to Charles le Moyne this morning and he told me."

"Then you know . . ." Philippe paused. He looked down before adding, ". . . you know that I wanted to marry Félicité and that M'sieur Charles has refused to give his consent."

"Yes, my son." The old priest looked at the lowered face of the unhappy suitor and shook his head sadly. "Do you know that the baron talked to her after you left?"

"Yes, monsieur. He told me he intended to."

"And have you any idea what course she's going to decide on?"

Philippe looked up at that. "Yes, monsieur. Of course! There's only one thing for her to do. She must"—he swallowed as though he found it hard to get the words out—"she must do as the baron says. It's her duty."

Dollier de Casson was not surprised at this reply. Although it could not have been entirely unexpected if Philippe had shown a tendency to fight, to claim Félicité in spite of all the pressure the baron might exert, the old priest knew him too well to anticipate such an attitude. He nodded his head again, and quite vigorously this time, saying to himself, "Here is the true spirit, the fine faith which moves mountains and builds cities in the wilderness."

"At first," Philippe went on, "I felt that I couldn't give in, that I would go to her and say we were under no obligation to M'sieur Charles, none at least to make us give each other up. She might have agreed with me if I had gone to her and said that. But it didn't take long, monsieur, for me to realize that to fight would be selfish and unpatriotic."

"Are you going to say this to her now?"

"No, monsieur. I'm not going to see her. It would only make it harder for her. But I don't want her to think that I'm angry or that I don't agree with her and that I'm sulking. It's hard enough to lose her without knowing that she thinks ill of me." He looked up with a hesitant air. "You have been kind to her, monsieur. Would I dare ask that you see her and tell her what I've said?"

"Hasn't it occurred to you, my son, that she may decide in favor of you and happiness?"

Philippe shook his head emphatically. "I know her too well to think that. I'm sure, monsieur, that her mind is already made up."

"Then, my son, I will see her and tell her what you have said. You are being very brave, and also very wise and right about it." He held up his hand in a blessing. "Let me give you a word of advice now. You are worn out. I suspect you haven't been off your feet since last evening. Go home and get to bed. You will sleep long and well, I promise you, and when you waken your spirit will be a little more at rest."

IV

The baron said nothing more to Félicité about this brief interlude which had threatened to sever their partnership. Things went on exactly as usual. They faced each other across the desk for many hours each day and transacted between them the complicated affairs of the house of Le Moyne. It occurred to him once or twice that she looked pale but in the press of business he forgot to speak of it.

Claude-Elizabeth, however, was more thoughtful as well as more observant. She did not know the whole story but she had heard something of it (and, having nothing of the gossip in her, had not pressed for more) and she realized that the girl was in need of sympathy and attention. She would interrupt proceedings in the cabinet by coming in with a glass of warm milk, laced with a few surreptitious drops of brandy, or she would walk in around five in the afternoon and drive them both out, declaring that they had worked hard enough. Once she stood beside Félicité and said to her husband, "I don't know what you are doing, my Charles, but I suspect you're behaving like one of those dreadful characters of Monsieur Molière."

Félicité tried to put her bitter disappointment out of her head but, needless to state, she did not succeed. She did not sleep well. She would waken early always and toss about for several hours before the time came when she could get up.

On several mornings, when she lay thus in half-waking condition, she heard footsteps in the street below. She wondered about them and even considered speaking about the matter to the baron; for no law-abiding citizen would be out at such an hour. It was not the town watchman, who shuffled along at a slow gait, for the mysterious footsteps were quick.

On one such morning she decided it was foolish to torture herself by remaining in bed and going over and over in her mind the events which had resulted in the blasting of her romantic dreams. Acting on the impulse, she rose and went to the window. The sky was still gray and leaden and she shivered in the cold of the room. She was on the point of returning to bed when she heard the footsteps coming down the Rue St. Paul.

A few moments later the early walker came into view. It was Philippe. As on the previous mornings, he was walking briskly and his eyes were raised to the window through which she watched. Instinctively she stepped back so that he could not see her, but not far enough to prevent her from observing him. He continued to look up and she could see that he was pale and that his face reflected all the unhappiness within him.

"My poor Philippe!" she said to herself. Her eyes filled with tears and when he had vanished down the street she huddled under the covers and had a long cry. Her heart, nevertheless, felt warm for the first time and she hugged this proof of his fidelity to her all through the long hours of the day.

The next morning she was up at an even earlier hour and was dressed and standing behind the gate which opened from the street into the yard when his footsteps sounded in the distance. "Oh, Philippe, my faithful darling!" she whispered to herself. Snow was falling and she raised the hood of her old cloth coat with a hand which trembled.

He came abreast of the house with his eyes fixed on her third-floor window and so was considerably startled when she said in a low voice, "Good morning, Philippe!" He came to a stop and looked at her before returning her greeting in an even lower tone. "Good morning, Félicité."

He remained still for several moments and it was clear that there were many things he wanted to say. They remained unsaid, however. After several efforts to find the words he desired he shook his head in despair and resumed his walk. He raised a hand and waved to her before disappearing from her angle of vision.

There was a heavy fall of snow that night and the next morning she watched his approach over a white drift higher even than the gate. A path had been dug down the center of the street and she could see no more than his head and shoulders as he drew near. He had not expected to see her and his face took on the redness of one caught in an indiscretion. Nevertheless, he stopped long enough to say in a tone very little above a whisper, "I love you more than ever!" She wanted to answer that she would love him until the end of time but her throat became choked and all she could do was smile through her tears and wave to him over the barricade of snow.

They never missed their morning tryst after that. No matter what the weather conditions or the lateness of the hour at which she had gone to bed, Félicité was at the gate, and Philippe's approach could have served to set the time for all the clocks on the Rue St. Paul. He never stopped for more time than was needed to repeat his formula, "I love you more than ever," for it was clear that he was afraid their meetings might be observed and did not want to have the baron know about them. Félicité often made up in advance the things she would say to him but almost always forgot about them. She seldom did more than smile at him across the top of the gate and move her lips in unspoken messages.

On the few occasions when they met elsewhere they contrived to appear casual. When others were present his manner was one of such severe formality that she found herself compelled to respond in kind. Invariably, however, there were moments when they were free of observation and they would stare intently and silently into each other's eyes.

It was a mistake to say they never missed their morning meetings. There was one morning when Philippe did not appear. It was in the spring and Félicité had picked a bunch of daffodils in the yard before taking up her usual station and was wondering if she would dare to give him one. Before a decision was reached she realized that for the first time he was late. A few minutes passed and she became disturbed, knowing that he allowed nothing to interfere with his punctuality. When a quarter hour had elapsed, and she was momentarily expecting to hear from the rear of the house the sounds which announced the rising of the servants, she knew he was not coming.

Something had gone wrong. Félicité did not wait any longer but walked out into the street and made her way to the carpentry shop. As she came in sight of it she saw Polycarpe Bonnet emerge from under the sign and start down the street in her direction at a rapid pace.

"Carpe, what has happened?" she asked as soon as they had drawn close.

"The master is sick. I'm going to the chemist's to get medicine."

Félicité looked apprehensive at once. "What is it? Is he very sick?"

"It started last night when I was out." He winked at her in a way which said, Now prepare to be shocked with a tale of my depravity. "I came in late. It was *very* late when I got in and I found the master with his head over a slop bucket. I gave him some medicine we had in the place, a mixture of *huile de noix* and *bitaine,* but it didn't seem to have the right effect." He gave a puzzled nod of the head. "I thought he would be better this morning but he isn't."

"I'll go with you," said Félicité. "I'm sure your poor master is going to need attention."

Bonnet looked at her accusingly. "If you had followed my advice, ma'amselle," he said, "this wouldn't have happened."

Perhaps it was her presence which had the desired effect. Philippe, at any rate, recovered quickly when she returned with his assistant, so quickly that it was not necessary to use the rather nauseous medicine the chemist had given them.

CHAPTER XI

THE CLIMB of the Le Moyne family was so continuous and spectacular that any interruption was like a thunderclap from a clear sky or a sudden blow in the dark. There were interruptions, however, and the most serious of all was the news which arrived one morning in the spring following that year of anxiety when all the people of New France waited with muskets in their hands for the English attack; an attack which never came.

Félicité was in the cabinet when the letter from France was placed in the baron's hands. She was so busily engaged at the moment that she did not look up until the silence of the room warned her that something was wrong. She glanced at her guardian then and was shocked at the expression with which he was reading the letter spread out on the desk in front of him.

"M'sieur Charles! What is it? Are you ill?"

He gave no answer but continued to stare with white face at the closely written sheets. Then a flush spread over his cheeks and with angry abruptness he got to his feet. Taking the letter up, he tore it savagely into small pieces and tossed them in the air.

"It's always the way!" he cried. "Can fairness be expected any more? Not from ungrateful kings and their corrupt, grasping ministers! Men strive for the good of their country, they give all they possess, they sacrifice their lives—and the rewards are handed to others!"

He stared down at her but she was not sure he was conscious of her presence. His eyes seemed to be looking straight through her.

"And I was fool enough to think the King would never forget the services of the Le Moynes!"

With the same suddenness he had displayed in rising, the baron sank back into his chair. He dropped his head on his hands.

"M'sieur Charles, is there anything I can do for you?"

He heard this time, for he shook his head. "No, my child. Such a terrible blow has been dealt us that nothing will matter from now on." It was several moments before he could bring himself to the point of explanation. "All the trading privileges in Louisiana have been taken away from us and given to a rich merchant in France. This merchant, Antoine Crozat, is sending out a man as his representative, a Monsieur de la Mothe Cadillac, and this new administrator will have authority over Jean-Baptiste. My brother has been removed as governor of Louisiana!"

The girl was stunned by this blow and could find nothing to say. After a moment the baron began to vent his feelings in a voice almost breathless from his resentment. "Does His Majesty realize that the founding of Louisiana has been a Le Moyne enterprise? That we have done everything? Has he forgotten that it has cost the life of D'Iberville? What a grim twist of fate this is! We have done a great thing, for the King, for France, and for Holy Church, at the cost of our blood and our wealth, and now we are brushed aside! And all on the whim of an old man and his raddled hag of a mistress!"

For one moment of frank vehemence his sense of loyalty deserted him. "He has lived too long, this old man!" he said in a tense whisper.

He probably did not know that all over France this thought was being whispered.

After a moment of tense silence the baron straightened up in his chair. "De Mariat was in this," he declared. "This letter is from him and I can read the truth behind each lying sentence he has written. *He* has been responsible for this and it's plain he'll share the profits with his thieving partner, this Antoine Crozat. I'll declare war on the pack of them." He nodded across the desk at Félicité. "Send at once for Benoit. I have things to say to him!"

II

Félicité escorted Benoit up the stairs. When they reached the top she said, "You will go in, please."

For half an hour sounds of bitter debate issued from the cabinet. At the end of that time the baron came out and pointed to the stairs. "You will go at once, Master Benoit, and you must never come back. I shall refuse to see you if you do. Today I shall write to De Mariat and tell him I'll have no more transactions with him."

Benoit had walked to the head of the stairs and, as the baron's last words were accompanied by a vigorous gesture, he took a hurried step backward. He had grown heavier with the passing of the years and this made him unsteady on his feet. He was unable to check himself when he slipped on the top stair and proceeded to fall the whole distance to the first floor. Félicité, running out from another room, heard squeals of fright and pain and loud thumps as he rolled down the stairs. When he reached the bottom he lay perfectly still and the waxy look on his face made her fear he had been killed.

She was conscious, to her own surprise, of a feeling of pity for him. Although he represented to her all that was unpleasant and even evil in life, she could not help thinking of the loneliness of his lot and the burden of contempt he carried on his shoulders. She flew, therefore, to the nearest yellow sign with a basin suspended over it. The *barbier-chirurgien* (the functions of barber and surgeon were still combined) was at home, fortunately. "Come at once, please!" she said. "The man may die from the bad fall he's had!"

Arriving at the house, the surgeon took one look at the injured man and asked, "Will it be a matter of much regret if he dies?" Having indulged in his little pleasantry, however, he instructed the servants to carry Benoit to a bed as fast as they could and to remove his clothing; an order which they obeyed with every sign of reluctance.

"No bones broken," he announced after making an examination of the body. "But never have I seen a larger and blacker set of bruises and contusions. It won't surprise me to find that he's hurt himself as much inside as out. Well, I shall now devote myself to a task on which men of medicine spend most of their time, the saving of a useless life."

He proceeded to try out a multitude of measures, bleeding and oiling and dosing. As he did so he commented to himself on the results he was obtaining or the lack of them. "No running of the reins. Hum, too bad, I have a splendid oil for *that*. . . . A fall like this will often unsettle the reason; perhaps he will offer me a fair fee for my services. . . . I appeal to St. Yves if any lawyer should ever get as flabby as this!"

Nothing seemed to do the injured man any good until the surgeon called for a dozen hens. After they were killed he had them slit and fitted one at a time over the skull of the patient. When the last of the chickens had been sacrificed on the altar of medical ingenuity Benoit moved and emitted a faint groan.

The surgeon nodded his head with satisfaction. "It has never failed," he said. "There was the case of a King of Denmark who had the palsy and who stirred after the sixty-seventh hen had been put on his head. That, I believe, was the most stubborn case on record. It has been comparatively easy with this one, this illustrious limb of the law."

After an examination of the prostrate frame he announced that Benoit would live. "Perhaps," he added, looking at the baron, who had come into the room, "my zeal has been somewhat excessive."

The baron made no comment but he gestured disgustedly to one of the servants to remove the bodies of the dead hens. "See that they're burned," he said. "I don't want them cropping up in a meat pasty!"

After three days of poulticing and dosing with queer concoctions and applying cataplasms to the injured skull, the surgeon permitted Benoit to rise from his couch and don his clothes preparatory to returning home.

"It is a miracle," he said, "that you are so well."

"I give thanks for that miracle to this young lady," said Benoit, nodding in Félicité's direction. "You, Master Surgeon, shall have your fee but if it had not been for this nice child's kindness I am sure I would have died."

The surgeon made an offhand gesture. "After all," he said, "a fee is more useful than gratitude. I'm paid too often in the latter coin to take offense when all I receive is money."

When the surgeon had left, Benoit motioned to Félicité that he had something to say to her. "You came to see me many times, you obtained little extras for my tray. You even smiled at me once." The patient put a hand in his pocket as though in search of a purse of gold. If that had been his purpose he changed his mind suddenly and brought the hand out empty. "You will enjoy my everlasting gratitude."

The baron came in to pay him a visit before he took his departure. "For the harm you've suffered," he said, "I beg your forgiveness, even though it was to your own clumsiness that the fall was due."

The lawyer said magnanimously, "It was an accident."

"As for what passed between us previously, I take back nothing that I said. The partnership, if it could be called that, is broken. I desire no more communications from De Mariat. As for you, Master Benoit, I intend to have nothing more to do with you."

"But you will. Oh yes, you will indeed."

"If you ever come to this house you will find a closed door."

CHAPTER XII

I T WAS the first day of the year 1717. The old King had been dead
for two years and as the new King was a minor there was a regent
ruling in France, Philippe of Orléans, a reckless individual who was
falling under the influence of a banker from Scotland named John Law.
Rumors were reaching the colony that John Law had great schemes in his
head which would either make France the richest nation the world had
ever seen or bring it to complete ruin. The war with the English had
come to an end and prosperity reigned along the St. Lawrence.

It was so cold on this first day of a new year that it was an easy matter
to follow the custom of scratching the names of all the children on the
frosted windowpanes; a proud occasion for Jules Dumounchel, who had
the largest family in Montreal, nineteen, and had to carry the writing over
from pane to pane, ending up with six-months-old Hippolyte at the very
bottom of the kitchen window; but an embarrassing event for the next-
door neighbor, Georges Cadel, who could not write and so had to scratch
nine crosses on his windows. There had been daily alternations of frost
and thaw with the result that now great icicles hung from all the eaves
like the beards of giants and the people who had dressed themselves in
their best to make their *jour de l'an* visits found it wise to walk in the
middle of the streets. The crunch of their heels on the hard snow was a
constant reminder that winter had now started in grim earnest.

The Baroness of Longueuil was finding it necessary to receive in an
armchair before the fire. A handsome cover of *brocart,* which was silk
embroidered with silver threads, was muffled closely around her knees.
She was no longer strong and had drawn rather too heavily on her re-
serves the previous evening.

The evening, of course, had been given over to the *Ignoleux* (the singers
who went about town caroling the *"Ignolée"* and collecting food, mostly
in the form of chines of pork, for the poor) and she had acted on a sudden
impulse to invite them in. Hot chocolate and cakes had been served be-

tween the rendition of favorite songs for which she asked, such as *"Dans les haubans"* and *"Qui n'a pas d'amour."* Félicité had been so busy attending to the wants of the singers that she had not realized Polycarpe Bonnet was among them until she heard a deep voice ask, "Am I suiting you in the bass, Bénigne?" and the leader answer, "if you sing any louder, Carpe, you'll crack the glass in that eye of yours." Before they left she had managed a word with him and had asked some of the questions she was storing up, all about Philippe. His answers were to the effect that his master was busy and prosperous but that he seemed in low spirits most of the time. He volunteered one piece of information with many confidential winks and mysterious nods of the head.

"He's been approached. Several times, ma'amselle. Parents in this town seem to think he'd make a good son-in-law. But he just thanks them and says no; he isn't suited yet. It's my opinion he's never going to be suited. Not unless you act on that advice I gave you." The winks and nods continued. "You'll save him trouble if you do. Father François has been after him. He comes regularly and gives it to the master hot and heavy. You know, there's a law against staying a bachelor."

The baroness had been in a gay mood all evening and had enjoyed the singing, even joining in the refrain of *"Dans les haubans."* And now she was paying for it. She had slept fitfully and had not touched any food since. She was finding it an effort to talk to the visitors who came and went in droves. Nevertheless, with her soft white hair fluffed about her face, she looked like a very pretty doll. Many compliments were being whispered in her ear.

Félicité had been aware from the first that the baroness was watching her with a rather disconcerting intentness and was certain she had something to say when a favorable moment arrived. The favorable moment came when there was a brief lull between visitors and the baron slipped out to the kitchen, jingling the bag with the gold coins he distributed to the servants on New Year's Day.

"Félicité!"

"Yes, madame?"

"I've been thinking back. I always do on New Year's Day. It's a bad habit because it makes me feel very sad. Today it makes me angry. Angry with Charles."

Félicité answered lightly. "Come, madame! You can't be angry with M'sieur Charles on New Year's Day."

"But I am. Very angry. He's been such a planner and schemer, that husband of mine. Jean-Baptiste was to become a great diplomat, a governor, perhaps even a minister of the King. And what has happened? My poor Jean-Baptiste! For nearly twenty years he has been in a swampy pesthole, living in a most miserable way. All his youth gone and the best years of his manhood passing him by! And now he's no longer governor and has to take orders from someone else. Jean-Baptiste was my favorite and I get very angry when I think how his life is being wasted. But when I say this to Charles—and I do, often—his nostrils begin to flare and he says I don't understand. He says in this matter the lives of individuals are of no importance."

"And he's right, madame. It's quite certain things are going to turn out well after all. This Monsieur Las,[1] who has so much influence with the Regent, is planning to fill Louisiana with settlers. It's going to be a wealthy and important colony. It wouldn't do to give up after all these years when victory is in sight!"

"But will victory do us any good? The rewards have been taken away."

Félicité was silent for a moment. "I don't believe, madame, that the rewards are important. If we succeed in holding the river for France, that will be reward enough for everyone."

"And now," said the baroness, "we'll consider what Charles is doing with *your* life. Oh, I know he pretends to be very fair when you receive a proposal, saying you must make the decision yourself—but always letting you see how much he's against it. How many proposals have you had?"

"Four."

"That illustrious match he talks about! It won't ever come about, not unless he sends you to France and lets it be known that the *dot* is a considerable one. And then what kind of a husband are you likely to get? Some impoverished old widower with a title and with a sharp pair of kneecaps and a sniffle to go with it."

"But, madame, there's plenty of time still."

"Plenty of time!" The tone of the baroness had become sharp. "You're twenty-one. At twenty-one most girls have been married for years and have several children." She stopped and indulged in an unexpected laugh. "I must be fair and say as well that at your age most girls have lost their bloom and their hips are beginning to bulge like feather squabs. You've been spared that at any rate."

"There's something more important in life than marriage, madame."

"Not for you! Not for any woman." The baroness gave her head a shake to show how completely in earnest she was. "There's that poor young carpenter. I agreed with Charles at the start. I was sure marriage with him was quite out of the question. But now I'm not so sure. He's a gentle young man and quite handsome in a quiet way. I'm beginning to wonder if he wouldn't have made you the best possible husband."

Félicité had no desire to continue the conversation now that it had arrived at this point. Her face became white and she shrank back into her chair as though to avoid a blow.

"I've been keeping an eye on that poor young man. After it was decided

[1]John Law was generally referred to by this name in France.

you were not to marry he seemed to change. Before that he had been such a brisk and pleasant boy and then he became silent and had no interest in anything but his work. I saw him on the street the other day and I noticed how his hair is growing gray over the ears!"

Félicité said in a tone scarcely above a whisper, "It started to turn more than a year ago."

More visitors arrived at this point. The baroness looked at them in dismay and said to Félicité under her breath: "Sainted Mary, what a day this is going to be! How I long for the comfortable sheets of my bed!"

Félicité went about her duty of looking after the visitors in a perfunctory way for the next half hour. Her mind was on what the baroness had said about Philippe. It was true that he had changed. He had always been lively and cheerful but from the evening when he took his proposal to the baron he had become quiet, austere, unhappy. Worse than that, he seemed conscious always of the difference in their stations and on the few occasions when they had met recently he had addressed her as "Mademoiselle." He never spoke any more of extending his trade. Was he going to be a humble artisan all his life, content to stay in what he now conceived to be his ordained station?

One of the late arrivals created some consternation in the household staff. It was Benoit, wearing a coat which had originally been of fur but now was so old and worn that one could no more than guess at the identity of the beast which had worn it first. One of the maids came to Félicité and whispered in her ear: "You know the orders, ma'amselle. He's not to be admitted. What can we do?"

Félicité saw the sallow face of De Mariat's representative staring at her from the doorway. No one had offered to relieve him of his coat and he was holding his moth-eaten hat in his hand.

"But he *is* in," she said. "I'll speak to him, Jeanneton."

Benoit seemed more interested in her than he had ever been before. His sharp eyes took her in from head to foot and he kept nodding and muttering to himself. When she crossed the room to him he said, "I judge women by their walk and *you* are as light and full of grace as a cat." Then he raised his forefinger abruptly and pointed it at her. "It's no use. You can't put me off. I'm here to see him. For over three years I've been barred from this house and I've done nothing about it. I could have forced him to see me but I didn't. I bided my time. And now I'm here, and I'm going to see this great and mighty Baron of Longueuil."

"Is it a matter of importance?"

The lawyer cupped a hand behind his ear and leaned closer toward her.

"Never mind." Guests were arriving now in droves and she did not want to precipitate an argument with him. She raised her voice. "I'll speak to M'sieur Charles. It will take no more than a minute so you will stay here in the meantime, if you please."

II

The servants had not expected their master to occupy his cabinet on New Year's Day and so the potted plants from the window sills (the baron was an ardent botanist), which had been carried to his desk the night before to save them from the cold, had not been replaced. There was, as a result, a green barricade between the baron and Benoit when they seated themselves.

Reaching an arm between a geranium and a begonia, the latter laid in front of the master of the house a miniature painted on ivory. The baron took it up and glanced casually at the face.

"He is handsome, is he not?" demanded the visitor.

"I suppose he is."

"He has courage, spirit, intelligence?"

"I didn't look closely enough to read any of those qualities in the face."

Benoit retrieved the miniature and laid it on the desk beside him. "We'll lay it aside for the time being. I'll come back to it later."

He launched then into talk about the man who was dazzling all France, all Europe in fact, and who had established such an ascendancy over the Regent. "As you know, Baron, John Law plans to use Louisiana as the bait to make all the people of France invest in the funds. To give substance to his dream, he must see to it that the colony has a remarkable and immediate growth. I have definite word that he plans to send eight shiploads of new settlers within the next two years. A town must be established at once. I needn't ask if you realize what this means?"

The baron had no faith in the grand schemes of M'sieur Las. He snorted indignantly. "I've heard rumors of the eight ships. Is it official then?"

"It is official."

"I realize," said the baron, "that the colony will grow like a mushroom. But will the prosperity continue after the schemes of this Scot have brought France to the brink of ruin? I think it may, but time only can supply the answer." His voice raised. "This clever foreigner may benefit Louisiana but his mad schemes will bring about the ruin of France!"

"The Regent doesn't think so. He's determined to proceed with the plans."

"The Regent," declared the baron, "thinks it more important for him to have his way than for his way to be beneficial to France."

Benoit remained silent for several moments, his eyes fixed on his companion's face. Then he leaned forward, thrust the flowerpots to each side, and planted his elbows on the table.

"You are a shrewd man, Baron, the very shrewdest I know. I have something important to tell you. You must have guessed it when I took advantage of your house being full to force myself on you."

The baron waited for him to continue.

"Antoine Crozat has relinquished the trading privileges," said Benoit. "It didn't prove a profitable venture for him."

"Nor for those who shared the privileges with him. In particular, Joseph de Mariat."

Benoit spoke slowly and emphasized each word. "Joseph de Mariat is in a position to have your brother, the Sieur de Bienville, reinstated as governor of Louisiana."

The baron was too experienced a trader to permit any emotion to show on his face. Outwardly he seemed calm and disinterested and he continued to toy indifferently with the sander on his desk. Inwardly, however, he was filled with excited speculations. What had been proposed to him, he realized, was the establishment again of the Le Moyne family in control of the Mississippi country. Was it possible that De Mariat had enough influence in the councils of the Regent to redeem such a promise? It was a dazzling prospect. His lack of faith in the plans of Law did not hide from him the possibility that the sudden impetus the home government would supply might start the colony toward a permanent prosperity.

Benoit continued to speak in the same deliberate tones. "You're thinking that De Mariat is making promises he can't fulfill. Monsieur Baron, sweep such doubts from your mind! He has the ear of the Regent. He has your brother's fine record to lay before Law at the proper moment. The Scot will want the best man in control through this crucial period. Baron, if the strings are pulled expertly your brother will be governor again, and in time to take full advantage of the great boom. But unless you move quickly some outsider will be handed the plum."

The baron had gained full control of himself by this time. He demanded in a dry and skeptical tone, "And the price, Master Benoit?"

The lawyer became immediately the expert go-between, the bargainer. He began to speak quickly. "Little enough, Baron. Little enough. I'll be honest and tell you everything, even though my candor may put me at a disadvantage. As it happens, De Mariat has had reverses——"

The baron interrupted, "In the Crozat company."

"All I know is that certain speculations on which he had counted heavily and into which he had sunk more than he could afford to lose have broken in his face like bubbles. He finds himself short of funds at the one golden moment of history when men with brains, and with money at their disposal, may make incredible fortunes."

"And he expects me to provide the funds with which he'll plunge into the wild schemes of this mad Scot?"

"Baron! No!" Benoit shoved his hands from him, palms up, as though repelling such an absurd notion. "How can we be sure, you and I, of what is in the mind of Joseph de Mariat? Isn't it possible he agrees with you and wants ready funds to take advantage of the ruin which will follow the pricking of this great soap bubble? There will be properties to be picked up for a song, fine estates, houses in Paris, inherited concessions."

"That's the first thing you've said to which I can subscribe. De Mariat is more likely to let other men take the risks and get his profit out of their failures. Well, come to the point. What is the price he asks?"

Benoit reached for the miniature and proffered it a second time. "This is his son. Auguste Joseph Goadrey de Mariat. He is, I'm informed, the possessor of splendid qualities."

The baron had some recollection of hearing the elder De Mariat sing the praises of his only son. He said impatiently, "I'll subscribe to anything you say about this paragon, this youthful Bayard, if you'll come quickly to the point."

"The son has been married once. His wife died. It hadn't been a successful match. There was—well, a whisper of scandal. This makes it difficult now for this comely young gentleman to find another wife in the desired level of society and with an adequate fortune. Have you already sensed what I'm coming to?"

"I am expected to find a wife for this amiable young man who doesn't seem to have made a good husband in his one attempt."

"That, Baron, is the bargain. The son is to be given a post in the provinces. You are to make a settlement of such size that the young couple will have enough to start off well and to feel assured about their future. And there must be a share of it for De Mariat to use as a working capital."

The baron cried impatiently: "But the bride, Benoit? Who is to marry this scapegrace son?"

Benoit's eyes opened in surprise. "Who? You haven't guessed yet? I'm surprised at your tardiness. Who but the little ward, the owner of the busy fingers which labor so cleverly with your papers and books, the little lady of the nice gray eyes and the very neat figure, your Ma'amselle Félicité herself?"

The surprise of this was so great that the baron ejaculated, "Félicité!" in a tone of complete disbelief.

"Of course. I've been singing her praises to De Mariat in every letter I've written him. I think very highly indeed of your tall young lady."

An intense preoccupation had replaced the look of surprise on Charles le Moyne's face. He thought the proposition over from every standpoint before saying anything more. "This much is clear to me," he said. "De Mariat sees danger in accepting money in any way which could be construed as a bribe——"

"Exactly. I'll supply the details later."

"In the meantime, what was the nature of this scandal? Was the De Mariat cub responsible for his wife's death? Had he been guilty of some abomination of conduct? Why is he being exiled to the provinces and why is his once proud and doting parent willing to marry him to a girl of no family?"

"I don't know the answers to any of your questions, and there's no time to find out. If the Sieur de Bienville is to be reinstated, it must be done at once. We can't sit here for months and twiddle our thumbs waiting for reports on the moral character of this candidate for your ward's hand. We must accept the proposition at once so De Mariat can forestall any plan to appoint a new man."

The baron kept his eyes lowered. Exhilarating thoughts were racing through his mind. To control Louisiana again! To save the huge continent back of the Mississippi for France!

"I must have time to think," he said. "This is a—a difficult decision to face. If she, my ward, has no wish for the match, that will end it. You understand?"

Benoit answered in brisk and relieved tones which suggested that he had feared another answer. "If she has qualms, send her to me. I think I can make her content. In fact I promise it."

The baron was so torn by conflicting emotions that several moments passed before he found it possible to make any response. "I'll speak to her," he said, slowly and reluctantly. "That's all I can say to you now, Benoit."

III

When she entered the apartment of Monsieur Benoit a few days later Félicité was wearing her beaver coat, which was still almost as good as new, and a cloth hat with blue ribbons. She was looking well, and Benoit, from his chair by the fire, welcomed her with an approving smile.

"You look nice, very nice. Our handsome young man will be well pleased with his bride. He will indeed."

He was most inelegantly clad himself in a woolen dressing gown, his hands tucked into the sleeves in search of warmth. A pair of cloth spatterdashes covered his ankles.

Félicité, who had taken a chair on the opposite side of the fire, said, "He won't have a chance, m'sieur, to like or dislike me."

Benoit's air of approval vanished. "Come, ma'amselle!" he protested. "I expected better from you than this. Not in all France could a finer match be found."

When she remained silent he leaned toward her, his eyes searching her face for a clue to her real feelings. "It's time you were married, ma'amselle. You are twenty-one! Do you want to be an old maid? Such a waste that would be! You must marry, and soon, and so why not take this young man who has so much to offer you? He will have a title someday and a high official position. He will be wealthy. What more could you ask?" He was realizing that he must bring every possible argument to bear. "Don't you know that by remaining single you are sure to involve a certain young man in serious legal complications?"

She sat straight up in her chair at that. "What do you mean?"

Aware that he had scored a point, Benoit went craftily to work. "If this certain young man doesn't marry soon himself, he'll find he's in trouble with both church and law. You know, of course, that there's a regulation against singleness after a certain age. It may be invoked in his case. It happens"—the lawyer was leaning so far forward that his face was close to hers—"that the royal judge has three unmarried daughters. It has come to my ears that he offered the oldest one, who is plain and rather fat, to this young man and that he was seriously annoyed when the suggestion was rejected. I would have little faith in the fairness of the royal judge if the case should be heard before him."

"But, M'sieur Benoit," said Félicité, frowning anxiously, "that law hasn't been in use as long as I can remember."

"A law remains in force until it's repealed. It may fall into disuse but it can always be invoked. As it happens, none of the regulations of the late King, foolish though some of them were, have been repealed." He then swung back abruptly to the real issue, raising a forefinger as he did so. "It's clear you haven't given this matter sufficient thought. Are you aware that the appointment of the Sieur de Bienville hinges on this marriage?"

"But why, m'sieur! Why must I marry this young man? Why can't they be content with the money? That's all they want."

Benoit seemed glad of the opportunity to explain the situation fully. "Our new master, the Regent of France," he said, "has a great regard for what you might call the niceties of administrative practice. If he found that one of his officials had accepted a large sum of money for influencing him in the matter of an appointment, he would see to it that the culprit was destroyed, promptly and utterly. It follows that the transaction must be given a legal guise. A marriage settlement! What could be more satisfactory?" He began to smile and bob his head, in appreciation of the fine web he and his principal had spun between them. "A rare good bargain all around, this! The baron gets back into family hands the power which has been taken from them. Joseph de Mariat becomes the possessor of the money he needs. M'sieur Auguste gets a pretty and clever wife and a marriage settlement which will allow him a fresh start. You, my child, will take your place in a society much above anything you might have hoped for. I receive a reasonable commission for my services. Could anything be more satisfactory for all concerned?"

"I wish I could make you understand how I feel." Félicité was losing her self-possession. Her hands, which she kept in her lap, were trembling. "I have a feeling that this marriage would prove to be a mistake, perhaps even a tragedy. I've tried so hard to reconcile myself to it but I've failed. M'sieur, I'm afraid, I'm afraid of it!"

Benoit allowed his eyes to rest on her face in the most intense study to which he had yet subjected her. Then he got to his feet and walked to the other end of the room. As he encountered the chill which existed a few feet from the blaze he shuddered and said, "On days like this I regret the poverty which forbids me the luxury of a good fire." In a very few minutes he was back with his hands full of papers.

"Mademoiselle Félicité," he said, seating himself again, "I like you. In fact, my child, I am quite fond of you. And so I had hoped it wouldn't be necessary to proceed to extremes. I would have preferred not to use my final argument." He tapped the papers in one hand with his other fore finger. "I have here certain proofs which—— You must be aware, being so fully in the confidence of your guardian, that when the war was going so badly for France there were merchants here who sold their fur to the English. The trade went on for nearly three years and, if the facts became known to the Regent, it's certain that drastic steps would be taken against all who participated. These papers refer to the case of one merchant who figured in it. Do you care to look them over?"

"No, m'sieur."

"No? You would be very much surprised to learn the name of the merchant in question."

"You are wrong, m'sieur. I wouldn't be surprised at all. I haven't forgotten all the hints you've dropped and the half threats you've made when you were angry with us. I know you mean the Baron of Longueuil."

"Your baron *was* one of them. The full proof is here."

She stood up and faced him. "There's no need for us to talk about this—this monstrous charge!" she said. "I know as well as you do that those papers in your hand are forgeries."

"They would convince the authorities in France if they should fall into official hands."

"Yes, M'sieur Benoit. I'm sure you've done your work with great cleverness."

" 'A good bone never falls into the mouth of a good dog,' " he quoted with a smile. "These proofs could be sent to France with the most perfect safety. It was I who stumbled on them and, if I sent them to De Mariat it would be for patriotic motives. He would lay them before his master for the same motives. That would absolve us if the point should be raised that *we* were active in the trade ourselves. You realize that, of course?"

Félicité did not answer at once. She knew now what her decision must be. Her tears, which had been close to the surface for some time, began to flow.

Rubbing her eyes with her handkerchief, she asked, "How can we be assured that the appointment of the Sieur de Bienville will go through?"

"The word of his appointment will reach you here before you set sail for France."

"M'sieur, this is all a pretense," said Félicité in a last effort. The intensity of her emotions had left her physically weak. Her knees were trembling. "You are trying to frighten me, that's all. You've no intention of making such a charge."

All hint of amiability drained out of the lawyer's face. "Do you think," he demanded, "that I would go to such pains for no other purpose than to frighten you? My child, my little *méchante,* I have every intention of following this matter through to the end. You, and you only, have it in your power to call a halt. Let me impress this on you: if the story gets to the ears of the Regent, the house of Le Moyne will crumble and fall like the pillars of Samson!"

CHAPTER XIII

IN SPITE of the cold, the baron left early the next morning for a visit to his fief at Beloeil, where he was considering the purchase of additional lands. Félicité was alone in the cabinet, therefore, when one of the maids came up in a state of mild excitement.

"He's here, that Petit Poucet, with his glass eye and his hints and his silly winkings. Doesn't he know I'm spoken for? And that I wouldn't look at a low-pockets like him, even if I wasn't?"

Félicité looked up from her work. "Do you mean that M'sieur Bonnet is downstairs?"

The maid tossed her head. "Yes, ma'amselle. He's walking about as though he had the itch and he says he must see you without *any* delay, if you please."

Carpe's nervousness had not been exaggerated. He made a pounce across the room when Félicité entered and began talking at once.

"He's been taken, ma'amselle! To court. He'll be fined and perhaps sent to jail if we don't help him right away. It starts in a few minutes and we'd better be there or that judge will make things bad for him."

Félicité's heart sank because she had no illusions whatever as to what this meant. "Is it your master?" she asked, knowing quite well that it was.

The assistant nodded his head several times. "They came half an hour ago. When they saw everything was gone they said he had broken the law both ways and would have to pay for it."

Félicité laid a restraining hand on his arm. "Please keep cool and tell me exactly what happened. What do you mean when you say everything was gone?"

"Ma'amselle, it was my fault. I brought in the trader from the Sault and showed him Old Kirkinhead's stuff. He paid a round sum for it, ma'am selle, and he's going to trade it off to the Indians instead of the usual beads and calicoes. He bought everything except the wigs. Eight of them, ma'amselle, and where Old Kirkinhead got them is a mystery."

"But, Carpe, the goods belonged to your master. They were willed to him. Why shouldn't he make a sale if he wants to?"

The assistant sank his voice to a dramatic whisper. "My master is a bachelor. Under the laws no bachelor can take any part in the Indian trade. It was put that way to discourage them from being bachelors. They say my master engaged in the Indian trade when he sold the goods and that it's brought him under the law."

"When does the hearing begin?"

Carpe allowed excitement to take possession of him again. "It's coming up in a few minutes! We must get over there at once or they'll have him in jail!"

Félicité found herself in such a panic that it was difficult to slip her coat over the wool dress braided with tavelle which she was wearing. "If M'sieur Charles were only here!" she said to herself desperately. "He would know what to do."

They had barely reached the Rue St. Paul when Benoit came stumping up the street with the aid of a thick cane. He stopped when he saw Félicité and her companion.

"Then you've heard," he said. "I was coming to give you the news myself. This is a petty thing the judge has done! By St. Joseph, they'll be arresting me next for not having my chimney cleaned once a month!"

"Why did they pick on my master?" demanded the carpenter, giving way suddenly to his resentment. "There are dozens of bachelors in Montreal. Are they going to take all of them to law? I'm a bachelor. Are they going to take me?"

"The law," said Benoit impatiently, "applies only to bachelors *by choice*. Everyone knows, Polycarpe, that you've proposed for a dozen girls and been refused each time."

"That's not true!" cried Carpe. "I suited one of them. Did it matter that she was a widow and had six children? She had land on the river and a house with pink shutters and a red door, and the walls were two feet thick and there was a sign on the lintel to keep witches off. She had money, too, and a house and two cows, too."

"We haven't time to hear all this if we're to reach court," said Benoit.

But Carpe was determined to establish his right to be considered a law-breaker as well as his master. "I could have married her but I didn't," he protested. "She was of a roundness and I was reconciled to all six children, Thérèse, Angélique, Guillaume, Henriette, Blanchefleur, and Dominique, the baby. But I couldn't put up with her habit of stringing the baby's steaming diapers on a line across the room so they flapped me in the face every time I came in the door. I told her I wouldn't marry her and gave her back the gold seal which had belonged to her first husband. So I'm a bachelor by choice and I could be taken by the law too."

"If you jilted every widow in New France, Polycarpe, they would pay no attention," declared the lawyer. He turned to Félicité and said in a low tone, "You must know that it's the Le Moyne family, and the baron in particular, they're striking at through you and your faithful Philippe."

Félicité remembered the voices of the three small girls on the bench in front of her at school and felt again that twitch in her foot which had caused her to send them sprawling on the floor. The same ill-natured gossiping had gone on ever since but in quarters where it did not matter. This, if Benoit were right, would be the first instance of serious aggression.

It became apparent as they approached the Sénéchaussée, which was located in the old Seminary on the Rue St. Paul, that the public was taking a keen interest in the case. People were hurrying down all the streets and there was already a crowd in front of the building. The arrival of the curiously assorted trio created a ripple of comment but it was evident at once that the feeling ran against the law. They heard such comments as "It's a disgrace!", "Such a fine young fellow!" and "Will they be telling us next when we must go to bed and how often we should wash our feet?"

One man with red hair and a hot brown eye got up on a hitching post and said in an angry tone of voice: "Ten years ago there was a soldier in the jail, waiting to be hanged in the spring, but the prison was so cold that they hanged him at once, saying it would be cruel to make him live in such discomfort. The royal judge seems to have that same idea of justice in his head. He doesn't want any man to exist in the discomforts of bachelorhood and wants instead to string him up with the halter of matrimony!"

It was apparent that there was no more room in the court but a party of husky young fellows formed themselves into a wedge and forced a way inside for Félicité. The leader winked at her and said, "You have a right to be in there."

II

The courtroom was filled to overflowing and from the corner where she stood Félicité could see no more than the head and shoulders of the judge. The head looked vain and unimpressive when thus cut away from the dignity of a well-padded body but the shoulders would have redeemed it somewhat if it had not been known to everyone that he had paid out of his own pocket for the robe he wore with its ermine collar and cuffs. On the wall behind him was a brass plaque with a phrase lettered on it in Latin.

"You give us no reason for your obduracy, young man," the judge was saying. There was an unctuous quality to his voice and a description of him which she had once heard the baron use went through her mind: "that pompous old clinchpoop."

She could not see Philippe but his voice came clearly from somewhere to the right of the dais which held the judge and his *procureur fiscal*.

"Marriage is a contract for life, Monsieur Judge," he said. "I feel that what I do with my life is my own concern."

To hear him and not see him was more than Félicité could bear. She began to inch her way forward, smiling and apologizing in whispers, until she reached a more favorable position. She could now see all of the judge, even to the tips of his small and fastidious boots, and off to the right the profile of Philippe.

"Marriage," declared the judge sharply, "is an institution governed by laws. You are allowed no option, Philippe Girard. By not marrying you have gone against the King's law. By engaging in a transaction which involves goods for the fur trade, you have laid yourself open to the highest penalty provided by the regulations."

The eyes of the man on the bench roved along the well-packed rows of spectators as though seeking approval of the sentiments he had uttered. They passed quickly over Félicité, then stopped and came back with a jerk of surprise to study her face intently. When convinced of her identity, he indulged in a sly smile.

"Is it possible," he asked the defendant, "that you hold out against the demand of your sovereign lord the King because the lady of your choice refuses to marry you?"

Philippe made no answer.

The judge asked the next question with his eyes fixed on Félicité. "Have you made the mistake of raising your eyes too high?"

As no answer was forthcoming to this, the judge brought an indignant fist down on the table in front of him. "I am not addressing questions to you for the pleasure of hearing my own voice but to elicit information. I demand an answer."

"My reasons for not marrying are my own, monsieur. That is all the answer I can give you."

The judge frowned but decided to try a new line. "You came from Longueuil?"

"Yes. I was raised on the seigneurie of Monsieur le Moyne."

It began to come out now, the hostility which men of the judge's stamp felt for the famous and wealthy Le Moynes. The occupant of the bench said, "Is it perhaps that you feel yourself above the laws governing the lives of men who can claim no special protection?"

Philippe answered, "No, monsieur."

"It surprises me that a certain great and titled man is not here to say that this court must not touch one who may be needed for mysterious duties, here or elsewhere, and at the sole discretion of the aforesaid great and titled man." The voice of authority fairly dripped sarcasm. "And these special duties, I may add, seem to many humble citizens more necessary for family aggrandizement than for the good of the state."

Having thus delivered himself of a shaft at the pretentions of the dynasty of Longueuil, the judge proceeded to ask more questions in a tone of voice which had suddenly become almost amiable. Did the defendant ever intend to marry? Was there any physical reason for his refusal? Was it that the needs of his business absorbed all his present funds?

Listening to the subdued negatives with which Philippe answered, Félicité said to herself: "How he has changed! If he had any heart left in him he wouldn't let himself be trampled on by this bully but would stand up and fight! Ah, Philippe, Philippe! You were never afraid of anyone before."

The briefly assumed cloak of amiability slipped suddenly from the shoulders of the judge. He glared down at the defendant. "Do you intend then to go on playing the brokenhearted lover for the rest of your life——"

"Monsieur!" cried Félicité. "I beg the privilege of asking a question."

The judge seemed pleased, as though he had been phrasing his questions with the intention of drawing her into it. He nodded briskly and smiled, fancying himself the cat which sees the head of the mouse come within reach of his claws. "Very well, mademoiselle. The court will hear what you have to say."

Félicité stepped clear of the spectators and took a few paces forward. Philippe turned to look at her with consternation written on his face. He began to say in a low tone, "Mademoiselle, this is very unwise——" when the judge, glaring at him, demanded that he make no further attempts to address the new witness. Félicité, looking at no one but the occupant of the bench, was thinking sadly, "You won't say it for yourself, my dear Philippe, and so I must!"

"And now, mademoiselle, what is it you desire to ask?"

"I desire to ask, Monsieur Judge, if it is your intention to throw our city into such confusion that its people will have to spend all their time here? If it's your intention, moreover, to bring about a complete bankruptcy?"

The judge glowered. "This—this question has no meaning and no purpose other than to distract attention from the case now being heard."

"On the contrary," declared Félicité, "it has a definite meaning and it's of importance to every man and woman living in Montreal." She looked back of her before going on and saw faces which reflected interest and approval. It was quite clear that the spectators were with her. "Everyone in this room knows," she went on, "that the regulations covering marriage, which haven't been enforced for more than thirty years, are outdated and absurd. Everyone knows also that, as they have not been repealed, it is your privilege, monsieur, to invoke them, as you are doing in this case. I have, therefore, another question to ask. If this one regulation is still in force, are all the other regulations issued at the same time in force also?"

The judge nodded his head. "All of the late King's regulations are still in force, never having been repealed."

"Then," she cried, stepping forward until she stood immediately beneath him, "if one old law is invoked, I demand that they all be invoked at the same time!"

This brought such a demonstration of approval from the spectators that the judge could not make himself heard by pounding on the desk. He glared angrily and took a ruler from a drawer with which he proceeded to pound on the brass plaque. "The room will be cleared if there is any more noise!" he shouted.

This brought silence, the spectators having no desire to miss the rest of the proceedings. The judge then said, frowning down at Félicité, "The old laws will be invoked at any time I consider it necessary. Is that clear, mademoiselle?"

"It's clear enough but not satisfactory. I demand," she cried, "that the law compelling parents to marry off their children or pay fines be invoked at once, today! The ages at which children must be married is fixed at twenty for sons and sixteen for daughters. Monsieur, there are many citizens who pay no attention to this regulation. I know of one case"—she paused and looked first at the judge himself and then at the eager row of faces behind her—"where a well-known citizen of Montreal has three unmarried daughters of ages nineteen, eighteen, and seventeen——"

The judge, his face an angry red, interrupted. "I'm sure the father in question has arrangements pending for the marriages of all three daughters."

"It is sincerely to be hoped so, monsieur," said Félicité in a sympathetic tone. "He has already broken the law three times and so would be in a most difficult position if *this* old law were revived. Don't you agree with me, monsieur?"

The judge, looking down at her with a set face, made no response.

"And now, monsieur, there is the matter of licenses for domestic servants. It is provided that all citizens having servants should procure a license or pay a fine. I know that you employ a servant, Monsieur Judge, but I'm not going to ask whether you have the license because, after all, it may not be fair to single out any one person when it seems that all citizens who have domestic help are equally at fault. It is my understanding that no licenses have been issued in the city for more than twenty years. If I'm wrong, I hope you will set me right."

The occupant of the bench did not reply. He continued to stare at her with so much enmity that she should have felt alarm. The only effect it had, however, was to send her on to still more dangerous suggestions.

"It was ordained in the council of His Majesty, King Louis XIV," she said, "that a bounty of twenty livres should be paid each youth who marries by the age of twenty and to each girl at the age of sixteen." She turned her back on the bench and addressed the spectators. "How many of you were married by the ages stipulated in this regulation?"

Cries of "I was!" came from at least a score.

"And none of you ever received your twenty livres! My friends, I propose that a petition be sent at once to the King, demanding that the bounties due be paid now, dating back thirty years or more to the time when the officials of the King ceased paying them!"

The applause with which this suggestion was greeted filled the court-room and the judge had to lift his ruler again and pound on the brass plaque before order was restored.

"And what of the bounty for children?" demanded Félicité as soon as she could make herself heard. "It was decreed that all citizens having children to the number of ten should be paid out of the moneys sent by His Majesty to Canada pensions of three hundred livres a year! It was decreed further that those with twelve children should be paid the yearly sum of four hundred! I wonder how much money would be owed to the people of Montreal with large families if *this* regulation were considered to be legal and binding still? Remember this, the decree read *in future*. It has not been repealed. Monsieur Judge, think of the hundreds of people who will stand before your door demanding their share of the King's money if you decide to continue with this sort of thing! The government of New France will become bankrupt and the courts will have to close, and there will be no money to pay the salaries of royal judges!"

Pandemonium broke loose at this point. It was of no avail to pound with the ruler or shout for order in the court. The judge made every effort and then motioned to the court *huissier,* who was seated in a chair at the entrance. The latter took his pipe from his mouth (as smoking was prohibited in court, he had not lighted it) and threw the doors wide open.

"The court will be cleared at once!" he shouted.

The spectators may not have heard what the *huissier* said but they understood what he had done. Quiet was quickly restored.

The judge sat in silence for several moments in a bitter unwillingness to take the only course now open to him. Then he made a gesture of disgust, said, "The case is dropped," and got up from his chair.

Benoit had managed to fight his way into the court and had followed the proceedings with the liveliest interest. He shook his head as he saw Félicité and Philippe leave the room together and said to himself, "I'm afraid this girl will be wasted on the De Mariat cub!"

III

Even in the middle of winter the Place d'Armes, which served also as the town market, was a busy spot at noon. It was filled with groups of men, chaffering and bargaining and arguing. Sleighs went jingling across the square with much whoaing and slapping of reins on unresponsive flanks. The taverns were full and whenever a door opened a cheerful odor of hot food reached the nostrils of those near by.

Félicité and Philippe were oblivious to all this activity as they made their way along its northern boundary, which was the Rue St. Paul. The Hôtel-Dieu loomed up in front of them before either spoke.

"The judge was very angry," said Philippe.

"Does it matter? He's an unfair, leering, ugly old man. I hope none of his three daughters get husbands!"

"It was brave of you to stand up in front of him and talk that way."

They had reached the entrance to the chapel of the Hôtel-Dieu and without a word, and with what seemed like a single movement, they turned and went inside. There were a few people kneeling before the shrines and a stooped old sacristan was standing at the head of the aisle. They took possession of the end pew. Here they knelt down, crossed themselves, and lowered their heads in prayer.

After several minutes, and without raising her head, Félicité whispered, "Philippe."

"Yes, Félicité?"

"There is—something I must tell you." She had not risen from her knees and her head was still hidden in her hands; an easy position for the telling of anything as unacceptable as what she had to say, but it was hard for her nevertheless to find the words. "Philippe, I—I am to be married!"

He did not move for a long time. She was beginning to wonder if he had heard when he said in a low tone of complete hopelessness: "I knew this had to happen sometime. And that—it couldn't be much longer."

The door behind them swung open and enough draft was created to set the candles spluttering. They waited until the newcomers had passed them on their way up the aisle.

"Who is it you are to marry?"

"The son of Monsieur de Mariat. I'm to be married in France sometime this summer."

He raised his head at that and looked at her, his eyes full of startled inquiry. "A son of De Mariat!" he said. It had been his intention clearly to make some further comment. After a long and anxious glance he changed his mind and lowered his eyes again.

The old sacristan, who shuffled along with his eyes closed and seemed almost beyond the exercise of any physical powers, stopped in the aisle beside them.

"There must be no talking, young people," he said in an admonitory whisper. "Here one comes to adore and to say prayers, not to talk."

They might have told him that they had come to pray and that the one prayer they had already said together would be repeated countless times, even though they would never be together again. But they got to their feet instead and went out through the door.

They lingered by the font of holy water, reluctant to part. There was so much to be said. For many moments, however, they remained silent. Words are useless and stale when the emotions are deeply stirred, a feeble effort to explain the poignant and unexplainable workings of the heart. They might have parted without another word being said if Félicité had not felt she could not let him go that way.

"Do you remember," she asked, "the day when the word reached us of the death of D'Iberville? Perhaps, if you do, you will recall that I said they would be needing assistance and that everyone, even a girl like me, should be ready to help in any possible way?"

"I knew it without being told." He managed to smile at her as he said this. "You've found a way to help."

"Yes, Philippe," she whispered. "I've found a way to help."

There was another long pause. "I've come to a decision," he said. "No matter how much I may be needed here, I'm going to Louisiana. Perhaps I can be of some use there."

"I think"—she found it hard to complete what she had started to say—"you will be happier if you go."

They parted then. Félicité went out to the street by the right door, Philippe by the left.

CHAPTER XIV

BREAKFAST was nearly ready when Philippe returned to the rooms over the carpenter shop after a walk which had taken him along the waterfront but not past the house on the Rue St. Paul. He had not passed the house once during the months which had elapsed since he and Félicité had parted in the chapel of the Hôtel-Dieu. Nor had he seen her in that time.

He looked about him with the sense of satisfaction which comes from the completion of a difficult task. The rooms were stripped bare and in one corner all his belongings, and those of Carpe Bonnet, were packed and strapped in canvas.

"Tomorrow at dawn!" he called to Carpe, who was testing a strip of meat with a fork.

Carpe looked up and nodded, not too happily. "I hope we're not making a mistake, master. Are there unmarried women in Louisiana? You've told me so but—are there enough to go around?"

Philippe intended to say that nothing in the world concerned him so little as that when the thought of a happening on his walk drove everything else out of his mind.

"Carpe," he said, "I saw a ghost today."

The assistant's good eye seemed to grow as large and round as the glass one at this statement. He dropped the fork into the frying pan.

"The ghost of M'sieur Jean-Baptiste." Philippe nodded his head to lend further weight to his words. "It must have been his ghost because, of course, he can't be in Montreal. And yet—Carpe, I swear that I saw him with my own eyes not more than half an hour ago."

"He must have died!" declared Carpe in a frightened voice. "Like the Sieur d'Iberville!"

"He was standing on the Place d'Armes and staring about him. He looked older, naturally, and there was some gray in his hair. But I couldn't be mistaken. It was M'sieur Jean-Baptiste, the same features, the same expressions, the same ways of moving."

Carpe shook his head. "No, he couldn't be here, master. It's just a month ago we had the word he had been made governor again. He would be at his post—if he was still alive!"

"Does a ghost clear its throat and take snuff?" asked Philippe. "Does it take a strip of dried meat from a pocket and eat it? It seems impossible that he can be here in Montreal, particularly as all the family are at the château, but I'm sure that it *was* him, and that he's alive. I'm sure enough to give you a word of warning. He doesn't want it known that he's here— *that* we can be sure of—and so you must keep your mouth closed tight over what I've told you."

Carpe's feelings were hurt that it had been thought necessary to say this. "Master," he said, "I can't be suiting you!"

After the two men had breakfasted, speculating the while on the meaning of what Philippe had seen, the latter made a last tour of inspection of the rooms to make sure nothing had been overlooked. All that he found were a number of wood carvings he had made since coming to Montreal. They were standing in a row on the window sill of his bedroom, soldiers and priests and peasants, some painted, some not, but all showing a highly individual skill. They all seemed to have woebegone expressions as though they knew they were being left.

He picked each one up in turn and examined it. In some of them he appeared to find reason for pride in his craftsmanship but most caused him to shake his head. "My talent is small," he thought. Gathering up the lot, he carried them to the rubbish box. "There will be no time in my life from now on," he said, dropping them in, "for this kind of nonsense, even if I had enough talent to make it worth while; and God and St. Luke know that I haven't."

His face seemed to have lost the capacity to smile and there was a determined gravity about everything he did. His assistant, who had grown accustomed to his smiling ways and his jokes and to hearing him whistle as he worked, was at a loss to understand the change in him. "You don't seem happy at leaving, master," he remarked as he cleaned up after the breakfast. "Don't you want to go, now that the time has come to leave?"

Philippe answered with what seemed an unnecessary degree of emphasis. "Yes, I want to go, God knows!"

"Then is it because Ma'amselle Félicité is to marry the man in France?"

Philippe stared at his companion for several moments with an air of such severity that Carpe realized he had stepped over a forbidden line. "Hop-o'-My-Thumb," said Philippe, "that is a subject we won't discuss from now on, if you please."

Nevertheless he went back to the rubbish box and hunted hurriedly for one of the discarded figures. It was unfinished but showed unmistakable signs of the steady development of his gift. He held it on the palm of his hand and studied it with eyes from which all the severity had melted. It was a head-and-shoulder study of Félicité.

"I'll keep this," he said aloud. "I can finish it from memory."

How easy that should be! Her face was as clear in his mind as though she stood in front of him. Why had he thought he could throw this away with the rest? He must never part with it. It was all he would have.

II

After a dubious tap on the door, as though he knew he should not be asking admission, the baron entered his wife's boudoir, which for several days had served as headquarters for an orgy of dressmaking. The baroness was sitting in a corner in an armchair and with the inevitable coverlet over her knees (outside a May sun of unseasonable ardor was shining) and conducting a discussion with a woman who looked like an animated pincushion and over whose arm dangled samples of satin and lawn and tabby and lutestring. Félicité was seated in another corner, wearing a white linen kirtle which clothed her in complete modesty from head to foot, with the exception of her bare arms. On a stool beside her were a pair of the gloves worn to conceal the arms when sleeves were short. They were of a delicate gray kid and more than two feet long. They were unusual in having no fewer than three drawstrings of pink silk cord, with the most frivolous tassels.

The table in the center of the room was given over entirely to shoes. There were at least a dozen varieties, arranged in pairs with an effect of demureness, and presenting as much range in color and form as, say, the animals which entered the Ark. There were shoes of white kid and brown leather and soft rabbit skin, and Indian moccasins elaborately beaded and as striking in colors as the cloak of a Mayan prince. Some were beautifully embroidered in blues and yellows and many had tasseled drawstrings. All of the shoes had red heels; for this great fad, which had persisted nearly a century, was still maintaining its hold.

"I don't agree, Madame Fruteau," the baroness was saying. "Venetian point lace is too elaborate for the falling bands. It's much too ostentatious." At this point she became aware of her husband standing in the doorway. "Yes, Charles?"

"I would like a word with you."

The baroness sighed as she got up from her comfortable chair and began to cross the room with the aid of a cane. None of the doctors had been able to do anything for her rheumatism, although she held the belief, secretly, that in Paris there were physicians who would soon have her skipping about like a young girl. She never dared mention this belief for fear she would be sent back.

In the hall the baron spoke to her in a whisper. "We have a visitor. An unexpected one."

"Please, Charles, I don't like surprises. Who is it?"

He smiled. "I don't dare mention the name for fear the sound would travel down this hall and finally reach the ears of my enemies." Dropping his voice to a melodramatic whisper, he added, "He's in the eastern tower room."

The occupant of the tower room got to his feet as soon as they appeared in the doorway and greeted them with a bow of exaggerated respect. He had been sitting at the council table, and the chair he had selected should have offered the baroness a clue to his identity.

She did not, however, recognize him at once. He was tall and rather thin, and with quick and intelligent eyes. Although he looked worn and worried, and his dark hair was liberally shot through with gray, he still in some indefinable way gave a suggestion of youthfulness.

The baroness advanced toward him slowly. Then, suddenly, she began to hobble as fast as her crippled joints allowed.

"Jean-Baptiste!" she cried ecstatically. "It's you! Ah, what a wonderful surprise! What a beautiful surprise! And that Charles of mine, refusing to tell me. What a trick to play on a poor sick woman!"

De Bienville took her hands in his and kissed them. Then he put an arm around her and pressed his cheek against hers.

"You are as lovely as ever, sweet sister," he said. "How often I've thought of you! How often I've recalled your kindness to me!"

"I'm an old woman, Jean-Baptiste." The baroness sighed. "I'm old and crippled and full of aches and pains." She began to cry softly with her head against his shoulder. "And you are the governor of the great new colony, and such a wise and famous man! Why aren't you wearing bay leaves in your hair, my Jean-Baptiste?"

"To me you haven't changed," declared the baron, pumping his younger brother's free hand. "And it's twenty years since you left! Twenty years! It takes a long time to write a single page in the book of history."

"But why," demanded the baroness, stepping back and drying her eyes with a handkerchief, "has it been necessary to arrive like a thief in the night? Why must you stay hidden up here? I don't understand this at all!"

"I think," said her husband, "that I can give you the explanation. But first we must make you comfortable." He found a cushion and put it behind her in one of the wooden chairs. "Jean-Baptiste doesn't dare let it be known he's here because the Regent and M'sieur Las would be angry if they knew he had left his post."

De Bienville nodded in agreement. "Luckily," he explained, "there was some trouble with Indians up the river and I gave it out I was going on tour of the delta country. My people seemed to think me a brave man to start out on such a mission with such a small company." He smiled. "How we've raced! We'll have to make the trip in a record short time if suspicions are not to be aroused."

"Going back, you'll have the current of the river with you," said the baron. "That will make it easier."

"We'll travel night and day as I must settle this Indian trouble on the way back. All the men I brought with me are Canadians. I couldn't put full trust in any of the others."

"But, Jean-Baptiste!" cried the baroness. "What brought you back now? All the way up that terrible river and with Indians everywhere! Why did you take such risks?"

De Bienville's mood changed. He became intensely serious. "I had good reasons, you may be sure, Claude-Elizabeth. It will be enough to give you one. I had to come back! I've been twenty years in the south, cut off from the world, hearing and seeing nothing. I felt the need to set eyes once more on the cross up on the mountain, to watch the cold blue waters of the St. Lawrence rolling by, to live if only for a few hours with the people of New France! I had to see the towers of Longueuil again and sit here at this table with some of my brothers around me!" He had begun to pace about the room. "I had been away too long for the good of my soul. I had to come back—to renew my faith!"

After this outburst they were silent for some moments. Then the baron smiled and said, "I can tell you another of your reasons. You were in the dark."

"Yes, Charles, and I'm still in the dark. All I know is the official instructions I receive. I know nothing of the political forces at work in France, although I suspect that among the Regent's advisers there are men determined to see that the Law plans fail. I've been told that men are to be sent out to assist me who'll act in reality against me. I won't know who to trust and who not. And I've had no way of finding out. Every letter I write is opened and read and all the mail I receive has been opened first. I had to come, Charles, so we could arrange some way of getting information back and forth. Letters must be smuggled in and out if I'm not to be like a—a card player who doesn't know the rules of the game."

The baron nodded his head apologetically. "This is my fault," he declared. "I should have foreseen the difficulties you would face. It will be easy to get letters in to you through members of ships' crews. And I must keep closer in touch with what goes on in France so I can advise you."

De Bienville returned to his seat at the table and sat down. The sudden flare-up in feeling had been short-lived. He looked infinitely tired. He lifted the cup of coffee, which had been in front of him when they entered, and took a sip. "Can you imagine, Claude-Elizabeth and Charles, what it means not to taste coffee for twenty years?"

After finishing the cup, he regained some energy of mood. "It's not only my need for enlightenment on royal policy which brought me back. Charles, I come in a demanding mood! I need money, supplies, men, women. No letter could give you any conception of the situation. We're in desperate plights! Why, if I were to take off my coat you would make the discovery that the governor of Louisiana has patches on the seat of his breeches!"

"I've sent money continuously," said the baron, veering quickly to the defensive.

"I've no complaints about the past, Charles. Your purse has always been kept full in some magic way. But now no ordinary magic will suffice: we're going to need miracles."

He had risen to his feet and was standing in front of them. He had again become fanatical in his earnestness. "Charles, the human wastage they send us from France is of little use. There are no looselatches among the women but so many of them are soft and useless. The men are worse— failures, malcontents, misfits, as sour a lot as Luskard grapes."

He pointed a finger down at his brother. "Charles!" he exploded. "I've come to demand the best men that New France has raised. Bakers, millers, farmers, builders! I need them fast so the land can be prepared and homes built for the complaining town spawn that I'll be receiving in shiploads next year!"

The baron tried to answer but the torrent of words continued to sweep over him.

"A city must be built quickly on the bend of the river which Pierre picked. It's a perfect location, Charles. Give me the help I need and in a few years a great city will stand there. All I have so far is the site and a name, a name like music. *Nouvelle Orléans!* Do you like it?"

III

De Bienville did not waken until the rays of the sun touched his face. He stirred, stretched, and sat up.

His first thought was that he was in his house on the compound at Fort St. Louis de Mobile. Then, with the realization that he was in a tower room at Longueuil, he felt a sharp sense of dismay. Hundreds of miles lay between him and his appointed place, an endless, weary distance to be covered by canoe. Would he be able to get back before suspicions were aroused, before the real reason for his absence had been uncovered?

Dismissing such thoughts, he walked to the window in the carnation-colored camisole he had found in his old chest. He peered out cautiously, because his presence in the château must be kept a secret except to members of the family and one servant. His first impression was wonder that the common surrounding the château had become so large. The edge of the forest had been shoved far back, so far that the danger of a surprise attack by Indians was gone forever. The trees, he saw, were beginning to show green. The fine warm season of the settlers' content was starting. How unfortunate that circumstances would keep him a prisoner in this one room! He wanted to go from one end of the seigneurie to the other, to find all his old friends, to hear the gossip of Longueuil in the cheerful exuberance of habitant talk.

Henri, the servant selected to share the secret, brought him a bowl of coffee before he began to dress, saying in an aggrieved tone: "Five times I come to the door and find you still asleep. Five times I make fresh coffee."

The homecomer sprawled out in a chair and began to drink with the greatest enjoyment. "It's marvelous, Henri," he said. "I sometimes think the small things in life are what we need most, that it's better to be able to count on a good cup of coffee in the morning than to succeed in your greatest ambitions."

"Ten Le Moyne brothers!" the servant said. "What good is it to us that there are so many? We never see them. M'sieur Charles condescends to visit us once a year, twice perhaps. The rest? They are here, there, everywhere. There might only be one instead of ten."

"You forget, Henri," said De Bienville, in a mood which had become completely sober, "that there are only four of us left."

"But there were ten once, and it was always the same! Always you were away. When you were big enough you were sent to France to be trained. And when you came back? You went away at once to fight Indians!"

The homecomer nodded his head. "You are right, Henri. We've always been a family of rolling stones." He laid down the cup and got to his feet. "I hear no sounds in the house. Where is your master, Henri?"

"He has the cariole out. He and the mistress are driving. The cariole had to be taken off the snow runners and put back on wheels. Hyacinth had to do it all himself."

"And where is my brother's ward?"

Henri gave his head a vigorous nod. "She's here. In the salon, M'sieur Jean-Baptiste. The dressmaker from Montreal's there with her. Holy Mother Mary, what a mess! Patches and bolts of cloth and feathers and thread everywhere! And a dummy figure for fitting on. Madame had to be dragged away to go driving. How they were gabbling in there!" He nodded his head and grinned. "If I put my head in, it would be snapped off, Holy Mother Mary!"

De Bienville, anxious to lay eyes on the daughter of the beautiful lady who had commanded his devotion once (and whose image, it must be confessed, had become very shadowy in his mind), decided he would risk having his head snapped off by putting it in at the door of the salon. Before acting on this rash resolve, however, he had a much safer thought. He had remembered the squint.

When Charles had set about building the château he had wanted to include in it everything that was to be found in the great houses of France. He had wanted circular towers for decoration, and flying buttresses set anglewise, and flamboyant balustrades, and the handsome dormer windows which had become such a feature of French architecture; and he had been seriously irked that the need for defense had made it impossible for him to satisfy such desires. However, he had insisted on a squint among other things, a small niche in the top of the salon wall from which it was possible to observe what was going on below through a minute observation hole. It was such a very small squint that, once inside, it was hard to move the arms.

De Bienville, accordingly, paid a visit to this little-used niche. Pressing his face close to the aperture, he found himself overlooking a scene of confusion. Tables and chairs were piled high with materials. The buxom dressmaker was engaged on a fitting operation and was indulging in a flow of exclamations such as, "Ma'amselle, stand still, *if* you please!" and "No, no, no!" and *"Voilà!"* and "By all the saints, ma'amselle, keep those hips of yours from moving or——" When his eyes came to rest on the central figure in this scene, however, they stayed there and he failed thereafter to notice anything else.

Félicité was draped in a white gown with a square neck and sleeves of elbow length. The dressmaker was stooped in front of her and pinning into position on the front of the bodice no fewer than five bands of puckered ribbon, each with a bow in the center. The girl's hair had been loosely bound up on the top of her head and gave the impression that she had just emerged from the bath. She was in a gay mood and he could hear her say, "And would the skies fall, Madame Fruteau, if the ribbons were not spaced just that way?"

De Bienville's ideas of feminine beauty were vague and made up of details such as heart-shaped faces and eyelashes which fluttered and eyes like dark pools into which luckless admirers could sink and be forever lost. There was nothing of this kind about the girl on whose slender figure the dress with the puckered ribbons was being fitted. She was different in a way which commanded his instant admiration. Her eyes were clear and direct and her eyelashes, although long enough, did not flutter. Her features had a cameo distinctness and had never, it was clear, been smeared with pomatoms and salves and rouges, and most certainly did not need the assistance of beauty patches. She was so different from his faint remembrance of her mother, in fact, that he found himself entertaining doubts of the relationship.

The dressmaker, it developed, worked quickly. With an impatient "This skirt doesn't sit right!" she had stripped it off before he realized what she was doing and had thus revealed to his startled eyes other things about Félicité which he found easy to admire.

Knowing that to stay longer would be unthinkable, and that he should not have come in the first place, the young governor of Louisiana backed out of the squint and closed the panel after him, taking infinite care not to make any noise.

As there were continuous sounds of activity about the château, De Bienville decided to remain in his room for the balance of the day. He was pacing up and down, and finding the confinement extremely irksome, when there was a knock on the door. Opening it cautiously, he discovered Félicité on the threshold.

"M'sieur Charles will be delayed," she said, bowing. "One of the tenants, Georges Catin, is so ill that his life is despaired of. M'sieur Charles is very fond of him and is paying him a visit."

"Old Georges Catin was doddering on the brink of the grave when I left twenty years ago," declared De Bienville. "And you are Félicité-Ann Halay, I think."

"Yes, M'sieur Jean-Baptiste."

"Won't you come in? There are reasons, as you probably know, why it's dangerous for me to show myself, even at a tower door."

She entered the room, closing the door after her but continuing to rest a hand on the knob. She was wearing a simple blue dress with a flounced skirt which made her look very young.

"Is there anything to be done for your comfort, M'sieur Jean-Baptiste? I was told to see that you lacked nothing."

"I lack nothing, except the freedom to walk about Longueuil and see my old friends." He studied her face for several moments and then said abruptly, "I knew your mother, Félicité."

"Yes. I—I know about it."

"I was very much in love with her. So much in love that Charles, whose plans didn't include an early marriage for me, found it necessary to break things up. I don't believe he found it hard. The devotion was entirely on my side."

"I've known the story for many years, M'sieur Jean-Baptiste. And I've always thought my mother shouldn't have agreed to return to France."

"Naturally I felt that way. At first, I mean. Later I realized that she had acted with good sense."

Félicité asked eagerly, "Would you have recognized me if you hadn't known who I was?"

"You don't resemble your mother. And yet it's because of seeing you that I'm able again to remember how she looked. You see, mademoiselle, memories have a way of becoming dim, even in the matter of people to whom you've been most devoted. I'd retained only the vaguest recollections. But a moment ago you raised your head quickly in a way she herself—and suddenly her image came flooding back into my mind!"

"Isn't it strange that I could bring back your memory of her when you say I don't resemble her at all?"

De Bienville's mind had gone back to the past. He smiled reminiscently. "I remember the first time I saw her. She was coming out of church and I fell in love with her at one glance. A drop of rain fell on her face and she looked up quickly, just as you did." His smile began to show awareness of the present and of her. "And now that I can recall her face again, I can see there *are* points of resemblance. She was dark and you are fair. Her eyes were a very dark brown and yours are gray. But the shape of your face and your mouth are much the same as hers."

The girl's eyes were shining eagerly. "I can't tell you, M'sieur Jean-Baptiste, how happy it makes me to hear that I take after her a little."

"You should be happy, Félicité, that you are—just as you are. I couldn't consent to any changes in you at all."

As he showed no intention of relating more about his romantic first meeting with her mother, she said, "Please tell me more about seeing her come out of the church."

"There's nothing more, I'm afraid."

"What did she wear?"

He thought this over. "A cloak and a hood. I don't remember what color but I recall thinking her beautifully dressed. She started away from the church, not wanting to be caught in the rain. And I followed."

"Naturally, M'sieur Jean-Baptiste."

"It began to rain almost at once and she drew the hood up over her head, so I didn't catch another glimpse of her face. Then she began to run. I remember being surprised at the grace with which she ran."

"And you still followed, of course?"

"Of course. I was in such a dazed condition that I kept right on, even after she reached the house where she lived and went in. I don't believe she had seen me. I was drenched to the skin before I got back to my brother's house."

"If you had only been a more determined lover!" She shook her head at him. "You should have married her in spite of everything. And then I would have been your daughter, wouldn't I?"

"Yes, I—I suppose you would."

"I would have liked that very much."

He was not sure he would have liked it as much as that. Discovering her in this way for the first time, he was aware that the sentiment she inspired in him was not a fatherly one. After she left he gave a great deal of thought to her coming wedding, which Charles had mentioned in one of his letters, and was disturbed to find himself wishing it did not have to be.

That afternoon he had a talk with Charles about the matters which had brought him north. He found that Félicité kept coming into his mind and that, when this happened, his interest in everything else slackened.

"Charles," he said finally, "I'm not sure I approve this marriage you've arranged for Félicité."

The baron hesitated before answering. "I'm not sure I approve of it entirely myself," he said. "But the bargain hinged on it, naturally."

The wave of color which swept over De Bienville's face made it clear that this was his first intimation of anything back of the approaching nuptials. "Bargain? *Mon dieu,* Charles, what do you mean?"

The baron decided to tell the whole story, although he became doubtful quickly enough of the wisdom of doing so when he saw the effect it was having on his brother. The latter was deeply disturbed.

"And so," interrupted De Bienville, before he had the whole story, "this poor child is being forced into a marriage which may turn out badly so that I could be reinstated as governor of Louisiana!"

"I prefer to put it this way," said the baron quickly. "There was only one man with the proper knowledge of the country and the people to be put at the head. It wasn't done to further your ambitions or mine; but so the colony could prosper and all the continent beyond the river might become part of France."

The flush ebbed slowly from the young governor's face. "There's still time to undo it, Charles. She isn't married yet."

"It can't be undone! They've fulfilled their part. You are governor of Louisiana, as they promised, and now we must live up to our side of it. It's not proving easy as it is. I may tell you that I'm having great difficulty in making up the dowry. Do you care to guess at the extent of De Mariat's cupidity?"

"No!" declared De Bienville. "I find it hard to discuss this matter at all. I can see one way of getting out of your agreement. I can resign my post, Charles! Had that possibility occurred to you? If I resigned there would be no need to marry her to this fellow."

"Yes, you could resign your post," said the baron. Then he gave his head an emphatic shake. "But you won't! When you've recovered from this first shock you'll realize that personal feelings can't be permitted to govern your course. There's too much at stake. An empire, Jean-Baptiste! An empire for France!"

There was another long pause. The younger brother had realized at once, however, that Charles was right, that when it came to a decision he could never let personal considerations interfere with his work. The strange and beautiful land to which D'Iberville had taken him was in his blood. He would never be happy away from it.

"You are right," he said finally. "We must keep on, all of us. But why must the hardest part fall to this poor child?"

IV

The young governor overslept again and it was Félicité's voice which finally wakened him the following morning. It came from the direction of the inner court and he heard her laugh as he crept cautiously toward the window which faced inside. He stopped when he saw her below, talking to a wizened old man with thin white hair who sat in an armchair outside the smithy door, because she saw him at the same time. The smiling expression she had been wearing changed to one of dismay and she gave her head an almost imperceptible shake which he took to mean that he must be careful. He raised a hand in a hasty greeting and retired from the window.

In a few minutes there was a cautious tap on the door and Félicité entered, carrying a tray with his breakfast. There was a pot of chocolate and a loaf of crusty bread straight out of the oven.

"Good morning," she said. "This is quite an improper proceeding but it was a case of breaking the proprieties or letting you go without breakfast. I could tell the cook the breakfast was for Madame but Henri couldn't if I'd left it to him."

"I will enjoy my breakfast doubly."

She placed the tray on the table and then turned an accusing glance in his direction. "M'sieur Jean-Baptiste," she said, "you will have to be more careful. Already there are stories going around among the servants. They say there must be a ghost in the château. They've heard footsteps in strange places and seen faces at windows which disappear at once. Sooty-Arms was telling me about it when I looked up and saw you."

"Was that old man Sooty-Arms?" De Bienville's face wore a look of incredulity. "I remember him as a big, strong fellow who had been a soldier and wore his old regimental white coat and buff jacket when he wanted to be dressed up. The red distinctions on the coat were badly worn but I always thought he carried himself like a marshal of France."

"That was twenty years ago. The poor old man is so weak now that they have to carry him out to his chair and keep moving it so he stays in the sun. Hyacinth was saying last night that he ought to be tied in so the wind wouldn't have a chance to blow him out over the walls."

"Does Sooty-Arms believe in this story of a ghost at large in the château?" asked the governor with a smile.

Félicité shook her head. "He's too wise still for that. In fact he has guessed the truth. He was saying to me that the château had *a visitor from the south.*"

"Trust him to hit on the truth." De Bienville was beginning on his breakfast with an eagerness which could be credited to the appetizing odor of the hot bread. "I wish he had the strength to climb these stairs. Now that he knows I'm here, there would be no harm in having a talk with him."

Félicité turned to leave the room, her flounced skirt rustling as she walked, but he called her back in an indignant tone. He put his cup down and shoved the platter of bread to one side as a sign that he now intended to devote himself to talk.

"Félicité," he asked, "are you content with this marriage which has been arranged for you?"

She was taken aback by the unexpectedness of the question and a flush crept into her cheeks. She proceeded, however, to answer without any reservations. "Sometimes I'm so frightened at the thought of going to France to marry a stranger that I—I feel like running away and hiding." Then she added hastily: "Isn't that natural under the circumstances, M'sieur Jean-Baptiste? There have been many marriages between people who've never seen each other and I think the brides must always have felt as I do. I'm told that such marriages have generally turned out well——"

"Who told you that? Charles?"

She hesitated. "Yes, it was M'sieur Charles. But I'm not always that way. At other times I say to myself that, after all, I have some common sense and should be able to—to——"

"Charles says you have a gift for management." De Bienville was keeping his eyes fixed on her intently. "He also tells me you were in love with Philippe."

She had faced about and was standing with a hand on the knob of the door. Without lowering her eyes or indulging in any of the customary symptoms of maidenly modesty, she answered simply, "Yes, M'sieur Jean-Baptiste."

The governor began to speak with sudden vehemence. "I am against what Charles has done. It was wrong to involve you in our affairs. I know what the purpose of it was and I find it hard to look you in the face when I realize what a sacrifice you're making for my sake."

"We must all make sacrifices. No one has been more unselfish than you, M'sieur Jean-Baptiste."

"I'm angry at Charles for his scheming. The fact that I'm governor again because of it adds rather than takes away from the feelings I hold at this moment toward the head of the family. But I'm sure he was right in the matter of your boy-and-girl romance with Philippe. There couldn't have been any lasting happiness in such an uneven match. From what Charles tells me you are capable of climbing high."

She opened the door. "I think now I must go, m'sieur."

She brought him his tray again at noon. It was loaded with dishes and he crossed the room in such a hurry to relieve her of its weight that some of the soup was spilled.

"How very hungry you must be!" she said.

She did not immediately release her hold of the tray, perhaps through fear of what might happen if it were entrusted to him. Accordingly they remained facing each other for several moments, each holding one side and anyone who could not see the expression of his face might have suspected they were disputing possession of it.

"Yes, I'm hungry," he said. "But the appetite which consumes me doesn't necessarily have anything to do with food. There are many kinds of hunger, Félicité."

"That is true," she said, nodding across the tray. "M'sieur Charles eats very little and I think *his* appetite is for the accomplishment of great things. Yours too, perhaps?"

"Mine too, perhaps. But there are still other kinds of hunger."

"Come! Your food will get cold. And it's such a very fine dinner. See, there's a fish soup, which is very hot and good, and a ragout, and the last wood dove laid down in the fall. The cook just discovered it and I bespoke it at once. I must remind the baroness to thank the cook for it, although she doesn't expect one bite of it."

She placed the tray on a table and, as he still lingered and seemed interested only in watching her, she drew up a chair for him and insisted that he sit down. He did so but only after obtaining her consent to sit beside him.

"I'm starved for talk!" he declared. "It will be a most wonderful kindness if you will indulge me in some news of old friends."

Accordingly, as he went on with his dinner, she chatted about the people of Longueuil and the country at the junction of the rivers, telling him stories of Old Kirkinhead and Polycarpe Bonnet and the lawyer Benoit and Tante Seulette. She told them with spirit and several times he laid down his knife and fork and laughed out loud.

When he reached the cheese stage of the meal she got to her feet with a determination which he made no effort to combat. "I must go," she said. "How am I to explain to the cook this sudden increase in the appetites of the family?"

The afternoon was devoted to a consideration of what would be needed in the way of supplies and settlers and De Bienville was not surprised that Félicité arrived with the baron to take part in the discussion. She seated herself between them at the table, spreading out a sheaf of papers in front of her, and proceeded to prove herself a well-trained assistant, serious, alert, full of suggestions. She had the answer to every question the baron asked almost as soon as it was out of his mouth. How many of the largest-sized canoes could be obtained at once, and what would they cost? Did the military stores still contain any of the musketoons which had been put on sale after the declaration of peace? Where could adequate supplies of flour and salt and sugar be obtained? Her prompt answers contained all the needed information.

When it came to consideration of the people who might be induced to go to Louisiana she was equally helpful, for she contributed bits of personal information and such pertinent remarks as, "No, no, he wouldn't do; he has a weak stomach and would be a great nuisance," or, "He's strong and brave enough but his wife's a great flirt and there would be trouble from the first day."

When the discussion reached the question of the need of a builder she was prepared to speak up for Philippe and was taken completely by surprise when the baron said, "That's filled already."

De Bienville asked, "Who are you giving me?"

"The best man in Montreal. Philippe Girard. He left on the boats for Quebec yesterday at dawn. You couldn't find a better man anywhere, Jean-Baptiste."

The younger brother observed that Félicité was hurt as well as surprised at thus hearing of the builder's departure and he asked himself with a sinking of the heart, "Is she still in love with this young Philippe?"

Félicité was disturbed beyond measure by the fact that Philippe had left without making any effort to bid her farewell. She tried to explain it on the ground that she had been at Longueuil for over a week. But could he not have spared a few hours to cross the river and see his old friends before leaving? "He thought it better not to come!" she said to herself disconsolately. "And now I shall never see him again!"

She had become pale and there was a pained look in her eyes. The young governor thought, "I was feeling sorry for Philippe but now—now I find myself envying him."

The baron glanced at the papers in front of him. "I believe we've covered everything. You'll be able now, Jean-Baptiste, to return with an easy mind."

"Then I'll start after dark tonight. Every hour counts in getting back. My men will be waiting for me farther down the river." De Bienville gestured toward the south with his hand. "Only one of the mad Le Moynes would come two thousand miles to spend fifty hours or so at home. Levelheaded citizens would have a good laugh if they knew. What foolhardiness, what waste of time and effort! And yet, Charles, it's been well worth it. I can return to my post with a feeling of confidence that everything will be well." He fumbled in his pocket and brought out a sheet of paper. "Here, Charles, are the names of the men who came with me. All of them, as you'll see, come from hereabouts. See to it that something is done for the families of these men, who came all this distance with me and are now going back without having seen Montreal or a single familiar face. That's devotion in the highest sense! These fellows of mine are of the stuff of Adam Dollard!"

Félicité rose from the table and gathered up the papers. Finding it hard to keep her voice under control, she said, "I'll begin on these matters at once, M'sieur Charles."

De Bienville followed her to the door. "There's nothing to compel you to marry this man," he said. "If I return my commission you will be freed of all obligation."

She answered in such a startled tone, "No, no! That would never do!" that the baron heard and looked at them with an air of surprise.

"You need have no fears for me," she declared in a low voice. And without giving him time to say anything more, she left the room.

De Bienville seated himself again at the table. He fingered the narrow gold chain around his neck which was almost concealed under his cravat "Charles," he said, "when I found you had arranged with Marie to leave for France, I took it very hard; much harder than you realized at the time. The first night I nearly threw myself in the river. It took me a long time to get over it. The cure, of course, was complete when it came." His lips drew up in a wry smile. "It's strange how near history has come to repeating itself."

The baron was so surprised that he stared at his brother with rounded eyes. "What's this? You're not telling me that you've fallen in love with Félicité?"

"If my feelings haven't progressed quite to the stage of falling in love," said De Bienville, sighing deeply, "it's so close that I find it hard to tell the difference. What a wife she would make! Isn't there some other way, Charles, of contenting the De Mariats, father and son?"

"You should know that there's no other way."

"Twice I've stood on the threshold of happiness. Twice duty, in the guise of my eldest brother, has closed the door in my face." De Bienville sighed again. "She's put a spell on me, this brave, gray-eyed child! It's a very good thing for my own sake that I'm leaving tonight."

CHAPTER XV

THE DAYS which followed the departure of De Bienville were busy ones for Félicité. The baron found it hard, seemingly, to take much share in the work involved. He preferred to talk over plans for tearing down the house on the Rue St. Paul and building a new one on much more ambitious lines. The idea of a trip to take in most of Europe, and even England, had gained possession of him and he discussed it continually. When she brought matters to him for his approval, even lists of purchases, he would sigh and say that, if she knew what should be done, he would rely on her judgment. Some days he would say at breakfast, with a half-guilty air, something as follows: "I'm going to be busy all day, my small one. Those letters which have been accumulating: I'm going to spend this whole day clearing them up, once and for all. You mustn't bring anything else to me." This was all the intimation she needed that he would spend most of the day with Father Benignus, an amiable little priest who also was enthusiastic about native silverwork. They would spend uninterrupted hours gabbling happily about pap bowls and *écuelles* and *burettes* and *cuillers à potage*. The next morning she would find no diminution in the pile of unanswered letters.

She had noticed this tendency to slacken ever since the day when the news had reached him of the handing over of Louisiana to Antoine Crozat and his trading associates. That blow had stolen some of the fighting spirit from him and he had never succeeded in recovering the hot white glow of crusading zeal which had driven him before into such excesses of planning and preparing and saving. But now it was becoming noticeable to everyone, and he was inclined to boast of it. "I slept late this morning," he would say. "What a thoroughly lazy hound I'm getting to be!"

Gradually she took most of the work in charge. This was a good thing for her as it kept her busy and gave her little time to think about the certainty that she would never see Philippe again in this life. It was only when she was through with her labors for the day and had climbed the

stairs to her own room that she could relive in her mind the last moment
they had spent together in the chapel at the Hôtel-Dieu and count ove
the few words they had exchanged like the beads of a rosary.

To her intense relief, a postponement of her wedding became necessary
Word of the change of plans reached her in a letter, her first, from Au
guste de Mariat. It seemed to her a stilted piece of writing, couched i
classical style and full of high-flown phrases. His appointment, it seemed
had been most inexplicably delayed and so it would be wise for her t
delay her departure until more definite plans could be made. He regrette
the postponement of the much anticipated day when he would first se
eyes on his bride. And he remained her devoted, disconsolate, and hopefu
servant.

She was so overjoyed that she found it hard to keep her relief out of th
answer she wrote. She took the final draft of the note to the baroness, wh
gave her the accolade of immediate approval.

"It's a nice and polite letter," said the baroness. "I think it much to
nice for this conceited, ill-bred bourgeois my Charles has picked as
husband for you."

The summer wore away. Barges and canoes plied busily up and dow
the river against the day when the ice of winter would lock off eac
town of New France from the others and, of course, from the rest of th
world. Félicité sat oftener in the baron's cabinet than he did and trans
acted unaided a large share of the business of the ever-growing house c
Le Moyne. Her trousseau had been completed but she had not stored an
of it in the chest with the *till*. One day the miniature of Auguste d
Mariat was knocked to the floor and was stepped on; so that thereafte
its dented face wore a squinting and unpleasant expression. The baro
and Benoit finally completed arrangements for the raising and depositin
of the excessively large marriage settlement.

And then autumn came with its haze and it curious manifestations c
light and its radiance of crimson and gold and russet, turning slowly int
purples and browns. *La Grosse Gerbe* was celebrated in every commu
nity and the thrifty housewives were up to their elbows in the puttin
away of food for the long winter ahead.

The baroness seldom left her chair now and so it devolved on Félicit
to see that the work of preserving, and the pickling of cucumbers an
onions and samphire leaves, the storing of smoked hams and veniso
and eels, and the filling of the winter pits with turnips and carrots an
apples, went on satisfactorily. She found the work thoroughly uninte
esting, her mind being at all times in the countinghouse and filled wit
lists and invoices and deposit slips.

She was in the kitchen one day in early October, wearing a huge apro
fastened over the shoulders and with a blue belt at the waist and two al

surdly large pockets, when the baron came running down the stairs with such haste that she rushed out to meet him, fearing that there had been bad news. He had an open letter in one hand and an expression of excitement on his face.

"Félicité! My small one!" he cried. "There's been a change of plan. Auguste de Mariat isn't being sent to one of the tax offices in the French provinces after all. He's being sent—by St. Chrysostom, you'll find this hard to believe!"

"Here?" she asked with an excitement to match his. "Is he being sent to Montreal?"

"No, not here! He's going to Louisiana! He's to act under Jean-Baptiste in a capacity to be determined when he gets there, and he'll reach the colony on the first ship from France in the spring. And you, my Félicité, are to meet him and be married there."

It took her several moments to grasp the full significance of the news. "I won't have to go to France!" she cried then. "I won't have to pass the inspection of disapproving matrons and I won't be criticized for my mistakes! I won't have to live so far away from everyone. I won't be an exile —oh, M'sieur Charles, I've been so frightened about it!"

"There will be many people from Longueuil in Louisiana and that will make it easy for you. Jean-Baptiste will be there to keep an eye on you."

"Yes—and Philippe."

The baron looked at her quickly. "Yes, and Philippe. He will be there, of course."

So great was her relief at the new arrangements that she paid less attention to the unpleasant side of the news, the fact that now her wedding had taken on a definiteness it had always lacked before. Gravity replaced the pleased expression on her face when she realized this, and it was then she noticed a corresponding gravity in the manner of the baron.

"I'm more convinced than ever," he said, replacing the letter in the crimson-flapped pocket of his waistcoat, "that the senior De Mariat is set on the failure of the whole Louisiana project. Why then is he sending his son out? Is he going in the role of a troublemaker?" Félicité became aware that he was regarding her with a sudden intentness. "This may make things very difficult for you."

"Why?" she demanded hotly. "Have you any doubts as to where I would stand?"

The baron shook his head. "At this stage, none at all. But marriages upset old loyalties. When interests merge—well, you may face a problem later on."

Winter settled down. The baron sat for his portrait to a young priest from Quebec, who whistled cheerfully as he painted, and who put down on canvas his impression of a man with a full face and an air of cupidity rather than the hint of nobility which was there. The baroness, whose

features were becoming thin and sharp, turned very religious and spen
much of her time with a returned Jesuit missionary. The old priest had
become fanciful from the hardships he had suffered and told her of hav
ing seen angels hovering in the mist over the great falls between the
lakes and of having talked with God, who came to him once in the guise
of a man when he was weary and discouraged. The baron seemed satis
fied with his portrait and the baroness was happy with the company and
talk of the frail missionary.

It proved a long and cold winter, the streets packed so high with snow
and rutted so unevenly that walking became an adventure. Snow backed
up on roofs and parapets and whitened the gargoyles on the churches. Al
narrow alleys were so drifted that they became impassable. Men said they
had never known a longer or more dismal winter; but finally, a full fort
night late, the ice went out in the river. A week after the current was
running free again, Jean Carrier arrived from Quebec in the King's
barge, and Félicité realized that the day of her departure had caught up
with her at last.

II

The afternoon light was waning as Félicité wandered over the commons between the Porte Lachine at the far west end of the town and
the houses on the Rue St. Pierre. A few of the houses had invaded the
once open space and were blocking off the lights from the monastery
of the Recollet Fathers at the north end. She resented this fiercely, knowing that it meant the coming of change. "I suppose the commons will all
be built up someday!" she said to herself. Although she would never
again see the palisaded town under the mountain, she wanted to believe
it would always remain as she knew it and as she would remember it.

She had intended to make an earlier start but she had found herself
with too many things to do. There was her packing to be finished, and
the baroness had been ill, and the baron had suddenly awakened to the
fact that he was to be left with all the management of the many companies on his own shoulders and had spent feverish hours with her, going
over lists and reports. It was now too late, she knew, for her to be on the
streets alone, and she hurried her steps.

She walked down the Rue St. Sacrement, her eyes fixed on the roofs
of the Seminary and the wish in her mind that she could see once again
the tall figure of the kind old man who had ruled there so many years but
who, alas, was now gone. Her steps became very brisk when she descended into the maze of streets and lanes about the market square and
she was glad to hear the voice of Pierre Prévost calling the hour somewhere in the direction of the Rue Capitale. She waited until the watch

man came around the nearest corner, lighting his horn lantern as he walked.

He recognized her at once. "It's you, of course, ma'amselle," he said, wagging his head at her. "I've been expecting you. Indeed I have, ma'amselle. I knew I would see you before you left in the morning." The man who had wept in front of the old Le Moyne house on the day when the word of D'Iberville's death had been received shut the slide of the lantern and held it up in front of her face. "You're a little pale, ma'amselle. It won't do! You must go to your wedding with roses in your cheeks. Do you wonder why I talk this way? I'll tell you, ma'amselle. I've always been interested in everything concerning the Le Moynes. I've always felt like one of them. I was born on the same day as Pierre and *at the very same moment!* Yes, ma'amselle, I was indeed. The great D'Iberville and I should have been as much alike as two peas out of one pod. But he, that Pierre Le Moyne, had the marks of greatness on him from the start. And I? I was nothing. He used to laugh at me and push me about, and he had a dozen nicknames for me. And as for me"—he smiled wistfully— "I worshiped the ground he walked on!"

A man was coming down the Rue St. Paul with hurried steps. She recognized the baron at the same moment that he saw her and came to a halt.

"Praise to our Father, it is you!" he said.

"Yes, M'sieur Charles." She looked at him apprehensively. "Is there bad news?"

"I became worried when I couldn't find you in the house. I waited an hour, two hours. As you hadn't returned then, I started out to look for you."

Pierre Prévost, who was as meek as a lamb in the daytime but became bold and even assertive at night when he felt that he had the town in his keeping, said at this point: "I can tell you why Ma'amselle is out so late. She's saying her farewell to Montreal."

"Yes, M'sieur Charles. I wanted to see everything again once more. I love it all so much! I want to carry away in my mind such a picture that I'll never forget a single thing." They were passing the intersection with the Rue St. Joseph and she came to a halt. "There! The cobbler's window! I hope it's still light enough to see."

Alcide Lasource, the cobbler, kept a booth in front of his shop and there had on display, as an inducement to others to buy their footwear of him, the wooden lasts of many of his best customers with cards attached. It had become a common saying in town, "He must be getting rich because Alcide has put his last on display." When Félicité was fifteen years old, and her feet presumably would not grow any more, he had made lasts for her and had placed them out in front. They had been there ever since and she had stopped at least a hundred times, to look at them and read her name on the dusty card and say to herself, "I think I have a rather nice foot."

The watchman understood what she meant. He stepped over to the booth, which was still unshuttered, and held his lantern close to it. "In the right corner," said Félicité. But in the spot where the pair had always been there was on display instead a huge last with lark-heels and turned-up toes with the name on it of a man who was getting wealthy in the river trade. "He has been changing things about," said the watchman, running the light along the rows of shoes. Félicité, however, knew better. Alcide Lasource never changed things about. It was clear that he knew her for a lost customer and was using the space to better advantage.

She drew a disappointed sigh. "Of course he has to think of his trade," she said. "But it makes me realize that I'm no longer a part of Montreal!"

The baron called in a peremptory tone, "Alcide! Come out here, man!" He nodded his head to Félicité and said, "I'll give him a piece of my mind!"

She protested at once. "Please, no, M'sieur Charles. I don't want any trouble on my last night at home!"

The cobbler, who was old and shortsighted, came out from behind the booth, holding a candle and saying in a reedy voice: "It's clear, Alcide, that you're getting old. You have no mind left. Here is the proof of it again: you've forgotten to put up the shutters." He raised his candle and peered out at them. "Has Alcide's stock been stolen, messires?"

"No," said the baron shortly. "Only one item is missing. What, will you tell us, have you done with Mademoiselle's last?"

The cobbler turned and blinked at Félicité. "What has Alcide done with Ma'amselle's last? Ha, he will show you!" He turned and went back into the dark recess where he had his working quarters. In less than a minute he was back with a neatly wrapped parcel in his hands, which were trembling with eagerness. He thrust the parcel out in front of him, not being sure where she stood. "They are yours, ma'amselle," he said. "When Alcide heard you were going away several days ago, he said to himself, 'Never will the little ma'amselle have a neater last than you made for her, Alcide. You must give them to her.' Take them with you, ma'amselle, and when there is a need for new shoes go to a cobbler and say to him, 'Here, these were made by Alcide Lasource, the best cobbler in New France, and I want shoes made from them.' You will do well to tell that cobbler he must not deviate by the hundredth part of an inch if he wants to make the perfect shoe for those neat little feet of yours, ma'amselle. Get that into his head and you will always walk in comfort."

Félicité took the parcel, saying to herself, "There's not an inch of space left but I must make room somehow!" Aloud she said, "I can't thank you enough, M'sieur Alcide, for this very kind gift."

"A maker of shoes," said the cobbler, beginning to expand in the light of the approval he felt about him, "knows his customers by their feet. He thinks of them in his own mind as M'sieur High Bunions, or Madame Lark-Heels or old Broken Arches. You, ma'amselle, I've always thought of you as Young Deerfoot, for your feet are as slim as a fawn's. They tell me you've grown up into a very pretty lady. In all honesty Alcide might not recognize you if you didn't speak but if a million feet came walking past him he could pick yours out without fail."

The trio walked slowly up the Rue St. Paul. The watchman had decided to consider himself a member of the party and he stalked rather importantly in front, swinging his lantern back and forth to facilitate the recognition of familiar places. In addition he took on himself the role of cicerone. "See, ma'amselle!" he would say. "The house where Adam Dollard lived! You must never forget it, you must remember everything about it, even the way the paint has been allowed to peel off."

"It's a disgrace!" declared the baron. "I shall go tomorrow and demand that there be no more of this neglect of historic places!"

The watchman halted when they reached the Rue St. Gabriel. "Have you ever stood here, ma'amselle, and looked between those two houses to the left?"

"Yes!" she answered eagerly. "You can see the cross on the mountain from here."

"You see it in the daytime, ma'amselle." The watchman nodded his head with a suggestion almost of pomposity. "I see it only by night. My eyes have become so accustomed to the dark that I can perceive things no one else can. Would you believe that, as I stand here, I can see the cross up there very clearly?"

"I would *not* believe it!" declared the baron after one indignant glance at the black space between the two houses. "Must we stand about while you indulge in your silly boasting, Pierre?"

"But I *can* see it!" protested the watchman. "I tell you I can!"

At this point they heard the banging of shutters a short distance up the Rue St. Gabriel and realized that Alcide had not been the only merchant in Lower Town to forget this important task on this particular evening. Monsieur Gadois, a gentle old man who kept a shop where he sold a little of everything (but, alas, not much of anything) and had raised a large family by some miracle of industry and frugality, was correcting the same oversight. He saw they were watching him and, with a final impatient shove at a recalcitrant shutter, walked down curiously to the intersection of the streets.

"So, Baron, it is you," he said. "And the little lady who is leaving us in the morning. Ma'amselle, I am indeed glad of this chance to beg forgiveness for my third daughter Annette, who serves as a helper to Madame Fruteau."

"Your Annette is very bright and nice," said Félicité. "I became very fond of her while I was in the hands of Madame Fruteau. Why should there be any talk of forgiveness?"

"Because," said the old merchant, who was quite short and on that account had fallen into the habit of holding himself up straight, "she took a great liberty. When no one was about she sewed a small lock of her hair —she wanted to be sure, so she used a whole lock instead of just one hair —into the hem of your wedding gown. I have told her, ma'amselle, it will be of no avail, because control of the future does not come out of deceit. But she is sure, my Annette, that it will bring things about so she will be married herself within a year after you."

"Isn't she too young to be thinking of marriage?" Félicité was worried, remembering the childish slimness of the dressmaker's helper.

"She will be fifteen soon," said Gadois, as though that disposed of any possible objection. "I will walk along with you for a few blocks, if there is no objection to my company. I can see you are making your farewells and so would prefer to be alone, ma'amselle; but inasmuch as there are two with you now, a third will make no difference. And there is something I would like to say to you."

The baron was thinking, "Both of these simpletons knew what brought her out and I didn't!" The possibility that there was something lacking in him reduced him to such a pliable mood that he said to the little shopkeeper, "Join us by all means, Edouard."

"What is it, m'sieur, that you want to tell me?" asked Félicité as the now augmented party resumed progress up the main street. They were passing a tavern from which issued the sound of vigorous fiddling and over the latch of which hung the red indienne cover of the minstrel's instrument as an invitation to enter and hear the music. Félicité wished she could add to her memories a glimpse at the inside of a Montreal tavern on an evening when a wandering player was on hand.

"Ma'amselle," said the shopkeeper, "marriage is an important step and a difficult one. Fortunately there are the old proverbs for guidance. What I wanted to urge on you was to have belief in our proverbs, ma'amselle, because truly they've grown out of long experience. Let me give you an example.

"Here is Pierre Prévost with us," he went on. "Did you know that Pierre's wife forgot the warning against any sweeping in the house after supper because it condemns a couple to poverty for the whole of their lives, and that she actually began to use a broom on the evening of their marriage, just as Pierre was getting ready to go out on his rounds? He's a very conscientious man, our Pierre, and did not stay at home, even on his marriage night. And what was the result? Will you tell her yourself, Pierre?"

"It's a fact," said the watchman, nodding his head solemnly, "that we've been poor ever since."

"Both Pierre and his wife know that they'll always be poor and are reconciled to it."

"That is true." The watchman nodded again. "I've never said this to my good wife but it's also true that I've never been able to stand the sight of a broom since."

"And now there is my own experience," said the shopkeeper. "You've heard the saying that the one who gets into bed first on the wedding night will be the first to die? You have heard it, of course, but do you believe it? Let me tell you then that my little wife forgot about it and, as she was very modest, she was into the bed and had the covers tucked up around her neck before I knew it. Ah, ma'amselle, how careless of me that I didn't send her out of the room and get into the bed myself! I knew I would never be happy without her and I wanted to be the first to go." He gave vent to a deep sigh. "She died a year ago, as might have been expected under the circumstances."

Félicité was walking beside him and she could see that his deeply lined face had taken on an expression of the utmost melancholy.

"How long were you together, M'sieur Gadois?" she asked.

"Forty years!" Another sigh. "Forty happy years! And it might have been fifty if I had shown the proper care on our first night together." He brushed aside his own memories to apply the moral for her benefit. "It's said you are marrying a man who is quite a few years older than you are and so it would be a very great pity if you were the first to die. Let him, then, be the one to make the first move."

In a few minutes after that they found themselves in front of the Le Moyne house. There were lights at many of the windows and it was clear that there was much activity inside. Some of the neighbors had dropped in, Félicité concluded, to wish her Godspeed.

Then she began to cry. One moment she was standing in the midst of her three elderly escorts and smiling at them gratefully, the next she had buried her face in her hands and was weeping with a suddenness which took them completely by surprise.

"You've been kind to me," she said between sobs. "You've made my last evening so pleasant and you've said and done all the things I needed to keep my mind free. But now it's over, and there's nothing left and tomorrow I leave you! I love Montreal, I love all the people here! I love you, M'sieur Charles, and Madame Claude-Elizabeth, and all the companies and the offices and the warehouses, and the clerks and the sailors and everyone I've worked with! It's going to be hard to do without you!"

III

The circumstances under which Félicité departed the next day could not have been more impressive if she had been a princess of the blood. Jean Carrier had bedecked his barge as though the governor himself were on board. The blue silk coverings which on such occasions were draped over the well of the barge had been brought out. There was a chair for her with a fine plum-colored cushion. The fleur-de-lis floated at the masthead, with the marine flag of three fleurs on a shield with crossbars.

"It's as fitting to do honor to a pretty bride," declared the King's messenger as he helped her aboard, "as to one of these stiff-necked courtiers they send us nowadays from France. The old comte, how different he was! When Frontenac was with us this little craft seemed to know it had greatness in its care. How lightly it skimmed the water, how proudly it carried its canvas!" He glanced down at her face, which was pale in spite of the excitement of the moment. "But why do you have to be married to one of these mincing clinchpoops from the court when there must have been plenty of fine Canadian lads clamoring for you?"

The waterfront was crowded with people, all of whom seemed genuinely sorry she was leaving. As the barge nosed its way out into the current of the river they began to sing *"Là-haut sur ces montagnes."* The tears streamed down her face when they came to the words,

> *"Pas plus que vous, belle bergère,*
> *Vous qui ête' en danger d'amour."*

But she was not haunted by the fear of love, as it was natural for them to expect her to be on leaving to marry a man she had never seen. Instead she was filled with the bitter knowledge that she had lost her love.

Putting such thoughts from her with a considerable exercise of will, she stood beside the blue-draped rail until the roofs and spires faded into the distance and all she could see was the great cross on the crest of the mountain.

The baron, turning to leave the waterfront and trying to dislodge the lump in his throat with a cough, discovered that Benoit was standing beside him. The lawyer lifted his cane and pointed it at the fast disappearing barge.

"A fine child!" he said. "She's much too good for Joseph de Mariat's whelp. You know that, don't you?"

"I've been afraid so." The baron was looking thoroughly unhappy. "The decision was hers, Benoit. She made it freely, willingly."

The man of the law peered up at him, with a hand behind his ear. "What did you say?"

When the remark had been repeated Benoit spat noisily at the side of the road. "Why must there be hypocrisy between you and me? You're trying to salve your conscience, M'sieur Baron. St. Joseph, who am I to blame you! It may ease your conscience a little when I tell you that I consider myself the chief villain in this affair. But we have this consolation: it had to be. I wish this pestilential cub had earned a better reputation for himself. You know, of course, that there was talk when his wife died?"

"Benoit! What do you mean?"

Benoit smiled unpleasantly. "Ordinarily you would have taken the precaution of finding out all about him. If you didn't know this it must be that you refrained from getting reports on him through fear of what you might learn."

"You insisted there was no time!"

"That is true. But should you have acted on my insistence?"

The baron's voice rose to a high pitch as he asked a question. "Did you know this when you brought the proposal to me?"

Benoit gave a negative shake of his head. "I didn't know it then but I liked the girl and I regretted the rancid streak in the De Mariats. Later I made inquiries." He frowned. "It had to be, Baron. We both knew that. I think we'll find this splendid young Auguste didn't beat his wife, as rumor has it. I do think we'll discover that he broke her heart and wasted her fortune before she died."

The baron gave vent to his feelings in a low tone. "I think you knew all about it from the start and didn't tell me. You're a crooked stick, Benoit, a treacherous dog, a scoundrel, an archvillain, a Judas!"

"Be careful, M'sieur Baron. I've heard every word you said!"

People on the Rue St. Paul were surprised to see the two men walking along together, shouting bitterly at each other and waving their arms.

Book Four

CHAPTER I

THE YOUNG governor stood at the edge of the quay and watched the first barge land opposite the Place d'Armes. There was another ship anchored at the mouth of the Mississippi and for the next few days the river boats would be bringing up the new settlers sent out by John Law. The governor's mind was filled with calculations as the sailors began to bring ashore the luggage which constituted their load and to pile it in a pyramid at the edge of the cobbled quay, calculations as to how he could accommodate several hundred more people in a settlement already filled to the brim and spilling over.

With a shrug of the shoulders, which meant that he could do no more than his best (as he had been doing for over twenty years), he turned back across the square. On each side of it were the *casernes* (barracks) which he had seen were built first for the troops. Facing him as he crossed was what one day would be Cathedral Square. All that it possessed now was a shrine with a covering of canvas so that as many, perhaps, as fifty people could remain dry when mass was celebrated in rainy weather, and at the southwest corner a single-story frame building which was facetiously called the Hôtel de Ville and which succeeded in housing all the administrative officers. Streets had been cut through the brush in all directions but the peaked tops of tents were seen more often in the trees than the roofs of houses.

"I will now hear much more talk," said De Bienville to himself, plying a fan of palm leaf vigorously, "about the city with slate roofs and church spires which these new people expected to find."

His own cabinet in the squatty Hôtel de Ville proved to be one of reasonable size in which the furnishings, which had been sent out with an eye to the day when New Orleans *would* be a city of slate roofs and church spires, contrasted almost ludicrously with the rough planking of the walls and ceiling. There was a desk which had come right out of

Versailles from the satiny look of the wood and the perfection of its detail, a walnut commode with a marble top (which he used for the storing of papers), and handsome hangings of heavily corded paduasoy at the windows.

Within a few moments of his arrival here he was so absorbed in work that it took a loud clearing of the throat on the part of the Sieur de Balne to announce his presence. The Sieur de Balne was *procureur général* of the colony and it was apparent that he was much disturbed about something.

"Excellency," he said when he had managed to capture the governor's attention, "there are three more Spaniards reported in the settlement. That makes seven all told. Frankly, Excellency, I'm worried about it. Why are they here? Is it the sign of a conspiracy?"

De Bienville remained for a few moments in silent consideration of the problem. "They may be refugees from Spanish ports," he said. "On the other hand their presence may mean exactly what you fear." He nodded his head as a solution occurred to him. "We must have a special corps to handle this situation and to keep order in the settlement, with a provost at the head of it. After all, it's a matter for police work rather than military."

The Sieur de Balne said insistently, "That may be a wise step. But whatever we do we must do quickly."

"They'll be pouring in on us, these new settlers, in a very few days," declared the governor. "We'll require a gendarmerie to keep order, quite apart from the more serious need you foresee. I'll attend to this at once." He swung around in his chair to face his visitor. "Sieur de Balne, I'm disappointed, sorely disappointed, in the people they're sending us. I don't know where they recruit them but certainly they're not the poor people of the city slums who need so badly the fresh air and the food we can supply here. That was my idea when I first came to Louisiana, that the New World would take the poor for whom there doesn't seem to be room in France, or in any part of Europe for that matter. What I'm becoming convinced of is that we could populate the whole of this great new continent without doing anything to eliminate the slums!"

"People from the cities," said the *procureur général,* "would be even harder to handle than those we're getting."

Another official put his head in at the door a few minutes later to announce that a large part of the food supplies sent out from France on the previous ship had been found to be bad. "We just opened a barrel of salt meat, Excellency," he said, "and the stench drove us out of the place."

De Bienville's face became red with anger but he did not speak until he had mastered his indignation. "What do the government contractors care if we starve to death?" he asked. "They must have their profits, of course. *That* is the first consideration. Fortunately there are food supplies coming on the ship from New France. As my brother is paying the bill, it will be an honest shipment we receive."

"But, Excellency," said the official, "that ship from Canada, as you know, is two weeks overdue."

The red flush faded out of the governor's cheeks and he looked out of one of the windows with an air of solemn absorption for some time before replying.

"Yes," he said, "the ship from Canada is overdue. I very much fear, m'sieur, that I was giving scope to my optimistic tendencies. The ship from Canada is *dangerously* overdue."

When the official had left, De Bienville brushed the papers on his desk to one side and got to his feet. "I shall be away for an hour," he said to the secretary who hurried to bring him a hat. "Not longer."

His walk took him down a cypress-lined road which still had no name but would in a short time thereafter be called the Rue de Chartres. It ran in a westerly direction and at the end of it he could see the roof of a house which promised to be much more ambitious than any of the other residences in the settlement. It was set in an extensive plot and it actually boasted a rough fence. The house itself proved to be wide and low with a gallery on three sides, and the cypress trees draped their branches over the roof in a protective alliance. Although built of logs and daubed with mud and Spanish moss, there was a gracious air about it and the governor smiled approvingly as he turned in at the gate.

"Philippe!" he called.

A sound of hammering inside stopped and Philippe appeared in the door with a hammer in his hand. It was clear at once that the new life had been good for him. He had filled out and his color was ruddy.

"Good morning," he said. Then a look of mingled hope and dread crossed his face. "M'sieur Jean-Baptiste, has there been any report of the ship?"

De Bienville answered with a degree of confidence he did not feel. "No word yet. But I can't believe there's any reason for fear. It's a long voyage and unfavorable winds will cause delays. We'll have some word of the ship soon."

Philippe swallowed hard and said, "I hope so, M'sieur Jean-Baptiste."

The young governor gave the builder an understanding smile. "You're very fond of her, Philippe. I've been watching you and I can see that you haven't enjoyed any peace of mind the last ten days or so." He gave his head a sober nod. "I, too, am very fond of her."

Philippe did not seem in a mood to be optimistic. "It's not the season for unfavorable winds. I'm frightened about it!"

"I came to talk about the house," said the governor, having no desire to continue with a subject so trying. He gave his arm a sweeping motion to indicate the whole domain. "I'm completely satisfied with what you're doing for me here, Philippe. It will be in every way worthy of the office. You've conceived, in fact, the perfect type of house for Louisiana. It has dignity and it will be comfortable in summer. Now we must begin to move in the furniture I've been having sent out to me and storing against this happy day." He nodded his head with sudden vigor. "I must move in before someone gets the idea that I should give it up as a home for missionaries to the Indians or as headquarters for unmarried officers."

"I'm glad you approve," said Philippe. "Carpe and I will see to the furniture as soon as you say, M'sieur Jean-Baptiste."

A soldier turned in at the gate and came to a stop on the path. "Excellency," he said. "You're needed at once."

The Sieur de Bienville paid no attention to this familiar summons. He was too interested in the prospect of taking possession at last of a house of his own. "My grandeur will stagger you," he said to Philippe. "There's a fine crystal chandelier for this room, a serpentine table made of rosewood, some very fine rugs——"

"Excellency," repeated the soldier, "you must come at once. The lady refuses to come down until she sees you."

"The lady refuses to come down!" The governor indulged in a puzzled frown. "You must be more explicit. What lady? And what does she refuse to come down from?"

The soldier flushed and stammered at facing the necessity of addressing so great a personage at such a length. "She arrived—the lady, I mean, Excellency—on the second boat up the river. The luggage which came on the first was still piled on the quay. The lady is on top of the pile, Excellency, and refuses to come down. She demands to see you."

"Then I suppose I must find who this lady is and why she's behaving in such a strange way."

As he returned to the Place d'Armes, the soldier walking three paces behind him, the Sieur de Bienville's mind was on his plans for the immediate development of the town, the designing of the Church of St. Louis, which would face the open square, the finding of a safe and yet convenient location for the *poudrière* (powder store), the soundest method of facing the Rue du Quay so it could resist the action of the water.

Although New Orleans was still little more than a collection of log huts and empty streets, it had begun to take on some of the aspects of a frontier town. The Place d'Armes buzzed with life. The one tavern, just around the northwest corner from the square, was as busy as the most popular inn could conceivably have been in Paris itself. Groups of people were praying at the shrine under the canvas cover. Loud talk, loud laughter, loud song, reached his ears from all directions.

"We're growing, we're growing fast," he said to himself with an air of pride as he passed the governmental building and turned onto the square.

The pyramid of luggage had grown since he had seen it first. It contained portmanteaux in all stages of age and decay, bags, canvas sacks with mail, a few trunks of curious design, and even an article of furniture which might have been a chest of drawers. The chest stood in the center and the rest was piled up around it; and on its flat top the lady was seated.

Soldiers were standing in the doors of the *casernes* to watch her and men had gathered in small groups on the square for the same purpose. A lady of any kind was a fascinating spectacle in New Orleans and one who sat openly on a chest in a public place and refused to move a phenomenon which demanded the most careful attention.

The sun was pouring down with such intensity that the watchers on the baked clay square had a damp and wilted look about them but the lady had drawn her feet up on the chest and was keeping her skirts wrapped most determinedly around them. In further despite of the heat she wore a scarlet cloak of the kind known as a cardinal and her only concession had been to allow the hood to fall back on her shoulders, thus exposing to view a mass of red hair elaborately coifed and curled. The cloak opened at the neck and it could be seen that the voluptuous figure of the lady was clothed in a black *contouche* with bows of ribbon in red down the front.

"I am your humble servant, Excellency," she said when De Bienville had arrived in front of her improvised throne. Then she smiled archly and said in a low tone: "So! We meet again, my Jean-Baptiste."

At first he had no idea who she was. But gradually, as he studied her, he became aware of a change in her outward guise. Her face seemed to lose its roundness and high color and her features began to hint at an earlier delicacy of outline. The hair no longer asserted flamboyantly its redness but became again a warm brown. The amplitude of the figure receded to the gentler curves of youth.

"Marie!" he gasped. "You must forgive me for not recognizing you at once. It's been a long time since I saw you——"

"I'm not sensitive, Excellency," asserted his visitor. Her voice had been one of her chief sources of charm when he had made her the object of his hopeless worship, a slightly throaty contralto. Now it could not be called anything but heavy. "I'm even willing to be honest about the lapse of time since we last met. It's over twenty years." She laughed and there was in her amusement a quality of heartiness. "I'm not at all surprised, Jean-Baptiste, that you didn't recognize me at once. Some people still find me attractive but I'm no longer a slip of a girl looking forward to life with dewy-eyed wonder. And, if it doesn't partake of disrespect for authority,

I may add I wouldn't have known you if you hadn't been wearing a wig. Only the governor would wear a wig in this crude pesthole of nature!"

De Bienville laughed in turn but there was no hint of heartiness in his mirth. He was disturbed and unhappy about this most unexpected encounter. What had brought her, his once lovely and slender Marie, to Louisiana? The instructions under which he conducted the affairs of the colony left him no latitude in the matter of unattached ladies, particularly if any cloudiness could be found on the title deeds of their pasts.

"Marie, what brings you here? You must forgive my surprise but, in all frankness, I can't conceive of any good reason you might have had for coming."

Marie laughed. "You haven't changed at all," she declared. Out of respect for the governor the watchers had withdrawn to a sufficient distance for the conversation to go unheard. "What an earnest and proper little man you were in Montreal! What an earnest and proper little governor you've become! But you may put all your fears aside, Jean-Baptiste. I haven't come in pursuit of you after twenty years during which, to be perfectly honest, I gave you no more than a dozen affectionate but fleeting thoughts. I haven't come here to live on the fruits of—well, you have a favorite word for it yourself, no doubt. No, Excellency, I've come under the most proper and flawless auspices. I'm a married woman. My husband is a man of substance, of fine reputation, of great wealth, *parbleu!* In short, I'm none other than the wife of Claude André Achille Jouvelt."

In his desk at the governmental offices was a letter from Joseph de Mariat. The name of Jouvelt recalled to him at once a clause which he had studied with the greatest care. It read as follows:

Among those on this next ship will be M. Jouvelt, a banker of considerable wealth. His errand ostensibly is to decide what will be necessary in the way of banking facilities if the colony flourishes in accordance with the rosy predictions of M. Law. I have a feeling, however, that he has another purpose in undertaking a long sea voyage with its dangers and hardships. The bankers of France are apprehensive of the Law policies, to phrase it conservatively, and yet at the same time they quiver like game dogs at the prospect of profits. If John Law is right, they must have their share. I strongly suspect, therefore, that M. Claude Jouvelt goes to Louisiana to look over the ground and determine what may be expected so that the banking people will know which way to face. I solicit for him your full co-operation and the most constant attention.

M. Jouvelt, I may add for your personal information, is a bilious and ill-natured individual. He recently married a well-known courtesan. Still thinking her the beauty she once was, he is afraid to leave her behind and consequently Mme. Jouvelt will accompany him to New Orleans.

The young governor assured her that, having been advised of their coming, he had made every possible arrangement for their comfort, two rooms having been engaged in the one tavern. This brought him to the question which had been in his mind from the moment he saw her. Why had she chosen this particular place to sit?

Her face became pale and she looked about her with renewed apprehension.

"Jean-Baptiste!" Her voice quivered. "I didn't dare go a foot farther. As we came up the river I saw the most terrible-looking creatures along the banks. They say there are no dragons in the world—but these were dragons! They were ugly monsters with huge jaws and teeth like knives!" She paused to shudder and to draw her feet up closer beneath her. "As I set foot on land there was a great splash in the water beside me. Jean-Baptiste, I don't know how I got here! All I know is that I found myself on top of this chest when I could think and see again. I'd never been so frightened in my life! I could feel those terrible jaws snapping at me!"

De Bienville found it hard to keep from laughing. "Alligators," he said, "aren't as dangerous as they look. You're as safe here as on any square in Paris itself."

It happened that a bull alligator in one of the marshes back of the townsite chose to express his mood of the moment, which seemed to be one of rage and defiance. Marie's arms clutched her knees convulsively and her face became still paler.

"I won't take a step!" she cried. "You must send your carriage for me, if you please, Excellency! And what's more I must have an escort of soldiers with loaded muskets."

"My dear Marie, I'm afraid you have many painful surprises in store for you. I have no carriage. If I had, there isn't a horse in the whole of Louisiana." Then, seeing that she needed to be reassured, he added: "I'll summon a guard of honor for you. If there's any comfort in my presence, I'll walk beside you." He held out a hand to help her down from her perch. "Before the soldiers come, Marie, I want to tell you that I—I saw you in Paris the winter after you returned to France."

She gave him a suspicious side glance. "At the theater, no doubt?"

"Yes, the Comédie Française. The night they produced the two drolls."

"I remember now." She was completely at her ease. "I was with—but there's no sense telling you his name. I broke off with him soon after. He was so conceited and selfish that he thought I could be content with feasting my eyes on the purse in which he kept his money. That one! If he had ever swallowed a gold piece, all the purging in the world wouldn't make him give up more than some change in silver."

The governor turned the subject hastily. "Where is your husband?"

Marie got down slowly, casting anxious looks about her as she did so. She continued to hold his arm after reaching the ground and he could feel her fingers trembling.

"My husband?" she said in a whisper. "Jean-Baptiste, I don't know."

De Bienville raised a hand and summoned one of the officers. After giving his orders for an escort, he asked if anything was known of the whereabouts of Monsieur Jouvelt.

"The man with the cane, Excellency?" asked the officer.

"That would be Monsieur Jouvelt," said Marie.

"With all due respect, Excellency, to you and to the lady," said the officer, "I never saw a man run faster than that one, cane or no cane. While Madame was climbing the luggage he was running and before I could turn my head he'd vanished from sight. I've no idea where he went, Excellency."

"Perhaps," remarked Marie in an indifferent tone, "it will be like the man who took up his bed and walked. Monsieur Jouvelt may never need his cane again."

They began to walk in the direction of the tavern, with a file of soldiers on each side. Marie seemed to have regained her composure in part but he noticed that she took care not to look at either side. She winced when the bull alligator elected again to voice defiance but made no other sign.

"Monsieur Claude André Achille Jouvelt," she began to explain in a low tone, "not only suffers from gout but from a sour condition of the stomach. After drinking wine his conversation is punctuated with eruptions in the throat which good taste impels me to leave unnamed. He's never quite free of colds and he has a rheumy condition in one eye." She paused and indulged in a deep-throated laugh. "I'm telling you this, Excellency, so you will be prepared for the full fascination Monsieur Jouvelt exercises on all who come in contact with him."

The governor thought it wise to make some explanation of the tavern to which he was taking her. "It has one room only under roof. Back of that the guests sleep. I'm afraid, Marie, you'll find it somewhat primitive."

"What will the alternative be?"

He motioned up at the hot burnished bowl above them. "In that case you will sleep under the moon and the stars. Was nothing told you of the conditions you would find here?"

She shook her head. "From what I heard, I expected to have the use of a palace, with thick cool walls and an army of servants, across a paved square from a great cathedral. I expected to be lulled to sleep by the soft chiming of the bells."

He was glad to be able to say, because of the chance it gave him to escape: "Here is the tavern. From the description you gave me, I judge the gentleman standing in the doorway, watching us, is Monsieur Jouvelt."

"That is indeed the gay seeker after adventure with whom I shared a cabin, six feet by six, for four months." Marie sank her voice still lower. "It will be best, Jean-Baptiste, to let him believe we had never met before. When he hears I've known a man in the past he has an unpleasant habit of—of jumping to conclusions."

The banker was a short man with dark eyes which rolled in their sockets with the curiosity of a malicious ape. It would be a difficult matter to describe him because on seeing Monsieur Jouvelt for the first time one's eyes never got beyond the yellow waistcoat he wore. Yellow was a color men shunned in choosing their clothes, for it had come to denote one of two things, a traitor or a deceived husband. "Does he wear it," thought De Bienville, "to show his indifference to her past? Or is it a gesture to prove his superiority to all idle beliefs?"

Monsieur Jouvelt acknowledged his introduction to the governor by reciting a long bill of complaints. The voyage up the river had been a nightmare. It had been necessary to get under sleeping nets hours before sundown because of the numbers and viciousness of the mosquitoes. The boatmen had refused to halt while passengers went ashore to honor the demands of nature. A valuable trunk had been lost . . .

"And now, Your Excellency," concluded the banker, "we come to the question of this inn. It might make a decent pesthouse and it's conceivable that the lowest beggars of Paris would regard it as suitable. But for Madame my wife and myself, it is impossible. This," he added with a gesture of disgust, "is what I expected. Incompetence, lack of preparation, indifferent planning, official sloth! It was promised that a city would stand on the river by the time we arrived."

"It's easier to promise miracles than to perform them," said De Bienville, keeping his temper in leash.

"I demand a minor miracle at once!" Monsieur Jouvelt hawked so violently that he seemed on the point of an explosion. "Suitable living quarters must be provided for us, Your Excellency. How you achieve it is of no concern to me. My interest is in the results only."

The young governor reached a reluctant decision. "My own residence is nearly completed," he said. "I've lived in temporary quarters for more than twenty years and so I can contrive to wait a little longer for something better. My house is yours, monsieur and madame, for as long as you stay."

The banker darted a triumphant glance at his wife, looking very much like a monkey which has successfully raided the larder. "Madame, you will observe, if you please! I provide for your comfort always. I contrive, I improvise, I make the best of things. I even procure for you a house on the very edge of the earth!"

"My thanks nevertheless go to His Excellency," said Marie, giving De Bienville a grateful smile.

The latter made no response. He was watching a young man who had emerged from the door of the inn and was glancing about with an air which conveyed to everyone the disdain he had already conceived for this New World. The newcomer was most handsomely attired. His coat was a knee-length *capot,* belted in at the waist with a scarlet sash. He wore a *audebec* of ostrich down on his head and a long sword clanked against his calves as he walked. A servant followed him, carrying his master's fan in one hand and a raincloak over the other arm.

"If I am not mistaken," said the governor, "that is Auguste de Mariat."

The banker nodded his head. "Who else," he asked, "could carry himself with such overweening pride? He came out with us and he made it clear at once that he considered banking a middle-class occupation and anyone engaged in it as beneath notice. He made it clear also that he has a good opinion of the role he expects to play here. He sees himself as another Richelieu or, at the least, as the Mazarin of the Mississippi."

"I found him very witty and amusing," declared Marie.

"I must have a talk with the young man," said the governor, "after I've escorted you to your house."

II

The governor of Louisiana lived in a tiny room back of his cabinet and his servant had an even smaller niche behind that which served the double purpose of a kitchen and a bedroom for himself. De Bienville was supping that evening in his own part of these domestic quarters when he received a call from the official who had complained earlier of the condition of the meat supplies.

"Excellency," said this official, "there is trouble."

The governor continued his efforts to separate the stringy flesh from an ancient drumstick. "There is always trouble," he said.

"But this time, Excellency, it is serious. The passengers insisted on coming up the river with all the barges available. No fewer than three loads have arrived within the last hour. Is that trouble, Excellency?"

"Not if they brought the tents with them which were on the ship."

"Excellency, they didn't bring the tents. There were no tents to bring. The contractor, or the naval inspector, one of them or both, had forgotten about the tents. We have this night three hundred new people in New Orleans and no place for any of them to sleep. Is *that* trouble, Excellency?"

The answer to his query was supplied by a sudden outburst of sound from the direction of the Place d'Armes. De Bienville rose hurriedly and went to the window which commanded a view of a small part of the square. He could see that the place was crowded and that a noisy meeting of protest was under way.

"They're in an ugly mood, Excellency," said the official. "If you want my advice, you should go out and speak to them."

De Bienville found, as soon as he issued from the administration offices, that the crowd was indeed in an ugly mood. The sky was overcast and it was rapidly becoming dark on the square, a condition which was being helped very little by the one torch the new arrivals had lighted. One of them had mounted the chest which had served Marie as a refuge from danger that afternoon, and was haranguing the crowd.

"Every promise made us has been broken!" he was shouting as the governor skirted the crowd and reached a position close at hand. "We were herded on a ship fit only for cattle and capable of accommodating no more than half of us. We were fed like beasts of the wallow, on rotten meat and wormy biscuit. We were told New Orleans was a beautiful city and that fine homes were ready for us here. What do we find? A few log cabins built on a swamp! A stinking hamlet, reeking of fever and death! There's no place here for us to sleep unless we lie down in the bogs with alligators for bedfellows!" He paused for breath and then raised a clenched fist in the air. "We have arms. I propose we drive out the people who now occupy these hovels and take them for ourselves!"

A loud cheer greeted this bellicose suggestion and it was clear that the new arrivals were in a mood to act on it. De Bienville pushed his way forward until he stood beside the chest.

"I would like a chance to speak to you," he said in a tone loud enough to be heard over the square.

"And who are you?" demanded the speaker, staring down at him belligerently.

"It happens," said De Bienville, "that I am the governor of Louisiana."

An uneasy silence settled over the square as the governor stepped up on the chest, after motioning to the speaker to make way. He looked about him for a moment and then nodded and smiled.

"First, let me say," he began, "that I can't blame you for feeling discontented. It's clear that you've been badly treated. I am not responsible for the treatment you received on the ship nor for the fact that the navy contractors neglected to send tents for your use until houses can be built for you."

"We were told," came a voice from the crowd, "that houses would be ready for us!"

"I don't know what you were promised but this I can tell you now. You were not sent out to live in a ready-made city. You were sent out to assist in building that city. You are better off than the first settlers to arrive, for they found nothing but swamps and cypress clumps. Would you try to drive them out of the houses they built for themselves?" He raised one arm above his head. "I solemnly swear that I shall do everything in my power to ease for you the hardships of pioneer life and to protect you in every way. The first step will be to make the best possible arrangements for your immediate accommodation. If you'll remain quiet for a short time I shall proceed to do this."

"Where am I to sleep with my six children?" demanded a woman standing immediately beneath him. He could see that she was a big

woman with a commanding eye and a stern mouth. In her arms she was
holding a baby less than a year old.

"I'll discuss that with your husband, madame."

"That you won't, m'sieur!" she said. "My husband always managed to
fail me when I needed him most. He took sick on our wedding night,
he frittered away the *dot* I brought him, he let the moneylenders get our
and from us. It was his idea to come to Louisiana and two days out from
France he had no more sense than to take sick and die!"

"Madame," said De Bienville, "I shall see to it that you and your family
are well looked after. But you must wait until I can discuss the situation
with my officers. It will take half an hour perhaps. I beg you to be patient
in the meantime, all of you. If you are not I shall be compelled most
reluctantly to resort to severe measures."

It took an hour, however, to decide how many of the new arrivals could
be quartered in each house and tent. De Bienville relieved the pressure
considerably by throwing open the administration offices and the living
quarters behind for the temporary accommodation of the unhappy settlers.
He pointed out to the incensed officials, who were thus deprived of their
beds, that they could do what he proposed to do himself, wrap up in their
blankets and sleep under the canvas cover of the shrine.

"It will be for one night only," said the governor, to silence their complaints. "There's a supply of canvas in one of the *casernes* and tomorrow
we can fashion enough tents to relieve the pressure. In the meantime it
will sweeten the mood of these unfortunate people if we display a willingness to share their discomforts."

"Very well," said the Sieur de Balne in a plaintive tone, "but it will do
my rheumatism very little good, Excellency. And may I ask what you
propose to do with the outspoken widow and her large family?"

"They will share my house with the banker Jouvelt and his wife." The
governor smiled. "I shall take them there myself in a few minutes to make
sure they are fairly treated in the division of the space."

III

It was Marie who answered the governor's knock on the door. She had
been on the point of retiring and had slipped on a *gorge-de-pigeon* robe
over her nightclothes. Her eyes opened wide at the sight of Madame
Gauthier and the children who streamed after her like the tail of a comet.

The explanation caused her eyes to open still wider, if possible. "I'm
sure, Jean-Baptiste," she said, "that you wouldn't do this unless compelled
by circumstances——"

"Every one-room hut in New Orleans," he assured her, "contains at
least two families tonight."

Marie sighed. "There's one small source of satisfaction for me in this—

the rage my husband will feel when he wakens in the morning and find
the place overrun with noisy children."

"My children," declared Madame Gauthier, who had overheard, "are
not noisy. They are well-trained children."

"I'm sure, Madame Gauthier, that they are model children and that you
are a model mother. But will you pardon me if I wonder why you had
quite so many of them?"

"Monsieur Jouvelt has retired?" asked the governor.

Marie drew him aside so their conversation would no longer be heard.
"My husband, as you guessed, has retired. There's as much ceremony to
my husband's retirement as to a court reception. He takes off each article
of clothing carefully, examines it carefully, folds it and lays it aside. I then
hand him his nightgown, and then his nightcap, and I knot it for him
at the back. Then I bring him a small book—with a lock and key, mind
you!—and a pen and ink. He writes in the book for at least half an hour.
I think he enters down all the transactions of the day, so much received,
so much paid out, so much profit. Then he puts under his pillow a leather
case containing all the money he brought with him—at home it's two
boxes, one under his head and one under his feet—and he goes to sleep
with his head on it."

"There is a matter of some importance," said the governor in a low
voice. "Have you heard that Auguste de Mariat is to marry a girl from
New France who is coming on the next ship?"

"I heard some talk of it."

"The girl who's coming to marry him," looking about him to make
sure that Madame Gauthier was still at a safe distance, "is your daughter."

Marie gasped. She regarded him for several moments with unbelieving
eyes. "My little Félicité! I can't believe it! Jean-Baptiste, this can't be true!
It's impossible, it's absurd! Why should he, this proud and important
young man, be willing to marry my daughter?"

"In the first place, neither of the De Mariats, father or son, has any
idea that you are her mother. I'm taking it for granted that you were
wise enough to tell Joseph de Mariat nothing about your affairs when you
crossed back to France on the same boat with him."

She shook her head instantly and decisively. "I told him nothing. He
didn't know I had a child."

"All that the bridegroom knows, then, is that Félicité is an orphan who
has been raised in my brother's family. For reasons which seemed good
to them, they arranged this match, my brother and Joseph de Mariat, and
my brother made a large marriage settlement. I'm not free to make any
further explanation than that. This I may say: my brother was deeply
attached to Félicité and the match was arranged with her full consent."

"What is my little girl like? She was plain enough as a baby."

"I've heard," replied the governor, "that she's very attractive as well as

lever. I know she proved a great help to my brother, the Baron of
Longueuil, in his business affairs."

Suddenly Madame Jouvelt began to cry. She buried her face in her
hands and wept so violently that her shoulders shook. It was some time
before she recovered control of herself and the governor took advantage
of the opportunity to set Madame Gauthier to arranging where the children were to sleep. When this difficult operation was under way he returned to Marie and found her wiping her red eyes with a perfumed
handkerchief.

"I beseech your pardon most humbly, Jean-Baptiste, for behaving in this
silly way. Mother in heaven, why should I feel badly! I left my little girl
because I wanted to get what profit I could out of my good looks. I wanted
ease and admiration and good position and money. And I succeeded."

She produced a small mirror from a bag at her belt and examined her
face critically. "I should never allow myself to cry," she said in a tone
which implied irritation. "When I was young I was irresistible if I gave
way to tears. And how I gave way! But now—now I only succeed in
making myself look like a bad-tempered old she-bear!"

After a few moments she shook her head and returned the handkerchief to its receptacle. "I may tell you quite honestly that I've no regrets
as far as I'm concerned myself. I still try to look as well as I may with
what's left of my looks but I'm more interested in a comfortable shoe than
in this leathery flush I call my complexion. Now that I desire security and
comfort above everything, I have a husband who supplies the first need
and some of the second. Haven't I every reason to consider myself lucky?"

Her eyes filled again. "I thought I was lucky until you told me about
my little girl. Then I knew that I wasn't. I knew that I had a problem
to face, a decision to make. Well, Jean-Baptiste, I've made the decision.
Félicité must never know who I am."

The governor nodded his head. "I'm happy you see that," he said. "I
intended to suggest it if necessary."

"I knew right away how it would have to be. It would be better, in fact,
if we returned to France before she arrives but my husband will leave
when he's ready and not before. My little Félicité is going to have enough
difficulty as it is," with a shake of the head, "without having to acknowledge *me* as her mother."

CHAPTER II

THE GOVERNOR rose early each morning but never early enough to forestall Philippe and his volunteer helpers. Every able-bodied man was assisting in the work of building the needed homes for the overflow of new arrivals. The sound of ringing axes and the scream of saws filled the air from dawn until sunset. The governor worked late into the night also but it was doubtful if he outlasted Philippe there, for the latter and his leaden-footed helper spent many hours of darkness each night raising the timbers for a house of ambitious size on the narrow road running north from the church site which later would be called the Rue d'Orléans.

One morning the governor sallied out a little earlier than usual and found both Philippe and Polycarpe Bonnet engaged in sizing beams. It was arduous work and in spite of the early hour they were showing the effects of the heat.

Philippe suspended work as soon as he perceived the broad-brimmed hat of the head of the colony approaching down the road. "I don't need to ask if there's been any report of the ship," he said. "You would have told me."

"There's no report yet." De Bienville shook his head soberly. "I begin to think you'll finish that house for her before the ship arrives."

"We've made a start on it. That's all." Philippe lifted his ax and tested the edge with his fingers. It was easy to see that he did this to conceal the expression of pain which had taken possession of his face. "M'sieur Jean-Baptiste, the ship is lost! I had a dream last night and I saw it go down as clearly as—as I see the roof of the tavern through the trees over there. A dream like that means something. It means that it's gone, the ship and every soul on it."

"Dreams mean nothing. They reflect only the fears you feel when you're awake." De Bienville voiced this opinion with more assurance than he felt.

Don't abandon hope yet, Philippe. I'm not allowing myself to give up.
still believe that a fast canoe will come up the river soon with word the
hip has been sighted on the gulf."

"God and St. Cloud grant that you're right!" said Philippe fervently.

The governor turned to continue his morning rounds. "Don't let your
ears prevent you from finishing the house," he said over his shoulder.
We must have a suitable nest for our bride when she arrives."

"What do you think of M'sieur de Mariat?" Philippe asked.

The governor paused. "He's polished and a gentleman to his very
finger tips. At first I had grave doubts about him, as a husband for Félicité,
but now I'm not sure. This I will say: he's the most amusing man I've
ever met."

The savage way in which Philippe proceeded to ply his ax after the
governor had departed was an indication, without a doubt, of the estimate
he had formed of Auguste de Mariat.

Some minutes later the helper dropped his ax point and looked at Philippe with a questioning eye. "It's new for me to swing an ax all day,"
he said. "Am I suiting you, master?"

"You've been as industrious as an Ottawa beaver, Carpe."

In spite of this favorable answer, Polycarpe did not immediately resume
his work. "Master," he asked, "what do you think of this Madame
Gauthier?"

Philippe was not missing with a single stroke of his ax. "Do you mean
the widow who's sharing the governor's house?"

"Yes. That's the one. She's big, isn't she? And of a roundness?" Polycarpe's face became so serious that Philippe, catching a single glimpse
of it as he worked, found it hard not to smile. "Master, do you think it's
intended I should be suited only by a big widow with six children?"

When his master made no comment he went on: "There was the widow
in Montreal. *She* had six children and she was the only one in New
France who had no need for these new bustles. The youngest of the six
was a year old just like this one. And with the same name, Dominique.
Would you say, master, that it looks like—like it was all planned and
that it won't matter whether I'm suited or not?"

"I think, Carpe, it will depend on how often you go to see this widow
with her brood of children. Don't you realize that where big women are
concerned you're like a moth at a flame?"

"But that's not all, master. The strangest thing is still to be told. Yesterday I was there——"

"And what were you doing there yesterday?"

Polycarpe drew himself up with an air of importance. "I had a reason
for being there," he said. Then he lowered his voice. "When I got there
what do you suppose she was doing? She had a rope strung across the
room and she was hanging out wet clothes on it! Does that seem to you,

master, like—like what they call the hand of fate? I took one look and
then I ran away."

"You'll be safe, Carpe," commented Philippe, "if you continue to run
But, mind you, you must run in the right direction."

II

When the governor reached his cabinet he found that it already had
a visitor. Much to his surprise, the visitor was the one man in New Orleans
he would least have expected to meet at such an uncivilized hour, Auguste
de Mariat. That perfect gentleman was defying the heat by wearing a
wig, a *perruque à circonstance,* moreover, which fell far down over his
shoulders in pole-locks. He was wearing gloves with black fringe.

"You are up early this morning," said the governor, seating himself at
his desk. "I'm surprised, considering the late hour to which we continued
our talk last night. I may say, m'sieur, that I found your anecdotes of court
life most engrossing."

Auguste de Mariat seemed pleased but he made no comment. He
thumbed the end of a mustache and then said, "My reason for being here
is that I want the matter of my administrative duties settled."

The governor seemed equally desirous of getting his new lieutenant to
work. "Your experience seems to be nil," he said. "I may tell you, however, that I was in the same position when I was first in command here.
I've had to create rules of my own. I can't find fault with a similar lack
in you."

The man from France looked surprised and perhaps a trifle annoyed.
"It wasn't in my mind," he declared, "that there would be faultfinding
of any kind."

The footing of amiability on which they had begun seemed to evapo-
rate. De Bienville resented both the tone and the words and he made no
effort to conceal his feeling. "My instructions were that I might make use
of you in any capacity which seems most fitting," he said finally. "Perhaps you'll oblige me with an opinion."

The courtier gestured indifferently. "I have a head for figures."

"Financial matters are in the department of the intendant. Would you
like a post under him?"

"Not at all." Auguste de Mariat swung one leg negligently over the
other and flicked a spot of dust from the satin-ribboned garter he wore
under his knee. "I prefer a department of my own. In fact I've no hesitation in demanding that I be given a post where the responsibilities will be
mine and where I'll receive the credit."

"And the blame if things go wrong?" The governor asked this with
a smile.

"Blame!" The young man snorted with amusement. "I think I may
elieve your mind on that score. I'm equal to any problems which may
rise in this——" He gestured expansively. "Out of respect for your feel-
ngs as the originator of all this magnificence I suppress the far from
omplimentary references which were on the tip of my tongue."

"It's quite evident, m'sieur," said the governor sharply, "that you will
oon correct all the mistakes I've made and take off my shoulders the
roblems I'm incapable of solving myself." Then, realizing the need for
ordial relations between them, he forced himself to smile. "Come! We
eem to be getting at cross-purposes. That is not good, for we are to be
onnected by matrimonial ties as well as administrative. The ship with
ny brother's ward will arrive soon now. We mustn't allow ourselves to
all into disputes in the meantime."

Auguste de Mariat toyed with the tip of one sharply upturned mus-
ache. There was a finicky suggestion about the motion of his fingers but
is eyes, which were hard and uncompromising, made it clear that any
uch affectations of manner were not an index to his character.

"That you are to marry our Mademoiselle Félicité," the governor con-
inued, "makes it doubly necessary to find the right niche for you—so that
ou will achieve much credit and no trace of blame whatsoever."

De Mariat helped himself to snuff and then proffered his box to the
governor. The latter refused with the explanation that he never indulged
intil later in the day. "A curious restriction to place on yourself," com-
nented the new arrival. He whisked the brown grain from his face with
scented handkerchief. "There are some questions I should like to ask,"
ie said, "about my future wife. As you are no doubt aware, I know noth-
ng of her except what was reported by the attorney in Montreal who
eems to have been the agent in the matter."

"I know little, m'sieur. But I'll strive to satisfy your natural curiosity."

The prospective bridegroom leaned forward and began to ask questions
bout Félicité: her weight, her height, the color of her eyes, the pitch of
ier voice, her education, her manners, her antecedents. He made no com-
nents on the answers he received except to say, when the last query had
een discussed, "You may depend on this, M'sieur de Bienville, I shall
trive to make the best of it."

For a moment nothing more was said. Then, having suppressed the
harp retort on the tip of his tongue, the governor returned to the ques-
ion of a post for his visitor. "I have an idea, Monsieur de Mariat. The
need for a provost has arisen, with so many new people pouring in.
You've had military experience, which would be useful. It will be exacting
nd important work, and sometimes not at all pleasant. Does the idea
ppeal to you?"

Surprisingly enough it did. De Mariat's manner made this clear im-
nediately, although he was guarded in his comments. "Provost?" he said.

"It's an honorable post and there's no nauseous reek of clerkship about i
I'm prepared to consider it."

"Do you feel you would be fitted for the post?"

"I've an inquisitorial turn of mind," asserted De Mariat. This was tru
The questions he had asked about Félicité had been sharply phrased, i
sistent, to the point. "I may tell you also, since you seem determined t
probe into my qualifications, that I'm in no sense adverse to the use c
violence. I confess, in fact, to a bent for ruthlessness when occasions d
mand." He nodded his head brusquely. "It is settled then?"

"It is settled. I'm sorry that I won't be here to help you get the ne
department organized but I must leave at once. The secretary writes m
that M'sieur Law is sending out on the next boat the German peasants h
has selected to settle the land reserved for him. I can no longer delay a
examination of the tract and the making of the necessary arrangements.

"Germans will make poor settlers," declared De Mariat scornfull
"They'll die in this country like flies."

"I fear you're right. The Law tract is good land and quite high bu
these poor German peasants will be like children. They're accustomed t
neat farms and easy habits. They'll be a sick lot when they make th
acquaintance of alligators and see how the Mississippi can flood in th
spring."

"When do you leave?"

"At dawn. I'm taking a single squad of men with me. I should be bac
in two weeks." De Bienville gave his head a shake. "You'll soon realize
M'sieur de Mariat, that a new country isn't governed by sitting at a des
in a comfortable cabinet and issuing decrees. It's one continuous roun
of expeditions against the Indians, of peace missions, of explorations, o
inspections, of battling against the elements. I've had twenty years of it.
He came to a sudden stop and, leaning across the desk, looked with th
utmost gravity into the eyes of his visitor. "Monsieur de Mariat, there i
the deepest affection among the members of my family for this young gir
who's coming here to marry you. They desire her happiness above every
thing. It's very easy for marriages to go wrong when the contractin
parties have never seen each other. It's possible she will arrive before
return and so I'm asking you now to exercise the greatest kindness an
tact with her."

"I hardly think, Excellency, that it will be my fault if the marriage is a
failure."

"From the reports which reach me," went on De Bienville, "she's a
veritable prize. She's quite lovely, and my brother, the Baron of Lon
gueuil, can't say enough about her cleverness. On top of that she seems t
possess all the virtues. A paragon indeed, m'sieur! Of course, she has live
all her life in Montreal and she'll know nothing of the things which inter
est you the most. She has never seen a play. Her reading has been limited

She'll have none of the talk of the salons on her tongue. You'll find it necessary to make allowances."

"I'm quite prepared to do so." De Mariat's attitude, as well as his tone of voice, evinced impatience.

"On the other hand she'll find it necessary to make allowances for *you*. She is most devout, as are all the people of New France, and she'll find the levity of your conversation both strange and distressing. May I suggest that you—well, that you show some consideration for her feelings in this respect?"

"Excellency!" De Mariat's brows had drawn together in a frown. "I see no reason at all for this lecture you're reading me. How I conduct myself in my married life is my own concern. I'll have no interference at all. Is that clear? I may tell you that I resent all this advice."

"I may tell you," declared the governor, "that I shall resent it if I find you are making your wife unhappy. Shall we leave the matter there?"

"Unless," said De Mariat, getting to his feet and dropping his gloved hand on the hilt of his sword, "you prefer to continue the discussion with swords instead of words."

"The sword of the King's representative," declared the governor, "can't be employed against those who serve under him. If it were not for that"—he tapped the hilt of his weapon in turn—"I would find a dispute on the lines you suggest a great pleasure."

CHAPTER III

A WEEK had brought about a change in Auguste de Mariat. H
sat at a table in the small cubicle which had been assigned hin
in the Hôtel de Ville and was so busy studying the reports whicl
reached him that an inkstain on the braid *amadis* of his sleeve went un
noticed and there was even a hint of limpness about the ends of hi
mustache. It was clear that he was finding the maintenance of order i
the new town an exacting task.

The afternoon passed before there was a lull. He called then to his secre
tary: "Tell the people who keep inquiring that the report brought up th
river today has no mention of the ship from Quebec. It's still missing. Yo
might as well give it out at the same time that His Excellency the gover
nor has been taken ill up the river and that it may be weeks before he'
well enough to get back. And now have that Englishman in."

The Englishman was brought in from the cells which were immediatel
behind the office of the provost. He was a mild-faced individual wearin
a copper chain around his neck.

"M'sieur," he said, "that cell you've got me in will be the death of me
I've been there five days, m'sieur, and it's the exact shape and size of a
coffin. I'm down to a skeleton now and another two days will finish me
Walk me up, m'sieur! Have you any idea of the abom'nable stink of tha
place back there?"

"We're short of space and can't think of the comfort of criminals," de
clared De Mariat. "What was your purpose in coming to New Orleans?"

"I'm an Indian trader. It's an inoffensive business and I, with all du
respect, am an inoffensive man. Our countries have stopped fighting and
so I saw no reason—but I may be wrong, of course—why I shouldn't come
here."

The new provost consulted a paper in front of him. "Your name?"

"I'm Melvin Jack Adoo, m'sieur."

"You're a liar as well as a scoundrel! I have your record before me. It';

ere stated that you go under the name of Jack Melvin in the islands
lthough your real name is Jack Beddoes. You claim to be a sea captain
ut there's no evidence that you've ever commanded a ship."

"Walk me up, m'sieur! A man's name gets changed in these parts. I've
nown some that had half a dozen names and found it dangerous to use
ny of them. We're free and easy about names in the islands. As for being
captain, I've owned a ship of my own. Certain, it was a turtler; but when
ou've owned and sailed a turtler you're a captain by every right and not
ll the admirals and the judges and the courts in the world can take it
way from you. Certain, it was a small turtler." He paused and winked
miably. "In fact, m'sieur, it was a *very* small turtler."

The provost looked at him down the length of his long nose for several
noments. Then suddenly he brought his hand down sharply on the table
1 front of him and chanted in English:

Have you not a promise made that you will marry me?

The prisoner straightened up and grinned excitedly. Then he slapped
is thigh and responded in a singsong voice:

That I have, that I have, for am I not the parson?

De Mariat's expression changed to one of triumph. Seeing this, the Eng-
ishman began to realize that he had been tricked into an indiscretion. He
ooked sheepish as well as uncomfortable.

"Voilà!" said the provost. "You've given yourself away nicely, fellow.
You *were* with the Bahama pirates, just as this paper in front of me says.
You were with a murderous scoundrel named Jack Rackham when he
aptured a ship off one of the islands after promising to accept the English
King's pardon and quit the sea. This Rackham was better known as
Calico Jack because—ugh, the barbarian!—because of his habit of stripping
ff his clothes and fighting in his dirty calico shirt and drawers. These
evolting details are contained in a report I've just received about you.
The parson song was used in the capture of the ship as a signal between
he boarding party and the confederates that Calico Jack had on board."

"Walk me up, m'sieur! I *did* give myself away! But it was such a gaudy
rick we played on them."

"You were captured later," went on De Mariat, reading from the paper
n his hand. "You were tried at Kingston——"

"Tried, m'sieur? We were chained to a rail, hand and foot, and every
ime any one of us opened a mouth the judge bellowed he wouldn't have
he atmosphere of the King's court polluted by speech from such as us.
When one of us, a Welshman named Jones but we called him Taffy
Mustard, tried to make a speech, they came and clamped sacks down on
ll our heads. I was nearly smothered. Walk me up, m'sieur, would you
all that being tried?"

"You were all convicted and sentenced to hang. It seems that you and
wo others escaped. The rest, I expect, were hanged in due course."

"Aye," affirmed the Englishman cheerfully. "And in the main, m'sieu they deserved it. They were a bad lot."

"And you came here." De Mariat folded up the paper and shoved back into a drawer of the table. "If we send you back they'll lose no tim at all in hanging you. You know that?"

"Walk me up, I know it! But you wouldn't give them that much sati faction, not those English governors and those judges with their grea wigs and those fat shipowners, crying out their eyes over the bottoms we sunk for them! Not you, m'sieur, you're a Frenchman!"

"And you, gallows bird, are a pirate. It may be that Monsieur de Bie ville will decide that the best way to deal with you is to hang you here. would be a splendid example to all evildoers. It's my intention to recon mend that we build a gallows on the Place d'Armes and let you dance o air in the full sight of everyone."

There was a long pause during which the prisoner kept his head dow and shuffled his feet nervously. De Mariat watched him closely, strokin the tip of his nose with two fingers.

"There's one other possibility," said the provost finally. "There's a mi sion to be undertaken. A dangerous one, I must tell you. If you wer disposed to try it——"

"Aye, m'sieur, aye!" exclaimed the prisoner, looking up with renewe hope. "I'm the man for it!"

"Are you likely to jibe at the nature of the task? To protest this or tha to get scruples all of a sudden, to hold out for terms?"

"M'sieur! I'm like a lamb in your hands. I'll scalp an Indian or cut white throat in the wink of an eye if that's what you want."

"Do you know a Spaniard named Don Miguel? It's a nickname, believe."

"I've heard of him. A bad one, m'sieur."

"His real name is said to be Manuel Sanchez Maria y Lopez. I agre with you fully that he's a bad one. He's in New Orleans now and he' agreed to go on this mission of which I speak—for reasons not entirel unlike your own. You would take orders from him."

"And where are we to go, m'sieur?"

De Mariat motioned over his shoulder with a thumb. "You will go u the river. The mission is with a certain tribe of Indians. As I've alread said, there's danger in it. But you, an Indian trader, would know best ho to meet it."

"M'sieur! I lied. I'm not an Indian trader. I'm a sailor. A deep-sea man I've no liking for Indians, m'sieur."

"Then," declared De Mariat with an air of finality, "you'll be sent bac to Kingston, where they'll see to it that you bless the world with you heels. Or we'll save them the trouble by hanging you here."

There was a lengthy silence. The prisoner watched the unfriendly fac

ehind the table in the hope of detecting some signs of relenting. When
his prospect failed him, he sighed, shuffled his feet, wiped the perspiration
rom his brow, and gave in.

"I'm your man, m'sieur," he said. "I'll go with this Spaniard. I'm afraid
f Indians but I'm more afraid of hanging. It's a poor kind of a death,
h'sieur. A miserable, strangling kind of a death!"

"Go back to your cell," said De Mariat sharply. "I'll release you in the
horning and have your instructions ready for you. You'll have enough
nse to keep your mouth closed? A word out of you and the kind of fate
ou'll face will make you whine to be hanged!"

"Walk me up, m'sieur! I'll be as quiet as a mouse that's escaped the
laws of the cat."

II

Auguste de Mariat seemed well pleased. When the prisoner had been
aken back to his coffinlike cell the provost paced up and down his small
abinet, nodding his head at intervals and smiling to himself.

"His Royal Highness would need no more than one look at conditions
ere to realize that no profits will come out of Louisiana for a generation,"
e thought. "As we can't get him here for the purpose, we must bring the
ruth home to him in some other way." He gave a triumphant twirl to
oth mustache ends. "I shall accomplish it at one stroke."

He stopped before a cracked mirror on the wall and adjusted his cravat.
A veritable stroke of genius!" he said to himself. "It must be a quick
ttack. They'll strike at night and be well up the river again before the
roops can be rallied to meet them. If someone of sufficient importance is
illed or carried off a prisoner, a wave of revulsion will sweep over France
or everything connected with this accursed colony." His mind began to
lay with a choice of victims. "A priest? No, the public has been satiated
vith stories of the martyring of priests. We'll have to do better than that.
A beautiful woman? Where could a beautiful woman be found? The
anker Jouvelt, and his wife, perhaps? The Sieur de Balne? The gov-
rnor?"

He gave his fingers a sudden snap and nodded his head. "The banker,
think. It will be easier that way. And when we get him back he's certain
o raise a hubbub which will be heard from one end of France to the
ther. Yes, the banker it shall be."

He seated himself in his chair and began to consider the instructions he
nust give the next day to his agent. "He's not to be trusted, that hangdog
Englishman," he thought. "But I have him in a cleft stick. He can't go
ack to his own people. The Spanish are only too glad to hang an English-
nan on any pretext, so he can't run to them. It's only by doing what I
lemand that he can hope to save his miserable neck. I think that Jack

Melvin or Jack Beddoes or Melvin Jack Adoo—or whatever his real nam
happens to be—is going to be very valuable."

He began to write in a small neat hand on a tiny square of paper. Ap
parently he had made up his mind as to how the Indian raid was to b
managed, for he smiled and nodded with every evidence of satisfactior

He was still engaged in this task when a rap sounded on the cabin
door. De Mariat placed the slip of paper, which was now covered with hi
careful notes and symbols, in a waistcoat pocket before calling, "Come in!

It was one of his aides. "I have them!" the soldier announced trium
phantly. "They're outside. And as mad, both of them, as cats with singe
tails."

De Mariat got briskly to his feet. "You have Duguest and Brossard?

The crowding which had resulted from the constant influx of new se
tlers had led inevitably to trouble. Street fights were a daily occurrenc
Women screamed at each other when they met, and children carried o
the feuds of their elders. Continual readjustments had to be made in hous
ing arrangements because of the bad blood engendered by the enforce
sharing of small rooms. All this had seemed to come to a head in th
furious feud between Jules Duguest and Antoine Brossard, and their re
spective families.

The Duguests, who had come out from Rouen on the first boat, and th
Brossards, who had arrived on the last, had shared one of the smalles
huts. Because the space was so very limited and because both familie
were large, the initial friendliness had degenerated within two days int
snarling hatred and the exchange of insults and threats. Charges anc
countercharges had been bandied back and forth. There were hourly tus
sles between the two men, with more noise than actual bodily damage
The feud had become even more bitter after arrangements were made to
separate the families; and the whole community had begun to take sides
In no time at all, it seemed, the population was divided into two camps
the supporters of Duguest and the adherents of Brossard.

"Yes, m'sieur!" The aide nodded his head vigorously. "It looked at firs
like trouble. Brossard had a knife and he said he wouldn't be seen i
public with Duguest. I got it away from him and then I gave them botl
a good booting and brought them along. People began to follow us. Ther
must have been a hundred of them tagging at my heels when we cam
across the square. They're outside now."

"I'm afraid all the cells are occupied," said De Mariat.

He opened a door at the rear and walked into a dark and narrow spac
lined on one side with the cells to which the Englishman had objected
There were two tiers of them, five to a tier (the cells were two feet higl
and two and a half wide and, as the length was a bare six feet, tall prison
ers found themselves badly cramped), and there was a small grating ir

each. There was no means of ventilation and the stench was so great that
the provost hastily stuffed a handkerchief over his nose.

"Just as I thought," he said, noting that a pale face stared at him from
behind each grating. "Every cell has its happy tenant. Whew! This place
is like the latrine of a slave market or a lair of wild beasts!"

He returned to his cabinet in such haste that the door slammed shut
after him, causing the board wall to shake. The mirror fell to the floor and
crashed into pieces. The provost said in a tone of the most intense exasperation, "This is a filthy mousetrap for a gentleman of France to be
caught in!"

He was aware that the early popularity he had won in the settlement by
his new clothes and his fine manners had been dwindling as a result of the
vigor with which he enforced the law and he decided it might be a wise
thing to treat the community to a spectacle.

"Joseph," he said to the aide, "there's no room back there for these two
unruly animals you've brought in. So—what are we to do with them? I'll
tell you. We'll try them tonight and we'll make a show of it. The trial will
be on the square so the whole population can attend and take sides. They
will all like it very much, you'll see, and they will say that this is the way
justice should be administered. You will go at once, my Joseph, to the
Sieur de Balne. In the absence of His Excellency, he will have to preside.
Tell him that the heat must be disregarded and he must wear his wig and
his ermine collar. . . ."

III

The Sieur de Balne had agreed, somewhat reluctantly, that it would be
well to allow the populace the enjoyment of the trial. He was, accordingly,
wearing a wig with the longest pole-locks anyone in New Orleans had
ever seen and his red robe with ermine collar, when he took his seat on a
bench at the north end of the Place d'Armes. Motioning to the *huissier,*
he said in an urgent whisper: "There will be interruptions and much
noise, I fear. You will have to be firm. Ring your bell and announce that
the trial will be held inside if there is any trouble."

"Inside?" The *huissier* was astonished that such an idea could have been
conceived. "M'sieur! There isn't a room in the town large enough to hold
the witnesses alone. And have you thought how warm it will be inside on
a night like this?"

"But," said De Balne, almost humbly, "with such a very large attendance, we must find some way of keeping order."

The court official looked about him at the people. "Everyone's here. All
except Philippe Girard and his Hop-o'-My-Thumb."

The Sieur de Balne, who was a bookish individual and did not keep in touch with the tides of life running so vigorously about him, looked puzzled at this information.

"Do you refer to the very small man who has, I strongly suspect, an eye of glass?" When the *huissier* nodded in affirmation the judge went on. "And they are not here, you say? May I inquire why they alone of all the people of New Orleans have refrained from attending?"

"They're much too busy, that pair. They have the house to finish for M'sieur de Mariat and his bride. *If* she ever arrives."

"But, my good man, it's most unfortunately true that the poor little bride is *not* coming. The ship is so long overdue that we must reconcile ourselves to believing it has gone down." He sighed deeply. "I am sure every family which came from New France has at least one relative or friend on this unlucky ship. I'm convinced that all the trouble in the town, all this quarreling and fighting, this screaming and shouting and going to law, is due to the strain under which the poor men and women are living."

The quarrelsome spirit to which the gentle Sieur de Balne had referred manifested itself at this moment in a loud demand from the crowded square for the trial to proceed. Accordingly the two defendants, both looking defiant of one another and of the court and of all aspects of law and order, were brought forward and placed in front of the bench, one at either end.

"There must be a proper degree of decorum," said the Sieur de Balne, looking about him with the sternest air he could assume, which, unfortunately, was not nearly stern enough to have any effect on the crowd at all. A lack of decorum, in fact, was manifested as soon as the questioning of Jules Duguest began. His idea of answering questions was to shout charges at his fellow defendant. The latter, naturally, responded in kind. If the exchanges between the pair did not seem sharp enough the spectators joined in and provided a keener edge. The insults mounted in virulence.

"He struck the first blow, M'sieur Judge."

"He lies. I didn't defend myself until he struck me three times."

"He served all the bits of meat in the soup to his own children. My wife and I watched him, the niggard!"

"You are a cheat as well as a liar. You stole a piece of silver out of my wife's purse."

"You are a muckworm, crawling on your belly! It wasn't safe to leave my wife and daughters within your reach!"

"You were hatched out of a serpent's egg!"

"You have fallen lower than a whale's droppings!"

Not content with this airing of all the details of the feud, one of the spectators marched to a place in front of the bench and began to criticize the management of the colony and to complain of the false promises by which they had been lured from their homes in France.

"We have been fed lies!" he charged. "And that is not the worst. We are fed nothing else. We haven't enough to eat and yet we know that there are stores of food in the *casernes*. Answer me this, Sieur de Balne, were we brought out here to starve?"

Another voice from back in the crowd raised a second point. "Why are so many native slaves being brought in? There's no work for them yet and won't be until we get those great estates the King promised us. There are so many of them here now that someday it will be Lachine over again. We'll wake up and find our throats cut!"

"Messires!" protested the judge. "It's not His Most Christian Majesty and His Royal Highness the Regent who are on trial here!"

It was at this point that a canoe pulled in at the landing below the square. A man sprang out and came at a furious pace around the edges of the crowd. The temper of the spectators had reached such a stage of bitterness, however, that no one paid any attention to the new arrival until he began to whisper in the ear of the Sieur de Balne. Then, sensing that something important was afoot, a silence took possession of the square.

The judge got slowly to his feet.

"Messires, friends!" he cried in a voice which cracked suddenly with excitement. "There is news! There is wonderful news. Messires, the ship from Quebec has arrived! It has been sighted off the mouth of the river!"

The spectators seemed to go mad. They cheered, they danced, they waved their arms. They embraced each other, they sang snatches of songs. Then, the first delirium having worn off, they dropped to their knees and joined in fervent prayers of thankfulness for the divine intervention which had brought the ship safely to shore.

No one thought it strange that in the first moments of wild excitement the two defendants clapped each other on the back with affectionate exuberance and that their wives embraced and wiped their tears on the same handkerchief. It seemed quite natural for the two families, the children included, to fall on their knees and to join in the prayers together.

The Sieur de Balne looked at the two slips of paper in front of him, which set forth the nature of the charges, and scribbled the word "Dismissed" at the bottom of each.

Auguste de Mariat heard the news with mixed feelings. Now, he said to himself, the marriage settlement was not lost. He had been indulging in some alarmed speculation as to what steps his father would take to raise the funds they needed so badly. His relief on that score, however, was balanced by the realization that he had not escaped after all the necessity of marrying a stupid provincial girl.

But he was all smiles when people rushed up to him, with tears of joy in their eyes, to say how fortunate it was that his bride had not perished and that now the great romance, in which all of them took the deepest interest, could go forward.

CHAPTER IV

DESPITE the steersman's gruff "Come now, keep back, do you want to swamp us?" all the special friends Félicité had made during the interminable voyage from Quebec and the delay for refitting when they drifted in to the Bahamas were crowded around her at the prow of the flat-bottomed boat. Little Madame Poitras, who had given birth to triplets, all daughters, as they passed St. Augustine (with Sister Agnes and Félicité acting as midwives), pinched her arm excitedly and said, "He'll be on the quay waiting for you, the handsome young man, with his fine curly wig and his fine buttons and the gold clusters in his garters!"

Félicité, eagerly watching the thick green mantle of shore line, through which a single rooftop had been sighted, answered, "Yes, madame, he'll be waiting."

But she was not thinking of Auguste de Mariat. She was thinking of someone else who would be waiting but who would not be wearing a fine curly wig nor gold clusters in his garters. There had been no word, of course, from either New France or Louisiana since the ship sailed, and she could only speculate as to what had befallen Philippe since his transfer to the new colony. Was he well, was he prosperous, was he content? She could only be sure of one thing: he would be waiting on shore to see her arrive.

Behind her she could hear much talking and shouting and stamping of feet. Here at last was the land of milk and honey, the prosperous new home they had been promised!

"It's a sweet land, so warm and peaceful!" breathed Madame Poitras. "What a pretty land to bring up my Félicité, my Agnes, and my little Florida!"

Félicité was acutely aware of two things. First, that she was pale and tired after the incredible hardships of the week spent in fighting their way up the river and, accordingly, would cut a very poor figure in the eyes of this fearsomely fashionable Monsieur de Mariat and, second, that poor Monsieur de Marest was watching her with his ardent soul in his eyes. He was a junior officer and had fallen in love with her before they had sailed out of sight of the Rock. In order to have that much longer with her, he had obtained from the captain the command of the first boatload up the river.

Their eyes meeting, the young officer nodded unhappily and said: "The moment of destiny approaches, Mademoiselle Félicité! You will achieve your happiness in a very few minutes now."

It had been impossible to prevent the other passengers from enveloping her mission in a warm aura of romance. How could it have been otherwise? A young girl from the land of frost and snow and danger, an orphan moreover, was sailing to meet and marry the son of a minister of France! Here were all the ingredients for roseate embroidery. She had soon discovered that her fellow travelers conceived her to be extremely lucky and were certain she was counting the days and hours until she met her handsome bridegroom. There had been no way of setting them right and so she had been under the necessity of smiling and nodding and acquiescing in the fiction.

"Don't you think, my lamb," whispered Madame Poitras, "that you should apply a—a mere touch of rouge to the cheeks? You must appear at your best for the young man."

"Do I look badly?"

"It's natural you should look nervous and pale." The little matron ran an appraising eye over the gray dress Félicité had selected for the journey up the river. There had been no chance for any of them to make a change of costume since the boat started; it had even been necessary, because of the lack of privacy, to sleep in their clothes. They were a sadly rumpled lot, Félicité as bad as any of them. "If only you had one of your pretty dresses! That Sèvres blue cherry with the laced *échelle!*"

Félicité began to feel doubly disturbed over the impression she was likely to make. There was no sense, certainly, in giving the man with whom she must live for the rest of her life a poor opinion of her at the start. But what else could she have done? To dress up for the river voyage would have been absurd in the extreme. Well, Auguste de Mariat would have to accept her as she was.

"If he could only have seen you for the first time when we had the dances on the ship! I'll never forget you doing the *jigue voleuse* with that very nice M'sieur de Marest."

The boat was swinging in close to the landing place and it was becoming only too apparent to the straining eyes of the passengers that the settlement was almost as new as the world on that third day when the first signs of order began to appear and God called the dry land Earth. Few buildings could be seen but there were many tents. The Place d'Armes was nothing but a muddy square. Enthusiasm on the flat-bottomed boat sank like a sack from which the grain runs out through an undetected hole.

"It will be mud we pick up on the streets and not gold!" declared a little rodent of a man who happened to be the father of five children. "We've been well taken in! We've been hooked and salted down like so much jack barrel—and sent here to rot and die!"

"There'll be no more talk of that kind!" declared the young officer, forgetting for the moment the tragic separation looming ahead and recovering some of his sense of responsibility.

But there was plenty of talk of that exact kind during the quarter hour employed in warping the boat in to the landing place. The newcomers looked with disillusioned eyes at the shrine under its canvas cover, the crude wooden barracks on each side of the square, the tents poking their heads up everywhere and creating the appearance of an army encampment.

Félicité was given, by common consent, the privilege of going ashore first. She stepped over the wet ladder to the firmness of the wharf with Monsieur de Marest carrying her portmanteau immediately behind her and two sailors after him heavily loaded with the rest of her belongings. It could have been an impressive entrance on a new life but instead it had the effect of making her feel still more conscious of the crumpled condition of her dress and the untidiness of her hair under her gray hood.

"He'll think me very plain and a dowd," she thought.

She kept her eyes on the ground as she followed the young officer across the planked wharf and onto the well-packed earth of the square, expecting to hear the friendly voice of the governor, the less assured greeting of Philippe and, of course, the well-bred tones in which the man she was to marry would speak to her.

Nothing of the kind happened. No man spoke to her at all! The watchers who crowded the edge of the square dropped back to make a lane through which she could pass. She was aware that they were inspecting her with the most active curiosity, and commenting among themselves, but nowhere did she see a familiar face, not even the round countenance of Polycarpe Bonnet!

A few more steps brought her face to face with a lady in a dress of some shade of purple which had all the fashionable trimmings without any conceivable exceptions. This remarkable costume boasted a Basque bodice and pagoda sleeves, and a flounced skirt which made all previous efforts at flouncing seem restrained. The skirt obviously had the advantage of the stiffened linen improvers known as *criardes,* and the high heels of her shoes were conspicuously red.

In keeping with such extreme adornment the lady in question should have been self-assertive and very sure of herself. When Félicité came close, however, she discovered that this overdressed woman was regarding her with a distinct trace of trepidation.

"You are Mademoiselle Halay." The tone of voice was unexpectedly friendly. "I, mademoiselle, am Madame Jouvelt. As no one else has appeared to bid you welcome, I am happy to assume that privilege myself."

"It's very kind of you, madame." Félicité, still at a loss to understand the failure of all three men to appear, was finding in Madame Jouvelt a fresh cause for puzzled speculation. "It's very kind indeed. I—I rather expected——"

"His Excellency was called away on duty. He's somewhere up the river —this dreadful ogre of a river which dictates so much of our lives! He hoped to be back in time to welcome you."

"You may have heard, Madame Jouvelt," said Félicité after a moment's hesitation, "that I'm to be married. It may be that my ship has arrived first——"

"No, mademoiselle, he's here, M'sieur de Mariat." Madame Jouvelt's voice had regained its normal heartiness. "I saw him a few minutes ago. But," glancing about her, "I don't see him now. He's provost of New Orleans and some matter of duty must have taken him away."

Félicité's heart sank. "He has taken one look at me and has gone!" she said to herself.

"It's just as well he's not here. Now you shall come with me. Through the kindness of His Excellency, my husband and I have the use of the only house in the place which has been finished. At least we have a part of it." Her tone became somewhat less assured. "He'll be angry but there's nothing else to be done now."

"*He* will be angry? Who do you mean, Madame Jouvelt? Do you mean my—M'sieur de Mariat?"

"His Excellency, the governor. He had other plans for you. But he's not here. Monsieur de Mariat isn't here. No one is here but me; and so I'm taking you in hand, and very gladly." She nodded her head encouragingly. "It will be better this way. You shall have a rest and a bath and then a most complete toilet. After that you'll select one of your most becoming dresses and put a little touch of rouge on your cheeks. Then—and only then!—we'll deign to let this M'sieur de Mariat see you."

Félicité began to feel an intense relief. "Yes, it will be much better that way."

The older woman looked about her with an air of surprise. "But where is your maid, child?"

"I have no maid, madame. It's—it's not usual in Canada."

"I had forgotten. Of course you would have no maid."

There was no mistaking the friendliness and solicitude that Madame Jouvelt was showing in her behalf. Félicité responded with a smile. Immediately the older woman took possession of her hands and pressed them

to her lips. "Ah, my small one!" she breathed. "You are pretty after all!
That smile, it gave you away. What was to be expected after that dreadful
journey up this river? When you've been in my hands for a few hours—
I, who know all the secrets of the toilet—you will emerge like a butterfly
with sunshine on your wings! That M'sieur de Mariat! We'll show him
what a lovely bride he has been lucky enough to win. Mother of God,
what a surprise we'll make of this for him!"

"It *was* a dreadful journey." Félicité was so tired that she could not
prevent her eyes from filling with tears. "I didn't sleep at all last night. I
kept thinking of what was to happen today. And, of course, it's a disappointment that—that no one was here."

Madame Jouvelt took her unsuspecting daughter into her arms and gave
her an ecstatic hug. "My small one!" she said. "You will need a very long
sleep. It's a great shame but there's no way of getting to this house save
by walking. Fortunately it's not far to go. Could this young man be persuaded to help us further with your portmanteau?"

"Madame!" The young officer's tone implied that it had been an affront
for her to hint at any limit to his devotion. "I would ask no better fate
than to carry Mademoiselle's belongings through all eternity!"

When Félicité wakened and found five pairs of eyes regarding her with
solemn interest she was convinced at first that it was part of her dreams.
It was not until the owner of the smallest pair of eyes, a dark monkey of
a boy of perhaps five, said, "She's awake, Nicolette," that she began to
realize where she was. She remembered then what Madame Jouvelt had
told her of the division of the house.

A voice of authority, proceeding from the largest of the five, answered
briskly: "Then you must run and tell Madame Jouvelt, Marcel. And the
rest of you—you, Urbain and Raoul and Saxe—you must go at once. Mademoiselle won't want her room filled with noisy little boys."

The possessor of the voice of authority was a girl of twelve. Still in a
half-waking state, Félicité watched her light a candle and draw the plain
cheney curtains on the one window. Her movements were light and brisk
and it was a pleasure to see how efficiently she herded Urbain and Raoul
and Saxe out of the room. She then walked over to the bed.

"It's getting dark, mademoiselle, and you will want to get up." She
added, as one woman of experience to another, "It's a very great nuisance
to have only brothers."

Marie entered a few moments later. "I see you've already made the acquaintance of Nicolette. That is good. Nicolette is a very useful little girl."
She shook her head in mock despair. "How you have slept! We'll have to

be right up on our toes now because M'sieur de Mariat has sent word he
will be here at eight-thirty."

On instructions from Madame Jouvelt, Nicolette brought in a pan of
steaming hot water, dragging it along the floor because of its weight. The
child then modestly withdrew while the ritual of a vigorous sponging was
carried out. "After I made that terrible trip up the river," said Marie, "I
took three baths before going to bed. I needed them."

After she had been thoroughly dried with the largest towel she had ever
seen in her life Félicité felt no more fatigue and was ready to take an
interest in the really important phases of the toilet which still lay ahead.
Marie dropped over her head the linen garment which served as the foun-
dation for all feminine attire, saying as she did so, "My skin was like yours
once, as fine as silk. And look at it now!" A pair of silk hose, with a
pattern in silver thread, were next adjusted and Félicité was hurried to a
seat in front of a mirror on the wall where the banker's wife proceeded
to apply all manner of unguents and salves to her face.

"I will do the best I can," said Marie, working with brisk fingers. "But
I assure you, child, that it will take weeks of constant applications to repair
the damage of so much exposure to sea winds. A fine skin is one of the
greatest of blessings and must be guarded as carefully as one's soul."

Nicolette, who had returned and was watching with an intensity of
interest, said, "My mother never puts anything on her face. She says she
believes only in water."

The next step was the dusting on of face powder. It was a very special
kind of powder, made of finely sifted starch and plaster of Paris, and most
seductively scented with a combination of musk and bergamot, a secret
which Marie had used in the past to good advantage. This was carefully
applied and then ruthlessly rubbed off, and the operation was repeated so
often that an uninitiated onlooker might have wondered why so much
trouble was being taken to apply it at all. The result, however, was most
satisfactory; the skin became smooth and white and all traces of the rav-
ages of the wind vanished, particularly after Marie had gently flicked the
cheeks with a mysterious substance which brought the faintest tint of pink
into them.

The banker's wife stepped back then and regarded her handiwork with
a critical eye. "What do you think, Nicolette?" she asked. "How does
Mademoiselle look now?"

"Lovely!" said the girl in an awed whisper. Then she nodded her head.
"Mademoiselle is of a type."

Madame Jouvelt left the room and returned almost immediately with a
quail pipe. Neither Félicité nor Nicolette had ever seen one before but it
was the child who asked, "What is *that,* please, madame?"

"It's used to spray powder on hair and wigs——" began Marie. But she got no further with her explanation. Nicolette protested in a shocked voice, "Oh no, madame! It is not for Mademoiselle! She has such lovely fair hair. It would be wrong to hide it."

Marie gave some thought to the problem and finally nodded her head in agreement. "The child is right. That honey color is so very rare. I think we must allow your M'sieur de Mariat to see it this once in its natural state."

"Will Mademoiselle's hair always be that color?" asked Nicolette. "Or will it turn dark like my mother's?"

"As to that, time will tell. But to use a lead comb will be of help."

The matter of dressing occupied almost a full hour; and had Auguste de Mariat arrived on time he would have been compelled to wait. Every second of the quarter hour that he was late was needed to complete the task of making his prospective bride as lovely as possible.

First, a damask petticoat with whalebone hoops was adjusted about her and on top of this came a blue skirt with side panniers of satin and a bodice of contrasting blue. The bodice was snug-fitting but the sleeves were bell-shaped, tight at the shoulder and flaring out widely at the elbow, where they ended in a cascade of white lace.

Such a dress made necessary a great deal of adjusting and even Nicolette was permitted to take a hand in the pulling and patting and tugging. Finally they were all satisfied and a little weary from the effort which had been involved. Marie sighed as she produced a bottle of perfume of curious design, saying, "And now comes the final touch." There were partitions inside the glass and different kinds of scent in the compartments thus formed. Each section had a funnel of its own and these were so arranged that the odors could be blended according to the fancy of the user.

Félicité held out her arms and turned slowly about. "My mother, who hasn't seen me since I was a year old, thought me a plain child," she said. "And she was right. I was a very plain child. I wish," indulging in a sigh, "she could see me now. I wonder what she would say? Perhaps she wouldn't recognize me."

Marie was so busy with the perfume bottle that she did not look up. She continued to spray lightly under the folds of the dress and Félicité could not see the expression on her face. Finally she said, "I'm certain that your mother, if she could see you now, would feel exactly as I do. She would think you had become a beautiful young woman." She seemed relieved when a loud knocking sounded from the front of the house. She smiled and nodded to Félicité. "We're just in time. Your bridegroom is here."

III

Auguste de Mariat had been at the wharf and had seen Félicité come ashore. Now, as he approached the house, attired in his very best coat and a waistcoat of red brocade, and with a three-cornered felt hat on his head, he was saying to himself, "Why did that fool in Montreal think this sickly-looking girl would make a wife for me?"

As he turned in at the gate he said to his servant: "Bousbach, your master is a punctilious fool who accepts with too good a grace the obligations laid upon him by others. I go, as many a king has had to do, to meet the plain bride foisted on me by family necessities."

A girl, who looked both small and wise for her age, answered his knock on the door with a nervous curtsy and a rapid succession of bows. "If you please, m'sieur," she said, "Madame Jouvelt is busy for the moment but you are to come in. I'll tell her you're here, m'sieur."

De Mariat did not get beyond the threshold, however. The main room of the house, as it happened, had been declared the territory of the Gauthier family and it had been taken over characteristically. There had been thefts in the settlement and so the clothesline, which had roused the apprehensions of Carpe Bonnet, was inside, stretched from the front of the room to the rear, while a second line, also laden down with newly washed articles of infant wear and use, crossed the first at right angles, thus cutting off most of the view from the door. In spite of this handicap, the visitor could see a succession of beds along the inner wall, made by the simple expedient of placing bed clothing on the floor. One of the beds was occupied by an infant which wailed incessantly.

An urchin of six or seven was bending over the occupied bed. On her way to summon Madame Jouvelt, the girl pushed him away in great haste. "Saxe!" she cried. "You ought to know better! Mother says it isn't catching but the spots are so large and red that you must keep away from him. Do you want to break out all over with them?"

This brought from somewhere in the rear a large and stern woman who shook a cane at the boy. "You, Saxe, you'll drive me to distraction with your shouting and your noise. How many times must I tell you to mind what Sister says?" Then, perceiving the visitor, the woman exclaimed, "Saints save me, it's the gentleman!" and promptly disappeared.

As if this were not enough, Auguste de Mariat became aware that someone was watching him from behind the blankets on the side line. It was a masculine face with an unruly thatch of hair and an eye which, even at the distance, was suspect. The owner of the eye, realizing that he had been discovered, parted the damp blankets and took a step forward. Nodding his head and smiling, he asked, "Are you suited with her, m'sieur, are you suited?"

It was fortunate that Madame Jouvelt arrived at once and led the visitor to the rear of the house. Here there was a small, and at present empty, room which someday would probably function as the cabinet of the owner. Here she left him, with an apology for the crowded condition in which he found them.

De Mariat said, "My thanks, madame," in a tone which expressed hi
dissatisfaction with everything. Leaning on his cane, he waited.

Félicité came into the room. She curtsied as she entered, then with colo
high walked slowly toward him. Although she held her head up, she go
no more than a hurried impression of arrogantly brushed-up mustaches
above which bold dark eyes stared at her out of a sallow face.

Not being prepared for such a change in her appearance, he did nothing
at first but stare at her. This could not be the dowdy creature he had seer
landing from the boat, that pale colonial in a crumpled cotton dress!

"Mademoiselle," he said finally, "I would have come sooner to pay my
respects but my duties are most exacting. You have, I trust, recovered from
the fatigues of your long journey. But that, assuredly, is an unnecessary
question. Your beauty, mademoiselle, supplies me with all the answer I
need."

"Thank you, monsieur. I've had a rest and so I feel much better."

The provost leaned his weight on his cane and stared hard at her.
"What kind of miracle is this?" he demanded. "You've been turned into
a very lovely woman by some magic. A kind of magic which I heartily
approve."

Félicité had regained enough self-possession to give him an appraising
look. He was rather handsome, she decided; but she knew, with the
instinct which is most active at a first meeting, that she would never be
able to like him. This became so clear to her as she continued to study his
face that her heart sank.

"We were more than a week on the trip up the river," she said. "It was
unfortunate that you saw me in the condition in which we arrived."

Still leaning on his cane, he nodded to her to come closer. "This banker
fellow is sparing with his candles," he said. "Although I've seen enough to
be sure that you please me very much, I would like a clearer picture of
my wife-to-be."

Félicité obliged by moving a step closer. He reached out with his free
hand and raised her chin. *"Parbleu!"* he exclaimed. "You have gray eyes!
I've always had a liking for fairness." He continued to study her face with
an intentness which was most embarrassing, although she contrived to
keep her head up while it lasted. "My sweet child, I've reached a decision
which surprises me as much as it may surprise you. Why should there be
any delay in accomplishing the purpose which brought you to Louisiana?
Why shouldn't we be married at once?"

Félicité was both startled and dismayed. It had never entered her mind
that there would be any haste in the matter. "How soon do you mean,
monsieur?" she asked. "In a few weeks?"

"In a few weeks?" De Mariat laughed. He took her hand, leaned over,
and implanted a kiss on it. "No, my very pretty Félicité, I don't mean in a
few weeks. You're a sweet child but there's much you must be taught and

I confess an impatience to begin with the lessons. We must be married——" He paused for a moment, frowning reflectively. "The Vicar General is here by the greatest of good fortune. I'll see him at once and will try to convince him of the need for a dispensation from the publishing of the banns. You need not look so horrified, my promised bride. It has been done before! And are we not living here under conditions which make it necessary for us to meet emergencies? The marriage contracts are already drawn up. We can sign them within the hour."

"But, monsieur! I—I had no such idea. There are preparations. There are so many things to be done! Madame Jouvelt has spoken as though she expects me to stay with them here for some time."

The first slight hint of impatience showed in his manner and in his tone of voice.

"This is a matter, mademoiselle, which concerns us and does not concern your Madame Jouvelt at all. What she may have planned, or what she may think, will have nothing to do with what we decide."

Félicité was completely at a loss. "But I think, monsieur, that I—I should speak to her. I am her guest and she's being most kind to me."

De Mariat had not taken his eyes from her face from the moment he discovered the change which had been brought about in her appearance. He shook his head now and demanded: "Is it a trick? Has there been a substitution? If there has, I shall refuse to recognize anyone else as my bride. I swear to that."

"But, monsieur——" She found it impossible to complete what she had intended to say. Her tongue refused its task and her mind was incapable of coherent thought. She had one desire only, to get away as far as possible from this demanding stranger who was so determinedly stating his intention of marrying her at once! The desire to escape, to hide, was so great that she did not stop to consider how she could get away or where she could find a place to hide.

Sensing what was in her mind, Auguste de Mariat laughed and then reached out suddenly. Drawing her into his arms, he kissed her twice on the mouth before releasing her. They were passionate, possessive kisses. "That was more to the point," he said. "That's how a bridegroom should talk to a shy and reluctant bride. And now, my sweet, you will seek out this tiresome Madame Jouvelt and inform her of my intentions."

"But, monsieur——"

Auguste de Mariat shook his head with a hint of impatience. "Mademoiselle," he said, "there's another reason beside the fact that you've taken my fancy. This is no place for you. Madame Jouvelt's reputation—well, mademoiselle, it is not of the best. If the governor had been here to greet you he wouldn't have allowed you to fall into the clutches of this loud-talking woman of tarnished antecedents. No, no, it can't be allowed to continue! There's only one way now to avoid the scandal of further association with this banker's wife: we must be married at once and take possession of the house the governor has prepared for us. The Vicar General will see the wisdom of an immediate marriage as soon as I tell him what I know."

"I don't know what words to use to make you see that it would be a great mistake!" protested Félicité.

"Mademoiselle!" Auguste de Mariat spoke with an admonitory sternness. "I am a man of the world. You are an inexperienced young woman from the colonies. You must be willing to allow that in all matters I will know what is best, particularly on questions of propriety. I tell you it would be a mistake if you remained any longer under the same roof with this woman!"

"What will Madame Jouvelt say? What will she think?"

"What Madame Jouvelt may say and think is of no consequence. I will explain to her what I think and that will suffice." The new provost smiled at her, drawing upon all his resources in the desire to make himself agreeable. "What greater compliment could I pay you, mademoiselle, than this desire to wed you at once?"

"I am happy, m'sieur, that I find favor in your eyes."

The possessive gleam showed itself again in De Mariat's face. "I consider myself very lucky, mademoiselle! I am happy in the wife selected for me."

CHAPTER V

BOUSBACH walked ahead, carrying a ship's lantern to light them on their way. The canebrakes and scrub mulberries loomed up on each side and from the thick brush came sounds of rustling and of stealthy life. A black shape swung back and forth across the sky, sometimes so close that they could hear the flap of wings.

"Fair bride of an hour," said Auguste de Mariat, his feet unsteady as a result of the wedding potations, "this is a sleazy home-coming. You should be riding a white steed with a train of servants behind you."

Behind them came Madame Gauthier, carrying a tremendous bundle of bedding, and Nicolette, whose arms were filled with articles of clothing. They were too far back to share the light of the lantern and Madame Gauthier could be heard muttering, "You will have to raise your brothers, Nicolette, for I know I'll never get back alive this night."

One thought kept running through Félicité's mind as she stumbled along on her husband's arm. "I am married! The step has been taken and there's no backing out now! I'm married to a stranger, to a man with whom I have nothing in common, a proud and selfish man who'll soon come to despise me. What manner of life have I to expect?"

The hope had been in her mind from the start that the man she was to marry would prove companionable at least and that her life with him might become tolerable. This hope had now been most thoroughly and rudely snatched from her. There could never be any happiness for her in a life shared with Auguste de Mariat. She disliked everything about him which she had discovered so far, his looks, his arrogance, his self-will. Every mannerism he possessed went against the grain. And yet they were married and tonight she must begin to share a bed with him!

It did not occur to her to blame those who had arranged the marriage. There had been no other course open, unless they had been prepared to let the control of the Mississippi fall into the wrong hands. Although the price was a high one, it had to be paid. She had no thought of refusing to carry out her part of the bargain but her heart sank with her realization of the nature of it.

"Have we stumbled into purgatory by mistake?" the bridegroom demanded. "I swear that I would rather wear a hair shirt and sleep on a bed of spikes than live in this hot and horrible land! Ah, beautiful France! Ah, that safe, busy, lovely Paris! Life elsewhere is a mere existence and I hope our recall won't be long in arriving."

Félicité was stirred from her thoughts by the need of protesting what he had said. "But, m'sieur, one doesn't come to a colony for a short time. One comes for life! We must stay here, and work very hard, and do our full part in making New Orleans into a great city!"

The bridegroom threw back his head and indulged in a scornful laugh. "I've no objections to New Orleans becoming a great city at some time within the next century or so. But it must achieve its greatness without the refining presence of Auguste de Mariat. It's my most ardent hope that I'll receive my recall before the summer is out."

The house proved to be a close copy of the first one Philippe had built but it lacked the gallery. De Mariat looked it over gloomily in the light afforded by the lantern. "Behold, madame," he said, gesturing about him, "the magnificent domicile to which your spouse has brought you. At any rate," he added in a grumbling tone, "it will be an improvement over that malodorous beehive of an inn where I've had to exist."

Félicité laughed. It was a brief and slight laugh and did not suggest any great degree of amusement. Nevertheless De Mariat stopped at once, as though surprised. He said to his servant, "Give me the light, rascal!" Holding the lantern close to her face, he studied her intently.

"You laughed," he said. "You have actually found something in what I say to amuse you. Can it be that you have a sense of humor after all? I was beginning to doubt it. All through the ceremony and the drinking of the toasts you sat like an owl on a dead branch. May I depend on hearing more laughs like that if I strive very hard to amuse you?"

They walked up the narrow path which led from the gate to the front door. Félicité had heard of the valiant efforts Philippe had made to have the place finished before she arrived. She looked up at the dark mass of it looming above them and forgot her own troubles in thinking of him. Where was he? Why had he not been at the quay when she arrived that afternoon? Was he ill? Had he been hurt?

The stillness of the house added to her fears. She was certain that only something unforeseen, something beyond his control, could have kept him away.

De Mariat said to Madame Gauthier, "This will pay you for your pains," and threw a few small coins behind him. Madame Gauthier cried, "Thank you, my lord!" and began to scramble for them feverishly in the dark. Nicolette did not follow her example until a furious outburst of, "Ungrateful child! Would you have us lose them?" brought her also to her hands and knees.

"Bousbach, open the door!" commanded the bridegroom. "Throw back your shoulders and hold the lantern up with some attempt at style. We must contrive between us a suggestion of dignity in making our entrance." He turned to his newly made wife. "Draw on your imagination, my sweet spouse. Try to believe that inside this door there are two rows of flunkies in handsome new liveries, bowing and smiling and bending the knee to the new master and chatelaine of this princely domain."

If he had drawn on the fullest resources of his own imagination, he could not have conceived the kind of reception they met. As they stepped inside the door a sound of heavy breathing reached their ears. The bridegroom came to a prompt halt.

"It appears," he said, "that our house already has occupants!"

The door opened directly on a long room with a fireplace at one side. The sound came from the far end. When the servant stepped forward with the lantern raised above his head, it could be seen that a man was sleeping there on a pile of shavings.

"What impudence is this! Bousbach, waken this fellow with your foot!"

Félicité laid a restraining hand on her husband's arm. "I know who it is," she said. "Please let me speak to him first."

He acceded grumblingly. "Unless he has a better excuse than any I can think of, I'll put him in irons for this," he said.

Félicité stepped forward and called, "Philippe!"

The sleeper moved and, after a moment, raised himself to a sitting position. He frowned at the darkness, unwilling seemingly to accept the fact that night had fallen. Then he recognized her and sprang quickly to his feet.

"Félicité!" he cried, then hastened to correct himself. "Mademoiselle, I didn't know you had arrived. I"—he glanced at the nearest window—"I must have been asleep a long time."

Auguste de Mariat decided to take the matter into his own hands. He advanced several paces into the room. "Come a little closer," he said to Philippe. "I want a good look at this intruder who addresses my wife by her first name."

Philippe obeyed. He had started visibly at the provost's reference to Félicité and now he carefully refrained from meeting her eye.

"What explanation have you for this strange conduct?" demanded De Mariat.

"The only excuse I can offer, m'sieur, is that I had instructions from His Excellency to finish this house before—before Madame arrived. I worked the last two days without stopping. When the walls were completed this afternoon and we had moved some furniture in I—I thought it would be safe to allow myself a short rest. I didn't intend to sleep for more than an hour but it seems I've been here ever since. I beg your forgiveness, m'sieur."

The bridegroom was toying with the well-spiked ends of his mustache in a way which might have been considered an amused acceptance of the situation. "I can have no quarrel with your reason for falling asleep. But this doesn't explain the calling of my wife by her first name unless it's a quaint colonial custom of which I'm ignorant." He suddenly dropped his hand and gave his thigh a resounding slap. "I have it! You are the unlettered native son I was told about. You are the faithful lover, the mute adorer who remained in the background like another Jacob waiting his seven years. I heard all about you from the attorney in Montreal."

"Philippe and I are old friends," said Félicité. "We grew up together at Longueuil."

The bridegroom did not look in her direction but kept his eyes fixed on Philippe. "What a charming idyll! Is it true, Master Philippe, that you were in love with my wife?"

When Philippe made no answer Félicité said, "Yes, m'sieur, it's true."

"Ha! Perhaps it's well that I insisted on having the ceremony performed at once since I find old admirers of my wife sleeping at the very door of the nuptial chamber." The facetious note disappeared from his voice. "And you, madame, were you in love with this bucolic admirer?"

She did not hesitate in answering. "Yes, m'sieur."

Apparently he had not expected an affirmative answer. He turned and stared at his wife.

"This much I'll say, one doesn't see a spider here at noon every day,"[1] he declared finally. "Curious things seem to happen. It is natural, of course, for girls to fall in and out of love. It means nothing. But I find it hard to accept that *my* wife's fancy should have fallen as low as this."

Félicité was thinking, "What am I to say if he asks me how I feel about Philippe now? Will I dare give him an honest answer?"

Auguste de Mariat did not ask this question. He continued to scowl. "I must warn you, my good carpenter, to keep a proper distance from now on. Any falling asleep that you do away from your bed had better be at the doors of other men's wives. As for you, madame, I see no point to keeping alive these youthful memories. You must never speak to him again."

"M'sieur, I haven't thanked him yet for striving so hard to have this house finished." Félicité turned to Philippe and smiled. "I haven't thanked him for a thousand great kindnesses in the past. It's nearly a year since we last saw each other in Canada and there are many things I must say to him." She walked across the floor to Philippe and placed

[1] An expression meaning to be bored.

a hand on his arm. "Come, I'll walk with you to the gate and that will give me time to say some of the things which are in my mind."

De Mariat watched them leave the house with a heavy frown but he made no effort to stop them. "My wife," he said to himself, "seems to be a lady of spirit."

II

The bedroom was sparsely furnished. The bed, which the servant had made with the clothes brought by Madame Gauthier, was of cypress wood and quite plain, with a battered linen sleeping frame. There was an armoire of sassafras wood and one chair of cherry. A small black dog-skin rug was on the floor.

De Mariat followed his wife in and turned the key in the lock after them.

"You must give me credit for both patience and tact," he declared, dropping the key in a waistcoat pocket. "I allowed you to have a farewell scene with your honest young workman. And I did not ask if you still cherish your girlish fancy for him." He walked over to the bed and considered it with a critical frown. "We shall have to draw on our imaginations again, my spouse. We must close our eyes and conceive this lumbering thing to be a handsome *lit d'ange* with satin *bonnes grâces* and armorial bearings in gold." He indulged in a shudder. "I very much fear this dreadful mattress is stuffed with Spanish moss!"

Félicité had been thrown into a state of inner panic by the click of the key. She thought, "He has locked me away from the past, from everyone and everything I love!" Like a newly caged bird, she looked at the window, wondering if the frame could be broken to let her through.

When she made no comment he looked at her curiously.

"You're frightened!" he charged. Then he gave vent to a high-pitched laugh. "My little bride of an hour, filled with virginal doubts at what's ahead of her! You are a simple gosling, a little rabbit who seems very much afraid of the wolf. Well, madame, you must accustom yourself to the ways of a husband who has eaten many little rabbits in his day!"

He would have said more in the same vein but was interrupted by a sound of loud voices, the clatter of sticks on pans and the braying of horns. It grew more distinct as they listened. A drum had joined in. The sound was coming closer.

De Mariat frowned uneasily. "What can this mean?" he asked.

"I think," said Félicité, "it's another of our quaint colonial customs. The charivari."

"The charivari? Do you mean they're going to serenade us? But there's no sense to that. There's nothing irregular about our marriage."

"In New France, m'sieur, there's nothing cruel about the charivari.

Most often it's a sign of good will. They're so friendly, the people there, and they don't try to cause pain." She hesitated as though she found it difficult to talk about themselves. "It may be, m'sieur, that ours is the first marriage in New Orleans and so they feel there should be a celebration."

The serenaders had reached the grounds by this time and were pouring through the gate. Not content with the torches which some of them carried, they proceeded to build a high pyramid of brush on the road. A great blaze resulted when fire had been set to this and the square around the house became as light as day. Watching through the window, Félicité got the impression that the whole town had turned out to do them honor. There seemed to be hundreds, women as well as men, and they were laughing and singing. To the accompaniment of the drum and an assortment of horns, they began to intone the serenading song:

Come out, come out, m'sieur!

De Mariat, who had joined Félicité at the window, asked impatiently, "Must I go out?"

"Oh yes. They would take it as an affront if you didn't."

"It wouldn't cause me any concern if they did." His frown deepened. "I suppose it will be necessary to give the rogues some money so they may go back to the inn and get themselves drunk."

"Yes, m'sieur. It's customary."

The singing of *Come out, come out, m'sieur!* was becoming more insistent.

"Please, I think you should go out at once."

Grumblingly he obeyed her. His appearance in the doorway was the signal for an increase in the uproar, the serenaders shouting at the tops of their lungs and pounding furiously on tin pans. The drummer, who was one of the provost's own men, went into a positive frenzy of activity with the drumsticks. One of the ringleaders came forward with a pan of liquor and tendered it to the bridegroom. De Mariat accepted it willingly enough and raised it to his lips.

Félicité remained at the window, scanning the crowd eagerly. She was finally rewarded by a glimpse of Philippe standing far back on the road as though he had no intention of intruding himself again but could not make up his mind to leave.

"My poor Philippe!" she thought. "How unhappy he looks! He doesn't like this. If he could, he would send them all about their affairs."

The serenaders were still singing loudly but the words had been changed to: *Come out, come out, madame!*

Knowing that she must respond, she wiped away the tears which the sight of the lonely figure of Philippe had brought into her eyes, and went to the doorway. There was an immediate outburst which transcended the welcome accorded the groom.

The leader came forward with the pan of liquor and held it out to her. She raised it to her lips and took a cautious sip. It was well that she had exercised caution, for it proved to be brandy and of the rawest variety. She choked and spluttered to the great delight of the crowd.

"A strong drink for little rabbits," said her husband in her ear. He took the pan from her and helped himself a second time. "But the perfect brew for me. I'm pleased, after all, that your friends from New France decided to pay us this visit."

Someone in the crowd shouted, *"Le reel à quatre!"* The idea found immediate favor and in a moment the cry was coming from all sections. The leader, getting rid of the pan of brandy (it was nearly empty by this time), made his way over to Félicité.

"Madame, will you dance with us? It would make us very happy."

"Of course, m'sieur. Brides always dance in the *reel à quatre.*"

"You will have M'sieur as your partner. But at first only. We must all have the privilege of one turn with the lovely bride."

She did not perform more than a step with her husband as partner. The first effort he made to swing her about caused him to stagger and, after staring about him helplessly, to drop back into the ranks of the spectators. The leader came prancing forward at once, calling, "Madame, I claim the honor."

She thought it would never come to an end and that she would never be free of faces smiling broadly and emerging from the clutter of other faces to say, "I claim the bride this time!" She danced forward and back, bowed, pirouetted, until she thought she would drop of fatigue. And yet she was enjoying it, the fast tempo of the music, the stamp of many feet, the happy smiles on every flushed countenance. But she was relieved when the leader offered her his arm and escorted her to one side.

"Madame, you don't know who I am," he said, smiling and nodding to her. "But I am from Longueuil and once I carried you on my back. My name is Jules Latour."

She identified him at once. He had not been with the first party which had set up their camp at the mouth of the river but he had gone south at an early stage, about 1706, she thought. In and about Montreal he was remembered as a gay blade, a deft hand with the fiddle, and a great success with the ladies. Now he was thin and a little stooped, and his face was sallow and leathery.

He was infinitely pleased when she told of seeing him preside at a celebration of *La Grosse Gerbe* at the château even though she had no recollection of the occasion when he had carried her back from a picnic.

"You were a very small girl then, madame," he said. "And you have—you have changed very much in the years which have passed. This is a strange land you've come to, a heady land, madame, and I'm sure you'll come to love it in time, even though——" He paused and gestured expressively. A black figure had bounded out suddenly in front of the fire and had begun to dance wildly like a scarecrow in the grip of a windstorm, with curious caperings and fantastic improvisations. "There, madame! That is what I mean. The fixed dances of New France seem out of place here. It is all so different. This is a gay land as well as a strange one. Every moment of our lives isn't controlled by rules and regulations. We are loyal and devout but—we live on the edge of the world and we are natural and carefree, and the sun warms us to happiness."

His dark face had lighted up with eagerness to make her see what he meant. "And now, madame, there is something you must do," he went on. "You must come over in front of the fire where everyone will be able to see you clearly. You are from Longueuil and they will be proud to see how beautiful you are. You must be properly introduced. Then we will say good night and go. You are very tired and it is clear that—that too much drinking is being done."

When they had stationed themselves in front of the blaze, where she could be seen by all the serenaders, he made a brief speech. "We are happy to welcome Madame de Mariat to New Orleans. She is one of us and we are very proud that she is so lovely and that she has danced the *reel à quatre* with us. I'm sure that this occasion will remain long in all our minds."

Félicité was conscious of smiles on the faces confronting her. She could hear close at hand a feminine voice saying in a whisper, "Of course I saw her when she came ashore but what could you expect after a week on the river without a chance to change her clothing?" It was clear they had been agreeably surprised.

Jules Latour continued with his speech. "It has been very kind of M'sieur de Mariat and his fair bride to accept our visit in such friendliness. I am sure that you all join me in wishing them a long and happy married life. And now it is late and there is, I'm sure, a limit to their indulgence. I propose, my good friends, that we say good night at once and make our departures."

III

Félicité was standing at the window, watching the last of the serenaders vanish down the road, when she heard the key turn in the lock a second time. She swung about quickly and saw that her husband was fumbling over the simple task of extracting the key. It was clear that Jules Latour had been right; there had been too much drinking.

"My bride of two hours," he said in a thick voice, "your friends stayed a long time. But now they are gone and we, my love, are alone."

Drink had blunted his powers of perception and he was not aware that she was shrinking back against the wall. He came toward her slowly, nodding his head.

"If I hadn't swallowed so much of that brandy I would ask you a question. I would demand your—your assurance that you no longer entertain any absurd sentiments for your honest but very dull carpenter. I intended to—to get that point cleared up at once." He was so unsteady on his feet that he almost toppled over when he made a gesture with his arm. "My small rabbit, it was a heady brew those yokels brought with them and at this moment I'm not interested in your past at all. But, ah, my pretty bride, what an interest I take in the present!"

He came toward her, walking with great care and holding out both arms. A panic took possession of her and she moved quickly to evade his embrace; so quickly that her feet became entangled in her long skirt. She pitched forward to her knees and saved herself from falling on her face only by catching hold of a corner of the armoire. Scrambling into the corner between that piece of furniture and the wall, she drew herself back as far as possible and wrapped her arms about her knees.

Standing above her, Auguste de Mariat laughed until his sides shook.

"My little rabbit!" he said. "Are you as afraid of me as that? Or is this a playful form of country coquetry?"

And then, with a suddenness which was surprising in view of his condition, he pounced forward and seized both her ankles. Backing away, and roaring with intoxicated amusement, he began to drag her about the room.

Félicité cried, "Stop it, m'sieur!" and kicked furiously to free herself. "This is vile! This is infamous!"

The only effect of her struggles was to increase the disarrangement of her clothes. Her skirts fell back around her hips. Frantically conscious that her thighs were exposed, she stormed at him to desist. She snatched at the rug and floor.

"Vile? Infamous?" he said, still laughing boisterously. "Don't you know this was the favorite sport of the lovely Duchess of Bourgogne, who would have been Queen of France today if both she and her husband, the Dauphin, hadn't died together of some pox? She used to allow two valets to drag her about on the grass, and she would laugh and wave her arms with delight. *Parbleu!* Her whole household had reason for knowing that she had nice thighs. As nice as yours, my fair bride. Is it possible that you think the diversions of a dauphine unfit for a simple little gosling from the colonies?"

Félicité succeeded in catching one of the legs of the bed and she was then able to kick her feet free from his grasp. With frantic haste she pulled her skirts into place, sobbing meanwhile with humiliation.

"You're very angry with me, my most proper wife," said De Mariat.

"It is possible that your yokel admirer didn't smooth the floor properly and that you picked up a splinter?"

Félicité got to her feet. She was still sobbing and still so angry that she could not see him clearly. When he stepped close to her with the intention of taking her in his arms she had no thought but to repay him for the indignities she had suffered. She slapped him resoundingly on the cheek.

Although she did not regret what she had done, she realized immediately that it had been a mistake. Her husband stepped back and glared at her.

"Some men like violent resistance, thinking it sweetens the surrender in the end," he said in an ominously low voice. "I don't share the feeling. I've never condoned a blow in my life. Because it's a woman who has struck me, and my own wife moreover, makes no difference. I promise you, madame, that you will long regret this—this stupidity!"

"Let me go!" she pleaded. "This is a mistake. A terrible mistake!"

He was so amazed at her suggestion that there seemed to be some moderation of his anger. "Are you proposing that we separate?" he demanded.

"Yes," she sobbed. "Let me go back. To Montreal. You can get an annulment of the marriage and then you'll be free."

"This," said De Mariat, "is unbelievable. It's—it's almost amusing! I should be the one to chafe at the bond—I, a gentleman of France, married to a stupid little country prude!"

"If that's how you feel, then surely you'll be willing to agree that this marriage is a mistake."

"Madame! Is it possible you know as little as that? Marriage is a life bond. You've been delivered into my hands. You belong to me, your body and your property and even perhaps your soul. No law of God or man can deliver you from me. Nor can I, heaven help me, be freed from your insipidities and the annoyance of your inexperience!"

"Marriages can be annulled," she pleaded. "They're not binding if they are not consummated. Let me go now and—and you will be able to free yourself of me legally."

"If they are not consummated!" He reached out and drew her into an embrace of such strength that she could not move. "Do you think I'll allow you to leave this room as virtuous as when you came in? When you struck me, you simple-minded goose, I swore to myself that to lie with you was the last thing I desired on earth. But that was the effect of a most unpleasant surprise and shock. I seem to have recovered from it. I find you desirable again. I intend, my little spitfire, to destroy all chance of an annulment at once!"

CHAPTER VI

THE SUN rose over New Orleans, the brown pelican stretched his long legs and looked about him for a handy breakfast, the ivory-billed woodpecker began to labor with such a burst of energy that it sounded as though a whole corps of carpenters was at work. Carpe Bonnet rose from his couch. It had become his habit to go to the well at one corner of the Place d'Armes and fill a large bucket which he would then carry to the house shared by the Jouvelt and Gauthier families.

The following morning, arriving a little earlier than usual, he was surprised and disappointed to find Madame Jouvelt in the kitchen. Always before it had been Madame Gauthier who was there to receive the bucket (with no more than a grunt of thanks) and thus he had been privileged to stand about and ponder on the amplitude of her proportions.

It was apparent that Madame Jouvelt had just risen. Her face, lacking all aids to middle-aged pretense, was tallowy. She wore a tattered camisole over which wine had been spilled.

"On behalf of Madame Gauthier, who has been saved a trip to the well, I give you thanks, M'sieur Bonnet," she said.

"I always find it a pleasure, and an honor, to bring the water in the mornings, madame."

"Oh!" She looked at him rather sharply, noting that his hair had been dampened and smacked down on his head and that he looked in consequence surprisingly neat. "So, you come each morning. Is it to see Madame Gauthier?"

"Madame," said Carpe, "yes."

"Will you pardon me if I say that you surprise me? I've always been interested in what attracts men in women." As indeed she had. "Do you find Madame Gauthier attractive?"

"Madame," answered Carpe, "no."

"What then is the fascination she has for you?"

"Madame, she's like taking a bath in a barrel of cold rain water. You don't plunge right in but lower yourself slowly, inch by inch. You grow to like her by degrees. And she's not bad-looking. No indeed, madame."

"This is very interesting, M'sieur Bonnet."

Carpe nodded his head energetically. "To see her at her best, madame, you must look at her from behind." His face began to beam. "Ah, how she must burst her stay bobbins!"

It became clear, after Philippe's assistant had departed, that the banker's wife was in a depressed frame of mind. She sighed as she beat eggs in a bowl for an omelet. "The poor child!" she said aloud. "The sweet little innocent!"

The widow came into the kitchen, looking even more severe and taciturn than usual. "He has brought the water?" she asked. She nodded her head with satisfaction when she saw that the daily chore had been performed. "He is useful, that one. But still you could pick him out of a shell with a pin."

"Will you see that none of the children disturbs her? They shouldn't find out she's here because we don't want it known around."

The widow nodded her head. "It will be hard because they are like ferrets, they poke their noses everywhere. As soon as they're up and have their breakfasts I'll drive them out of the house. Nicolette could be trusted and I think we might let her know about it."

"Yes, Nicolette will be useful. Is—is our visitor still sleeping?"

"No, Madame Jouvelt. I looked in a moment ago and she said she hadn't been asleep at all."

"Then she'll be ready for something to eat. I must get this omelet on the fire."

"She says she doesn't want anything," declared the widow. "She says she doesn't think she'll ever eat anything again."

The handle of the fork gave an angry tap on the edge of the bowl. "That means my husband will have to be given this omelet." Félicité's mother dropped the fork and raised her hands above her head. "I knew it would end this way but I did nothing about it. I should have driven him out of the house. If I had been in my right senses I would have told the priest it was wrong to marry them so soon, that he was forcing her into it. But I didn't. I did nothing. I sat there like a ninny and let him have his way!"

II

Auguste de Mariat wakened late. When he sat up in bed a pain shot through his head of such an excruciating nature that he thought for a moment a blade had been driven from one temple to the other. He groaned and rubbed a hand over his brow. "That foul brandy!" he said aloud.

Then he became aware that the other half of the bed was empty. His forehead wrinkled in a reluctant grin. "She'll accustom herself to my ways in time," he thought.

He crawled out of bed, keeping a hold on the bedpost to steady himself. He called in a subdued voice, "Bousbach, have you coffee ready, rascal?"

The servant put his head in at the door. "The coffee's been ready for hours, master."

"Then bring me some at once. I've a headache." He raised his arms gingerly. "Where is Madame de Mariat?"

"She's gone to the Jouvelt house, master."

The bridegroom grinned again. "That was to be expected," he thought. "She's gone to exchange confidences and beg for sympathy. Perhaps I was a little too demanding." Then his face clouded. "But I told her she must never see that woman again!"

"One of your men is here," said the servant, lingering in the door with an expression which would have puzzled his master if he had been as observant as usual. "He says he has reports for you."

"Send him in then. I'll talk to him while you get my breakfast ready."

The soldier was a lean fellow whose regulation coat, once of white-gray, had become almost black from long usage and whose bandoleer and belt of bleached leather were cracked and painted. He came in with a jauntiness and confidence which hinted at a degree of understanding with his commander.

The conversation which ensued would have puzzled any listener who did not know that in France there was a large body of opinion which desired the failure of the Louisiana schemes of John Law, and that a few men, looking to profits in the inevitable breaking of the bubble, were prepared to hasten by any means the disintegration of the colony.

"Another good rain to swell the river and it'll go, patron," announced the soldier.

"The dike, Jean?"

"The dike, patron." During the winter De Bienville had built at considerable expense and trouble a stone dike to protect the settlement from the danger of spring flooding. "It's been weakened in half a dozen places."

"You used only men who can be depended on?"

The soldier had the effrontery to wink. "Only the ones you picked yourself and who've had their pay in advance. They can all be depended on."

De Mariat gave his head an approving nod. "I'm told a good flood would wipe out everything that's been done here. And now how many people are sick in town?"

The soldier's expression changed to one of soberness. "Too many, patron. Sixty-six cases reported so far. It comes from the exposure and the sleeping in tents. All the men with the yellow signs," a term applied to doctors, "are so busy, patron, that they'll need new coattails."

"Any deaths, Jean?"

"Six. There will be plenty more, I'm afraid."

"And we've had nothing to do with it. That's a great satisfaction."

When he found that the soldier had nothing more to tell him De Mariat dismissed him with a wave of the hand and remained seated in a deep study. "I'll have a report to send back soon," he said to himself, "which will convince all France that John Law is mad. But I must wait for Don Miguel and the Englishman to carry out their part." He nodded his head with satisfaction. "I don't believe my father could have done better if he had come himself."

The news he had received seemed to have had a good effect on him. He was even able to smile as he walked to the rear of the house.

"When did Madame de Mariat leave?" he asked the servant, who was broiling a piece of meat on the end of a long fork.

"I don't know, master. She was gone when I got up."

De Mariat's brief moment of good nature came to a quick end. He stared at his servant as though he found it hard to believe what he had heard. During the time which passed before he spoke again he was turning an unpalatable possibility over in his mind. "Then she didn't go on an innocent visit," he thought. "She has run away from me!"

To make sure of what had happened, he began to ask more questions. "At what hour did you get up, rascal?"

"At five-thirty, master."

"And she was gone then? How can you be sure?"

"Master, I wondered if you were in need of anything. I—I opened the door a few inches and looked in."

"But could she leave the house without you hearing it?"

Bousbach shook his head. "I was tired, master, and I slept like a bear. I didn't hear a sound until habit wakened me at my usual hour."

De Mariat said to himself, "There's no doubt about it, then." The end of his nose quivered with the intensity of the feeling which had taken possession of him. His eyes seemed to have drawn together. "I must get her back before it becomes known or everyone will be laughing at me, the deserted bridegroom!"

His next question was accented with a silent fury. "If she was gone when you wakened, how do you know where she went? Are you guessing, you simpleton?"

Bousbach was not sensitive, for once, to his master's moods. He drew back the toasting fork and examined the meat on its prongs. "It's ready, master," he said. He laid the meat on a wooden plate and reached for the loaf of bread. "Will you have ale, or will the coffee do?"

De Mariat seized him furiously by the arm. "Answer me, you rogue!" he exclaimed. "How do you know where she went?"

"It wasn't a guess," the servant answered in an aggrieved tone. "Jean told me just now."

"Jean? How would he know anything about it?"

"One of the watch saw her on the way. It was just before dawn and he called to her. As he got no answer, he followed her. She was in such a hurry that he had to trot to keep up. The watch told Jean that she had nothing on her feet."

Such a wave of passion surged through the bridegroom that coherent thought was impossible. He took hold of the collar of his servant, saying, "Fool! Dolt! Rascal!" and shaking him furiously. He then began to dress himself with such hasty abruptness of motion that Bousbach, recognizing the signs, betook himself to the comparative safety of the kitchen.

"Everyone in town will know by this time!" The provost forced on his hose with impatient tugs. "They're laughing at me now! The tavern is ringing with merriment at my expense. The fine courtier deserted by the simple country maid! How delighted they must be!" He shoved his feet into his shoes with angry stampings. "There's no figure so comic as a deserted bridegroom!"

Then he brought himself to consider the situation with some degree of calm. "I must bring her back at once," he decided. "No explanation need ~~ever be made. They'll probably go on laughing behind my back but that~~ can't be helped now. And it won't last long."

He called in a loud tone to Bousbach, "Come at once! I need you. There are things for you to do."

III

Auguste de Mariat, outwardly, was a picture of easy composure as he approached the house. The five Gauthier boys were playing in the yard and when little Saxe, the first to sight him, shouted, "Here he is!" and vanished behind the house, the others were not slow in following his example. Even this incident did not disturb the calm of the provost. For the benefit of any eyes which might be trained on him, he smiled and walked leisurely to the door. There was no urgency in the way he manipulated the knocker.

It was Madame Jouvelt who answered. She opened the door no more than a foot and looked out at him with a truculence which almost matched his own.

"Go away!" she said in a tense whisper.

"I've come to escort Madame de Mariat back." His tone was natural and easy. Without any change of expression, he dropped his voice. "Let me in, you troublemaking fool, or I'll crash the door with my heel! Do you want a scene? We're being watched, you may be sure."

Reluctantly she allowed the door to swing back wide enough for him to enter. Without closing it, she whispered: "You might as well know at once that your wife won't see you. She never wants to see you again."

"What my wife wants is of no importance whatever. *My* wants are what count, madame." He forced her hand from the knob and closed the door. "And now, if you please, where is Monsieur Jouvelt? I want him to hear what I have to say."

The suppressed anger which she perceived in his face caused Madame Jouvelt to lead the way through a door opening into the bedroom she had shared with her husband since the division of space became necessary. The banker, who was sitting in a chair by one of the windows and wearing a cotton dressing jacket, said, "Good morning, monsieur," in an uneasy tone of voice.

"Master Banker," said De Mariat, walking over beside him, "you must know enough of the law to be aware that a runaway wife has no rights at all. Come, then, produce her at once, and make an end to this farce."

Jouvelt, speaking in a far from assured voice despite the stern look his wife was bending on him, said, "Madame de Mariat is a guest in my house at the moment. If she prefers not to see you that is her right and her personal concern."

De Mariat indulged in a short laugh which did not suggest he was amused. "Do you think me as ignorant of the law as that, Master Banker?" He became instantly sober again. "Before my first wedding I studied the laws relating to matrimony with the greatest care. I assure you that I'm familiar with every phase of them. I understand every little turn and quirk."

"Indeed," said the banker, nodding his head. "That is interesting. I doubt if many bridegrooms go to such lengths."

"I can tell you in detail what my rights are. I can tell you what my wife may and may not do. I know, moreover"—the provost looked sharply at Jouvelt at this point—"the penalties imposed when outsiders attempt to come between husband and wife. It generally proves to be a costly indulgence." De Mariat had continued to wear his hat, which had a long yellow plume dangling over one shoulder. He glared down contemptuously over the plume at the seated man. "When a wife runs away she may not be given shelter by anyone, not even by her parents."

"We make no claim of standing in the stead of parents," declared the banker hastily. "Madame de Mariat came here at some hour of the night —I can't be specific as I was asleep at the time—and she was admitted, of course. As for the law, M'sieur the Provost, you must be aware there is canon law as well as the civil code. I understand your wife intends to place her case with the good father who acted as her confessor on the ship from Quebec."

De Mariat laughed again, and this time there was a hint of amusement in it. He stopped abruptly, however, and shook a gloved forefinger at the banker. "Canon law? It's much more lenient with wives, as we both know. But, Master Banker, my foolish little wife has closed the portals of the Church in her own face by her ill-considered departure. Canon law can be invoked only if the confessor is consulted before any action is taken. Action taken on his advice has a legal basis. By leaving me as she did, my wife has barred herself from appealing to the Church."

It was apparent from the expression on the banker's face that he was aware of this unfortunate truth. He slumped farther back into his chair and stared up at the bellicose visitor with a look which announced his personal willingness to surrender.

"Allow me to expound the law a step further," said De Mariat, who seemed anxious to complete the discomfiture of his opponent. "Under the civil code, Madame de Mariat may apply for a separation—while still living under my roof. But there are only two grounds on which she might hope to win a decision—the impotence of the husband or his harsh treatment of her." He burst into a loud laugh. "After last night Madame de Mariat is in no position to claim me impotent. On the contrary, monsieur, on the contrary! As for the question of harsh treatment, the law defines the point with great clearness. I may beat my wife, provided I don't do so with unnecessary severity. If she were disabled permanently, she would have a basis for a claim. That I wouldn't do under any circumstances.

"I want to go still further, so there can be no misunderstanding between us. I may waste my wife's property and she will have no legal grounds for complaint. I may commit adultery, even in my own house and in front of her, if I so desire—nay, I may use my wife's bed for the purpose—and the law will have nothing to say about it. Is it now clear, Master Banker, that my wife is completely in my power?"

Jouvelt asked in an unhappy tone of voice, "What do you want me to do?"

"I want you to produce my wife and turn her over to me. To deal with as I see fit and as the laws of France allow."

Madame Jouvelt had been watching and listening with growing apprehension. Although she could tell from her husband's face that De Mariat was stating the case accurately, she had no intention of giving in.

"She will stay here with us!" she declared. "Go to law if you like, M'sieur Despoiler of Innocence, M'sieur Drunkard, M'sieur Bully! The law is two-edged and we'll fight you at every turn!"

"Come, come, my sweet!" cried the banker, winking at her in desperation. "You mustn't antagonize the young gentleman! We must keep calm, we must be ready to talk things over quietly. The law is the law, my fair spouse."

His wife turned on him. "I'm not a coward, m'sieur. I'm not frightened by all this superior talk of the law. If you were half a man you would order this insolent creature from the house." She turned back furiously to the bridegroom. "You are full of the law, it seems. Will the law help you if the story is spread everywhere of your lack of respect for virtue and innocence?"

The banker repeated in a quavering voice, "The law is the law, madame."

Félicité chose this moment to appear, wearing the red wrap which had been the first thing her hand had come in contact with when she began her flight, and with a pair of Madame Jouvelt's shoes on her feet. The shoes were at least a size too large and they clumped as she walked.

"I've heard what has been said," she declared, avoiding her husband's eye. "Enough to know that I have no legal right to be here and that I must go at once."

"Félicité!" cried Madame Jouvelt. "I won't let you go! I'm not afraid of this man and all the rights he claims! I snap my fingers at the law! If my husband hasn't the courage to stand up for you, I'll walk out of this house when you do. We'll go away together."

Félicité gave her a grateful look but, nevertheless, shook her head. "I'm afraid it would be of no use." She turned to face De Mariat. "It may be that no one is allowed to offer me shelter but there's nothing to prevent me from going away and—and disappearing. I would rather die in a swamp than continue to live with you!"

"You lack any understanding of the full meaning of the law," declared her husband. "I may follow you wherever you go and bring you back, by force if necessary. Anyone attempting to interfere would be subject to fine or even imprisonment." The red tinge in his eyes deepened. "You've seen fit to leave me. You've held me up to scorn." His face flushed as he said this, making it clear that the blow to his pride was the chief stimulant to his resentment. "I intend to make you pay to the fullest extent."

A bird was singing in a thicket outside the window at which the banker sat. It was a full-throated song, rising at intervals to such an ecstasy that the room was filled with it. Auguste de Mariat broke into a laugh.

"There you have the proper note for the first morning of a honeymoon. Both the bride and her lucky spouse are supposed to be as full of rapture as that. I deny that I am to blame for this lack." He walked to the window and called through it: "Where are you, rascal? Well, come in. And bring the cane."

Bousbach, keeping his eyes down as though not pleased with the part he was being forced to play, brought a cudgel into the room. It was about three feet long and all the bark had been removed from it, leaving the surface smooth. De Mariat took it from him, hefted it, and then held it out for the banker's inspection.

"Observe, if you please. It's not thicker than a man's thumb, the exact size specified by the law."

He gave a cut at the air with it. Then he reached out with his free hand and pinioned both of Félicité's. She struggled to break his hold but was unable to get her arms free. His strength was much greater than anyone would have expected.

Then he began to beat her over the back and legs, bringing the stick down with enough force to send sharp pains through her body.

He counted as he struck. "One! Two! Three!" He paused, out of surprise at her lack of resistance. "So! You make a scandal by running away from me? You thought perhaps I didn't know how to deal with a disobedient wife. Let this be a lesson to you, madame. Four! Five!"

Félicité made no sound. Although her flesh shrank from the blows, she made no effort to defend herself or to escape from his grasp. "*They,*" she said to herself, meaning the Le Moynes, "have all suffered pain and hardships. Many have died. This is part of my share." She kept her eyes closed. After the first few blows it was necessary to bite her lips to keep from screaming. Once she winced away from him and the cluck of satisfaction he gave provided her with the fortitude to receive the remaining blows without any physical response.

"Six!" said De Mariat. "You will be a proper and docile wife from now on, I think. If not, I shall be compelled to discipline you every morning, my stubborn little pet! Seven! Eight!"

De Mariat desisted at that, holding the cane suspended over her. "Eight," he repeated. "Do you hear that, Master Banker? The law allows a husband to give his wife ten strokes if her disobedience warrants that much punishment. I have kept well within the limit. I call on you to make note of my moderation."

Félicité took a step in the direction of the door but her legs were so stiff that she found the pain of walking almost more than she could endure. She saw, moreover, that the sounds of the altercation had attracted the attention of the Gauthier family. The mother was standing a few feet back from the door where she could see what was going on, and behind her Nicolette. The child's eyes were round with fear and sympathy.

At the same time she became aware that a struggle had been going on between the Jouvelts. Madame Jouvelt had a pair of fire tongs in her hand, which she had seized with the intent of attacking De Mariat, and the banker was striving to take them from her. "You goose!" he was saying, panting with his exertions. "You thick head of a turnip! He may sue me for damages as it is. Do you want him demanding compensation for injuries to his person? This is no concern of ours, foolish woman."

"But it is!" cried his wife. She might have gone further and said something about the relationship but fortunately she perceived in time that De Mariat was staying his hand. She allowed her husband to obtain possession of the tongs.

"You are a beast and a coward!" she said to De Mariat. "A way will be found to punish you for what you've done."

De Mariat laughed. "I suggest, Master Banker, that you keep in mind
this lesson I've given you in wife training. Your own charming partner
seems badly in need of a demonstration." The light note left his voice.
He scowled at Jouvelt. "You will give it out that Madame de Mariat's
visit here this morning was a casual one. I've no desire to have the whole
settlement gabbling over what's happened. The matter of explaining I
leave in your capable hands."

He turned then to Félicité. "We'll now return. In order to avoid attracting notice, you must strive to walk naturally. Are you capable of it?"

"Yes," she answered without looking at him.

"Good! Take my arm, then."

Félicité found the effort of walking almost intolerable but she clamped
her lips tight and kept pace with him. Each step caused her such acute
discomfort that she thought with dismay of the long distance they had to
go. She would never be able to make it; of that she was sure. But she must
try.

She was so concerned with physical difficulties that she did not see
Nicolette break away from her mother's restraining hand. Finding a
broom, the child came charging after them, screaming in a shrill voice.
Before her mother could interfere she succeeded in landing a blow on De
Mariat's head which sent his fine hat flying across the room.

Madame Gauthier twined a knuckle in the back of the child's dress
and led her, expostulating loudly, to the rear of the house, while the victim of the attack, his face black with anger, recovered his hat.

"But, Mother!" cried the child. "Why shouldn't I beat him? He struck
the nice lady with a stick. I saw him!"

IV

"And now," said De Mariat when they reached the house after what
had seemed to Félicité an endless ordeal, "I trust you've learned your
lesson."

Félicité had seated herself in one of the two chairs in the main room of
the house and was enjoying the relief of resting her aching limbs. She
made no reply.

De Mariat watched her for a moment and then laughed. "I think I can
detect a trace of stubbornness in you still," he said. "Well, at any rate, tell
me this. When you were so injudicious as to think you could take matters into your own hands, how did you think you were going to live? You
couldn't subsist long on the charity of friends. Did you believe the story
M'sieur Las is spreading that gold can be picked up on the streets here?
Or did you think you could obtain some employment? After all, the op-
portunities for runaway wives are rather limited in this thriving city."

"All I thought about was that I had to get away."

"You're not giving me an honest answer." He took the other chair and, as he was warm from their long walk, proceeded to fan himself with his wig. "We are logical, we French. You had a plan in your head. You must have had some means on which you were counting."

"That is true." Félicité spoke with dignity. "Do you think my kind guardian would send me on a voyage with nothing in my purse? I had a little money left and some pieces of jewelry. I could have looked after myself."

"So!" He sprang from the chair and walked over close to her. "You've acknowledged it! You've confessed."

Félicité was startled. "M'sieur!" she gasped. "What have I done now?"

"Don't you know," he demanded, "that from the moment you became my wife you ceased to have possessions of your own? The gold you had in your purse——" He stopped and glared down at her. "How much was it?"

"Not much, m'sieur. I had expenses."

"All the money you had, your jewels, have ceased to belong to you. They've become communal possessions. You can't spend a sou, you can't drop a white in the poor box, without my knowledge and consent. If you sold your jewelry it would be a theft. You would be stealing from me, madame, me! Don't you understand that?"

"I know about communal possessions, of course. But these were gifts. From my guardian, the Baron of Longueuil."

He leaned down closer, his eyes sharp and acquisitive. "I think perhaps you had already sold something to that banker, that cunning fellow Jouvelt. Come, you must answer me."

"Yes, m'sieur, I did. I thought I would be in need of more money. He was kind enough to make me a fair offer."

"What did you sell this designing rogue?"

"A cameo, m'sieur. It was a present from M'sieur Charles and it was my right to dispose of it as I saw fit."

"Must I explain again that you've no right to sell as much as a discarded ribbon or a torn stocking without my consent? What did he pay you?"

She named the sum. His eyebrows went up with surprise and even a degree of satisfaction. *"Mordieu!* The attorney in Montreal was right. You have shrewdness, madame. The price was not bad." He snapped a finger and thumb. "The time has come to take things into my own hands. The money, if you please. Should proper occasion arise, I'll let you have what you need. I'll take the jewelry also."

Félicité, who had been keeping her head lowered, looked up. "Since you say it's the law, you may have the money and the jewels. They mean nothing to me now. I have only one wish in life, only one thought."

He allowed this to pass without comment. "Sometime later in the day

I'll call on Master Jouvelt and demand the return of the cameo. What I'll have to say to him won't sit well on his stomach. It will be an unpleasant surprise for him, I think."

Félicité roused herself to defend her friends. "What he did was intended as a kindness. I was in need and he helped me. I ask that you bear this in mind when you talk to him. You'll find what he paid me in my purse and so it can be returned to him."

De Mariat seemed to consider this a very good joke; at any rate he threw back his head and laughed. "I wasn't a party to any transaction with this banker. He dealt with you—you, who had no right to sell him the cameo. If he desires his money back, let him come to you. After I'm through with Master Jouvelt, however, he won't think it wise or safe to importune you in the matter. Of one thing I'm quite certain—I'll have no difficulty in getting the cameo from *him*."

v

Night had fallen when Auguste de Mariat returned to the house. Bousbach was hovering outside the door. "Must you pounce on me like an evil spirit or a ghost?" demanded his master.

"There's a bottle of wine in your room. And a loaf of fresh bread. The new oven back of the east *caserne* was finished this afternoon and the baker turned out the first batch an hour ago. St. Alexis, what a rush there was!"

As he spoke, Bousbach opened the door and hurried inside to light a candle. De Mariat accepted it with a critical look. "Rascal," he commented, "there's something odd about you tonight. Have you been up to some mischief?"

"No, master, no."

"You can't deceive me. I can always tell when you have something on your evil conscience. What are you hiding from me, you hangdog rogue?"

When Bousbach protested vehemently that these suspicions were unfounded, his master walked to the bedroom door and glanced in. The bottle of wine was there and the fresh loaf of bread. But the room had no occupant.

"Where is your mistress?"

The servant motioned toward the rear of the house. "Madame has retired," he said. "She had me put a mattress for her in the pantry. It was mine I gave her, master, and so I think she'll find it very hard. I've a pile of shavings in the kitchen."

"Be off, then."

De Mariat opened the door into the pantry. It was dark inside and there was a pleasant smell of sugar and spices.

"Are you awake?"

"Yes, m'sieur."

He held the candle above his head and stepped inside the door. The mattress had been spread in one corner and Félicité was sitting on it with a sheet pulled up protectingly around her neck. It was certain she had not been asleep, for her eyes were wide awake and her hair showed no signs of disorder.

He made it clear at once that he was in an angry mood. "The banker's efforts at explanation fell flat," he said. "Everyone knows the story of what happened. No one dared laugh at me but I saw the desire in every pair of eyes."

Félicité said in a low voice, "There's a way to end this, m'sieur."

"I have no intention of agreeing to a separation, if that's what you mean." The indignities under which he had suffered all day lent an extra sharpness to his tone. "You'll be very much interested in one thing which happened today. Your friend the carpenter, that honest young workman, is in prison."

If he had expected her to show alarm or surprise he was disappointed. She remained silent for several moments. When she looked up, however, he saw that her face was white.

"This was done by your orders?"

"Yes, madame. I ordered his arrest."

"I'm not surprised. I had no doubt you would find some way of making him suffer also. What excuse have you found for putting him in jail?"

"I had no need of an excuse. The great hulking ox came at me with threats. If I ever struck you again he would have my life's blood. It's a criminal offense to utter threats against the life of an officer of the King and so I had him taken into custody at once. He'll have every reason to regret his insolence before I'm through with him."

Félicité held out a beseeching hand. "I can't bear to think he must suffer through me. Release him, m'sieur, please!"

"Your solicitude for your faithful suitor is very touching. I think it will be best to let him stay for a time in the cell I selected for him—the top one, where it's hotter and more cramped. A good baking will teach him a proper respect for his superiors."

"Please, if not for my sake——"

Her husband did not seem to be listening. "I secured the cameo. The banker whined to have his money back but I soon convinced him of the absurdity of that. It's a very handsome cameo. The best piece, perhaps, in your *extra-dotaux?*" He did not wait for an answer. He stared down at her belligerently. "It seems that you're determined to oppose me."

Félicité's hand strayed unconsciously toward the inside edge of the mattress. "I intend to sleep here," she said.

He had noticed the motion of her hand. "An idea occurs to me," he said, grinning. "You've acquired a weapon and you have it under that mattress. A knife? In another minute, I'm sure, you'll be telling me that if I try to force you to my will you'll plunge the steel into your own virginal heart. Is it not so? I saw a play in Paris with a scene like that. The heroine was a lovely little creature with a very fine bosom. *Parbleu!* How the audience shivered and wept!"

"You are very clever. Yes, I have a knife, m'sieur. And I shall use it as you say."

" 'Rather would I die by mine own hand than yield myself to you,' " he quoted. He now seemed to be enjoying himself. "Another idea has entered my head. You have that knife of Bousbach's. I know the rogue. He would do anything to harm me."

"I found it." She tried, not too successfully, to make the falsehood sound convincing.

"I don't believe you, my most faithful spouse. That fellow has been whispering ideas in your ear. I'll beat him until he whines and grovels for mercy."

Félicité was so tensely concerned that she had forgotten to keep herself covered with the sheet. By allowing it to slip down, she had exposed her shoulders to view. Over the lace-trimmed neck of her *chemise de nuit* he could see the delicate white lines of her throat and the curve of her breasts.

"What you fail to understand," he said, going into a long disquisition, "is that women, because of the provisions of nature, are actually the prisoners of men. When a woman marries she belongs to her husband just as much as his horse or cow or sheep. If he so decides he can keep her from showing herself in the outside world. What's more, madame, this is a wise act of nature, most women being foolish geese without a grain of sense in their heads." As he talked his eyes had remained fixed on her and it was clear he approved the slight suggestion of the plumpness of maturity about her shoulders. He interrupted his discourse to say: "You have a very pretty neck. By St. Luke and the arts, you are quite a picture as you sit there!"

His contemptuous assumption of superiority had roused her to such a degree of indignation that she proceeded to say something she had intended to keep to herself for the time being.

"It may be a surprise to you that a mere woman, one of these chattels, these prisoners who exist under the eye of a jailer husband, can be as far-seeing sometimes as the cleverest of men. You took the precaution of studying the marriage laws. M'sieur, so did I!"

He could not conceal the fact that he was startled. "The lawyer in Montreal said you were a wise minx. *Voilà!* You studied the laws. What gems of information did you stumble upon?"

"I found that men were not perfect at all, that sometimes they allowed themselves to make a slip. Wives have one right, m'sieur, which the god-like creatures who drew up these vicious laws seem to have overlooked. They must accompany their husbands wherever they go, if they so demand, except *outside the country!* If we had been married in France I could have refused to accompany you to Louisiana. As we were married in Louisiana, I have the right to refuse to go back to France with you. And that, m'sieur, is what I shall do."

He made an impatient gesture. "Enough of this! You will now get up, madame, and come to bed with me."

Félicité did not move and she continued to look at him with steadiness and determination. "I shall stay here. Not only tonight but all other nights that we remain married."

De Mariat tossed his arms above his head in angry abandon. "I can't brawl with you every night, you obstinate little fool! I can't pick you up and carry you, kicking and screaming and threatening me with your knife, to the nuptial couch. I have too much of a sense of proper dignity to turn our marriage into a prolonged rape!" The ends of his mustache were twitching and it was clear that he was quite beside himself. "If you continue to defy me in this way I swear that every morning of our married life, if necessary, I'll give you as sound a beating as you received today. If you remain obstinate, my little pet, you'll feel the weight of my arm again tomorrow! That I promise you!"

CHAPTER VII

AS SOON as he returned from his long stay up the river the governor of Louisiana heard the whole story. The Sieur de Balne met him at the quay with all the details and informed him moreover that he, the *procureur général,* had reviewed the evidence and was convinced there was nothing to be done. Auguste de Mariat, unfortunately, was acting within the letter of the law and could not be called to account.

The governor then heard Louis Rapin addressing a meeting on the Place d'Armes. Louis, who was called Le Babillard (the Gab) because he always had so much to say, was asking questions of his audience. Standing well back, where he could not be seen, the governor listened.

"Is chivalry dead among the men of France?" Le Babillard was demanding to know. "Has it come to this, that an innocent young wife can be beaten in the presence of witnesses and then locked up in the house to which her husband has taken her and not permitted to see anyone? Must we stand about with our thumbs in our mouths while one of us is thrown into prison for protesting? Are we cowards or have we enough courage to do what brave men should do under the circumstances?"

Old Jules Panletet, the minstrel, was standing at the edge of the group, his pear-shaped lute hanging over his shoulder. "And what, my brave Louis," he asked, "do brave men do under these circumstances?"

Louis raised both arms in the air and exclaimed, "They don't stand around and talk, they act!"

"And what form does the action take?" The minstrel was now asking the questions. "Do they carry off the unfortunate young woman? And if so, where do they carry her to?" He then raised an entirely new point. "Do any of you beat your wives? Because, if you do, any action you take now will be thrown up to you later. Being a single man, I don't know about such things. But the point deserves some thought, does it not?"

Louis le Babillard brushed these matters aside impatiently. "Every man within sound of my voice," he declared, "has been at the house and has been refused admittance. Every one has been told that Madame will not see visitors. We know that her husband beats her each morning because the servant was trapped into admitting as much. But we don't know how she is standing this punishment. She may have been seriously injured. She may not survive this harsh treatment."

"Perhaps," suggested one of the listeners, "she's dead already and they're afraid to let anyone in because then the truth would come out."

"No, she's not dead," declared the speaker. "I saw her this morning. She was looking out of a window at the rear of the house. She left the window at once but not before I had seen that she was pale and sad." Louis le Babillard raised his voice excitedly. "Are we going to do nothing about it?"

"If we had him in Canada," shouted one man, "we would ride him on the *chevalet*—and we'd see to it that the edge was sharp and that he had weights on his feet!"

"If His Excellency were back——"

De Bienville stepped forward. "I am back," he announced. "And so it will no longer be necessary for you, Louis Rapin, to ask what course of action should be taken. I shall take the proper steps at once." He looked at the tense faces closest to him. "I must have the whole story first. Three of you, those best able to give me the facts clearly and honestly, will please accompany me to my cabinet."

When the three men selected had told him all they knew and had left, De Bienville said to his servant, "Groissart, you will tell Monsieur de Mariat to attend me here at once."

II

De Mariat obeyed the summons promptly. "Excellency, you are back at last! Your friends were beginning to entertain fears."

"By what right," demanded the governor, "do you take it on yourself to speak for my friends?"

The angry eyes of the two men came together at that. *"Voilà!"* said De Mariat. "It seems that war has been declared. What will be the first overt act, Excellency?"

"The first broadside," declared the governor, "has already been fired. I've ordered the release of Philippe Girard."

"I have witnesses to swear that the man made threats against me. The law in such cases——"

"In the final analysis I am the law!" declared De Bienville. He rose to his feet and leaned across the desk. "I know all about the infamous way in which you've behaved. And of the great pains you take to keep within the law."

De Mariat, who had gained control of himself, began to speak with studied deliberation. "You as governor are the upholder of the law. The law declares that a disobedient wife may be punished. My wife has been disobedient. The law states what a husband may do to bring a foolish wife to a more reasonable frame of mind."

"I'm quite sure you've been calculatingly correct in everything you've done. You have all the cunning of a Levantine moneylender, Monsieur de Mariat. I'm equally sure that you've already planned the protest you'll send to Versailles if I take any action which might be construed as improper." He indulged in a short laugh before proceeding. "As it happens I have no thought of invoking the law or acting on my powers as governor of Louisiana. I prefer, monsieur, to deal with you in a private capacity."

He picked up a glove lying on a corner of the desk. With this he slapped De Mariat across the cheek.

For a moment nothing was said. Then: "You must fight me for this," declared the provost.

"There's a law against dueling. As the head of the state, it's my duty to uphold the law, as you have reminded me. Instead, m'sieur, you and I shall break the law together."

"As soon as possible!"

"Tomorrow at dawn?"

"Tomorrow at dawn!" De Mariat seemed to be breathing with difficulty. "I have choice of weapons. The sword!"

De Bienville nodded in agreement. "The sword, of course."

They proceeded to make the necessary arrangements, deciding to fight on the space already cleared to the west of the settlement for the erection of a storage house for powder. Lacking seconds to give an air of formality to the occasion, they faced each other like a pair of angry schoolboys who found it hard to wait for the fight to begin.

The provost bowed ceremoniously when the details had been settled but immediately tossed the pose aside. He snarled at his opponent, "You ignorant woodsman!"

De Bienville retorted with equal feeling, "You court fop!"

"You ill-mannered colonial!"

"You cowardly wife beater!"

The provost took a step closer and rested his hands on the desk. "Say your prayers tonight, Excellency!" he advised. "As it happens I'm quite skilled in the use of the sword. The best arms master in Paris was my teacher and I have a bag of tricks in my repertoire. I'm promising myself the pleasure of opening a way between your ribs with the point of my sword. I assure you, Excellency, it will be a great pleasure."

The young governor threw back his head and laughed heartily. "Am I supposed to spend the night tossing in my bed with fear? M'sieur, I am a Le Moyne of Longueuil. Do you know anything of the Le Moynes of Longueuil? We are a rather exceptional family, I may tell you. We were

all taught the use of the sword, the saber, the pike, and the bill as soon
as we had the strength to lift a weapon. Each day I spent hours in the
armory at practice. Sometimes there would be half a dozen of my brothers
there, cutting and slashing and lunging. What's more, our training was
not all theoretical. All of us had occasion to test what we had learned in
battle. You've never faced an Indian brave in his war paint or charged
against English cannon, have you, m'sieur?" His laugh was replaced by a
belligerent frown. "Do you think a Le Moyne need have any fear of a
parade-ground soldier, a skipping little dancing master? Spend the night
at your own devotions, m'sieur!"

III

Two days and nights in the top cell without a single opportunity to
leave it had left Philippe in such a state that he went at once, on attaining
his liberty, to the tent he occupied with Carpe Bonnet. It had been pitched
at the edge of the clearing for the powder house. Carpe was amazed at his
appearance.

"Master!" he cried. "You look as if you'd been in prison for a month!"

"I've been living like a rat in a sewer!" said Philippe, giving his body
a twitch of disgust. "Heat some water for me, Carpe. It must be steaming
hot if I'm to become clean again!"

After a thorough scrubbing he laid himself down on the mattress he
used as a bed while Carpe washed his clothes and hung them out to dry.
He slept soundly and dreamlessly, and darkness had settled down when
he wakened. He felt like a new man and capable of carrying out the
purpose in his mind.

Carpe had a hot stew ready and had brought a fresh loaf from the
baker's oven. Philippe ate with the furious appetite of one who had
starved himself rather than swallow the noxious foods of the prison.

As they dipped into the mutton and sopped up the gravy with the fine
crusty bread Carpe proceeded to talk about his personal problems. "Master," he said, "I'm not suiting her. I don't understand it but there you are.
I'm not suiting her."

"If you mean the Widow Gauthier, I thought you had decided to keep
away from her?"

Carpe shook his head with a full appreciation of his own lack of will.
"I did, master. But I must admit it, there's a flaw in me. I can't resist
her. I think, 'Let her support her six children herself, I had nothing
to do with bringing them into the world,' and then I find myself getting
up at dawn and drawing water from the well for her, and begging for
other things to do. There's no use fighting it, master."

"And yet your devotion is having no effect?"

"None at all. I ask her questions. Which is better on a cold winter night, an extra blanket or a bedfellow? Are six children enough? And what does she answer, master? She says the nights are never cold in this country and six children *are* enough, more than enough. It seems to me that such answers are discouraging. Sometimes she makes no answer at all. She just says, 'Shoo!' "

Philippe had been paying small attention. Since hearing of the way Félicité had been treated, he had been filled with a hate which seemed like a thick black mist. Of naturally gentle instincts, he had always accepted life's mishaps and rebuffs with fortitude and resignation. Even when the provocation had been great he had never before allowed himself to feel a desire for revenge. He had heard someone say once that every man had a murderer inside himself and needed only the incentive to let him loose. He had never believed this. But now it was different.

At the back of his mind a voice kept saying, over and over again: "There's only one way out of this. If the law won't free her of this man I must."

It had started to rain but they were fortunate in having a tent which had served an officer in the European wars. This meant that it had a double canvas roof, the outer one overlapping the sides by several feet and thus providing complete protection from sun and rain. Philippe, listening to the drip of the water, said to himself, "This is lucky, there will be few out tonight."

A voice from the darkness called, "Are you there, Philippe?"

Carpe showed signs of annoyance. "It's old Jacques Besse," he said. "He's been here twice already, asking if you were awake. The old solan goose, he wouldn't tell me what he wanted."

Philippe walked out of the tent and called, "Yes, M'sieur Besse?"

The old man came close enough to see inside the canvas walls. "No one with you but Carpe," he said in a satisfied tone. "Philippe, this is *very* important. Go to the tavern at once and ask for M'sieur de Marest. Ask the landlord and don't let anyone hear you. Is that clear?"

"Do you mean the officer on the ship from Quebec?"

"Yes, Philippe. He leaves at midnight for the trip back to the mouth of the river and he must see you before he goes."

"Thanks, M'sieur Besse. I'll see the officer at once. And I'll be very cautious."

Philippe walked back into the tent, whispering to Carpe, "Give him a glass of wine." A corner of the tent was cut off from the rest by a sheet of canvas and this served him as a bedroom. A crucifix was attached to the tent pole, one he had fashioned himself on the long journey from Quebec.

He knelt down in front of it for several minutes, his head bowed in prayer. There were many things he had to say to the God he knew would listen. When a man is aware that he may die soon or be responsible for the death of another he must enter his plea for forgiveness, not only for the great sin he may commit but for all the transgressions of the past.

When he stepped out again under the sheet of canvas the old man was gone. He tried to be casual in his manner but Carpe sensed there was something in the wind. "Be careful, master," he urged. "This is no concern of yours. Leave it to His Excellency."

The tavern, as the governor had once explained, was a purely temporary structure. It had been thrown together hurriedly when the first word had been received of Monsieur Law's plans. It consisted of a single long room, where food and drinks were served, and back of that a bark palisade with a canvas cover over the enclosed space. Under this canvas roof sheets of barraca had been stretched on ropes to serve as partitions; and in the tiny cubicles thus provided the guests slept on mattresses spread on the ground.

Philippe paused and looked up for what might be the last time at the Latin reference to St. Theodotus which he had carved over the front door on instructions from De Bienville. He did not know what it meant.

The place was filled to overflowing. As Philippe waited for the officer to appear he could hear the loud complaints of guests, the shouts of servants carrying platters of food on upstretched arms, the clatter of dishes. Through an open door he could see into the sleeping quarters. The use of lights had been prohibited there because of the danger of fire and, to supply the lack, a brazier was burning at the door. About this insects were swirling in amazing numbers.

It was apparent that many of the guests had already retired to their beds. Sleep being out of the question, they were tossing remarks back and forth. Philippe heard the contentious voices of men and the querulous tones of their wives, complaining of this bitter discomfort in which they existed.

Lieutenant de Marest emerged from this noisy warren. When he saw Philippe standing expectantly inside the door he approached him with a questioning smile.

"You are M'sieur Philippe Girard?"

"Yes, m'sieur."

"Good! I've something to say to you." The officer allowed his voice to drop. "We have an interest in common, Philippe Girard, a desire to be of help to a certain lady." He raised his voice to normal again. "Let us leave this dreadful din and find a spot outside where we can talk. A sailor doesn't mind a little rain. Do you?"

"No, m'sieur," answered Philippe. "I won't mind a little rain tonight."

IV

Philippe approached the house with cautious steps. It seemed to him that menace hovered over the place and that a taint of evil was on the still air. The rain had stopped and the trees swayed in a light breeze without making any sound, as though they, too, were aware of the need for silence and caution. The impression grew on him that he was expected, that eyes watched him in the darkness.

He stopped several times to heft the weapon he was carrying. This he had secured at the east *caserne* after leaving Lieutenant de Marest. An old friend from Montreal had been on guard and had responded to his whispered request for a weapon by motioning inside. "No one's about, Philippe. Help yourself to a bill, a brown bill. It's a gaudy fine weapon to use against a sword. Many a fine gentleman has gone down with sword in hand with the point of a bill through his ribs. If there's trouble, forget you saw me; and oblige by leaving through the door on the other side." The guard began to whistle *"Dame Lombarde"* when steps were heard approaching but paused long enough to whisper, "Good luck, Philippe!" The latter had vanished quickly through the door of the barracks.

Since coming close to the house he had taken some reassurance from the fact that there was a light showing through a side window. Auguste de Mariat had not retired, then. The visitor turned cautiously through the gate. Leaving the path, he walked on the grass, keeping in the darkest shadows he could find. That he had been wise to take precautions became evident when a sound of heavy breathing reached him.

He remained without moving for several moments. The sound came from the front of the house and he listened with the closest attention before allowing himself to be convinced that someone was sleeping there. He walked back with infinite care and found, to his great relief, that it was Bousbach who shared the garden with him. De Mariat's servant had propped himself up against the front door and was breathing evenly and loudly, in blissful ignorance of the insects which buzzed about his head.

This discovery had the effect of dispelling the fears with which Philippe had approached the house. There was something so earthy and commonplace about the recumbent figure that he said to himself, "What a timid rabbit I've been!" He smiled with new confidence as he skirted the house toward the window from which the light was pouring.

It was a french door and instead of glass it had sheets of sheer linen. He found it necessary, therefore, to rip the material away at one side, using the blade of his knife. This he accomplished with skill and dispatch, making no sound whatever. Shoving the linen back with the point of his knife, he leaned close and peered into the room.

Auguste de Mariat was sitting at a small table. Philippe had made it himself, thinking it would be useful for Félicité. It had been designed to play the double purpose of desk, having shallow drawers beneath it. The provost was filling sheets of paper with a pen which moved angrily as well as fast, leaving the impression that he resented the necessity of what he was doing. He was wearing a purple camisole, open at the neck, and on his head was an elaborately embroidered and tasseled combination of velvet and satin which probably was a nightcap. His task engrossed his attention so completely that Philippe had no hesitation in opening the french door and stepping into the room.

The intruder saw several things in the first instant of entry. De Mariat had placed his pistol on a chair perhaps fifteen feet from where he sat. His sword was nowhere to be seen and so, obviously, had been left in the bedroom when its owner disrobed. There was a bottle and a glass on the table and it was clear that the provost had been lightening the hardships of composition by steady application to the wine. All doors into other rooms were closed.

De Mariat dropped his pen and got to his feet, glowering with surprise and indignation. It was not until he had risen that he recognized his visitor.

"The honest artisan!" he exclaimed. "I half expected you tonight, having already had proofs of your stubborn turn of mind. I instructed my man to keep a sharp lookout for you. It seems he has failed in his trust."

Before making any response Philippe walked across the room and stationed himself between De Mariat and the chair where he had deposited his pistol. Having thus placed himself in an advantageous position, he turned to the provost.

"I waited long enough to let him fall asleep."

"And I also, perhaps?" De Mariat's resentment at the intrusion was growing visibly. "Well, what is the purpose of this visit? What have you to say?"

"It was my purpose to come here tonight and kill you."

De Mariat nodded easily. "And what caused you to change your mind? A belated sense of caution, perhaps?"

"The last boat down the river leaves at midnight," said Philippe. "Under the circumstances I decided to follow another plan. I came to escort Madame de Mariat to the boat, so that she could catch the ship back to Quebec."

This was so unexpected that De Mariat studied his visitor's face before replying. "A most curious plan," he said. "I'm sure it wasn't hatched in that far from nimble brain of yours, Master Carpenter. Who's with you in this? That naval officer who's been wearing about town the sick look of a mooncalf which is supposed to denote a broken heart? And how do you propose to carry it out in the face of my opposition? Do you think I'll sit by and watch you carry off my wife?"

"What you may think and what you may try to do are of no consequence, m'sieur." Philippe had been tongue-tied when he entered the room but now he was beginning to feel at ease. Resting the end of the bill shaft on the floor, he drew from the pocket of his coat a small pistol which De Marest had insisted he would need. "I must warn you not to raise your voice or call for assistance. If you do, m'sieur, I'll be compelled to silence you by the easiest means. I mean what I say, so don't allow yourself to think otherwise."

De Mariat's attitude had become watchful but he gave no signs yet of uneasiness. "I doubt if you have much skill with firearms," he said.

"That is true." Philippe laid the pistol on the chair beside De Mariat's. Then he raised the bill and gave it a twirl in the air. "But with this, m'sieur, I have some skill. The point is sharp medicine. One dose would be ample."

"It wouldn't be hard to kill an unarmed man," declared the provost. "If I had my sword I'd have no hesitation in facing you, even with that barbarous weapon in your hand. Have you no sense of fair play?"

"Where you're concerned, m'sieur, none at all. I would kill you gladly. The only thing which counts with me at this moment is to put an end to your ill-treatment of the lady who's unfortunate enough to be your wife. I'm ready to use any means at all." His manner had become sharp and peremptory. "Sit down, m'sieur! We have much to talk about. I warn you again that if you try to resist or call for help I'll kill you without a single qualm—and face the consequences without a single regret!"

De Mariat was convinced at last. He said, "I've no desire to die this kind of a death," and forthwith sat down. He continued to scowl, nevertheless, with no diminution of enmity.

"And now, m'sieur, I'll explain what I propose to do. First, you must provide Madame de Mariat with the means for the voyage back to Quebec. After that I shall truss you up tightly and gag you. I'll do the same for your servant, who's sleeping soundly at the front door. Then I'll escort Madame de Mariat to the boat. After it leaves I'll come back and release you."

There was no hint of amusement now in the glitter of the provost's eyes. "Hasn't it occurred to you and your accomplices, whoever they may be, that this plan has one weakness? That in the end you'll all be laid by the heels and punished with the full severity of the law?"

"The future has no fears for me."

"Don't you realize how much influence I can bring against you? That I can compel Madame's return, even if she succeeds in reaching Quebec? Don't you know that this colony will fall like a house of cards and that the Le Moynes will tumble with it, when John Law's silly bubble bursts? The Le Moynes will be in no position to protect you then." De Mariat had spoken with so much heat that he paused for breath. "You are a clumsy bumpkin, Master Carpenter, and you're beyond your depth in this. I've a word of advice for you. Turn around and walk out of this house. And never obtrude yourself on my notice again."

Philippe said quietly, "You will produce at once the money your wife will need."

"I will produce nothing!"

"Then stand up." Philippe raised the brown bill. "Cross your arms behind you and then turn your back so I can truss them well together. Be quick about it! There's little time left. And let me tell you this, m'sieur: I would kill you now before taking Madame de Mariat to the boat, except that her departure and your death would be linked together. I desire to spare her more trouble and suffering, even at the cost of allowing you to live."

Félicité chose this moment to scream. The sound came from the rear of the house, a high-pitched cry and full of the most deadly fear; and it ended with an abruptness which allowed one explanation only, that a hand had been clamped over her mouth.

v

Just before Félicité's scream filled the house with its warning of danger Philippe had fancied that he heard the soft padding of feet outside. Suspecting it was Bousbach, he had changed his position so that he could keep the front door within the range of his vision and be secure from surprise in that quarter. It did not occur to him that the stealthy footsteps could mean anything more until her cry made it certain. He did not suspect Indians until the french door he had used in entering flew back against the wall and a naked brown figure, with dancing feathers above a round head shaved to the semblance of a skull, bounded into the room.

Philippe lunged out with his bill as the warrior rushed to attack him. It struck a naked shoulder and the brown body straightened up with the impact. The wounded man made no sound beyond a gasp. At the same moment that his opponent slipped and fell to the floor, Philippe saw an expression of horror on the face of De Mariat, who was turned in the other direction. A quick glance discovered for him that more Indians had already entered through the window on that side.

This, then, was the end! "God look down on us!" he said aloud. Having lived all his life under the threat of Indian attack, he had no illusions as to the fate he faced. If he were lucky he would be killed in the fighting. If he failed of this good fortune and were captured he would be dragged in a triumphal procession from one encampment to another, to be made the sport of old women and shrill children, and finally he would die at the stake. Félicité, already a prisoner, might be kept in captivity for the rest of her life.

What followed took no more than a few seconds. It was like a bad dream, a nightmare in which movement was not accompanied by sound. The earsplitting war whoop with which the Indians of the north always launched an attack had been missing. There was none of the guttural chatter of the Iroquois as they went into action. But these silent invaders moved with a celerity which proved that the attack had been carefully planned.

As Philippe swung around to meet the new danger he was conscious only of eyes: small and savage eyes which seemed to surround him on all sides, eyes which did not appear human but gleamed with an animal ferocity. Then he realized that they had begun the gabble of conflict, filling the room with an angry and obscene chatter.

He raised the bill again but had no opportunity of using it. A body landed on him heavily from behind and an arm was clamped around his throat with such furious strength that he thought his neck would break. He could not breathe and there was so little strength left in his arms that the bill was taken from him and he was thrown into a corner of the room. His head struck against the wall and he lost consciousness.

In this heated action of seconds he had thought he heard a voice raised above the sounds of conflict. It was, he was sure, the voice of a white man and it seemed to carry, strangely enough, a note of amusement. Could it have been real or was it due to an imagination stirred by the peril of his position? It had seemed to him that this mysterious voice had intoned a line in a language which he believed was English.

Have you not a promise made that you will marry me?

This had been followed by a laugh and then the voice had gone on. "Walk me up, m'sieur! Can it be that a mistake has been made in following out orders? What a trick to play on the bold, crafty provost!"

VI

The sun had a spectacular way of rising in Louisiana, bursting up over the horizon with an amazing exuberance of color. Even after twenty years Jean-Baptiste de Bienville was not quite accustomed to it and he looked at the ribbons of scarlet and mauve and pink which were making a huge bouquet in the east with an eye which acknowledged that this might be the last time he would see a dawn. He realized that there was, after all, a slight degree of danger in what lay ahead of him.

"He might get me with one of those trick thrusts," he said to himself with a feeling of reluctance and even disgust, for he could not stomach the thought of losing his life at such hands.

As he strode along in the direction of the cleared ground in the west he realized that he should have made his will. He had little to leave, except his interest in the Le Moyne concerns, which would, of course, revert to the remaining brothers, but there were other matters. If he died he wanted to be buried within sound of the Mississippi. He should have set this down instead of devoting all the time to official documents.

He could catch an occasional glimpse as he walked of the river rolling slowly past the town on its way to the sea. The Mississippi, he knew, had become the arbiter of his life. He was dedicated to its service, to providing a stately city at its mouth and creating a port so that in time great ships would ride at anchor where river and gulf met, and some at least of John Law's wild dreams would come true. He realized that he had grown to love the Mississippi.

He was accompanied by Pierre de Boitrac, one of his officers, who was to act as his second. The latter followed close on his heels and seemed to be looking forward to the duel.

"That fellow," he said, "is lucky to have such a fine morning for his last look at the sun."

"He claims to be one of the best swordsmen in France," said the governor.

The young officer gave a scornful sniff. "I've heard him boast of his skill. He boasts of so many things that I disregard everything he says. It's my belief, Excellency—as well as my sincere hope—that you'll have no difficulty in disposing of this very brave man who beats his wife."

When they came to the edge of the clearing they saw a tent on the far side and the disconsolate face of Polycarpe Bonnet staring out through the open flap. In spite of the earliness of the hour he was completely dressed. No one else was in sight.

De Boitrac looked the ground over and settled mentally on the spot where the duelists should stand. For the first time he became conscious of a feeling of doubt and chill. "What a tragedy it would be," he thought, "if this cowardly fellow should kill our fine young governor!"

De Bienville loosened his cloak at the neck. "Where is our opponent, De Boitrac?" he asked.

The officer replied with a puzzled frown. "He's the last man I would suspect of tardiness. Something has happened to keep him away."

At this point Carpe Bonnet approached them across the cleared ground. "Excellency," he said, taking off his flat cap and bowing over it, "my master didn't come back last night. I had my orders, Excellency. I was to stay here. I wasn't to follow him and I wasn't to open my mouth to anyone. But—but, Excellency, something has happened. What could keep him away all night in a place like this?"

The governor gave an anxious nod of the head. "Your master wouldn't have stayed out unless there had been trouble. I think, De Boitrac, we had better find at once what's detaining Monsieur de Mariat."

As the governor and his second approached the house, with Carpe following at a respectful distance, the former stopped abruptly and studied the place with a worried frown. "I can see nothing wrong—and yet I'm positive no one is there. There's an air of desertion about it."

The officer reached out a restraining hand. "Careful, Excellency!" he whispered. "There's a body on the ground. See, to the right of the door."

De Bienville drew the pistol from his holster pipe and made sure it was primed and ready. "It's a white man," he said after a moment. His mind jumped ahead and reached the conclusion that the dead man was De Mariat and that Philippe had killed him. He said in a tone of self-accusation: "I should have known something like this would happen. I should have put guards at the house. Now I may have to order the execution of a friend!"

De Boitrac was studying what could be seen of the body from where they stood. "I can't make it out clearly enough from here but somehow I don't believe it's either De Mariat or the carpenter," he declared.

On reaching the garden they found that he had been right. The body stretched on the ground beside the porch of the front door was that of Bousbach and it was evident that he had been dead for many hours. The slayers of the servant had not been content with killing him but had mutilated the body in a maniacal frenzy. The throat was cut quite literally from ear to ear, the nose had been severed, there was only a bloodied patch to indicate where the scalp lock had been.

De Bienville investigated inside and arrived at an accurate estimate of what had happened. He emerged from the house at a run, saying to De Boitrac, "There's no time to be lost!" and starting off in the direction of his own headquarters. Over his shoulder he told what he had discovered, adding, "There's no doubt in my mind that the raid was carefully planned and directed by someone here in New Orleans. But in that case, why was De Mariat himself one of the victims?"

There was no time for such speculations, however, when they reached the Hôtel de Ville. Never perhaps in the whole history of American colonization was a rescue party organized and started on its way in such a short space of time. The governor had a well-armed squad of forty determined men packed into canoes and on their way in less than twenty minutes. Even in that brief time he had scrutinized each volunteer carefully. His selections were all men from New France, with the exception of a few officers.

It was a grim lot who pulled away from the quay. De Bienville, in the first canoe, called: "Put your backs into it! The murdering devils have six hours' start of us!"

It seemed to the watchers along the waterfront that the party vanished around the western bend of the river with the swiftness of that magic canoe sometimes seen in the very far north against the horizon as the sun goes down. Almost until the last carrier vanished from sight they could hear the urgent voice of the governor. "Put every ounce of strength you have into it, men! Make every stroke count!"

CHAPTER VIII

THE RISING of the sun, which had seen the governor of Louisiana on his way to fight a duel, found the Indian raiders far up the winding river. All through the night the three captives had been kept in one of the long canoes, their arms tightly bound with withes. The pain this caused was so great that several times Félicité had whispered to Philippe, "I can't stand it any longer, I'm going mad!" However, she had managed to bear it, and gradually the pain grew less.

With the coming of dawn the mood of their captors changed. The silence with which they had paddled through the hours of darkness gave way to animation. They began to talk back and forth and to indulge in staccato bursts of laughter, occasionally raising their paddles in the air with a suggestion of triumph. The canoes lacked the ease of maneuver and the speed of the birch-bark craft of New France. They sank deeper into the water than even those of the Iroquois, which were made of elm bark. Philippe, watching everything with the sharp perception which danger supplies, realized that the rescue party, when it started, would make much better time. The gunwales were so low in the water that he wondered what would happen if a wind sprang up. The Iroquois never dared venture out in rough weather and these southern savages were even less well equipped. He began to pray, silently and fervently, for a wind, convinced that it was their only hope.

The leader of the party began to sing in a high and melodious voice and the rest of the warriors joined in at intervals with a resounding *Ho-ha-ho-ha-ho!* Hearing them thus, it might have been assumed that they were returning from a successful hunting trip in a highly pleased state of mind. Philippe did not allow this hint of amiability to raise his hopes. In one of the other canoes sat a glum warrior with bloodstains on his arm and a dab of mud on his shoulder where the point of the brown bill had entered. The enmity in his beady eyes was a surer indication of the fate awaiting them than the joviality of the rest. Philippe was convinced that this was the last dawn he would see. Félicité, whose arms were now so numb that all feeling had left them, shared his conviction. She was watching with fascinated horror the back of the Indian in front of her, which crawled with lice, and praying that the end would not be long delayed.

De Mariat had conducted himself quietly, and up to the present had shown no signs of fear. He was still wearing the embroidered nightcap and, as it had slipped down on one side of his head, he presented a ludicrous picture. His companions in adversity, however, had reached the state of mind where ordinary things make no impression and so had not noticed the incongruity of it.

He now spoke for the first time. "How far have we come?" he asked. All the arrogance had gone out of his voice.

Philippe answered: "Over thirty miles, in spite of the current. But these heavy canoes are slower than ours and if the governor gets an early enough start he might overtake us before night."

"Do you think they've already started after us?"

"If they haven't," said Philippe, crossing himself, "we might as well give up all hope. We're as good as dead in that case."

To the surprise of both of his companions, the provost made a sound which remotely resembled a laugh. "We've nothing to fear. They won't dare do anything to us."

"Why do you think that? Are we different from the other white people who've been captured in the past?"

De Mariat nodded his head with confidence. "I'm certain of it," he said. "There was an Englishman with them last night. Can you see where he is?"

Philippe had already studied each figure in the four large canoes. "I thought I heard a white voice last night," he said. "But there's no sign of him now."

Some of the confidence which had kept him buoyed up deserted the provost. "That's strange," he said, frowning. "If he were here we could come to some kind of an agreement at once. What do you suppose has happened to him?"

"He might have left by the portage to the gulf." Philippe glanced suspiciously at his companion in misfortune. "What do you know about this? Who is this Englishman?"

De Mariat answered in a voice which showed that he was beginning to share their fears. "I know enough. But I'm not going to talk about it now. If I could only speak to them I would be able to convince them they should let us go."

Aware that he had stumbled on evidence of something he could not understand, Philippe said quietly, "I know their language."

De Mariat turned to stare at him with such suddenness that he winced with the pain it had set up in his arms. "God and St. Adrian! Do you mean it?" He was so convinced that Philippe had made an idle boast that he added in an aggrieved tone, "Are you trying to tell me that you're like the apostles? That the gift of tongues has descended on you?"

"I was learning to speak Indian languages in Montreal with one of the Le Moynes, in the hope of making myself useful. An old Chickasaw, who had been sent up by the governor, taught me a little."

De Mariat's eyes were avid now with reawakened hope. "Do you know enough of it to make yourself understood?"

"I think so."

"Have you been able to follow their talk?"

Philippe hesitated, expecting a demand to tell what he had heard. "I've understood some of it."

"Then tell them," said De Mariat eagerly, "that there's been a mistake. Tell them I'm in a position to reward them well if they'll let us go."

"What have you to offer which would appeal to savages like these?" Philippe shook his head. "Gold? They have no way of using it, except to make trinkets. What else is there? Can you promise them to clear the country of all white men? That's the only boon they want from us, m'sieur, and make no mistake about it."

"You don't understand!" cried De Mariat. "I tell you this is a mistake. One word in the right pair of ears will secure us our freedom."

Philippe nodded in the direction of the canoe ahead of them. "I think the tall fellow who led the singing is the chief. Is it his ears you want to reach?"

"If he's the leader we must talk to him. Can't you make them understand we must see him at once?"

"I think, M'sieur de Mariat," said Philippe, "that I'm beginning to know what this mystery is. But if they've captured us by mistake they'll not be in any mood to let us go on that account. They risked their lives to take prisoners. We may not be the ones they wanted but we'll have to serve." His voice became hard and antagonistic. "I think the treachery you planned will cost us our lives, M'sieur de Mariat. To these people all white men are alike. As I understand it now, they came on this raid because they hoped it would discourage us and prevent more white men from coming out. What can *you* offer, m'sieur, to make them change their minds?"

The light from the rising sun was rousing the woods on each side of them to noisy activities and their captors were responding to the wild life which sang and trilled and whistled back and forth in the ecstasy of another morning. The voice of the Chickasaw leader was raised in a melody which rivaled the singing of the birds. The refrain, in which his followers joined, set a livelier time to the dip of the paddles.

But to the captives the coming of day brought only cause for increased fear. In the darkness they had felt the danger, now they could see it as well. Crouching together in the middle of the canoe, they watched the Indians with the deepest foreboding, sensing the cruelty in the wild dark eyes, the bestiality in the laughter. They were in the power of men whose strength had degenerated into obscenity.

Philippe looked up at the sky and his heart sank. There was no promise of bad weather there.

"They seem worse than the Indians of the north," whispered Félicité. "The heat has turned them into strange beasts!"

The chief's voice trailed off into silence. He raised his paddle high in the air and called out an order in his musical voice.

"They're going ashore," said Philippe. "He thinks they're far enough up the river to risk a stop for food."

"M'sieur Jean-Baptiste and his men won't stop," whispered Félicité. There was not, however, much trace of hope in her voice.

The canoes, so cumbersome in the eyes of Canadians, were brought skillfully to a landing on the north side of the river. On an order from the chief, the withes were cut from the arms of the prisoners and they were ordered, with savage gestures, to step ashore. A few moments later the chief came over to where they stood in a huddled group, finding comfort in bodily proximity. He towered over them by many inches and there was consciousness of this superiority in the way he studied them with his small but fine black eyes.

Most of the warriors were completely naked but the chief was wearing a *bagueiro* about his waist, a breechclout of deerskin, dyed to a violent red. Around one ankle he had a coil of copper, which was supposed to be a protection against disease. There was a great dignity about him. Under his wide brows he looked at them with an air which said as plainly as words, "Sickly white scum, you see in me what the free life of the woods can produce in the way of a man!"

His glance rested first on Philippe, then shifted to Auguste de Mariat, and finally came to rest on Félicité. He looked her up and down and his long features showed so much approval that he seemed almost to be smiling.

He began to speak to her, nodding until the single feather he wore on his head bobbed violently. Philippe, deeply apprehensive of the way things were going, translated his remarks as, "White maiden is pleasant to look upon." But the Indian leader had been praising her for the gentle line of her breasts and the slenderness of her hips. She made him think of "a little brown foal kicking up its heels."

Félicité sensed the nature of the chief's interest and kept her eyes on the ground. He found this to his liking and proceeded to indulge in a broad pantomime which expressed his intentions in regard to her and which caused his attendant braves to double up with laughter.

Then he ran to his canoe with long and graceful lopes and in a few minutes came back wearing a casaque, a mantle with huge puffed sleeves. It was of a silken material called ferrandine and was lined with black taffeta. Philippe had seen similar garments worn by chiefs in the Spanish possession of Florida and it surprised him to find one of them on the back of a Chickasaw from far up the river. The warriors, however, felt no surprise, either at this or the roughly done up bundle of old rags which he carried in his hands and which he proffered to Félicité with a grotesquely deep bow. They roared their approval of this travesty of the tribal marriage rites.

The chief's example was promptly followed by one of the braves, who sidled up to De Mariat and seized the nightcap from his head. Putting it on his own tonsured skull, the Indian began to strut about proudly. A sharp word from the leader, however, brought the cap to him (he would not have overlooked it if he had not been so concerned with Félicité) and to a place on his own head.

After this a third member of the tribe stripped the camisole off the provost's back, revealing the fact that he wore nothing under it but a flimsy pair of drawers made of silk and with embroidered edges. There was no suggestion of fun making about this brave. He ripped the garment into a multitude of strips, snarling and spitting as he did so, and giving every proof that, in thus destroying it, he was despoiling a symbol of the hated white race.

De Mariat had behaved with courage up to this point. The indignities to which he was being subjected, however, seemed to clear from his mind all misconceptions and, with them, all hope. His face turned white and he whispered to Philippe, "You said you understand the things they've been saying among themselves. What will they do with us?"

Philippe hesitated to answer. Finally he said, "It is clear that—that the best luck we can have will be a quick death."

De Mariat whispered in a stricken tone, "I'm not afraid of death." This was true enough, for he had on various occasions since coming to the colony demonstrated a personal brand of courage. His face became even paler. "But this is so horrible! I never could stand pain. If they torture me I'll—I'll——"

He had suddenly become unstrung. Philippe looked at him anxiously and said, "Come, m'sieur, don't give way!" But the provost was beyond the reach of reason or persuasion. He was looking up at the sky to which, he knew, must be addressed the only appeal open to him.

"Oh, God, save us!" he cried.

Then yielding to a blind and uncontrollable panic, he began to run toward the thick brush which grew a short distance back from the water. He ran with the wild speed which fear can lend.

Philippe shouted after him: "Stop, in God's name! They'll kill you! They'll kill us all!"

De Mariat paid no attention, if he had heard, which was unlikely, but continued to race wildly for the shelter of the trees. In a shrill voice he implored the saints above to lend him speed, to provide a hole into which he could crawl and hide, to save him, save him, save him!

What followed was an orgy of madness which would never leave the memories of those whose fate it was to watch. Félicité screamed as she saw the Indians take up the pursuit. Philippe said under his breath, "The fool, the madman!" Then they both dropped to their knees and started to pray.

The Indians took up the chase with a wild zest, screeching threats. They ran with long loping strides and the result was never in doubt, for De Mariat had not realized the need of kicking off his high-heeled shoes and running in his stockings. He stumbled repeatedly. The fastest runner in the pack soon overtook him. The tomahawk he carried descended on the head of the runaway and De Mariat sprawled forward on his face. After threshing about with both arms and legs he managed to get to his feet again. Before he could take another step, however, the brown-skinned pursuers engulfed him. He went down a second time.

"Don't look!" cried Philippe.

Félicité continued to pray with her head lowered and so was spared the spectacle of the last few moments in the life of Auguste de Mariat. The blows which sent him down the second time were more deadly than had been intended and the warriors exhibited a mad rage when he lay on the ground without moving. Robbed of the prolonged sport they had anticipated in slowly doing their victim to death, they expressed their disappointment by kicking the inert body and raining blows upon it. It might have been reasoned that the savages were responding to a high power which had decreed a careful measure of retribution; that a blow was being struck for every act of cruelty, every injustice, every wrongdoing of which he had been guilty in the course of his life. The space of time consumed was brief but when the savages finally desisted it would have been impossible for anyone who had known Auguste de Mariat to recognize that sprightly young courtier in the broken mass of flesh on the ground.

Philippe put an arm about Félicité's shoulders as they knelt together. "It will be over for us quickly now," he thought.

II

The redskins had gathered about the chief and were noisily disputing the disposition of the two remaining prisoners. Some, it was only too apparent, favored an immediate dispatch. The others seemed to demur, being in favor perhaps of reserving them for a more fitting and ceremonious end. The chief, who towered above them all, seemed to incline toward the idea of delay. He kept his eyes fixed on Félicité.

She began to speak in a low voice. "So many of the brothers have died. Six of them. Shouldn't we be glad, Philippe, to die in the same cause?"

Philippe made no response. He had straightened up and was watching the Indians with a thoughtful eye. To his surprise he realized that his fear was leaving him. "Why do we have such a dread of them?" he asked himself. "They're like children—wild, cruel children. There must be a way to make them see reason." The thought came to him that, for the first time, Félicité's fate was in his hands. He, and he only, could save her.

A resolution was forming in his mind. "Can it be that the hand of God has been in this?" he asked himself. "Why did M'sieur Jean-Baptiste send that old Chickasaw Indian to Montreal? Why did the idea occur to me to learn their language? Could it all have been planned so that I could talk to them now and, perhaps, save our lives?"

He got to his feet. Looking down at Félicité, and thinking how small and helpless she seemed, he said: "I'm going to speak to the chief. Do you remember how old M'sieur Charles frightened the Iroquois into letting him go? With God's help, I may be able to do the same."

She looked up at him eagerly. "Of course!" she exclaimed. "You can do it, Philippe. I'm sure you can."

Philippe was watching the contentious group around the tall chief. "I'm afraid he's being won over to the idea of a quick ending for us. So, if I fail, we'll have lost nothing. It's our only hope now. Pray for me, Félicité."

She did not obey at once. Her eyes followed him as he stalked across the clearing and she became aware of a great difference in him. He was no longer the quiet and unhappy man he had been for so many years. He seemed to carry himself straighter and there was resolution in the way he walked.

Philippe could feel in himself the change which Félicité had noticed. He was now so confident he would succeed that he walked up to the Indian leader and looked him in the eye with a smile.

"Great Chief from the lands of the mighty river, I come to give you a warning!" he declared.

It was clear that the chief had been taken completely by surprise. He frowned and hesitated. "How can white man speak in tongue of Chickasaw?" he demanded.

Philippe raised an arm and pointed upward. "The mighty God of the white man, who has taught him how to build the great ships and how to make the black guns with thunder and lightning in their mouths, speaks to you by the tongue of his humble servant."

The chief was uneasy. He looked about the circle of copper faces and saw in each one the same puzzled awe. No white man had ever spoken their language and so it must be as he had said, that it was the God of the white man who was speaking.

"What does your God want to tell us?" he asked.

It had been Philippe's intention to speak of the retribution which would fall on the Chickasaw tribe if they were not allowed to go free. Before he could begin, however, he felt a touch on his arm and, looking down, saw to his intense surprise that Félicité had followed him. She was showing no sign of fear and her eyes looked up into his as though to say, "We are in this together and must share the danger." Drawing her arm through his, she whispered, "Tell them of Jean St. Père."

He hesitated for a moment, not convinced that this would be better than the arguments he had intended to employ. Then he thought, "I can use it and save the threats for the finish."

"O Chief of the mighty river," he began, "the God of the white man bids me tell you of a curse which fell upon the warriors of the Long House many years ago. There was then in the city of the French from which I come, which is called Ville Marie de Montréal and is so strong that the Iroquois have always left it free of attack, a man named Jean St. Père. He was a gentle and peaceful man and had never done harm to anyone, but the fierce tribesmen of the Long House saw fit to shoot him as he went about his duties.

"That they killed him was not a matter for surprise. The Iroquois had killed many gentle and peaceful men for no cause at all save the hatred they felt for all white men. But this time they made a very great mistake. They cut off his head and carried it away with them. Ah, great Chief, that was a most grievous mistake! The God of the white man decided to punish them for what they had done. He is the only true God, and He made the land and the sea, and it is in His power to bring vengeance down on those who kill His people. Listen while you are told of what happened to the cruel warriors who carried off the head of Jean St. Père."

Félicité could see that he had won the full attention of the war party. They were standing in a silent, intent circle, taking in every word he said. She began to feel a faint stirring of hope. Would the miracle happen a second time?

Philippe was remembering how the Sieur d'Iberville had told the story and how the wonder of it had taken hold of him. He recalled every word the greatest of the Le Moynes had used and how he himself had shuddered as he sat in the darkness beside the bier of his friend Twelve-and-One-More. Could he tell it as well himself now that so much depended on it, his life and Félicité's?

"As they paddled off down the river which would carry them back to the Land of the Long House, a voice issued suddenly from the blanket in which the head had been wrapped. It spoke in the tongue of the Iroquois so that every one of them could understand. Now Jean St. Père, when he was alive, had not known a single word of Iroquois. So it was certain that it was the voice of the white man's God which was speaking to them.

"This, great Chief, was what the tongue of the murdered man said to them: 'You kill us, you commit a thousand cruelties against us, you want to destroy us; but you will not succeed and the day will come when we will be your masters and you will do our bidding.' The Iroquois warriors were frightened and they hid the head in many places. But it didn't matter what they did with it, the voice still reached their ears. It spoke to them all through the days and all through the long nights so that they had no rest and no peace. At last they removed the scalp and threw the head away. But still there was no peace for them. The voice began to speak to them from the scalp. It kept saying over and over again, 'Beware the wrath of the white man and of his God!' "

The chief's face showed that a sense of bewilderment and fear had taken possession of him. He looked at his followers as though seeking counsel but found them without exception staring at the white pair with as much fear as he felt himself. He turned back to Philippe. "If it is the God of the white man," he asked, "who speaks to us with your tongue, what is it the God wants us to do?"

"Great Chief," cried Philippe, "you may kill me as you killed my companion who had no weapons with which to defend himself. But you can't kill the voice which speaks to you now. It will go on speaking to you as the voice of Jean St. Père did to the Iroquois. You may destroy my body, you may burn it to ashes, you may scatter the ashes to the four winds: but the voice will continue to sound in your ears, telling of the vengeance which will be exacted of you and your tribe. You will never again have any peace. You will not be able to sleep. The voice will fill the air around you. You will hear it speaking to you in the murmur of the river. You will hear it in the rustling of the trees. You will hear it in the winds and the rumble of thunder, crying its threats from the skies above you!"

Félicité saw that the tall chief did not seem to stand so proudly erect.

"The voice will never stop!" declared Philippe, speaking in a tense tone. "It will so frighten your women and children that they will suffer from fits and the foaming sickness. It will bring a blight to your crops. It will sound so loud in the forests that the game will be driven away by it and your hunters will return empty-handed to their tents. It will never stop until it has brought madness to all the tribesmen of the Chickasaws. It will never stop, O Chief, until it has driven you to seek the relief of death in the waters of the river!"

With a gesture which said that he was through, Philippe turned his back on the chief. With Félicité on his arm, he began to walk slowly and easily toward the water's edge. "I think their one desire now will be to get as far away from us as possible," he whispered.

He had not overestimated the results of his long harangue. Over his shoulder he could see that the Indians were not pausing for the formality of a conference. They were running to their canoes, the long legs of the chief keeping him in the van.

III

After saying a silent and fervent prayer of thankfulness for their deliverance, the two young people ensconced themselves on the bank of the river where they would be able to see the canoes of the rescuing party when they arrived. They were so exhausted that with one accord they leaned against tree trunks and allowed themselves the luxury of complete relaxation.

Philippe spoke once or twice but Félicité was only vaguely conscious of what he had said and could do no more by way of reply than nod her head. She was too tired almost to think. The pain had left her arms and she wondered vaguely if this was because her body had lost the power to have any feeling at all. She was almost convinced that she had died and was in a suspended state between this life and the next.

Once she became conscious of a pair of horrible eyes gazing at her from what she had supposed was a log drifting by on the current and she suddenly recovered enough strength to shrink back and scream. Philippe laughed and said, "Alligators look more dangerous than they are." He was too weary himself, however, to change his position or to provide any further reassurance.

After as much as an hour had elapsed Philippe stirred and asked, without moving his head, "Do you realize that you're free now?"

The feeling of lassitude still gripped her. "Yes, I am free." She sighed and then asked, "Is it certain the poor man is dead?"

It was several minutes before he said, "His body will be taken back to New Orleans for burial—if there's enough of it left."

A second hour passed and then a third. The sun was climbing up high into the heavens with the promise of an intensely hot day. Félicité's wrists began to ache again.

Philippe's strength was coming back. He rose to his feet, stretched, and then suddenly let out a cry.

"Here they are! I can see the governor in the first canoe. St. Joseph, how fast they are coming! Is there any sight in the world to equal a large canoe with a full crew of the men of New France!"

He rushed to the bank and began to shout and dance and wave his arms to attract the attention of the oncoming flotilla. They saw him almost immediately and a loud hail of relief and jubilation came back to him. He saw Jean-Baptiste le Moyne raise his paddle in a salute.

Still without moving, Félicité said to herself: "Then we're saved. How fast they've been! They'll have to carry me out to one of the canoes, for I don't believe I'm ever going to walk another step as long as I live!"

CHAPTER IX

IT WAS in early spring of the following year. Jean-Baptiste le Moyne de Bienville was taking his usual morning walk before immuring himself in his cabinet for a long day of toil. He looked about him with pride: at the foundations of the church which had been started, at the site selected for the proposed Capuchin Convent (but on which work could not start for some time), at the gaping hole in the outline of the waterfront which would someday be the *Intendance*. He had every reason to be proud, he said to himself, of what had been accomplished.

At every step he passed someone whose cheerful, "Good morning, Excellency!" required a response in kind. Some of them he did not recognize at once, for John Law's ships had emptied so many people into the town that he now encountered unfamiliar faces all the time. This, however, was no drawback to the maintenance of a friendly atmosphere. He liked them all, even those he did not know, and they all liked him.

He was proud of the friendliness of his relations with the people he governed even though he knew that under the surface there was an undercurrent of tension. There was continual uneasy speculation as to what was going to happen and a general belief that the new colony would see black days if the Law schemes failed.

Madame Jouvelt was waiting for him when he reached his cabinet. She had arrayed herself in the most extreme version of the current styles. It was well that the doorways of New Orleans were wide, for otherwise the hoopskirts she was wearing (the most formidably whaleboned ever conceived by a dressmaker) would have kept her perpetually in the room where she donned them. On the other hand her bodice was so very confining that the governor found himself perturbed over the possibility that something would give way, with the most embarrassing of revelations. In spite of all this, he had to acknowledge that she was looking more like the Marie of earlier years. Her brown eyes, which sparkled in anticipation of the matters to be discussed, had recaptured some measure of their former beauty.

The nature of the skirts she was wearing made it difficult for her to sit down and so the conversation which ensued was carried on with them standing on either side of the governor's desk.

"Jean-Baptiste," said Marie, "I come to remind you of two things. First, my husband and I leave on the *Neptune*. I hear it has arrived off the mouth of the river."

"It will be a great loss, Marie," said the governor. It was easy to see that he meant it. He had acquired an affection for her during the six months she had spent in New Orleans. "But it may be very lucky for you that you *are* going. I feel all the time that we're sitting on a volcano which may explode any instant. The government has sent us plenty of settlers but not enough of anything else. The town is full of idlers. It would solve the situation if we could set them all to clearing their land. But—we lack everything that's needed, tools and seed and farm animals. Forty plantations have been started along the river and there are only thirty head of cattle in all Louisiana! Forty plantations may seem like a good start but we have the people now for—for nearly four hundred. What am I to do with them? They loaf about the town, and drink and demand that women be supplied for them. Should I establish brothels? The ministry would lop off my head if I did—and if I don't, no man's wife will be safe!"

Marie had not been paying much attention. As soon as he had finished his long speech she asked, "And now are you interested in hearing my second reason for coming?"

"Of course."

She moved closer, the metal bands under her skirts clicking as she did so, and held up an admonitory finger. "Philippe will be on the ship. His last letter said he would catch at Havana the first boat from France and come back to New Orleans on it."

The governor nodded. "I'm expecting him. He'll be returning with his head full of the good ideas he has picked up in the Spanish colonies. I'm sure he'll come back ready to give this town of ours a touch of the distinctive beauty of architecture of the New World."

"Jean-Baptiste! He'll come back with his head full of other things as well. His love for Félicité most of all."

A few moments passed without anything further being said. Then Madame Jouvelt burst into indignant speech. "Don't you see the need for acting at once? You must speak to her! You must get it settled! There must be a ring on her finger when her Philippe gets back. Do you want to lose her?"

"Marie," protested the governor, "I didn't send Philippe on this tour of inspection so that he would play Uriah to my David. I wasn't trying to get him out of the way so I could make love to Félicité. The arrangements were made on orders from the ministry." He paused and then gestured resignedly as though he did not expect to make her understand. "I've been careful not to take advantage of his absence by making love to her."

"Then you've been a great fool!" she declared tartly. "Haven't you heard from your brother in Montreal that he won't object if you marry her? *That* obstacle, about which you were so concerned, has been removed. You have her in your office all day long. She admires you very much." She threw both hands in the air. "What more do you need?"

"She hasn't shown the slightest hint of a romantic interest in me. Her manner, in fact, has always been casual."

"You are too modest. You, the Sieur de Bienville, governor of Louisiana, a famous man and on the way to becoming very wealthy. You're a hero in her eyes and a legend to the people of France because of the way you've struggled on here alone. I've heard her speak of you as though you were greater than all the heroes of history combined. In God's sweet name, what more could she ask?"

"Love," answered De Bienville.

"If I'm any judge, you are prepared to supply her with all she will need of that."

The governor swallowed hard. "I love her so much," he declared, "that sometimes I think nothing else counts. But she has experienced one marriage of convenience and if she marries again it must be on her own terms. It must be for one reason only—because she has found a man she can love herself. It's not enough that I love her."

"You're talking like a schoolboy!" she cried. "I've set my heart on this match. I was foolish enough to let you slip through my fingers when I was young and you were in love with *me*. I'm not going to let her make the same mistake I did. She's not going to lose you!"

"It's my greatest hope that she won't."

"Then you must act! You must forget this noble strain which is so strong in you and which is going to ruin your life. You must develop a healthy little streak of selfishness in yourself. Even a touch of good practical baseness."

The governor shook his head. "There's no use talking to me like this, Marie. I don't think you understand how I feel about your daughter. I love her, of course. I love her so much that——" He sighed and shook his head. "I love her so much that I desire her happiness more than my own."

II

After Marie had left, the governor stood for several moments in absorbed thought. He was not concerned, however, with what they had been discussing. He had the faculty, so important and necessary to men in high office, of putting one matter completely out of mind when the need to consider other things arose. He had dismissed his own personal problems and was pondering again on the dangerously upset state of the town. He was wondering specifically if the new cells which had been added behind the Hôtel de Ville (they were comparatively luxurious, with room for occupants to stand up and each supplied with a straw pallet) would prove sufficient in view of the disturbances he anticipated.

Then he closed another compartment of his mind and walked out to an office at the rear of the building which Félicité had occupied since he had begun to utilize her capacity for handling administrative detail. The office in question had been the first jail and it was hard to believe now that this curiously shaped cubicle, not more than twelve feet long and six wide, had once housed as many as ten prisoners!

Félicité was sitting at one end and the rough pine table in front of her was piled high with letters and papers of various kinds. She nodded to him cheerfully when he appeared in the doorway.

"This will be a busy day, M'sieur Jean-Baptiste," she said. "What a lot of troublesome detail! I shudder to think of the time when you had to do all this as well as your real duties."

"My handling of detail was masterly," declared De Bienville, smiling at her. "I disregarded it! I let it accumulate until there was no more room and then I threw it out. In no other way could I have carried the burden of work."

This offended her orderly mind. "But now that New Orleans is becoming so very important, you couldn't do that any more!"

He smiled again. "That is true. How lucky for me that I have you to attend to it!"

She touched one of the letters on the table which carried an impressive departmental seal. "In this note from the ministry," she said, "they report that the price of shares in the Louisiana Company is now forty times the original value. Has all France gone mad?" She paused and looked up at him with a puzzled gravity. "Can this keep up much longer, M'sieur Jean-Baptiste? What is going to happen?"

De Bienville replied with a gravity which matched hers. "The bubble will burst soon. Charles is sure it can't last long. When it does burst we'll have difficult problems on our hands here."

Félicité looked at him with the zealous interest he had found could be aroused easily in her. "We have a problem now. The need for a hospital, M'sieur Jean-Baptiste. I've been wanting to talk to you about it."

The governor was watching her in absorbed silence. From the moment he had guided the rescue party around the bend and had seen her with Philippe on the bank, waving excitedly to them, he had realized that the impression she had left on him after the days they spent together at the château at Longueuil had been deeper than he suspected. Seeing her again, he had known that he had been in love with her ever since. He had fallen now still deeper under the spell. No day could seem tiring or depressing any longer, for she was always near at hand and there was an hour of discussion between them over the work. Although he had been correct in telling Madame Jouvelt that Félicité's attitude was businesslike, it was also true that a most pleasant camaraderie had been developing gradually between them. Her presence never failed to raise his spirits, to drive away the cares of office.

She had turned her head away from him, as she always did when deep in thought, and he was thus given an opportunity for an uninterrupted view of her profile. He drank it in, saying to himself that never had a cameo been made which could compare with it.

It was apparent when she began to speak that she also had the faculty for closing her mind to all but one subject. "We have three women whose time is near," she said. "Two are married. The third—well, m'sieur, you know the facts of *that* case. Old Madame Feron is so doubled up with the rheumatism she can't hobble to her front door any more. Those two men who were caught in the fall of the cypress tree are still at the tavern. The other guests can't sleep because of their groans but the important point is that the two men are not getting proper care. One of them has mortification of the leg and will die very soon. And you heard the rumor last night that one of the sailors on the last ship, who was so ill he had to be left here, has a disease which may prove to be leprosy." Her gray eyes were filled with serious purpose. "M'sieur Jean-Baptiste, we need a hospital. We need it *terribly.*"

She had talked to him before about the need for proper care of the sick. He was, therefore, prepared with an answer.

"My child," he said, "you forget that the souls of men are more important than their bodies."

She looked up at him quickly. "I'm not forgetting. But we have Mother Church, and all the kind saints, and all our fine gentle priests to keep us thinking and acting as we should. But we do nothing for the sick and the injured except to have one ignorant little surgeon to attend them."

"Félicité," said the governor with a serious air, "you must see that we can't have a hospital until we've built a church. Everyone knows that and believes it."

"Yes, we all want a church!" she exclaimed. "No one will be happy until we can see a beautiful spire against the sky to tell us that this *is* France, and that God and all the blessed saints are with us even here on the edge of the earth. But, m'sieur, it will take many years to build such a church as that. And in the meantime our people go on dying, like poor little Henriette Catin, whose husband was always away on his river boat and so was never at home to help her after she fell and hurt her back so badly. She needed constant attention and care, that poor Henriette. M'sieur Jean-Baptiste! Can't we have a small church now—and a very, very small hospital?"

De Bienville's mind had gone back to that warm July morning when the family council had been held at Longueuil and it had been decided to risk everything on the Mississippi venture.

"My brother Charles said once that it would take many miracles to establish a French city here. It seems, my Félicité, that the time has come to perform some of these miracles. We must draw out from under the black cloth, where there is nothing at all, both a church and a hospital. Do you think"—he reached out and touched one of her hands, then drew back quickly—"do you think me capable of such prodigies?"

"Of course!" She surrendered both of her hands to him. "That there's a New Orleans today *is* a miracle. You've created a town out of nothing, M'sieur Jean-Baptiste. To build a church *and* a hospital will be small matters indeed to such a master magician as you!"

He continued to hold her hands and she smiled up at him with more interest than she had ever before displayed. This should perhaps have encouraged him to declare himself but instead it persuaded him to the opposite course. He realized that her happiness *was* what he desired above everything else. He must not allow any other considerations to stay in his mind.

"Did you see Madame Jouvelt just now?" she asked. "I spoke to her when she arrived and I could see she was in one of her demanding moods."

The young governor did not reply at once. He had compelled himself to look away in consideration of the decision he had reached. "Yes, Madame Jouvelt was in a demanding mood. She was demanding that I should become selfish enough to think of my own happiness above everything, that I should try to translate myself to a new and beautiful world where there would be nothing but happiness."

"I hope," said Félicité, "that you will find this new and beautiful world, M'sieur Jean-Baptiste."

After a moment's silence he shook his head and turned away without looking at her. "No," he said, "I'm afraid it's unlikely that I'll ever find it."

CHAPTER X

WHEN the word came that the first of the river boats would come in with its passengers in a matter of a few hours Félicité ran in great haste to her room. No bathtubs had yet been imported into New Orleans and, as a result, bathing was still accomplished by old methods. She spread a foot towel on the floor and then placed in the center a large and well-soaked sponge. Seating herself on the sponge and taking a small one in each hand, she proceeded to give herself a quick and thorough scrubbing. The pimpernel water she had poured into the bowl gave a pleasant glow to the skin and she emerged feeling well refreshed.

Not pausing to dress, except to drop a wisp of silk over her shoulders, she seated herself in front of a wall mirror. Dipping her fingers into a small silver receptacle called a *boist,* she began to knead her face with a preliminary ointment. She worked quickly, for the minutes were flying! Her fingers seemed to click like knitting needles as she applied a sweet-scented pomatum to her cheeks and to keep time with her thoughts through which surged one refrain, "He is coming, he is coming, he is coming!"

She had reached the final stage, the sparing use of a very light rouge, when a rap came on the door and Madame Jouvelt entered.

"So!" said the older woman. "Your eyes have that soft light in them, you are hardly aware that I've come into the room and am talking to you. I can see you are on the verge of making a very great mistake! I'm going to talk to you now as your mother would—if she were here to look after you!

"I must tell you first that I made a great mistake myself," she went on. "I was young and I was beautiful. If you find that hard to believe, you may ask His Excellency, who knew me—when I was in Paris. I had a chance for a home, security, a good husband. But I wanted something more than that. I wanted life, excitement, wealth, admiration, power. I got what I wanted. I may tell you, child, that there was a time when I was the toast of Paris. Life was all I had hoped it would be. I was sure beauty was power, and that beauty always lasted. Ah, such a deluded little fool! I didn't doubt for a moment that I would always find on my dress of mornings the little bit of white which promises a new lover. But instead I lost a garter and, certain enough, soon thereafter I lost my beauty and I lost—everything."

"But, Madame Jouvelt, I want nothing more than a husband and a home."

"But you, my Félicité, have a choice. You have only to reach out your hand! You may have a distinguished husband, who will be devoted to you, a high position, wealth, anything you may desire. And yet you seem set on marrying a poor young man, one who can never hope to get beyond his present position. It's a different kind of mistake from the one I made but—a mistake, nevertheless, a very great mistake! If your own mother were here to talk to you"—poor Madame Jouvelt, chained to her promise, had become red in the face in her earnestness—"if *she* were here, you would listen to her. You might believe *her*. Please believe this, my child, that she would say to you the same things I am saying!"

Félicité was surprised at the vehemence of her companion. She turned from her mirror and studied the face of her adviser. "I can see, Madame Jouvelt, that you are very much in earnest and that you're thinking only of my best interests. But, as it happens, I've no decision to make now. I made my decision the first time I ever saw Philippe. I was a small girl then but I knew my own mind. I've known it ever since."

"Do you know that the Sieur de Bienville is in love with you? That he—*that most honorable man!*—wants to marry you?"

"He's never said anything to me. But I—I think he does like me."

The older woman had much more she wanted to say but she refrained, with great difficulty, from voicing any further arguments. She began to walk about the room on the pretext of straightening the sparse furnishings. Her manner showed a curious lack of ease. Once, when standing behind Félicité, she allowed the mask to fall. She looked at her daughter with such an air of frustrated affection that it was clear she was struggling with a desire to confess their relationship. She held out her arms in a silent appeal. It was moments before she acknowledged the hopelessness of it by dropping her arms to her sides. Then, with dejection showing itself in every line of her ample figure, she walked to the door.

"I, too, will be noble," she said, "although I'm becoming more convinced every day I live that nobility causes nothing but trouble. It's a rich cake that sours on your stomach." She turned at the door. "Can you bear one more word of advice? Whoever you marry, don't have too many children. You're capable of so much more than childbearing; and if you get yourself a houseful of brats, you'll have to give everything else up. But have at least one daughter. Ah, my Félicité, keep as close to her as you can! Mother and daughter can have such a sweet and useful relationship! I'm just beginning to realize how much I missed by—by not having a daughter of my own."

She had intended to leave but was prevented from doing so by the arrival of Nicolette. The daughter of the Gauthier family had become so devoted to Félicité that the latter found it hard to enjoy any degree of privacy at all. The child was in and out of her room continually, seldom pausing to knock. She followed Félicité about everywhere, she sat and watched her with worship in her small, freckled face, she had even been known to climb up to the bedroom window, when the door was locked, and feast her eyes on her idol from a precarious position on a rose trellis.

"How lovely you look!" she exclaimed, walking over to where Félicité sat. "He won't know what to say when he lands and sees you looking so lovely, will he? It will be too much for him, won't it?" Then she remembered the mission on which she had come. She edged up closer to Félicité, fairly quivering with excitement. "What do you think's going to happen? My mother is to be married! Yes, she's made up her mind at last. She's going to marry M'sieur Bonnet and I'm glad because I like him. He's a very nice little man."

Both Félicité and Madame Jouvelt were taken completely by surprise. They had long ago become convinced that Carpe's courting was doomed to failure.

"Are you sure, Nicolette?" asked Félicité, turning around on her chair.

"Yes, madame, I'm sure." The girl nodded her head vigorously, delighted to be the bearer of such interesting news. "It's just happened. M'sieur Bonnet stopped working early because he wanted to wash himself and get dressed for the arrival of the boat. He dropped by here and my mother said to him—I heard her!—she said to him, 'You are a little beetle of a man but I'll marry you because I can see you'll never stop asking me if I don't.'"

"And was M'sieur Bonnet happy about it?"

"Oh yes, madame! He was so happy *both* his eyes showed it."

"The air seems filled with romance today," said Madame Jouvelt in a caustic tone.

The girl walked over beside Félicité and touched the handle of her brush with a reverent finger. "I did it, madame," she said in an excited whisper. "You know there are so many unmarried men here and they were always coming to see my mother. They would take me aside and ask me questions. 'How many children are there?' they'd ask, and I would say eight or ten, according to how eager they seemed. Sometimes, if they looked quite determined, I would answer twelve. They asked me about her weight and I always added thirty or forty pounds. And when they were leaving I would follow them and say, 'If you marry my mother, be sure you keep the carving knife locked up.' That would make their eyes pop at me and they would ask all kinds of questions but I'd shake my head and say, 'That's all I can tell you.' None of them ever came back, madame, and so at last my mother had to take M'sieur Bonnet, just as I wanted all the time."

Madame Jouvelt sniffed. "Make it a double wedding, Félicité," she said as she left the room.

II

Word of the coming of the river boat had reached town early in the afternoon. A short time later the townspeople began to gather along the waterfront, there being nothing more important in their lives than the arrival of ships from home. They waited, anxiously and eagerly, but hour after hour passed and darkness had fallen before a small light appeared down the river. The light was a very small one and it bobbed up and down continuously, announcing itself as a lantern suspended on the prow of the oncoming boat.

Félicité stood at the edge of the crowd with an anxious Madame Jouvelt at her elbow. She was so excited and happy that she could hardly stand still.

"Soon he will be here!" she declared.

"Then you haven't changed your mind?"

"I'll never change my mind as long as I live!" Félicité spoke with a passionate conviction.

The boat had come in to the landing place and a squad of troops with lighted torches formed a lane from the quay to the square. Félicité made a place for herself at the end of the lane where the new arrivals would have to pass her. In a moment she cried exultantly, "There he is!"

Madame Jouvelt squinted over her daughter's shoulder. "I see nothing. Nothing but a lot of faces."

"It has been a fine thing for him!" declared Félicité, watching Philippe step over the gunwale of the boat. "See how well dressed he is! He has become quite the man of fashion."

It soon became apparent, even to the unfriendly eyes of Madame Jouvelt, that Philippe lived up to this description. He was wearing a *claque* (a three-cornered hat), a very fine coat of light blue, and black gloves trimmed with silver ribbon.

Philippe looked about him eagerly as he walked up the lane. When he came to Félicité he stopped and allowed the stream of passengers to flow past him. His face had flushed and he found difficulty in speaking.

"It's the same as that other time," he managed to say finally. "I came off the boat—and there you were."

"You were returning from Fort Chambly. I was waiting for you."

"We had been away for many months. It was very cold and there was a sharp wind. The wind had brought the most beautiful color into your cheeks."

"But am I beautiful now?" she asked. "It has been—so many years, Philippe."

"You're more lovely now than you were then."

"You told me that day that I was beautiful." She was speaking in a cautious whisper. "It was the first time you had ever noticed how I looked. It made me very proud."

"You had on your new beaver coat and a three-cornered beaver hat!" he declared, the ecstasy of the recollection lending a rapt note to his voice. "You were no longer a little girl. You had grown up while I was away. And I realized suddenly that—that I loved you!"

History seemed to be repeating itself in many respects. They had started to walk away from the lighted square, with no more conscious volition than on the other day when they had found themselves walking over the snow-packed banks of the river back of the Church of Bonsecours. Their feet took them along the quay in a westerly course. For a short space they had the light from the torches to direct them. Then the shadow of trees intervened and they found themselves walking in complete darkness.

"People will think we're mad!" declared Félicité, unaware that she was repeating what she had said that day in Montreal.

They were passing a log hut which had been thrown up hurriedly when De Bienville and his party first arrived. It had been so quickly constructed that later, when the erection of a better class of house was started, it had been figured that to set it in proper repair would entail more work than to build a new house; and so it had been left without occupants except on occasions when the crowding of the town made any kind of roof welcome. It was in such a leaky condition that it was called La Passoire, the Colander.

If they had not been so absorbed in one another they would have noticed that a low murmur of voices was coming from the darkened hut. The sounds ceased immediately when she spoke. The happy pair passed on down the uneven quay without suspecting that La Passoire had occupants on this one night when all New Orleans seemingly was at the landing place.

"I've never stopped loving you!" declared Philippe. "Never for a moment. I don't believe you've ever been out of my mind in all these years." He paused suddenly. "When we parted that day after my return from Fort Chambly it was in the belief that everything was settled. The next time I saw you, everything was over between us. Is that going to happen again?"

Félicité said, "No!" and she said it with such conviction that his arms sought for her in the darkness. She yielded to them eagerly.

"Do you mean it?" he demanded. "Do you mean that you'll marry me now, even if pressure is brought to make you change your mind?"

"Yes, Philippe. There will be no pressure this time. But even if there was, I wouldn't let it count. I—I've never stopped loving you, my Philippe. Never! And I'll never stop loving you as long as I live!"

What did it matter now that they had been separated once and had lived for many barren years, Philippe in loneliness and despair and nursing a hurt pride, Félicité in a continuous round of work and responsibility which had ended in a calamitous marriage? It no longer seemed important that the De Mariats, father and son, had come into their lives, that she had suffered so much, that she and Philippe had faced death together at a time when the future had appeared so black that to die would not have seemed tragic. They had been forced to waste the sweet early years which are so important in married life and must now try to make up for them; but finally the path had been smoothed, the complications had been simplified, they could go on through life with a sense of duty well done and with the full right to enjoy their belated reward.

They did not know where they were; but that did not matter. The sounds from the landing place seemed far away. Philippe's arms were about her in the darkness. They whispered back and forth the assurances of love, the avowals, the promises, which are a part of all such moments.

"Félicité," he said finally, "we must be married properly. The banns must be published, even though it means three weeks."

She nodded slowly. "Yes. Everything was wrong the first time. It didn't seem to me that I was married when the ceremony was over." He heard her sigh. "We must be content to wait even though it—it seems such a very long wait!"

III

It was not surprising that La Passoire had shown signs of tenancy when the reunited lovers passed.

Perhaps half an hour before the arrival of the boat, two men had approached the deserted cabin through the growth of willow and mulberry trees which surrounded it. One was Louis le Babillard, who seemed nervous and was finding it hard to suppress an inclination to whistle, and the other was a short and thick individual who scowled and muttered to himself whenever he stumbled in the gathering darkness. They entered La Passoire through a rear door and Louis le Babillard tapped on the wall. It was, obviously, a signal, consisting of three short raps followed by a long and protracted one. Immediately there was a sound of stirring in the attic above and in a few seconds a trap door opened in the ceiling. A pair of legs appeared in the opening and tossed about as their owner sought to locate the first of several steps nailed to the wall. The owner proved to be the Englishman of many names who had conducted the raid of the Chickasaw Indians.

"Well, M'sieur Beddoes, here we are," said Louis le Babillard. "I trust we find you well fed, contented in mind, and in the very best of health."

"None of the three," said the Englishman. There was not, however, any hint of complaint in his voice. "I haven't had a bite to eat all day and I'm hungry enough to swallow raw alligator meat. And I may tell you, messires, that the heat up there is a proof of what the parsons say about hell."

The second visitor said in a voice which repudiated all social amenities, "We've come to get matters settled, Englishman."

It was too dark in the interior for the others to see the hostility with which Beddoes regarded the speaker. "Walk me up!" he said. "It seems we have a man of action with us, a rip-roaring tearer into things! There always has to be at least one of them wherever the jolly flag with the skull and the crossed bones flies."

"Jacques here can't wait to get his fingers into the gold we're going to earn for ourselves," said Louis le Babillard. "Ever since we had our first talk this Jacques has been figuring what his share will be and how he'll spend it. If he spends any at all, which is doubtful."

"You talk too much!" snapped the second man. He then said to Beddoes, "And now, Englishman, you'll tell us all about this scheme of yours."

Beddoes smiled slyly to himself in the darkness. "My good friends Louis and Jacques, I've nothing to offer you, not even a swallow of slosh-and-bite. There isn't a chair in this palace of mine and all the servants are having their day off. Still, we can all three sit down in a corner on our double-jugs and get our heads together. I've a plan for you. Walk me up, what a plan!

"The first boat must be in by this time," said Beddoes in low tones, when they had seated themselves as directed. "We'll give them a day to unload everything they brought up on it and then we'll take it over. To-morrow night, after the town has gone to sleep and we've made the head of the watchman acquainted with a piece of lead pipe, we'll act. It wouldn't do to move sooner because the boat must be light when we start out in it and ready to fly like a horse with turpentine under its tail. We must reach the mouth of the river before any word gets there of what we're up to."

The rear door opened and a head was put into the room. "Am I late?" asked a deeply resonant voice. The newcomer carried something over his shoulder which gave off a musical sound when it banged against the frame of the door.

"It's Jules Panletet, the minstrel," explained Louis le Babillard. "He's anxious to sign with us and I invited him to come here tonight."

"Come in, M'sieur Panletet," said the Englishman. "Sit down here and join us in a little talk of ways and means. You are a minstrel, m'sieur? What incentive is there for a minstrel to take a hand in the unpleasant things we're planning?"

"My incentive?" said Panletet, acting on the invitation to seat himself. "An empty belly, M'sieur Englishman. A thin purse. A sense of indignation over the official lies which brought me out to this new country."

"And what could a minstrel do to make himself useful on this little venture?"

"I'll be frank and tell you at once that I can't sit at the prow like Orpheus and set the ship to skittering over the waves by the magic of my music. But I can bring tunes out of this lute which will lighten the long hours of night. If need be, I can swing a cutlass. I even have a slight knack for cooking."

A moment of silence followed. It was plain that the minstrel's explanations had been found acceptable.

"The plan, then." Beddoes spoke in a different tone than any of them had yet heard him employ. His voice lacked the rough amiability of the deck hand. "We gather here at midnight. As I understand it, there are forty-four who've expressed their willingness to throw in with us. We seize the boat and make our way to the mouth of the river. I have confederates among the crew of the *Neptune*. There's no need to go into details but I give you my solemn assurance that the capture of the ship won't be a matter of any great difficulty. We'll take with us any of the crew who want to join and the rest we'll ship ashore. It may be necessary to cut the throats of a few officers but I'm not one to wallow in blood unless forced to it."

"The more throats we cut the better!" declared Jacques.

"You and I, my friend," said Beddoes, "look at things from different viewpoints. However, I'm sure we agree over what's to be done after the ship has been taken. We sail out across the gulf and then we cut into the lanes of commerce where the sails of helpless ships will greet our eyes!"

CHAPTER XI

"AREN'T we both married men now?" asked Carpe Bonnet as he and Philippe walked from the church with their wives riding in an oxcart ahead of them and their friends following on foot, the married men in couples first, the single ones after. "Why, then, all this ceremony? I don't know what it's all about."

Philippe's eyes were fixed on Félicité as she stood in the oxcart. Urbain Malard, the blacksmith, had kept the bellows blowing all day and the fire roaring in order to lengthen the vehicle and to provide a second pair of wheels. In spite of his efforts, it was a rickety affair, and each hole in the road made it rock dangerously. Whenever this happened Madame Bonnet would lose her balance and it would be necessary for Félicité to act quickly in order to avoid being pinned against the side. The latter would then look at Philippe and smile wanly, as though to assure him that she would do her best not to come to him in a damaged condition.

"We're following the marriage customs of the part of France where Madame Jouvelt was born," explained Philippe. "She begged us to do it. I didn't see any reason why we should but His Excellency came to me and said it was the only thing we could do for her and that it would give her a great deal of pleasure. So Félicité and I talked it over and we agreed." He indulged in a smile. "This is only the beginning, Carpe. There's worse ahead of us."

"I know there is." The second bridegroom spoke in a dismal voice but he soon brightened up as he watched the swaying figures of the two brides, his own wife in a very plain gray dress and Félicité with a coronet of white flowers on her head. He laid a hand on Philippe's arm to regain his attention. "Master," he said in an awed tone, "I married a lot more woman than you did."

Nothing more was said for the rest of the walk down the rutty surface of the road which would soon be the Rue de Chartres. Philippe kept his eyes on the slender figure in the oxcart and could think of nothing else.

The vehicle had been piled high with white flowers and Félicité, who was attired in the dress she had worn when De Bienville first saw her (on the day when he made use of the squint), had a sheaf of them in her arms. She looked lovely enough to keep him in a state of ecstatic wonder.

Old Jules Panletet, walking ahead of the cart with his lute over his shoulder, struck up an air as they drew near the house. All traces of uneasiness left Carpe's face. "That's better!" he said approvingly. "The music should never stop at weddings. It takes one's mind off the serious side of it."

Philippe broke the rules by helping his bride down from the cart. "My sweet and lovely wife!" he whispered.

Félicité gave her skirts a pat and looked down to make sure that the puckered ribbon bows on her bodice had not become disarranged. "This is very improper," she whispered back. "We're not supposed to speak to each other yet. You must control yourself and not look at me at all."

A supper had been prepared in the garden of the house although it was barely large enough to accommodate the guests. There was only one small table, at which the two brides sat, and the rest settled themselves on the ground or perched on top of the fence. The two new husbands stood behind their wives and attended to their wants. Later, of course, this order would be reversed but for once it was decreed that masculine appetites must wait.

"This is wrong," grumbled Carpe to his master, after depositing a plate of soup in front of his wife. "It'll put notions in their heads and we may have trouble knocking them out."

Observing the broad back of the mother of six, Philippe thought that it might be foolhardy for her diminutive husband to begin on any such form of education. Every time he looked at the oddly assorted pair he had a tendency to grin; but this was seldom, for his eyes were busy with the white neck and slender shoulders of his own wife which still kept him in a state of incoherent delight.

The supper was a substantial one. First, of course, was the soup, an excellent *bouillie de blé d'Inde*. Then came shrimps, smothered in a delicious sauce and served on mounds of rice. A lamb ragout followed and a cold boiled fish. Sagamité, the corn dish of the Indians which had become a favorite with the white invaders, was served as well as bread. There was an abundance of both red and white wine. It was an excellent supper and the hum of conversation, and the flood of bawdy jokes hurled at the newlywed couples, ceased as the guests proceeded to show their appreciation. Even the lute of Jules Panletet went silent as its owner settled down to a lively bout with the boiled fish.

Félicité ate very little but her companion more than made up for her abstinence. Madame Bonnet consumed huge quantities of everything and kept her anxious bridegroom busy attending to her needs. "Some more of the sauce, Polycarpe," she would say. Or, "If you were more attentive you'd see my glass is empty." Carpe obeyed with a dubious air and finally made an opportunity to whisper in Philippe's ear.

"This doesn't suit me at all, master," he said. "We shouldn't allow it. They'll be trying to keep us hanging around and waiting on them all the rest of our lives. Don't you think we should put a foot down right now?"

"Carpe," said Philippe in a tremulous voice, "I ask nothing better than to wait on *my* wife for all eternity."

Madame Jouvelt came up at this point and bent her head over Félicité's shoulder. "Are you happy?" she asked in a whisper.

"Yes, Madame Jouvelt. And I owe so much to you. You arranged everything beautifully."

The older woman was on the point of tears. "Tonight I feel that you *are* my daughter. It has been—it has been a great pleasure to look after things. It was kind of you to let me."

Félicité smiled up at her. "I'm enjoying it," she whispered, "but from what I've heard there are some masculine doubts about all this."

The older woman picked up a serviette and applied it to her eyes. "We leave tomorrow night, Félicité. When we found it impossible to take the boat back last fall M'sieur Jouvelt swore we would catch the first one in the spring. I'm—I'm afraid I'll never see you again!"

She turned her attention then to Philippe, even achieving a friendly smile. "You spoiled all my plans," she declared. "I might as well tell you I didn't want Félicité to marry you. Well, now that you're married, I'm beginning to think it was the right thing after all. My—Félicité looks so happy that I can see her heart was set on it. You must look after her well, Philippe. It's a sacred trust I leave with you."

"I'll devote my life to keeping her happy," declared Philippe fervently.

After supper an augmented orchestra began to play lively music and the guests lined up in the garden to dance. Félicité and Philippe should have led off the *reel à deux* but the former said she was tired and begged to be excused. Madame Bonnet volunteered at once to assume the duty and led her husband out to the head of the line. In the brisk dance which followed they resembled nothing so much as a large coal barge drawn along a towpath by a small mule.

Nicolette wormed her way in close and settled herself at Félicité's knee. "I think you're the loveliest bride that ever lived, Madame Félicité," she said in a rapt tone. Then she added severely, "I'm so glad you're not dancing like my mother. Don't you think she looks very foolish?"

At nine o'clock sharp Madame Jouvelt stationed herself in the center of the garden and clapped her hands for attention. "If you please," she announced, "the dancing will stop for a few minutes. It's time for the bridal couples to retire. As you know, we'll have a chance to see them later in the evening."

Félicité, who had been coached in her part, stood up in turn. While the guests applauded loudly she held out a hand to Philippe. On the palm reposed a key.

"To the door of my bedroom," she said, finding it hard to keep herself from blushing. "I give it into your care. It is yours, my husband."

A group of married people escorted them to the back of the house where they were to share the small room which had been hers since she joined the household. Another group was doing the same for the Bonnets and displaying a tendency toward levity.

Philippe opened the door and followed his wife into the room. To his surprise the escort party entered also. The women went through the motions of preparing the room, shaking up the pillows, turning down the covers, and closing the window curtains. While they were doing this Madame Jouvelt brought out a silk nightgown and a nightcap with forget-me-nots embroidered on it and placed them on the bed. The husbands meanwhile stood about and grinned foolishly. They winked at the bridegroom and whispered bits of facetious advice in his ear.

Finally, however, their departure could not be delayed any longer. Madame Jouvelt said, "We'll return in an hour," and led the way out of the room.

Philippe followed them to the door. He turned the key in the lock.

II

"When they return," said Félicité, "they'll bring wine and they'll stay a long time drinking toasts. They'd dance if the room was large enough. We'll have to sit up in bed and smile and drink wine with them. They'll stay until late into the night. Did you know?"

Philippe nodded. "It seems old-fashioned and—and barbarous. If we'd been married in Canada there wouldn't have been any of this horseplay. Our ceremony is pleasant and dignified."

"Why didn't M'sieur Jean-Baptiste come to see us married?" It was clear from the tone she used that Félicité was worried over the absence of the governor. "He took so much interest in the arrangements. I don't understand it."

"I heard that a party of Indian chiefs from across the gulf arrived this afternoon."

Félicité did not seem satisfied with this explanation. "I wonder if he had some other reason? Surely he could see the chiefs tomorrow! Do you suppose he was looking for an excuse not to come?"

Philippe was standing with his back against the door and smiling at her. "Does it matter?" he asked. "How patient you've been through everything! And how lovely in your patience!"

Félicité smiled back. She was happy and entirely at her ease. She felt no shyness at being alone with Philippe: and to feign it, as brides were supposed to do, would be foolish, she said to herself, even hypocritical.

She seated herself in a chair and raised one foot. "Will you be so kind, M'sieur Philippe, as to lend me a little assistance?" she asked.

He dropped on one knee in front of her and began to fumble at the buckle with fingers which had suddenly developed clumsiness. After several moments had passed he looked up. They drew together instantly, Félicité leaning forward and placing one hand on his shoulder, Philippe raising himself to an upright position and encircling her waist with both arms. "Everything looked so hopeless!" he said. "You were to be married and go to France. I was to come here, to New Orleans. Nothing seemed more certain than that I would never see you again in this life. And then, suddenly, everything began to change! Was it the intervention of our kind Father and the good saints in heaven which brought us together? How surely and wonderfully it all happened! And now we're married. And you belong to me!"

Her hand left his shoulder and touched the side of his head where a streak of white showed in his dark hair.

"We can't allow any more of this," she said. "I must make you so comfortable and happy that you'll never have another moment's worry." She pressed her cheek against his. "No more worries, my loved one! No more unhappiness, no uncertainty!" Her voice fell to a whisper. "And now, M'sieur Philippe, don't you think you should finish what you started to do?"

A light tap was heard on the window. Philippe sprang hastily to his feet. He looked at his wife with a puzzled frown. "And what is this?" he asked. "Is it more of their jokes?"

"I don't think so," she whispered.

Philippe went to the window and cautiously threw back the curtains. It had been raised for ventilation and he could see a face staring in at him.

"This is Jules Panletet," came a whisper. "I have a message for His Excellency. It's a matter of great importance and there is danger. Great danger. I need help, m'sieur."

"What can I do?" asked Philippe.

"He must be told at once what is happening," said the minstrel. He could no longer be seen and Philippe realized he had withdrawn into the dark at one side where the light from the window could not reach him. "I can't leave here. It would be noticed if I went; and afterward they would know who did it. Also they would be put on their guard at once. And, m'sieur, I dare not tell anyone else. I don't trust any of them enough. You, m'sieur, must get the message to the governor."

"I?" Philippe's tone told how much surprise he felt. "Do you mean I must go now? But, M'sieur Panletet, you understand surely——" He paused and indulged in a brief laugh. "Is it so important that you would drag me, a bridegroom, away now?"

"M'sieur!" The minstrel's voice from the darkness carried proof of the gravity of the situation. "There is a plot. Some men who are dissatisfied with the way things are going here want to get away. At midnight they will take the river boat which came in last night, and they'll go down the river and seize the *Neptune*. They intend to go into piracy, m'sieur."

Philippe did not change his position and it would have appeared to anyone on the outside that he had come to the window for a breath of air. "How does it happen that you know about this?" he demanded in a whisper.

"A hint was dropped and I pretended that I wanted to go. I was taken in as a member. Last night I heard the plan discussed at great length. That Englishman is in it——"

"Beddoes?"

"Yes, m'sieur. He's in hiding in the attic at La Passoire. The leaders are gathering there tonight. If His Excellency has the place surrounded at eleven-thirty he'll catch them all, the men who've planned this."

"Is that all His Excellency needs to know?"

"It's all that matters. There are nearly fifty men pledged to go. All unmarried, with one exception."

"I'll get the word to the governor. No one will miss me for the next hour."

Philippe stepped back from the window and dropped the curtains into place. He walked over beside Félicité.

"Did you hear?"

"A little. Philippe, can it be true?"

"I have no doubts. Panletet is honest. What purpose could he have in telling such a story if it were not true?"

"But the people here are so kind, so patient. I can't believe there are fifty men in New Orleans willing to become pirates."

"I must get the word to the governor at once. We'll soon find out how much truth there's in it."

They faced each other with rueful smiles. "My sweet wife!" He took her in his arms and kissed her passionately. "Was ever bridegroom placed in a less enviable position? I'll go as fast as my legs will carry me so that not as much as a minute will be lost in getting back to you!"

"Yes, Philippe. I know you must go—but get back quickly!"

He snuffed out the one candle before returning to the window. Cautiously he drew back the curtains. He remained there so long to be sure that no one was at the back of the house that Félicité had no way of telling when he finally climbed out.

"Philippe!" she whispered after waiting several minutes.

When there was no reply she lighted the candle again. She had the room to herself.

It was a long time before she moved from her chair. Troublesome questions had taken possession of her mind. Was there danger for Philippe in the mission he had undertaken? Would he get back in time? She became worried and unhappy, and there was nothing she could do. It was impossible to confide in anyone, even in Madame Jouvelt, because it must not be known that her husband was not in the room with her.

Finally she sighed deeply and rose to her feet. She must get to bed; and when this resolution had been reached a memory came back into her mind. She recalled what Monsieur Gadois had said that last night in Montreal: "Always put your trust in the old proverbs, ma'amselle." This started her thoughts in another direction and she lost no time in undressing. She had put her clothes away and was in the bed in as short a time as frightened little Madame Gadois.

"At least this much good has come of it," she thought gratefully. "If Philippe had been here he might not have let me get into bed first. But here I am, and so my Philippe will have more years to live!" She shuddered at the thought of anything happening to him. "I couldn't exist without him now. Perhaps it was intended for that old man to come to the window and take him away."

She wondered if she should put out the candle but decided it would be unwise as it would increase Philippe's difficulties in reaching the window on his return. She propped herself up on a pillow and deliberately directed her thoughts to the future and to what she conceived to be the uninterrupted bliss she was going to have in her life with Philippe. This became easy after the first few moments. Her lips curled into a smile and her eyes expressed nothing but happiness. She thought back over the years when she had not been sure that he would ever notice her. It had been the one black doubt which had haunted her girlhood.

"And now I have him!" she said aloud. "Kind Mother Mary, I thank you for giving me the man I love."

She had no clock and so was compelled to guess as to how much of the hour had flown. As a result, a new worry became lodged in her mind. What excuse could she give if he did not get back in time?

She kept her ears tuned for any sound of footsteps at the back of the house but before she was rewarded the dreaded summons came at the door. There was a peremptory knock.

"Who is it?" she asked after a moment of blank consternation.

"Who do you suppose?" came the voice of Madame Jouvelt. "It's time to open. We're all here, and we have wine. There are toasts to be drunk. Come, let us in!"

Félicité felt completely helpless. What was she to do? If she let them discover that Philippe had not been with her, the news of his absence would quickly reach the wrong ears. It might result in La Passoire being empty when the governor's men surrounded it. But what excuse could she give?

Another and more impatient rap on the door. "Let us in! How much time do you need?"

She called. "Not yet—please! Come back soon. In ten minutes. In fifteen minutes!"

There was a long silence, then a voice said: "So! In fifteen minutes we return."

"What will they think of me!" said Félicité to herself in agonized bewilderment. "What will they say? This is terrible, this is absurd, this is not to be borne! And yet what am I to do?" She held clenched fists to her mouth. "Philippe! Please come back, come back quickly!"

To her intense relief she heard cautious footsteps in the back yard a few minutes later. She blew out the candle and immediately heard a rustling sound at the window.

"How glad I was when you put out the candle," she heard him say. "There are people still in the garden and I didn't dare make a move while the window was full of light. It was quick of you, my little wife."

She heard him fumbling across the room and reached out a hand toward him. It encountered one of his in the dark.

"An important hour lost from our lives!" he whispered. "Perhaps the most important hour of all. But—it was well I got the news to the governor. There's no doubt now that Jules Panletet was telling the truth. The Englishman has been in the cabin for several days. When I left him the governor was making his plans to catch them."

Félicité put both arms around his neck and so discovered that he was wet from head to foot. "What has happened?" she asked in a tense whisper. "Philippe, have you been hurt?"

"No. I thought it unwise to appear on the streets and instead I cut back into uncleared land. I was splashing through marsh most of the way. I'm soaked to the skin."

Félicité reached for a flint to strike a light. "They mustn't see you in this condition. But where can your clothes be hung so they won't be seen?" She pondered the problem a moment. "There's no other way but to hide them under the bed. And you must hurry, my Philippe, because they'll be back soon."

"Then I'm just in time?"

She shook her head ruefully. "No. They came to the door a quarter of an hour ago and I refused to let them in. Can't you see them when they come back—all of them so very arch and leering at us and making silly jokes at our expense? Philippe, *what* are we going to say to them?"

III

The governor spent several hours interrogating each of the dozen leaders who had been captured at La Passoire. They had little to tell him, save that they were bitterly disappointed with the conditions they had found and that they were frightened of the future. He was forced to acknowledge to himself that they had much in their favor. Piracy, however, was such a heinous crime that even an intent in that direction could not be overlooked.

He was thoroughly weary when he sent for the Englishman last of all. The latter was brought in from a cell in which he had been confined alone.

"I happen to know," said the governor, stifling a yawn with difficulty, "that your name is not Jack Beddoes. Nor is it Melvin, nor Adoo."

"Your Excellency," answered the prisoner, "is well informed."

"Another report of you has reached me." De Bienville made a hasty search through the papers on his desk but soon gave it up. "Could it be that your name is Captain Cedric Goodchild?"

The prisoner nodded. "That is my name, Excellency. I was an officer in His Majesty's army until I was detached for special duties. It proved most unfortunate because I missed the chance of serving with Marlborough."

"The special duties had to do with the colonies, no doubt?"

Captain Goodchild nodded a second time. "Yes, Excellency. I have a gift for languages and I'm a bit of an actor as well." His voice and manner would have amazed all who had known him only in his role of an escaped pirate. He was making no effort to conceal the fact that he was well born and well educated. He leaned forward and asked his inquisitor eagerly, "Could you let me have a pinch of snuff?"

De Bienville found a box on his desk and handed it to his companion. It was a gift from the old King, a beautiful thing of blue enamel with rose diamonds in the filigree. Captain Goodchild inhaled the snuff with the most intense relish.

"The first pinch I've had for two years," he said. "My thanks, Excellency, for your great indulgence."

De Bienville continued with his questioning. "It's safe to assume, then, that you didn't serve with Calico Jack?"

"No, Excellency. That was a story which happened to serve my purpose when I first talked to the provost of New Orleans, who later died under such unfortunate circumstances. But"—he nodded and smiled—"I saw the pack hanged at Kingston."

"Are you conscious of having been the direct cause of the killing of Auguste de Mariat?"

"I've no intention of disclaiming the credit. And from what I've heard since returning to New Orleans, I realize that the death of your Monsieur de Mariat is regarded as a universally popular event. It seems, moreover, that I did no more than forestall a certain prominent state official who was preparing to run his sword through the De Mariat ribs when my savages stepped in ahead of him."

"Auguste de Mariat," conceded the governor, "had made many enemies in New Orleans. But the fact remains that he was an officer of the King of France and that his death can't be passed over because of personal feelings."

"I appreciate the difficulty of your position in this matter, Excellency."

"I must send you back to France to face the serious charges which will be brought against you. I have no alternative, Captain Goodchild." De Bienville paused for a moment. After studying the face of the prisoner with great intentness he went on. "But you can be of help to me, Captain, and so I am going to propose a bargain with you. You must give me a full statement of what happened. The whole truth, Captain, particularly as it relates to the part played by Auguste de Mariat. I need such a statement for several reasons. For one thing it will be valuable in vindicating my own course—should the need arise. It can be used also in the matter of the adjustment of a marriage settlement. Certain difficulties are being raised by the senior De Mariat and I can see that a statement from you would go a long way in convincing him of the selfishness of his position. If you will do this, I will agree to provide a certain chance for you when the ship reaches the island of Cuba. If it should happen that you give us the slip—well, you must give me your parole now. You are never to cross the Atlantic again and you must relinquish all the special duties which have been entrusted to you. I can see, Captain Goodchild, that you are a gentleman and so I have no doubt that you will keep your word."

"I swear solemnly," declared the Englishman, "that your conditions will be faithfully followed. It will be a fortunate circumstance for me, in fact, quite apart from escaping the unpleasantnesses prepared for me in France. I'm weary of the wilderness, Excellency. I long for the comforts of a berth at home, a cup of tea in the mornings, a comfortable pair of slippers after dinner, a good bed. How happy I shall be to give up this kind of life and resume the activities of a—well, a gentleman with a slight tarnish on his escutcheon."

They looked at each other in silence for several moments. Then De Bienville asked, "I don't suppose your special duties ever took you into Canada?"

"Indeed yes! I was there several times, looking around and sizing up the strength and the spirit of the place. As a matter of fact, Excellency, I once paid a visit to the Le Moyne château at Longueuil."

The governor heard this statement with unbelieving eyes. "Come, Captain Goodchild, that goes beyond the limits of my credulity."

"I was taken there, moreover, by your famous brother, the Sieur d'Iberville." The Englishman's eyes twinkled at the amazement reflected in De Bienville's face. "It was on an occasion when D'Iberville had returned from Newfoundland and was preparing to set out for Hudson's Bay, where, unfortunately, he gave us a thorough thrashing."

"Pierre was accompanied by a long train that day." The governor was close to the point of conviction. "Were you one of them?"

"I was, Excellency. Do you remember a minstrel fellow with a huge black dog?" The Englishman smiled reminiscently. "I have a good voice. I think that I rendered the songs of Normandy with spirit and fidelity."

CHAPTER XII

FÉLICITÉ looked at Nicolette with dismay. It was the morning after the double wedding. The household, it is perhaps needless to say, was in a disorganized state.

"Nicolette," she whispered, laying a finger on her lip to enjoin secrecy, "there's something I must tell you. I can't tell your mother about it nor Madame Jouvelt. I would be too ashamed. But you I can tell and be sure that it won't be repeated. Nicolette, I can't cook."

The girl seemed unwilling to believe there could be a flaw in her idol. "Madame means, perhaps, that she's not a very fancy cook?"

"Nicolette, I'm not any kind of a cook. Food has always been something which was brought in when you were hungry. Now I find that it's something which must be prepared, and that I, moreover, must do the preparing."

"Madame didn't have time to learn," asserted Nicolette.

"It's true that I was always busy with other things. But I should have realized that I would need to cook when I came to New Orleans." The new wife looked at Nicolette despairingly. "There's dinner today for my husband. He will come home very hungry and there must be a substantial meal ready for him. It must be a fine meal or I'll feel that already I'm a failure as a wife. But, Nicolette, how am I to cook such a meal?"

The child's eyes brightened with an idea. "Madame," she whispered, "I will go to my mother and I'll say it's time I was learning more about cooking. I will ask about one of the dishes she does best. I'll find out everything she does and then I'll come and tell you." She gave some thought to the selection of a proper dish. "Madame, what would you say to *ragoût Canadien aux pattes de cochons*? It's a wonderful dish and my mother does it best of all. Or perhaps *pâtés et cipailles*?"

Félicité was only too glad to accept assistance on this basis. "I think perhaps it should be the ragout," she said.

Philippe approached the house with the hurried and rather arrogant stride of the new bridegroom. Nicolette met him at the door, her eyes shining.

"Ah, monsieur!" she exclaimed. "Your wife is such a wonderful cook! I've been watching her prepare your dinner. It's going to be a good one, m'sieur!"

"What is it, Nicolette?" he asked.

"I'm not supposed to tell." The girl looked back over her shoulder to make sure that her voice would not carry to the kitchen. "It's a ragout of pig's feet. Cooked in a very special way, m'sieur."

"That has always been a special dish with me," he declared. Then he raised his voice. "Where are you, my sweet one?"

A voice from the kitchen came to him faintly. "I am here, my Philippe. You are early, are you not?"

"Of course I'm early." Philippe had reached the kitchen door. "What bridegroom ever failed to get home early on the day after his wedding?"

Félicité was bundled up to the chin in an enormous apron of an unbecoming gray which had been loaned her by Carpe's wife. Her face was flushed and there was a bandage on one finger, mute evidence of a disaster at some stage of the dinner preparations.

She gave him a worried smile. "I wanted so much to have everything on the table when you came. And to be cool and fresh myself." She gave a despairing gesture. "And look how you find me!"

"You are lovely enough as you are to upset this very humble and worshipful husband." He looked at the fire over which the ragout was simmering. A delicious odor filled the room. "I realize that not only am I desperately in love with my wife but that I'm hungry also."

"I'm not at all sure this will satisfy such a great appetite." Félicité spoke with a still more worried smile.

"My small one, you are full of surprises. I didn't know you were an accomplished cook as well as so many other things."

"Before very long, I'm afraid, you'll think that I'm nothing but a fraud." She looked at the iron pan which contained the ragout. "I think it may be done."

"I hope it is!" said Philippe, sniffing hungrily.

Félicité poked a fork into the meat with the lack of assurance of a bachelor godfather extending a finger in the direction of his newborn charge. "It seems tender enough. And now I must get it out of this and onto a plate for the table!"

"I think that I'm entitled first to a kiss from my beautiful bride."

"One only." Félicité looked down at the apron which engulfed her. "I'm not sure this is clean. And I know my cheeks are burning. I should always be nice and cool when you kiss me."

"Nice, yes—but cool? I'm not sure of *that!*" Philippe took her into his arms with such ardor that he forgot her injunction and kissed her many times. Félicité seemed to have forgotten it also. "There!" releasing her. "And now we'll perform this difficult feat of getting our very handsome ragout safely on a platter."

He took a large fork in one hand and a brass basting spoon in the other. The ragout was transferred without the loss of even so much as a drop of the gravy.

"I'll carry it." Philippe raised the platter high in the air. "We should have an orchestra with horns and drums to escort us in, like a king and his queen sitting down to meat. You look every inch a queen, my sweet one."

Following behind him, Félicité began to take some pride in her achievement. "First," she explained, "I boiled the pig's feet with salt and pepper and onions. Then I beat up flour and cold water to a"—she paused for a moment before recalling the right expression—"to a smooth paste. I mixed and mixed and mixed until there wasn't a trace of a lump. Then I poured the paste into the meat stock to thicken into a sauce; and as it thickened I stirred in many spices, cloves and cinnamon and nutmeg. Then the sauce was poured over the meat and I put it all on the fire to boil slowly together."

Philippe seated himself at the table while Félicité hurried to bring the loaf of bread and the wine in a cool earthenware jug. It was not until everything was on the table, and she had broken off an end of the long loaf for him, that she noticed he had fallen into an absorbed mood.

"What is it?" she asked. "What has come over you so sudden?"

"M'sieur Jean-Baptiste was at the quay just before I left." Philippe frowned to himself as he spoke. "He was looking very downcast. I think he's had bad news from France."

"I think so too." Félicité nodded her head solemnly. "It will come soon, the news that the schemes of John Law have failed."

"Something has gone wrong. He was telling them to hurry the unloading of the supplies. It was as though he feared some order might come to send everything back to France."

The ragout was steaming away unnoticed. Félicité took her place at the table but it was clear that they were too concerned with the probable fate of the colony to think of eating.

She asked, "If the Louisiana Company dissolves, what will happen to us here?"

"There will be black days for us, I'm afraid."

Félicité looked at him suddenly with reproachful eyes. "The ragout!" she cried. "It's getting cold while we talk. I made it for you with my own hands. Come, M'sieur Philippe, we must eat it at once. This ragout is more important to us than what may happen to the schemes of M'sieur John Law."

Philippe portioned out the meat between them and with an air almost of deference as though the dish, being of her making, was something sacred, if not actually one of the wonders of the world. After one mouthful he laid down his knife and fork and looked at her with worshipful eyes. "You are right! That you can make a ragout like this means more to us than anything that may happen to all of France!"

II

After supper that evening there came a knock on the door and they heard the voice of the Sieur de Bienville demanding in a cheerful tone to be admitted.

He came in, followed by two porters carrying bundles of various sizes. "Some wedding gifts," he announced, bowing to Félicité. "From the governor of Louisiana to the loveliest of brides and the luckiest of men."

He was wearing the plainest gray with coarse stockings of the same color and with a shabby *chapeau-bras* (a hat intended to be carried and not worn) under his arm.

He motioned to the porters to bring their packages into the room. "I've found new quarters for Bonnet and his family and, now that M'sieur and Madame Jouvelt are on their way down the river, you will have this house to yourselves." He began to explain about the gifts. "I've been bringing furniture over from France to be used when I had a proper residence of my own. A piece or two at a time. They've been stored in the east *caserne* and some have never been taken out of their casings. There's no reason why you shouldn't have some of this clutter of stuff. I won't have use for any of it for a long time. I'm beginning to wonder if it'll ever be of use to me."

Félicité glanced at him with affectionate concern. He happened to look in her direction at the same moment and a smile spread over his face. It was a natural and easy smile.

Philippe had left the room in search of a knife, as one of the parcels was tightly roped. The governor took advantage of this to ask a question, "You are happy, my Félicité?"

She nodded with a reluctance which was due to her appreciation of the delicacy of the situation. "Yes, M'sieur Jean-Baptiste. I am very happy."

"That is good." He smiled with such complete detachment that she began to doubt if his feeling for her had ever gone beyond friendship. "Your happiness is very important to me. If you always remain happy, then I'll be content too."

Philippe returned with a knife and the work of unwrapping the packages began. There were four presents in all: a clock for the mantelpiece which in later years would acquire a special value because it was the work of Boulle, a mirror for the wall with a gilded frame, a tapestry which depicted, as De Bienville pointed out, the story of the Seven Joys, and an astronomical dictionary in two volumes. Félicité's homemaking instinct awoke and she went into ecstasies of indecision over the placing of these handsome gifts. She was so delighted with them that for the time being all other thoughts left her mind.

The governor watched her as she moved about the room. He observed the grace and self-reliance of her carriage, the fine line of her profile, the glint of the candlelight on her hair. He sighed unhappily. "Twenty years of solitude," he thought, "and now it will continue to the end of my life." Félicité turned to ask a question and detected an expression on his face which was far different from the casual air which he had worn into the room. She remained still for a moment, feeling very unhappy about it.

The weather had turned unseasonably warm and the air in the room was sultry. A constant sound was caused by the insects bombarding the stiffened linen in the windows. De Bienville seated himself at the table and undid the blue tassels of his collar. He did not permit himself to look again in her direction.

"Come and sit down with me here," he said to them when the tasks had been completed. "I've something to say to you."

Félicité seated herself at the table and looked across it with an air as grave as his own. Philippe returned his tools to the kitchen before joining them.

"A letter reached me today," said the governor, "from my brother Charles, who is still in France. He hadn't dared send it through the regular mails but had arranged to get it to me by way of Spain and Havana. This care was necessary because he was discussing the situation in France and the position of John Law's companies."

Philippe remained silent through a habit of deference but Félicité felt no such restraint. "Is the news bad?" she asked.

"Charles says the bubble may burst before the end of the year. The Regent is as mad as John Law himself. He has authorized a new paper issue of over one hundred million! Can you conceive of such folly? When the crash comes it may bankrupt the French nation!"

After a moment of sober silence De Bienville went on. "Until the bubble does burst Frenchmen will go on trading in the shares and tossing their money about like maniacs. There's an uneasiness here already because of it. Yesterday a man from Canada insisted on seeing me. He said he had been hearing things which frightened him and he asked to be allowed to take his family back to Montreal." He straightened up in his chair and looked first at one and then at the other. "I've some advice for you. I want you to accept my word that, no matter what happens in France, it will be better for you to remain here. John Law is a madman but he's done more for us as a result of his madness than we could have hoped for in forty years without him. He made it possible for us to found New Orleans on a solid basis."

"But if he fails——"

"His failure," cried the governor, "can have no lasting effect on us! What we've done here is too important to be changed by the money-changing madness of France! Our roots have gone down into the soil. Soon the great river will be as French as the Seine or the Loire. Look about you! This bit of land has become in two years the beginning of an empire!"

He rose to his feet and began pacing about. "We've accomplished what we set out to do. We have a stayhold on the Mississippi!" He nodded his head vigorously, his eyes were glowing. "There are only four of us left. But I know this: the six who died would count their lives well lost if they could see today what has happened to the map of the world. You know what the old maps were like—all around the lands of the earth the waters of four oceans, and above the oceans a thick mist. The mist has been pierced in the west! First could be seen, rising above it, the Rock of Quebec and the cross on the mountain at Montreal. Then came the forts along the Great Lakes and the trading posts which secured the wealth of the north for Montreal, and then the forts along the Mississippi and its great tributaries. And finally we have here as our contribution the forts and the spires and the wharves of New Orleans, the last and most important link in the chain of steel. We have finished what La Salle died in trying. The great West is ours!"

He paused beside the table and stared down at them. "You must stay with me because you'll be needed. This is no more than a start. And the rewards, I promise you, will be great. If you'll stay, you'll become one of our first families. You'll become wealthy. Perhaps in time you'll be ennobled as my father was. When this little collection of huts grows into a fabulous city you must be here to share in the fruits.

"I've had a chance to do a great deal of thinking," he went on. "Twenty years to think, while I waited for what was coming. I reached a conclusion long ago with which, I'm afraid, my brother Charles will never be able to agree. I could see that this continent was too great to be nothing more than a collection of colonies.

"Sometimes, when the fever was on me, I would have visions. I would see this land teeming with cities, the cities of white men, and with towers rising higher than the Rock of Quebec. I've never been able to see what flag flies over these great high cities. It may not be the flag of France any more than that of England or Spain. Perhaps it will be the colors of a new race. But that won't mean defeat for us who dream now of keeping the fleur-de-lis over all of the new continent. What we are doing may be a part of something much greater, the nature of which we can't yet foresee.

"Whatever the future holds, this is the place for us. Here we must stay and make our stand, here at the gateway to the south and west."